BROKEN LIKE ME

KAITIE HOWIE

Broken Like Me

by Kaitie Howie

Trigger Warning: this book contains prominent themes of sexual assault, as well as mentions of domestic violence and miscarriage.

————

For Ariana,
who read the stories I wrote when they were nothing but notes app
ramblings typed during Dairy Queen breaks.

And for Rachel,
who met me at my lowest and somehow stuck around anyway.

1

Once upon a time, Rose had a Cinderella complex—hopes that some-day, somehow, someone would come sweep her away from the hell that was the only home she'd ever known.

(Now she knows better.)

No one is coming to save her, and they never will; she uses her own broken pieces as armor and drags herself through the fire.

(She's used to the flames now, the burn that once scalded her a defense against the very ones who'd caged her.)

She'd run away without looking back, but she's not naive enough to think that means she's truly escaped.

She's on guard, now and always, hypervigilant in the nearly deserted hospital wing. The lights are dim; it's the middle of the night, after all.

(An unfamiliar hospital, in a still unfamiliar state, full of unfamiliar people.)

(It's a blessing and a curse, knowing that she's escaped what she's running from whilst forever looking over her shoulder.)

Her wavy dark hair started out in a bun but has now effectively become a knot, a stark contrast to the light of her hazel eyes.

Rose is exhausted, and every part of her body hurts, but she won't be sleeping any time soon.

Her daughter's in her arms—hours old, defenseless and vulnerable.

(Her eyes can't close until she knows they're safe.)

She reaches to stroke a tiny rosy cheek with her thumb. Her daughter is an innocent, so new to the world but already so perfect.

It's...Rose knows it'll be hell. They're alone in the world and on the run, and...God, if she could give Scarlett the entire universe, she would do it.

(Scar is already the best thing in the world, the most important person that's ever lived.)

"You and me against the world, lovebug," she says in a soft whisper. "I won't let anyone hurt you."

(It's a promise she'll do anything to keep.)

———

The crying wakes Rose less than an hour after her head hits the pillow.

She shouldn't be surprised; she and the universe have never been on particularly good terms, and sleep is especially scarce with a newborn, but she'd finished her homework before 3 a.m. for the first time in weeks and had really been hoping for more than four hours of sleep.

The fumes she's been running on aren't strong enough to keep her going like this forever.

Slowly getting to her feet, she approaches the secondhand crib in the corner of the apartment and gently lifts her daughter, lips twitching toward a smile at the familiar sight of the wisps of black hair she'd passed on.

Scarlett's sobs quiet but don't stop, and after checking to make sure she isn't hungry and doesn't need to be changed, Rose sets her down just long enough to slip a hoodie over her head and wrap a soft blanket around Scarlett's tiny two-month-old body.

It's going to be one of those nights—the ones where nothing will calm Scar but walking, Rose's voice soothing her with stories, for at least an hour. She might as well do the meandering outside.

Slipping her phone and pepper spray into her hoodie pocket, Rose locks the apartment door behind her, hazel eyes looking around the building warily. They'd finally been able to move to a better part of town when her lease ended at their former apartment building, where her inability to sleep hadn't been helped by constant fear for her and Scar's safety, and while all of her research indicated that their new residence was a much less worrisome place to live, she can't help but feel on edge.

(Unsurprising. She hasn't been safe since her father died ten years prior.)

She stills for a moment, wondering whether or not stepping outside at night would be a terrible idea, but as soon as her movement pauses, Scarlett lets out a screech, and Rose rushes downstairs for fear of pissing off the neighbors on their first night in the building. Locks of dark hair escape her bun and brush up against the sides of her face as she moves.

Despite being from a bit farther north, she's been in Florida long enough now that the forty-degree weather she steps into makes her shiver; it's especially chilly for August, the humidity seeping through her skin. The street is by no means quiet, and she begins to meander along the dimly lit sidewalk while whispering tales to her baby of Peter Pan, of Mulan, of Nefertiti and Odysseus, weaving history and legend alongside the magic she's always loved.

She worries about Scar being in the cold, but hopefully, they won't be out for too long, and Rose has her well bundled. Taxis pull up to the curb as noisy passengers stagger from their seats loudly, perhaps belatedly celebrating the new school year, the semester only a few weeks in. Maybe merely celebrating their very existence.

(Maybe drinking away the darkness.)

Her new apartment building houses mainly college students like herself, which makes sense given its proximity to USF. She catches wind of many drunken mumblings about dreading having to go to class hungover the coming morning. Having a shift at the diner in merely three hours, she can sympathize with their exhaustion.

Had things worked out a bit differently, she would likely be in their shoes.

Less than half an hour later, Scar is sound asleep, and Rose's eyes revolt, attempting to flutter closed even as her feet carry her along the sidewalk. She goes back inside, pushing the elevator call button with more force than necessary at the thought of her bed all the way on the third floor.

Just after she steps inside the elevator, she hears rapid footsteps approaching as the doors begin to slide closed. "Wait, hold it, please!"

Her heart speeds up at the deep male voice, but the last thing she wants is an enemy in the building, so she hits the button to keep the doors open. At the sight of the broad-shouldered young man who'd called after her, however, fear spikes within her. She regrets the attempt to be neighborly now that she's trapped in a metal box with a man who could clearly overpower her in a heartbeat.

He's dressed all in black, a worn leather jacket thrown over a tight v-neck and black pants. His buzzcut hair is pitch, too, paired with dark brown skin pulled taut over a prominent jawline, a bright contrast to the bright hazel eyes that keep jumping around like his line of sight can't stay still.

Gorgeous, but she knows too well to be wary. The muscles visible through his shirt that are making her pupils dilate are exactly the reason she doesn't want to be alone with him.

"Thanks," he mumbles, pressing the button for the fourth floor himself. "I know it wouldn't have been much longer to wait or to just take the stairs, but I have an eight a.m. class, and I just got off work. Just thinking about losing those few extra minutes of sleep hurts."

She remains tense, hoping not responding will encourage him to leave her alone, but feels his gaze shift on to her.

"I don't think I've seen you around. I'm Josh Brooks. 427." He starts to reach a hand out but stops himself, a hint of a blush spreading across his cheeks. "Your hands are obviously full. Sorry."

His easy tone relaxes her somewhat; nonetheless, she doesn't want to speak, but the risk of not replying when he's clearly waiting for a response is even more anxiety-provoking, so she caves. "Nice to meet you. I'm Rose; you probably haven't seen me around because we just moved in today." She's pretty sure he notices that she doesn't give him her own apartment number, but by the light smile he responds with, he doesn't seem to mind.

"And who's this little one?"

"This is Scarlett." Rose's heart jumps, voice quiet.

"Like Black Widow?"

She nods, lips twitching upward. "I hadn't intended it to be, but yeah. Although her middle name is Bronte, so most people assume it's literary too, after *The Scarlet Letter*. Not sure what that makes them think about me as a mother."

Josh opens his mouth like a thought has struck him but shakes his head as though dismissing it. "Wherever it's from, it's pretty. And Scar is a badass nickname, so she has options depending on the vibes she wants to give off."

"Thanks. I hope she thinks so too when she's older. I mean, I didn't name her Gertrude, so she can't be too mad, I hope."

A deep laugh sounds from Josh's chest. "This is true, although the bar is low."

The elevator light blinks just before the doors open, and as nice as Josh seems, she's relieved to be on her floor—safety, space, and sleep all just a few yards away. *For less than three hours,* her brain reminds her, but she shakes away the negativity. "This is me."

And she's mentally berating herself because now he knows where she lives, knows where her daughter lives, and what has she done—

Stop being irrational. He's just a normal guy.

Josh waves as she steps into the hallway. "It was nice to meet you, Rose. If you or Scarlett need anything, feel free to come by. Two friends and I all room together and someone's normally around if you need a hand."

"Thanks, Josh. Have a good night." The word 'night' is clipped by the elevator doors sliding shut, and she takes her first deep breath since getting on the elevator, the hand not on Scar sliding within her pocket from its instinctive place on her pepper spray to her keys. Her heart is pounding strongly enough that she can physically see her chest stuttering back and forth.

She double and triple checks the locks before carefully laying Scar back in the crib, silently begging her daughter not to wake back up as she climbs into the twin bed in the corner of the apartment.

The conversation with Josh has rattled her for no reason of his own doing; he seems genuine, and it's promising to have an acquaintance in the building so soon. She won't go to his apartment, of course, but maybe the next time she sees Isa, the only friend she's made since running full speed from North Carolina almost a year ago, Rose can ask if she's ever seen him around campus.

The easygoing boy with the bright, tired eyes is the last thing running through her overworked mind before she falls right back into REM, her body too desperate for the two and a half hours she might still squeeze in to worry about tomorrow.

2

| **ROSE**

"Please don't let her take me back." Thirteen-year-old Rose's voice breaks.

(She feels so, so small.)

Bronte's jaw is clenched, her grip on Rose's hand so tight the younger girl is almost convinced there will be permanent damage.

(She doesn't mind. The pain means Bronte is still with her.)

Evan is outside, arguing with the officials that had shown up; he'd kissed them both on the forehead before promising to handle it, saying it was his job as the oldest to keep them all safe.

Rose can see the tension in his whole body, the way he's being so careful not *to piss the cop off, knowing his anger will make the outcome that much worse. The moment is too precarious.*

"They'll have to get through both of us to get to you," *Bronte promises, using her free hand to smooth down Rose's hair in an uncommon gesture of physical affection.*

For a moment, Rose is hopeful—thinks things might just work out in their favor.

(She should know better.)

Forty-eight hours later, she's back in North Carolina, her mother so relieved and well-meaning, having the respect of everyone in town and—

(The world can fall apart in forty-eight hours.)

———

Two days later, Rose can hardly keep her eyes open—but it's another five days till her day off, so she'll just have to suck it up. It's 9 a.m. on a Monday, one of the busier days of the week where breakfast is concerned at the diner; everyone is too tired and dreading the coming week to cook at home.

Not that she can blame them. She hasn't been cooking much herself; it's hot as hell outside and viscerally humid to boot, and using the oven makes the whole apartment feel like a furnace.

Her thoughts are far away as she approaches the table that was just sat. "Hi y'all, thanks for coming in, I'm Rose, and I'll be—"

(For a moment, she thinks she's imagining it—thinks she might be dreaming or hallucinating.)

There's a dark-haired guy seated at the table—the All-American type though tattoos peek out from his sleeves—and he looks familiar. She's pretty sure he lives in her apartment building, or she's seen him on campus or something.

(But he's not important.)

The thing that makes her jaw drop is the sight of the young woman across from him.

The shorn centimeter of hair so bleached it borders on white, eyes dark enough for the iris to blend in with the pupil...Rose's heart aches at the scarred arch of the woman's eyebrow, the one sliced by a would-be child abductor who'd nearly had twelve-year-old Rose inside his van until the blonde intervened.

(The hair had never grown back, a permanent reminder of the sacrifice made on Rose's behalf when she was still just a kid.)

"Bronte." Despite the wonder, the love, the apology in her mind, the word comes out in a whisper, conveying none of the above.

"Hey, kiddo."

8

Her steady voice takes Rose back, drowns out the ruckus of the busy restaurant until she's back to showing up at youth group, miserable and finding a kindred spirit, to things getting worse and them making a pact to run away and escape, Bronte's promises that she wouldn't leave without Rose, to planning so, *so* carefully and never looking back.

It takes her back to the best time in her life. The first time she was on the streets, away from her mother Cheyenne and her hellish home, maybe a bit hungrier than she should've been but happier than ever with Bronte.

They're her only fond childhood memories—the ones that made her believe happiness was possible, that things could be better.

After the cops cornered them two years later, Rose was sent back to her '*loving*' home, whilst Bronte's being nineteen meant they couldn't do much except take Rose away from her. They'd had each other's emails, and she'd memorized the number for Bronte's burner phone; they'd sworn to stay in touch until Bronte could afford a lawyer, until she could attempt to file for custody—an unlikely dream, but one Rose had wished on every candle and star for more years than she should've.

(Like everything other speck of happiness in Rose's life till Scarlett, Cheyenne ruined it.)

Rose had moved to Tampa like they'd always planned ages ago, telling themselves they'd find Bronte's family somehow, but Rose never imagined she'd actually manage to stumble into the woman in question. It had just been the only place she could imagine herself being happy after so many years of wishing.

"Te, I'm so...I—I tried, but she..." She gives up trying to excuse herself, closing her eyes in anticipation of how much Bronte must hate her for going ghost. For being the reason their contact had dissipated the way they'd always feared.

But the next thing she knows, familiar arms are wrapped around her, and while she initially stiffens, once she opens her eyes and convinces herself it's the older sister she never got to have, she returns the hug and starts to cry. She's at work, so she tries to rein in the sobs, but this is *Bronte. Here.* All these years later, and it's like no time has passed.

"I know. I always figured. It's okay. God, I can't believe I finally found you." Bronte squeezes her as Rose tries to remind herself of where she is. *Chill the fuck out; you're at work, and you're making a scene, and this is not the way to convince Bronte she still wants to be a part of your life.* "Holy shit, Rose, you're taller than me. That's not even *fair!*"

The exclamation draws a laugh out of the younger girl, and the two release each other as Bronte sits back down, but Rose doesn't take her eyes off her, praying to keep her in sight as long as possible. *Bronte.* There's nothing to tear them apart this time—no CPS, no Cheyenne; she would move heaven and earth to keep this string of happiness.

There's so much to say—so many questions and years of filling in to do. And she's so blindsided that she's blanking on all of it, her entire mind consumed by the fact that *this is actually happening.*

"Babe, you okay?" Isa approaches, softly pressing a hand to Rose's shoulder, and the touch of her best friend grounds her. "Marnie couldn't tell if you were upset, and she said if you need to take fifteen to go ahead, but if not, she really needs you on the floor."

"I—yeah, of course," she says numbly. "Isa, it's...this is Bronte."

"*Bronte* Bronte?" The only one Rose has told everything to, the only other person who could understand the significance of this moment save one, Isa's eyes go wide. "I...oh my God."

The guy sitting with Bronte merely watches the interaction quietly, looking afraid to interrupt.

"Rose! Isa!" their manager calls impatiently, and Rose knows she's been standing here for way too long, and the tips from the rest of her tables are going to be trash, but she hesitates long enough for Bronte to grip her wrist.

"We—we'll catch up soon."

Rose's heart thumps with joy at the thought of having the first person who ever loved her with her again, and she nods. "Definitely. I'll give you my number before you guys leave. I..." She can't finish the sentence; how can she even begin to put into words her joy at seeing Bronte, her love for her that hasn't shrunk in the slightest?

The feeling of your wildest dreams coming true when your entire life has been shit?

"I know. Me too, Briar Rose."

A laugh escapes her at the nickname Bronte has always known annoys her, one Bronte started using after a youth group *Sleeping Beauty* movie night.

(Rose is flooded with memories—the late-night conversations, meeting Evan, feeling seen for the first time.)

She's on cloud nine the rest of her shift, and she knows there's hard moments to come, knows they'll have to discuss what happened in the decade they were apart.

(Knows a lot of it won't be pretty.)

But it's *Bronte*. They've gone to hell and back together. They can handle whatever comes next.

———

On Saturday, Rose bites her lip nervously, foot tapping away beneath her wobbly kitchen table. Scar's favorite LeapFrog toy plays music in the living room where Rose can easily keep an eye on her from the rickety kitchen table.

The bills are piling up.

It had been a given that her regular expenses would hike after moving to a nicer, safer apartment building, and she did her best to brace herself (and her bank account) for that reality. But seeing the hits to her paycheck in action is brutal, and she's trying not to wince at the thought of those yet to come on the counter across from where she sits with Natalya.

Rose met her a few weeks ago, a neighbor from the first floor who'd been kind and clearly loves kids; she'd instantly earned brownie points with Rose for waving and smiling at Scar *without* planting kisses all over her, the way strangers seem to do all the time, no regard to how easily they might get her baby sick.

The older woman folds her hands and smiles at Rose. "I don't have my own transportation, which I know as a mother can be a cause for concern in case of emergency, but I have that new app. I did some looking around and found out the Lyft service requires background checks, so that would be the one I'd use."

Rose nods in response thoughtfully. "That works. The stroller has enough space for the base of the car seat in the storage part, I believe. I really appreciate you taking the time to find out which service is safest." Indeed, just hearing the woman's dedication to the potential employment made her feel better about potentially leaving Scar in her hands.

Nervous, still, because it's impossible to trust anyone in this world, and her daughter is the most precious thing in her life, but Natalya has great references, and...sometimes you can just see a person's goodness in their eyes.

She had few doubts to begin with; Natalya's husband had been killed in a construction accident just a few years after they immigrated to the US from Mexico, leaving her a single mother of three kids under the age of five with a thick accent that most assumed meant she didn't understand English and no diploma or degree— college or high school. Natalya busted her ass and came out on top, managing to keep a roof over her kids' heads and love the hell out of them. All four had either gone to college or enlisted in the military; the woman is everything Rose could hope to emulate as a single mother.

(She embodies the kindness that only comes from the greatest suffering.)

Rose is also fairly certain the woman reached out about the position for *her* sake because Natalya certainly doesn't need the money, but Rose is desperate enough for an adequate and affordable caretaker that she can suck up her pride and take the pity offer.

(It's for Scarlett; she can do anything for her daughter.)

"I have one more question: do you want me to only speak to her in English, or is Spanish okay too? I know different mothers have different preferences, so whichever you prefer."

"Oh! I mean, if you're comfortable with it, I'd love her to interact with Spanish. Language is one of the most valuable skills there is, especially living in Florida, and obviously, she's so young it might not make that big of an impact, but I could try to have her keep up with it later on. Regardless, I'll want her to eventually become fluent, but I don't expect that of you—just whatever you can incorporate day to day is perfect. Thank you so much."

"Sounds good to me." Natalya's smile is like being wrapped in a hug, and it feels like finally—*finally*—things are coming together.

"Well, ma'am, we'll have to figure out pay because I know I probably can't afford what you deserve, but I would really love to—"

A knock sounds on the door, and her breath catches in her throat.

They've found her. She'd known using her real name was a bad idea, knew they would catch up eventually and— *Focus, Rose, make a plan.* Climbing down a fourteen-story fire escape with a baby is not going to happen, but maybe she can—

"Rose?"

The voice is deep and slightly familiar. *Josh?*

(What the hell is he doing here?)

"Just a second," she says apologetically to Natalya.

She approaches the door cautiously, pressing her eye to the smudged peephole. Sure enough, it's him. She's only seen him twice, the once two weeks ago and bleary-eyed, and a few days later when they were both frazzled and running late to work, but even in the crew neck and basketball shorts he now wears, something about him seems stuck on her brain.

Opening the door, she gets a better view of him and sees for the first time the middle-aged woman standing next to him. She isn't tall by any means, dark hair streaked sparsely with gray, but her brown eyes sparkle.

"Hey." He fidgets, tugging at the gray collar of his shirt. The six-foot-something lean machine of a man actually looks *nervous*. "This is my godmother, Kathy Wilson. Aunt Kathy, this is Rose." He turns his eyes back to Rose. "I...sorry to just show up like this, but I heard about the new girl in 14C and figured it was you, and we wanted to bring you these."

Her attention is drawn to the container in his hands, which she hesitantly grabs. "Oh wow, thank you so much!"

"They're chocolate chip. Aunt Kathy's special recipe—the best you'll ever have." He smiles earnestly, blushing again when his aunt reaches a hand up to squeeze his arm.

Rose is touched at the gesture; she opens the Tupperware only to be more baffled. "But...these are the size of my head!"

For the first time since she's met him—granted, she's only had about twenty minutes of facetime with the guy, but she's a pretty good judge of character (she's had to be), and it's clear this guy radiates positivity everywhere he goes—his eyes flash briefly with something darker.

"It's just a tradition. Something JJ, his mother, and I have done since he was nine or so," his godmother explains with a gentle smile. "We wanted to welcome you to the building; I don't actually live here, but apparently my best friend and I didn't teach her son manners very well, or he would've done it more than a week ago," she chides, turning her narrowed eyes to the man towering over her.

"It's nice to meet you, Ms. Wilson," Rose addresses the woman slowly, double-checking to make sure she doesn't wear a ring before using the title. She realizes she's still awkwardly holding the open cookie tin, and her ears perk up when Scar begins to babble from within the apartment.

Rose hesitates, knowing it would be polite to invite them in but not thrilled at the prospect of strangers in her place. Natalya is there, though, so they won't be alone, and something about the softness in the Kathy's face possesses her to say, "I'll just put these in the kitchen, then. Come on in."

Aunt Kathy lights up, and it's this that soothes Rose enough to wave away Josh's words as he stutters that they don't want to intrude.

Scar is caged in by pillows and blankets despite the fact that she won't crawl or even roll over for a while yet. Her cooing turns to a more disgruntled babble, her signature *mommy-I-want-you-or-I'll-*

screech tone, so Rose quickly places the container on the counter and heads to scoop her daughter from her place on the floor, the light-up toy still in front of her.

"Hi, lovebug. Mama's here." Scar smiles up at her, eyes—the ones that used to make Rose feel sick on another but have become her favorite on her little girl's face—focused on her.

"Oh, my Lord, aren't you precious! Who's this?" Rose looks up to see Kathy's entire face filled with joy at the sight of Scar, and her heart swells.

"This is Scarlett; she's two months as of last week," she tells the older woman quietly.

"She's *not* named after the book or ScarJo," Josh says wisely, and Kathy's gentle laugh reverberates through the room.

"And this is Natalya. She lives downstairs, and she'll be helping take care of Scar while I'm at work. Natalya, this is Kathy and Josh." She gestures to the older woman seated at the table, who beams at her at the mention of being taken up on her offer and gets to her feet to greet the newcomers.

"Hola, Mrs. Rodriguez," Josh says kindly, reaching to kiss her cheek. "How are you today?"

"Very good, honey, thank you. This is your aunt?"

"The unlucky one," he confirms with a grin.

"You and your friend raised a good man," Natalya confers to Kathy, and the other woman smiles at her.

"Thank you. We can't tell him, or his head will get too big, but I agree," she replies, winking at Rose.

Scar, now content in Rose's arms, babbles excitedly without purpose, and the room's attention turns to her.

"Could I hold her for a moment? It's been so long," Kathy simpers and Rose is immediately at war with herself. Kathy seems nice—amazing, really if the last ten minutes are any indication—but only three other people outside the hospital where she gave birth have ever held Scar, and Rose watched all of them like a hawk. *Natalya* hasn't even held her yet, and she's about to be in charge of her well-being five days a week. The two people who previously took turns watching her while Rose was at work, she spied on for *days* before she allowed within ten feet of her daughter; Scar is her life, and she would do anything, risk anything, to keep her safe, to keep anything remotely bad far from her.

(She already has.)

Kathy's been nothing but polite, but Rose knows herself, and there's no way she's going to relinquish her grip on the baby until she knows the woman better. She braces herself to say no, cringing as she hopes the older woman doesn't lash out at the rejection, but before she can get the word out, Josh speaks.

"Come on, Aunt Kathy, she just woke up. The kid probably wants to cuddle with her mom. Besides, I happen to know you and Mama almost never let go of me when *you* were the ones with a newborn."

Thank God, he's given her an out.

Kathy scowls playfully at her grown godson, but his eyes are on Rose's, and given the way he's analyzing her, she has a feeling his perfect timing was not a coincidence.

"So, tell us about yourself, Rose. What brings you here?" Kathy asks, settling herself onto the couch.

"Here?" Rose croaks.

She knows. She knows I ran; she's going to try to be helpful and track them down because she's the kind that thinks family is important, and they'll come after us. They'll find us.

"To the building," Kathy clarifies, and the anxiety mounting in Rose jerks to a plateau.

"Oh, well, when I moved to Florida, I didn't have enough to get a place here, but my lease is finally up, and I really wanted to get us to a better part of town now that Scar is here."

She'd been a month shy of eighteen when she'd found out about Scar, the bean growing inside of her, and knew staying at home wasn't an option any longer, even if it meant living in a car till her birthday when she could finally sign a lease.

(which it did.)

Nati nods in understanding. "We did the same when my oldest was little. Did you move here to be near family once she was born?"

All the questions put Rose on guard, though she knows this is normal; most people just want to get to know the new neighbor.

She has to hold back a bitter laugh at this one, though, the opposite of the truth. She shakes her head definitively. "No, for school, actually." *In short.* "I'm taking classes at USF. Well, I say *at*, but they're all online so that I can do the work from home."

"Oh, how wonderful! More time with this precious one before she gets too big and doesn't let you kiss her cheek in public." Kathy winks at her as Josh rolls his eyes.

"Aunt Kathy, I *always* let you smother me in public. Don't lie to her, or I'll pull up the footage from my last game, which *aired on television* you sneak."

That gets a laugh from his godmother. "Fine, he's right. Josh goes to USF too, on a cheerleading scholarship," she tells the Rose and Natalya, beaming proudly. "He's the strongest base on the team—the one that throws the girls up," she explains further.

"No other way they would've let me in," Josh mutters, but the smirk on his face makes Rose think he might not mind so much. "They're trying to appear more well-rounded, so they've been recruiting a bunch of athletes to try and improve their ranking. I did football in high school, too, but there's a lot less male cheerleaders out there, and you kind of need them at the collegiate level, so it's a lot more feasible to get a scholarship."

Rose nods, brows lifted. "That's really impressive. You must be a pretty trustworthy guy if everyone lets you launch them ten feet high."

Natalya smiles at him. "He's a strong one, always helps me carry in the groceries and packages. Yells at me whenever he catches me on a ladder."

"My little Hercules, alright," Kathy teases, stroking the top of his head as he scrunches his face sheepishly.

"Don't you have any hobbies besides embarrassing me?" he half-jokingly begs.

"Not a single one," his godmother replies with a grin before turning back to Rose. "Well, dear, it's been lovely meeting you, but we have to get going so we can feed this one's friends before they start munching on the furniture. They're all helpless in the kitchen, so we take pity and do family dinner nights."

Rose rises to walk them to the door, feeling her body relax at the knowledge that all the strangers are leaving—that in just a moment, she can lock the door and know she and Scar are alone and safe. "It was really great to meet you too—and thank you so much for the cookies. I'm sure Scar wishes her teeth had come in already so she could try one. I'll wash the Tupperware and bring it by as soon as I can."

Josh waves an arm easily. "Don't worry about it; she has a million of those things. Whenever you get the chance is fine. And I'm sure she'll bring more over by the time Scar's on solids—the woman is the sugar industry's best customer."

Kathy laughs but leans in before following him out the door, and so only Rose can hear, she says, "If you need anything at all, go ahead and call me. Being a single mother is hard and terrifying; you never feel like you're doing anything right. I'm happy to help if you ever need anything or have any questions at all."

Rose swallows thickly. She's known Kathy for half an hour, and she's already been more motherly than the woman who raised Rose was in her entire life. "Thank you. Really, that means a lot."

Kathy smiles, "Of course, sweetie. I'll have JJ give you my number the next time he sees you. Bye, little one." She gives a little wave to Scar's drowsy form. "Bye, Rose. Have a wonderful rest of your day."

Rose bids her farewell, and she and Josh make awkward eye contact before he waves casually, and the two walk away, leaving Rose to close her door and wonder why she feels so strangely every time she interacts with Josh. She's seen hot guys before, but when he's around—

Focus.

She turns back to Natalya. "Right. Okay, Natalya—do you want to talk payment?"

The older woman rolls her eyes. "Listen, honey, I'm not worried about money. I have my retirement, and while a little extra cash is always nice, I don't need twenty an hour or whatever the going rate is these days. I'm not just saying that for your sake; you're doing me a favor by letting me spend time with the little one. All my grandkids live too far to see regularly. You give me whatever you think is fair that you can afford, help me decorate what I can't reach when the holidays roll around, and we'll call it even."

Rose starts to protest, but Natalya wags a finger at her. "No buts. You know why I'm here? Why my kids made it through high school, how we made it through it all? Someone else did the same for me. We women, we mothers, we have to help each other out, no? You let me do this for you and your baby like she did for me and mine, and one day when she's grown with her own children, and you see another one of us who needs a hand, you pay it forward. That's all I want from you in return."

Eyes watering, Rose nods reluctantly as Natalya squeezes her hand. "Yes, ma'am. Thank you. Really. I don't know what I would do if you hadn't offered to do this for us."

"We all have to help each other out, honey. Love the people around us, whether you believe in God or not. It's what makes the world go round."

3

She and Bronte both tense at the knock on the door; they've only been at this motel for a few weeks, and they're on edge in the unfamiliar space, surrounded by people that have them perpetually keeping a knife on their person.

"Hide," Bronte hisses, grabbing the baseball bat she keeps next to the bed as Rose pulls a blanket over her shoulders and slips under the bed, making herself appear as nothing more than forgotten laundry the way Bronte taught her when they first ran away.

(She peeks out the edge of the blanket, though, unable to help herself— worried for Bronte's safety, though she knows the older girl would prefer anything in the world to Rose getting hurt, especially on her behalf.)

Bronte undoes the bottom lock but leaves the chain up, cracking the door and bracing the bat behind her back. "What?"

The dark-haired man on the other side holds his hands up innocently, though his eyes sparkle with mischief.

(And something a different person might interpret as kindness; Rose knows better than to believe it.)

"Hey, relax, not here to bother you. Just made too many cookies and *figured if someone didn't help me eat them, they would go bad anyway. I've been offering them around."*

(Rose knows better than to trust it, and yet...it's been so long since they had something fresh baked. The longing seeps through her.)

Bronte scoffs. "Yeah, right. Out of the kindness of your heart? I don't think so. I've never even seen you before."

His smile wavers, but he doesn't relent. "Hey, I promise they're not laced with anything; you can ask any of the others who've already started eating them." He scratches at the back of his head with the hand not holding the plate of cookies. "I just...I've seen the kid around. Your sister, I'm assuming?" He lets out a heavy sigh. "I have a soft spot for kids. I remember what it was like..." A shake of his head. "I'm sure you know. Anyway, I just figured she might like some sweets. And you always look exhausted and terrified, so...thought you might like a bright spot."

Bronte stares at him; she doesn't move, but Rose knows her well enough to know she's shocked at the thoughtfulness.

"I'm Evan, by the way."

———

A week later, Rose had fought Isa on her taking Scar for the evening, but in this moment, she wants to send her best friend flowers. Her apartment is clean, her budgeting for the month is mapped out, and she still has time for a nap and an episode of something that's not *Paw Patrol*.

Basically, it's her dream night.

Returning Josh's Tupperware is her last errand for the day, and she nervously stands outside his door for at least three minutes, just building up the courage to knock. She knows full well that as soon as he opens the door, all smiles and cheekbones and smolder, she's going to be too frazzled for coherent thought.

(Just do it.)

Seconds after her knuckles touch the wood, it swings open, revealing Josh with a dishtowel slung over his shoulder and looking mildly out of breath. "Hey, you're—Rose!" His eyes widen comically at the sight of her. "What's up?"

"Is this a bad time? Sorry, I just wanted to return your Tupperware, but you look kind of...overwhelmed," she settles on, trying to be diplomatic.

"I'm the cook, and family dinner night is always a little bit chaotic," he admits. "But in the best way, even though they're all heathens."

"You talk a lot of smack for someone who pours his milk before the cereal," a familiar voice pokes.

Bronte comes into Rose's line of sight, and Rose's jaw drops, shock and confusion swirling together.

"Rose?" Before Rose can say anything else, Bronte yanks her into a tight hug.

"Bronte, what are you doing here?" she asks a little breathlessly. "I didn't think I'd see you till Tuesday."

"Family dinner. God, I'm so happy to see you. Do you want to stay for dinner?"

"I can't today, but...I'm so confused, you know Josh?"

"Yeah, Kai—the one I was with when I saw you—is Josh's roommate, and he's actually—"

Josh interrupts dryly, "Hi, this is super cute and all, and I love that you're comfortable enough in my apartment to invite others over, but Rose, how are you unlucky enough to know Angel Hair here?"

For a minute there, Rose had completely forgotten Josh's presence, but his commentary brings him back to the forefront of her gaze just in time to see Bronte elbow him in the ribs.

Bronte puts an arm around Rose, giving Josh a look. "Shut up, pain in the ass. Rose and I have been family for longer than I've known you or Kai even existed. We just found each other again last week."

Rose had worried things wouldn't be the same, but hearing Bronte say it for the first time in five, almost six years, just like they'd always said as kids...it's probably the second-best moment of Rose's life, after holding Scar for the first time. She feels a huge smile stretch across her face. Josh gives her a look, though she doesn't know how to label it. Maybe baffled?

Josh presses a hand to his chest, wounded. "Hurtful. I'll tell your cousin you said that."

"Cousin?" Rose asks, shocked. Her neck snaps back to Bronte. "You...you found them? Your family?"

Bronte grins. "I did. Mom apparently died when I was eighteen, while we were... Anyway, she mentioned who my father was in her will—she left everything to him, naturally—and I finally tracked his side of the family down and met Kai, my cousin; he's the one I was at brunch with when I saw you. That's how I got saddled with Josh here. Zeke, too; he's Josh's best friend since we met, so he's family. We normally drag him to brunch as well, but his boyfriend had a business conference this week, and he tagged along—you'll have to meet him next time. Anyway, Kai has four younger siblings, and my aunt is quite possibly the most wonderful person I've ever met. They're... even better than all the scenarios we came up with back in the day."

Rose presses a hand to her mouth. "I...that's *amazing*, Bronte. I can't believe you actually found them. Finally."

"Me too. But how do you know this idiot, anyway?" Bronte asks, tilting her head towards Josh, who looks too attractive for his own good in Rose's opinion.

"Rose is the new neighbor I told you about, the one Aunt Kathy and I went to see last week when you were making a ruckus about not getting your food soon enough."

Rose feels her face heat up at the memory. "I swear I meant to return the cookie tin sooner."

Bronte laughs. "Kiddo, I promise, Kathy couldn't care less how long it takes you. The woman is a legitimate saint—the only reason I'm ever in your building, anyway. I have my own apartment across town, and God knows this place is always a mess, so I normally make them come to me unless she's over."

But then Bronte's eyebrows scrunch together, and Rose can *see* the wheels in her brain turning, same as always, and knows she's in trouble.

"Josh," Bronte says slowly, still looking Rose dead in the eyes whilst her own start to burn with speculation, the beginnings of anger. Of *knowing*. "You said the new girl had a baby."

Shit. Bronte knows, and as nice as Josh seems, this is not a conversation Rose ever, ever, *ever* wants to have anywhere near him.

(or at all.)

"She does," Josh confirms, seeming a bit confused. "Super cute kid. I know I say that about every baby, but seriously, this one is commercial-cute."

Rose smiles lightly, though she knows it doesn't reach her eyes. "Thanks. I think so too."

"Rose." Bronte's tone is icy.

(Because she knows Rose is careful, meticulously so.)

The older girl stares at her, horror in the lines of her face. "Please tell me it wasn't—"

"Bronte, I have to get back to my apartment. And in any case, this isn't a discussion to have here." Rose's tone is even, but her eyes are pleading.

"Even now?" She completely ignores Rose's words.

Rose bites her lip and doesn't answer, knowing she's never lied to Bronte and never will, and even if she did, Bronte would know the truth anyway. She's always read her like a book.

"They don't know where I am now; they don't even know that I applied to USF. Why would I? They'll never come here to look." She's quiet to keep Josh from hearing.

Hoping to quell the rage visibly coursing through Bronte, she reaches into her apron for the burner phone she keeps solely in case of an emergency with Scar, opening it to show the blonde woman the picture of a smiling Scar on the home screen. "She—she's named Scarlett. Scarlett Bronte."

Bronte swallows, and Rose continues at a normal volume. "I thought she was going to be a boy; she was never in the right position during an ultrasound to see, and I guess I was in the thirty percent of mothers whose intuition is wrong because I have a baby blanket with *James Evan* embroidered."

Evan, the ally they'd met in the first shoddy apartment they rented upon Bronte turning eighteen. The first actual *good* guy she'd ever met. There'd been drama and authorities, a gang that moved into the same building who they'd had to run from, and they'd been split up without a way to contact each other. Not that it would have mattered even if they hadn't found each other shortly after, as they were separated for good just three months later.

The diversion does its job; Bronte presses a hand to her mouth, allowing Rose to catch sight of the tattoos snaking onto her hands.

"Evan? As in your Evan?" Josh ponders, and Bronte's nod only has Rose's eyes widening.

"You still talk to him?"

Bronte blushes, for the first time Rose has ever witnessed. "I managed to find his email after everything...fell apart. We'd always said we'd all make it to Tampa, so...he got here a year before I did, and we found each other a few months or so after I moved down. We actually..." She clears her throat nervously. "We're sort of together. He's at work tonight, but he was so fucking excited when I told him I saw you. He's planning on crashing our hang out on Tuesday."

"Oh, my God," Rose whispers under her breath. "That's..." She opens and closes her mouth, unable to put it in words. The elation coursing through her is like nothing else.

"Yeah." Bronte's mouth quirks upward, and she glances back at the phone, at the picture of Scar still dimly lighting the screen. "I can't wait to meet her, Rose. Ev will be so excited, too."

Her daughter will get to know the only family she's ever had. It warms everything inside her. "I...yeah. I can't wait. I have to get home, finish some stuff before I pick her up, but Tuesday," she promises.

Her mood is sky high by the time she goes to scoop Scar from Isa's place. She's on the verge of happy tears at the mere prospect of what Tuesday will bring.

She dreads it, too, though. Bronte has always been stubborn, and Rose knows it's only a matter of time until they have the conversation about how Scarlett came to be. Trepidation fills her at the thought alone.

(Bronte has always been like a dark angel of vengeance, and if Evan catches wind...)

Still. Bronte. Bronte and Evan. Her family. *Here*—and she's eighteen, so no one can tear them apart this time.

Nothing, not even the thought of Cheyenne, can darken her day.

———

A few days later, Rose steels herself before knocking on the door of Josh's apartment. She's in the midst of contemplating whether accepting the lunch invite was a bad idea when the door swings open, decision made for her.

"Hey, Rose," he greets her amicably, then bends a bit to look Scar in the eye, the infant cooing at the attention. "Hey, little angel. How are we doing today?"

"She's been in a great mood all morning. I think she's trying to be cute enough that I forget how little sleep she let me get last night."

"I'm sure she'd just rather hang out with you than miss out on the time together to sleep," Josh says wisely. He winks at Scar before he stage-whispers, "No worries, kid, I think she bought it."

Rose laughs in return, and Josh gestures inside the apartment.

She hesitates. "Is anyone else here yet?"

"Zeke and Kai are both around, but they have their own plans for lunch, I think."

So, she wouldn't be *alone* with Josh while they waited for Bronte. But then those are both his friends...but Kai is Bronte's cousin.

(And she can't always halt her life for this.)

She cautiously following Josh inside, and the place is...well, about as tidy and devoid of video games as one would expect from a space inhabited solely by three college-aged guys. Pictures adorn the walls, hardly a square foot bare here and there.

"What is that smell? Did you order in or something?"

"Oh, no, I...uh, I'm cooking. I have chicken parm in the oven. Shit, you're not vegetarian or anything, are you? I definitely should've made sure you didn't have any allergies or anything, I'm so—"

"Josh, honestly, no worries," she assures him, the ends of her lips turning upward. "I won't say I'll eat anything, but I'm not too picky—and Italian is probably my favorite thing there is. God, I don't know the last time I had anything more complicated than spaghetti." Her eyes close, and she hums in contentment at the aroma.

"Okay, cool, I'm glad to hear it. Te and Evan aren't here yet; they're late to pretty much everything—which is pretty ironic, coming from me. That's the real reason I always volunteer to host things. Makes it impossible for me to not be there on time."

A bit of tension fills her at the knowledge that she's the only woman in the apartment, but Josh seems like a genuine guy, and Bronte trusts him. Bronte has the best judgment of anyone she's ever known.

Anyone can be fooled, a little voice reminds her, but she takes a deep breath and turns her gaze back to Josh, who's kindly pretending not to notice her temporary breakdown while stirring at something simmering on the stove.

"Who's this?" She gestures to one of the larger pictures in the room, one of the only ones in a frame, hanging on the wall between the living room and the kitchen. It's a bright image of a lithe woman, the bottom half of her braids dyed a gorgeous silvery gray where they trail down her shoulders, cheesing widely at the camera with her arms around a vibrant redhead who looks just as thrilled to be there.

Josh turns to see where her attention is, and his eyes grow soft, a bit mournful. "My mom."

"Who's that she's with?"

"My mom," he repeats, coming to stand beside Rose with a small smile. "They got together in their early twenties. Decided to foster, since obviously, they could never have a kid biologically, and IVF is expensive as shit...adopted me out of the system when I was one."

"They look so in love," Rose comments wistfully.

"They were." Josh sighs, shaking his head.

Rose says softly, "You don't have to go into detail, of course, but... they're both gone?"

"Yeah. Cancer's a bitch. Mom—the one with auburn hair—died

when I was nine. Mama...my other mom, I mean, the one who was best friends with Kathy, just died two years ago." He doesn't elaborate on the manner of her death, and based on the look in his eyes, Rose gets the feeling it's something much darker—something that didn't come about naturally.

Saying sorry is tempting; it doesn't help, but it feels like the only thing to offer. Still, Rose decides against it. Josh seems to have made his peace with it. "Did she ever fall in love again?"

"No. She married my step-dad a year later, but...it wasn't anything like what she and Mom had. I hope they're together, whatever comes after this."

The mood, which has grown quite somber, is electrified when Bronte slams open the door without preamble; Rose and Josh both jump, Scar lets out a whimper.

Rose has to pinch herself at the sight of Bronte because it still doesn't feel real, even as the older girl comes to wrap her arms around her.

"You know I'm not much of a hugger, but I'm probably going to attack you every time I see you for the next year," she admits, and Rose says nothing but squeezes her back tightly with the arm not holding Scar.

"Bronte," she says hesitantly, stepping out of the embrace, "this is Scarlett." Her baby girl looks up at the stranger before her curiously, face neutral, grasping onto her fingers when Bronte reaches out to her.

The smallest of smiles creeps onto Bronte's face. "Hey there, little one. I'm your Aunt Bronte. Sorry it took so long for us to meet."

Scar smiles, likely having realized that the new face was going to continue giving her attention, and Rose looks to her friend questioningly. "Do you...you can hold her if you want."

Bronte's grin is like sunshine, like she knows relinquishing that much control alone is killing Rose, and she nods, reaching out to take Scar.

"Watch her neck," Rose warns her worriedly, scowling when Bronte bats away her nerves.

"Seriously? You make me park the car and leave without me *and* get your paws on the kid first?"

Rose whirls to face the door, pressing a hand to her mouth with a gasp.

She'd known he would be here, of course—seeing Evan was half the point of this—but nonetheless, hearing his voice, seeing him in the flesh, and so much older, nearly knocks her from her feet.

"Hey, squirt."

She moves to the door slowly, then abruptly presses herself into his chest without hesitation, surprising even herself as she can't even remember the last time she hugged a man. Evan's arms wrap tightly around her, and she holds back a sob.

Nothing can take them from her now; Cheyenne is completely out of her life, and no one and nothing but death itself can separate her from Bronte and Evan, but most of all Scar—the one good thing Cheyenne will never spoil.

"I hear the kid almost had a pretty great name," Evan says, muffled by her hair, and she laughs before tugging him over to where his girlfriend stands beside her neighbor, holding the child in question.

"This is Scar."

Evan reaches out to smooth her hair, face alighting when the infant grabs onto a finger. "I gotta hand it to you, Rosie, she's pretty perfect. Although I never would've imagined you'd be the first of us to have a kid," he notes almost as an afterthought. Rose meets Bronte's eyes, but she refuses to comment, glad for Josh's presence if only as a buffer.

Bronte hands Scar off to Evan, and his hand slides to support her neck before Rose can get the words out of her mouth to tell him to. Really, she's impressed by how quickly Evan slips the kid into his arms, his grip much more practiced than she'd expected.

"Food's ready!" Josh announces, shepherding everyone into the kitchen. "You two are lucky you weren't any later, or Rose and I would've eaten without you and had no remorse."

Bronte crosses her arms, smug. "That's a lie, and you know it,

Brooks; Kathy would have your hide for starting without all your guests present."

"Both of the guests *were* present, Whitman. You and Evan aren't guests, you're an invasive species."

The two continue teasing each other back and forth, and Rose's heart warms at seeing how happily Bronte interacts with her cousin's best friend; Evan looks on unsurprised, as though the ribbing is fairly regular, and Rose joins him in spectating as she eats with one hand, holding Scar in the other in a careful, time-honed manner.

"So, what are y'all up to, now?" She eyes Evan and Bronte expectantly.

Bronte shoots her a wicked grin and begins rolling up her sleeves. While Rose had noticed the swirls of ink peeking out on one wrist, she hadn't anticipated that every inch of previously covered skin would be adorned with intertwining quotes and images, masterful shading all the way up, extending to the collarbone beneath the crew neck of the shirt she tugs at. "Courtesy of my coworkers. I've been at it for six years; I always liked to draw, you know that, but I never thought anything would come of it. After I'd been in to get a few tattoos of my own—all of which I'd drawn the mock-ups of—Cal, my artist, showed them to the other guys, and he asked if I'd want to apprentice. Been there ever since."

"It doesn't terrify you?" Rose bites her lip. "Marking people? Knowing what you do—if you mess up, it's permanent?"

"After everything we've lost, everything we've had taken away...it's kind of nice to know some things are forever. That things I create will be forever." Bronte's voice is quiet, wistful, and Rose nods as understanding floods her.

To know something of yourself will last, regardless of anything else...in their former lives, it would've been an impossibility. Before Scar, she wouldn't have been able to imagine it.

"If I ever pluck up the courage to get one, I'll let you do the honors," she promises, and a delighted glint lights up Bronte's eyes at the prospect.

"Are you still painting, Briar Rose?"

Rose rubs at her forehead. "I suppose so, but I haven't really had the time or energy in ages."

"We'll make it happen soon," Bronte says decidedly. "Your turn," she tells her boyfriend, and he looks to Rose.

"I'm a youth counselor-mentor...basically a youth pastor, but without getting religion involved except when kids want to discuss their own faith. I run a community center on the other side of town."

"You know, I never would've pegged you for that, but that sounds so right. How did you get into it?" Rose asks curiously, but a pained look flashes across Evan's face.

"It's a long story. I'll tell you some other time."

She nods, understanding not wanting to bring sorrow into the atmosphere, and frowns at the guilt still alight in his face—at the implied history.

Another one of us with a dark history, with memories best left buried.

At this point in life, she's learned most people have gone through their own personal tragedy, a decent hand to play in misery poker.

(A game no one ever wins.)

4

She's reading in the room while Bronte's at work when the knock sounds at the door.

Normally she pretends not to be home whenever anyone stops by while she's alone, but they're expecting a package, and someone in the building has been stealing mail, so it's not worth leaving it out for longer than is necessary.

She keeps the bat at her side as she swings the door open to grab it and sees the dark-haired guy from the other day walking by as she does. She's contemplating whether it's worth risking Bronte's wrath to say hi to him when he spots her and makes the decision for her.

"Hey, squirt." He grins but doesn't move any closer—like he knows she's skittish, and doing so would send her running.

It's...oddly comforting. Makes her let down her guard, just the slightest bit.

"Hi. Thanks for the cookies," she says back, the words coming out quieter than she'd intended. "Sorry Bronte was a little...harsh."

"I'm sure she had every reason to be." Evan doesn't look resentful about it at all; his expression is understanding, empathetic if such a thing exists. "I'll bring more by the next time I make them."

Rose nods even as the prolonged interaction makes her antsy; he's tall and has to be almost twice her weight—it's all too evident he could over-power her in an instant.

Her breathing starts to grow shallow.

"You should get back inside," he says gently like he can tell his presence makes her anxious. "Tell Bronte I said hi. And anytime you two need anything, feel free to let me know, okay?"

"Alright. Um...thank you, Evan."

"Sure thing, squirt. It's no problem."

She hurries to re-lock the door once back inside, trembling a bit from the interaction.

And yet somehow, for the first time in recent memory, she's been able to walk away from a conversation with a man without spiraling into flashbacks.

———

It's 2 a.m. a week later, and Josh has every intention of going straight home. The five button in the elevator is lit, he's prematurely started unlacing his non-slip work shoes, the whole nine yards.

But when the box stops on the third floor to let out another resident, and he sees a crumpled form sitting on the floor in the hallway, his chest tugs him out without a second's pause.

"Rose?"

She looks up at him, rapidly wiping puffy eyes with the sleeves of her heavily oversized hoodie—the only thing she ever seems to wear outside of work. "Josh, hi."

"Hey, I...haven't seen you in a bit. You doing alright?"

"Yeah, I'm fine," she assures him, her face pulling into a smile that's so clearly fake it pains him.

He hesitates for a moment. He doesn't want to push, but she looks so downtrodden. He sits down a few feet away from her. "Sorry, I know we don't really know each other. It's just, asking if you're okay would be stupid, but...is there anything I can do?" His voice is pleading by the time the end of the mangled sentence escapes him, eyes flickering between her and the hall rapidly.

"No, that's—that's really sweet of you, Josh, but no."

"Come on," he encourages. "Something's obviously bothering you. It's okay to get it off your chest."

Rose hesitates, but he's pretty sure she can see the persistence on his face. She gives in and clears her throat. "I'm being ridiculous, really; nothing is that bad. It's...I haven't slept more than an hour or two in almost a week, and Scar is really sick, but I've already taken off two days of work to take care of her. If I don't go in tomorrow, there's no way I'll make enough to pay rent this month; I'll either be too exhausted to take care of her properly or too broke to keep a roof over her head."

His eyes widen, chest tightening with commiseration. "God, that sucks." He sits down next to her awkwardly, attempting to come up with something to say without sounding petulant or continuing to state the obvious. "Natalya won't take care of her when she's sick?"

"No, it's not that." She shook her head. "She's actually on vacation right now, visiting her daughter in Colorado for a week. She made sure I had plenty of notice, and I made arrangements for Scar to go to daycare while she's gone, but they won't take her when she's sick; they can't risk it spreading to the other kids. Honestly, even if Nati were here, I don't know that she'd be able to take her. Her immune system is just way too fragile; an illness like this could put her out of commission for months or worse."

"Damn, I wouldn't have even thought about that." Josh's heart feels constricted at Rose's clear misery and lack of options; the circumstances are exactly the kind of thing his mom had had to deal with the majority of his adolescence, in reality, if not legality while married to her piece of shit husband.

"Yeah. I asked Bronte for help, even though I hate to be a burden, so she's coming over right before I head out, but her shift starts two hours after mine, and she's closing, so I'll have to leave mid-shift anyway."

Knowing Rose would do anything she could for her daughter,

seeing the unnecessary obstacles in her way when she does nothing but work and love her kid...it's a familiar frustration that he has no power to fix. A moment of silence. "Is she sleeping right now?"

"Yeah, she just—" Cries erupt from within the apartment behind them, and Rose scowls at him, but beyond that, something behind her eyes crumples. "You jinxed this. It took me hours to get her down."

"Sorry. I have terrible luck, and it tends to be contagious."

The corners of her lips twitch upward, but she holds back the smile. Still, he's gotten her to look slightly less distraught, so he's counting it as a win. He's always been the class clown, and most people assume it's just him being naturally goofy, but the self-depre-cating humor is no accident. He'd been a kid still when he noticed his dumb jokes made a world of difference in his mom's mood. He was so desperate to make her day even the slightest bit brighter, and as he'd gotten older, he'd realized that most people could use that little bit of light in their day.

(It had been a costly habit when Geoffrey was around, but his mom's smile... *Worth it every time.*)

"Me too. Maybe us being near each other is a bad idea," Rose teases, and Josh is shaken back into the present.

She gets to her feet slowly and tentatively waves him into the apartment with her as she makes her way to pick up her daughter.

Josh has been inside once before, of course, but hadn't really looked around much then. He finds himself taking it in now. He spies a sink full of dishes, but otherwise, it's almost impeccably clean – a worn-looking pull-out futon and kitchen table, sturdy crib, vibrant colors on a bouncer and mobile.

She does the bare minimum for herself and spends all her money on Scarlett, then; Josh's heart swells with respect and awe.

(And other emotions it feels far too soon to have.)

He presses a hand to his chest, mock affronted, "And here I was prepared to sacrifice for the sake of our friendship. Besides, don't two negatives cancel into a positive?"

"I'll give you that," she concedes, rocking back on her heel and bouncing the crying baby.

She visibly relaxes a bit at his humor, and he breathes, glad that she's starting to seem a bit more okay around him.

He's seen her with Scar before, of course; it's pretty clear to him that he tends to make her uncomfortable, so he holds himself back from shouting to her from across the building or stopping by to talk often, despite their mutual family and the ease with which they've gotten along so far. But he sees her around all the time, usually clutching Scar to her chest like a mama bear ready to fight anyone and everyone to the death at the first hint of danger.

And she's beautiful. Always. It was the first thing he noticed, dropping on him like a brick, or a pile of bricks, really, when he saw her for the first time. But with Scar, when it's so clear how much Rose loves her, how much she's sacrificed for her, it's shines like a beacon.

Josh isn't an idiot, and he doesn't think it's a coincidence that Rose moved to Florida mere months after Scar was conceived, that she's never mentioned her family or the other half of Scar's genes' source. There's no way the omission is unintentional. It pulls on his heart-strings—and other parts of his anatomy because, really, the woman is a goddess. Not to mention the sight of Scar's adorable face, blue eyes bright and attentive. Every time he sees the kid, there's another spark of personality forming.

He opens his mouth to say something, to keep the conversation that's finally happening with this woman who's captivated him for a month now going, but he has no clue where to start. More than anything, he wants to learn all about her, how she became this vibrant, independent woman who works harder than almost anyone he's ever known.

Rose is a mystery, though, and she's made it clear she doesn't like talking about herself. So maybe the answer is to open up first, be vulnerable enough that she might feel comfortable around him.

"I bartend," he offers aimlessly. He starts to think the conversation is a lost cause, but she finally, *finally* produces that small smile he's seen glimpses of like she knows what he's doing and appreciates it. "I got an athletic scholarship—no other way I would've gotten into USF or been able to afford any kind of college because I'm incredibly bad at school, but you need a degree if you want to be a guidance counselor, which I do. Which sounds ironic, but it's *because* I'm bad at school that I want to work at one, so I can help kids suck at it less. Make them realize that being bad at traditional school shit doesn't mean they don't still have all the potential in the world, you know?

"But like, obviously commuting from Jacksonville wasn't going to happen, and with all of the debt—" He cuts off his monologue abruptly and looks up at Rose. He hadn't intended to mention Geoffrey, but something about the understanding on her face and knowing from Bronte that she ran away from home when she was eleven and managed to stay away for two years makes him think she might know something about going through shit. "Anyway. I ended up here. Slowly but surely working towards my bachelor's."

Rose nods in understanding. "And you cheer, which is pretty badass."

He laughs. "I guess you could say that." They sit in silence for a moment before Josh bites his lip. "Could I...could I hold her?" he asks, gesturing to Scar.

Rose nods slowly, looking surprised by the abrupt change of topic but not scared, which he figures is probably progress. "Make sure you keep your arm or hand under her neck at all times. She doesn't have the muscles to support her head yet."

He nods seriously, preemptively putting his arms into position as she carefully nestles the baby into them. He can feel her watching him, cautious and protective.

Josh sucks in a breath at the sensation. Scar is as light as a pigeon, her tiny body less cumbersome than a backpack, and his heart swells with some kind of instinctive awe at the sight of the vulnerable little girl in his arms. "Oh my God, she's perfect. This is the most amazing thing in my entire life."

Rose graces him with another small smile, and he decides right then it's going to be his mission to be both witness to and the cause of as many of her smiles as possible, for as long as she'll let him.

(That smile...it's something out of this world.)

"I think so too," she agrees.

"You—God, Rose, you *made* this little girl, how is that even real? You grew her like a plant, and now there's just this whole *person*..." He trails off, babbling incessantly, and Rose lets out a semblance of a giggle.

"Your first time holding a baby?" she presumes, and he doesn't even have it in him to blush at her smirk.

"Yeah. This is the coolest thing in my whole life, oh my God. I have to tell Aunt Kathy. She's going to freak."

Josh is hesitant to suggest it, is aware she might be reluctant to even consider the possibility. He knows he comes off as intimidating: muscular, typically dressed in the black standard bartender attire that seems to send out waves of foreboding.

"I could..." He takes a deep breath before voicing the irrational thought that has been popping up in his head incessantly throughout their interaction. "I could watch her tomorrow. So you could go to work. I mean, I know I don't know anything about babies, but I could come over while Bronte's here and watch her after she leaves till you get home. I mean, I would try really hard, and I could call Aunt Kathy if anything happens, and I don't have any classes, and there was supposed to be a performance with the team, so I didn't get put on the schedule and...yeah. I mean, only if you're comfortable with it, because obviously she's like, your *kid*, and you don't want to just let some rando have her for the day, which is so totally fair because I can't imagine how scary it is to trust anyone with your freaking baby, but I would keep such a close eye on her, and I know where the nearest clinic is if she were to get any sicker and...anyway." He sucks in a deep breath, looking up at her anxiously.

"I...Josh, that's so great of you to offer, but I couldn't impose on you like that, and she's really cranky when she's not feeling well."

(The look on her face, the love and concern so wholly directed towards her daughter; it's clear this is far outside her comfort zone.)

"That's okay! I know some lullabies, and I have literally nothing better to do, and her existence is just the most crazy amazing thing.

You know Bronte would make sure I knew exactly what I was doing, and honestly, I kind of just get the feeling if you don't get some sleep soon, you're going to collapse. Sorry. I just…Rose, you're not a burden. It's okay to ask for help."

They're both silent for a moment as she contemplates the offer. She's visibly torn and doubtful, but…she's in a tight spot.

(It's not really a choice.)

"Okay, if you're sure…"

"Yes! I'll be so careful, Rose, I swear. We'll watch movies, and I'll check her temperature every hour and make sure she eats and all of the things," he assures her earnestly.

"Okay. I have to leave at six, so I'm going to try to sleep now, but if you can be here at around five-forty, I'll show you and Bronte where everything is in the apartment and give you the spare key for the day."

"I won't let you down," he promises.

(He'll do whatever it takes to make sure it's not a lie.)

———

Josh, Kathy, and Bronte have all mentioned to Rose that Josh tends to run at least ten minutes late at all times, so when he knocked quietly on her door at 5:43 just a few minutes before Bronte, Rose was pleasantly surprised despite the terror coursing through her body at having to leave her baby with someone new.

Bronte had shot her a text to let her know when she was leaving, along with the reminder that she and Evan love her and an order for Rose to do more self-care that they've both been consistently adding to every interaction. So technically, she knows Scar is okay, but…it doesn't stop her mind from imagining the worst-case scenario. She's anxious all day at work, hopeful that Scar is feeling better, that everything is going well, that Josh didn't get fed up with the crying after Bronte had to leave and throw Scar out the window and into the bed of a truck driving to Canada and—

Rational, Rose. Be fucking rational.

When she turns the key in her lock, she's worried by the silence within until she enters to find the two passed out on the futon: Josh, drooling in his sleep with his head and upper torso propped up on the two pillows, Scar breathing quietly in her place across Josh's chest, thumb tucked under her own chin.

The sight has Rose's heart brimming with delight. And really, if she didn't already have a kid, it would give her one hell of a case of baby fever.

Josh's laptop—at least, she assumes it's his because it's not hers—sits on the coffee table beside him and has a sticker of the Bulls' logo with the words "**USF Cheer**" in big letters across the bottom. The screen long since faded into sleep like its owner. The kitchen is a bit messier than she left it; the formula she buys for when others have to feed Scar while she's gone and doesn't have any pumped milk frozen, four dirty bottles, a pizza box with three slices remaining, and a two-liter of mountain dew are strewn across the table.

Still, they're both alive, and Scar seems perfectly content, so Rose counts the day as a success.

"Josh," she whispers, shaking his shoulder gently.

"Wassamata Imup," he mumbles, then jerks awake, carefully rising to a sitting position with minimal baby jostling. "Rose, hey. You're back already."

"Hi," she replies with a smile. "Was everything okay?"

"Peachy," he says with a smile. "Her fever was gone by two, and I thought about bringing her by the restaurant so you would stop freaking out—don't deny it, I know you were." He gives her a look, so she closes her mouth and motions for him to continue. "She drank fourteen ounces, and we watched *Tangled* and *Big Hero 6*."

The smile on his face as he relays his day with her daughter is probably the most attractive thing Rose has seen in her entire life, and she knows the image will be imprinted on her brain for approximately the next year.

"Disney on the brain, much? There are kid's movies outside of their domain," she teases.

"They're not as *good*," Josh argues. "And songs are the easiest way to learn, so musical kid's stuff is important. Plus, all the Disney movies encourage independence and going after your dreams. Important stuff for kids."

Rose rolls her eyes jokingly. "Whatever you say, Flynn Rider."

He hands Scar off, and despite knowing she should just put her daughter in the bassinet immediately, Rose can't help but hold her close after being away from her all day. Maternal separation anxiety is the bane of her existence—and its defining feature since her daughter's birth.

"Sorry about the mess in the kitchen, by the way. I meant to clean while she was napping, but I obviously ended up napping too. I'll go ahead and sterilize the bottles; I know that's a lot of them dirty, but when I was online last night, it said if you made the bottle more than thirty minutes prior, you shouldn't give it to the baby, and once, I lost track of time, so I made a new one just in case, so they added up pretty fast, and—what?"

Rose swallows thickly, the feeling in her chest taking her aback. "You looked up how to take care of her last night?"

He hesitates, and she can see him struggle to read the look in her eyes, the confusion in her voice he doesn't seem to understand.

She waits for him to respond, and he flushes, scratching the back of his neck—what Rose has recently deduced to be a nervous tic. "Well, you were leaving her with me; I had to make sure I knew what I was doing."

"You're something else, Josh Brooks." *A marvel.*

He cocks his head at her. "How so?"

"You just...you care so much. About everything you do."

He blushes again at the compliment, then heads to the kitchen and starts tidying up as she curls into the edge of the futon, Scar pressed tight to her heart.

Minutes later, after her eyelids have drooped closed against her better judgment, she feels Scar being tugged from her arms, and she tightens her grip. "No!"

"Shhh, Rose, it's fine. She's okay. I'm just gonna put her in her crib. You need your rest."

"Okay. Thank you, Josh," she mumbles without opening her eyes, her ability to sleep with him still in the apartment a sure sign of exhaustion.

"Rose?"

"Hmm?" she squeezes her eyelids up just the tiniest bit.

"I'm gonna go now. I left the rest of the pizza, so you don't have to cook whenever you wake back up, okay? Make sure you eat some."

"Okay," she mumbles.

He leans forward, and she tenses up. Of *course*, he got past her defenses; it was all a ploy so that she would owe him. Her heart is racing, and she braces herself because now she's halfway passed out, and he can—

Josh presses his lips to her forehead, whispers goodnight, and she hears the door slide open and shut as her heart stutters and begins to slow its pace.

Before she can let herself think too much about it, she fades back into unconsciousness.

5

She's panting when she comes to, instinctively pushing herself to the bed frame as her eyes fly open and she takes in the room around her.

Evan gives her a worried half-smile, one arm still extended from shaking her shoulder to wake her. "You're okay, squirt. Just a nightmare."

(What to say when every nightmare is real—when waking provides no comfort because the horrors of your mind have already happened?)

She can see it in his eyes that he wants to soothe her, wants to brush back her hair and tell her she's safe.

But he won't. The first week they met, he picked up on her skittishness. He has been careful to always let her set the boundaries since.

(Which she knows kills him. He's an overprotective alpha male, and she's a wounded twelve-year-old; his instinct is to coddle her and fight anyone who dares to come towards her. But it's not what she needs, so he just...doesn't.)

(It makes her look up to him all the more.)

"Breakfast is ready."

Rose nods, trudging behind him toward the kitchenette attached to the room and nodding in thanks.

Their favorite country station is blaring on the shitty radio—which

43

Bronte hates, always trading favors and chores to convince them to play alt instead—and except for the fact that Bronte's not home, it's Rose's favorite kind of day.

Evan's phone rings eventually, and he looks surprised as he flips it open. "Hey, man, what's up?" Muffled talking on the other side, and he tilts his head thoughtfully. "Maybe. Let me ask my little sister if she's down. Hold on." He covers the mouthpiece and looks at Rose. "Barbecue at Esli's place, yea or nay? My other coworkers that you like will be there too, and I think he has the good cable stations."

"I...sure," she mumbles, surprised even still that he and Bronte always get her opinion before making decisions.

Later, when he gets off the phone and is putting on his tennis shoes so they can head out, Rose clears her throat. "You...you don't have to bring me along if you just want to hang out with them, you know. I can stay here. And...you don't have to call me that, either. Your—your sister, I mean. I...I don't want you to feel like you have to deal with me every moment of your life."

Evan moves to face her, expression serious. "Hey. You are my sister. Period. We're family. Not an obligation or something I just say; you and Bronte are the most important people in my world, okay?" He waits for her nod before continuing. "Second of all, it's my day off, and I told you we would hang out. I'm not bringing you along to be nice; we're going together because I told my sister I would spend the day with her, so she goes where I go. Period."

She eyes him carefully because...it's just so different than anything she's ever been told before.

(She's always been a burden or an accessory. Being loved by him and Bronte, it's...different.)

"I love you, kid. Bronte does too. You got that?"

Rose bites her lip before cautiously mumbling it back.

(Loving people—being loved by them—feels too good to be true.)

(But it almost seems worth the eventual heartache, even if she just gets to have it for a little while.)

44

By the time he leaves practice, Josh is pretty sure he's sweated out every ounce of water in his body.

He'd thought the same thing an hour previously when they'd practiced the choreo of the dance section of their routine over and over for an hour, and before that, when the coach had made them work intensely on one-man stunts wherein he held, threw, and caught a flyer by himself. But the icing on the cake was when, five minutes before they could go home, Coach shouted, *"Run through, from the top,"* and they had to do the entire routine again, slippery from sweat, muscles aching so badly they shook.

Their next competition is a week and a half away, so the grueling practice isn't surprising, but the more they practiced, the more sluggish he felt, and dread fills him at the thought of his shift at the bar in an hour. It was necessary, and if he had to work, he really couldn't imagine a better gig or better coworkers, but his body was sore, and God only knew how much homework had to get done before the next morning.

(Another all-nighter, then.)

"There you are!" Zeke greets him as he closes the door to the apartment. "Man, I feel like I haven't seen you in weeks."

"I know, sorry. You know how competition season gets. Things should start to let up a bit after the beginning of February."

"Good. I've been missing out on home-cooked meals."

Josh chucks a couch pillow at his older brother in every way except blood, who cracks a smile but then looks at him more seriously. "Anything you might want to tell me?"

"No, should there be?"

"Well..." He trails off, sounding truly nervous for once, and Josh narrows his eyes.

"Well, what?"

"I used your phone to get that link for the internship you showed me the other day, and when I went through your search history to find it, there was an awful lot of stuff about taking care of babies..."

Josh bursts out laughing at the trepidation on Zeke's face. "Dude, how long have you been stressing over my impending fatherhood?"

"Three days," Zeke mumbles. "So it's true?!"

"I don't even have the time to make dinner; how the hell would I have time to make a baby, man? I was babysitting for Rose and wanted to make sure I had my shit together."

"I can't believe she let you babysit." Zeke shakes his head in disbelief. "Not that I wouldn't trust you with a kid, because you already basically dad of a bunch of freshmen, but she doesn't know that, you know? She barely knows you. I can't imagine Dad ever letting someone outside of family watch one of us when we were that young."

Not that this is unsurprising, given that Zeke's father is incredibly overbearing, a quality only made worse by his oldest daughter's death three years ago.

"She doesn't really have any family in the area she could ask even if she wanted to; Bronte and Evan are as close as it gets. I offered, and Bronte was there most of the time. I was only solo for like a couple hours."

Bronte had read him the riot act afterward; they've known each other for years, but in that moment, it was clear that didn't matter when it came to Rose. It was a protective side of Bronte he hadn't known existed, eyes narrowed as she demanded to know his intentions and threatened him within an inch of his life if he so much as looked at Rose sideways.

Clearing his throat, he returns his attention to the conversation at hand. "And honestly, I think she was too sleep-deprived to think straight and didn't have the energy to argue why it was a bad idea. She was out of options."

"You seem to know an awful lot about her for only having met her a few times," Zeke comments innocuously. Josh scowls at him. "I'm just saying."

Kai strolls into the room with a yawn, surprising both his roommates, who hadn't realized he was home. He's only in the apartment part-time, at his family's house the other half of the time despite claiming to have moved out; he's too involved with helping raise his siblings to ever be away for long. Even when he plans on coming back for the day, he'll get distracted by a project at the auto shop and end up staying in his hometown for the night to get an early start.

"What'd I miss?" Kai asks, looking exhausted as per usual.

"Josh is going to fall in love with the new chick on the third floor, and her kid will be the flower girl at their wedding."

"Ezekiel snooped through my search history and gave himself an unnecessary heart attack and is now trying to embarrass me, so I don't notice that he's actually disappointed you two won't have a niece or nephew soon."

Kai raises his eyebrows, planting himself on a barstool near them with a bag of carrots in hand. "Sounds to me like if you and Rose get married, he'll get a niece anyway."

"At least you remembered her name," Josh mutters with an eye roll. "Melodramatic assholes."

"I see her all the time; she gets up for her morning shifts when I go on my run the days I'm not at the shop. I'll start talking you up when we bump into each other," Kai offers, earning a grin from Zeke.

"I don't need a wingman, trust me; Kathy already bragged about me when they met—if you do too, she'll think I need all the hype because something's wrong with me."

Zeke shrugs. "I mean, we want her to know the truth, don't we?"

Josh rubs his temples tiredly as his roommates cackle at his expense. "Yeah, I'll remember that next time you're feeling deprived of home cooking."

"Mockery is the highest form of flattery."

"That's mimicry, idiot. I have to go to work soon. Do you guys need anything while I'm out?"

"No, but invite Rose for dinner soon. I haven't gotten to meet her yet, and Aunt Kathy gave me some lovely baby pictures of you a decade ago that I've been saving for a rainy day."

Josh chucks another throw pillow at him before heading into his room to get ready. In undertones, Kai says, "Man, you *have* to show me those pictures."

———

On Wednesday that week, Rose is nine hours into a fifteen-hour shift, her feet aching and head pounding while she fumes about the table of middle-aged women she'd bent over backward for only to be left a five percent tip. She makes $2 an hour before tips, she has a baby to feed and rent to pay, and the women with fifty-dollar orders and bottomless mimosas can't be decent enough to leave a standard tip?

Her phone buzzes in the pocket of her apron, and without looking, she knows it's Bronte checking in and trying to wheedle her into coming over the following weekend. The thought is enough to put a smile on her face but only barely. Moments later, another table of horrible regulars walks in, Rose's shoulders tensing as she braces for the interaction.

She's just in a mood overall. With a project, two papers, and over a hundred pages of reading to do, she won't be having much time to relax in the next few days, and she knows there are other errands and chores she'll need to get done soon, too, the mere thought of which has her growing more and more agitated.

And while she loves the new apartment building, she can feel her neck muscles growing more and more tense as she does the math of how much she's made in the last few days and exactly how far that will (and won't) go towards rent and utilities alone, when she hears Isa's familiar voice cooing.

Which is confusing because Isa is watching Scar for the day.

She looked up to see her best friend grinning from the doorway of the near-empty diner, baby quiet in her arms as she stares up at the lights; Rose is pretty sure her daughter loves looking at lights more than she loves her mother.

"Isa, what on earth are you doing here?"

"Don't worry, my favorite niece and I are just fine," Isa reassures her, handing over the tiny infant immediately; Scar lets out a happy squeal upon seeing her mother, reaching a hand up to tug on her hair. "We were heading to the beach for the day so she could get some fresh air—*yes*, I have her hat and the baby sunscreen. Anyway, I figured we'd stop by on our way. You seemed stressed this morning, so I thought you could use a progeny-pick-me-up."

"Thanks love." Rose presses a kiss to Scar's hair, feeling her entire body relax at having her daughter in her arms. "She'll have a great time, my little waterbug. You want something to eat while you're here?"

She and Isa had worked together during her first shift at the diner, each of them new to both the state and the job, and she doesn't know what she would've done without her in the months since. When they met, Rose had only been in the city a month, starting to become visibly pregnant and surviving off soup kitchens and free food from filling out the survey on every receipt with the library computers, busting her ass, and constantly picking up extra shifts. While she was doing her best, she knew she looked like a mess, but Isa hadn't batted an eye.

Isa had run full speed from New York herself the day after she graduated high school and willingly estranged herself from the people who thought wealth a substitute for love; her father a CEO and her mother the head of a publishing firm, she'd spent her entire life in socialite circles. Despite her parents' wealth and status, Isa had never looked back and took on a ton of debt, attending an out-of-state school with no qualification for financial aid. She'd been working her ass off at the diner ever since.

Most people who grew up well off couldn't handle sudden poverty, but Isa took life in stride and hasn't complained once since the abrupt change. She works almost as many hours as Rose, and almost every week, she takes care of Scar on her day off.

(She's the best family Rose could ever ask for, for her daughter and herself.)

"You didn't tell me Z lived in your building, chickadee," Isa chides.

"That's probably because I've never heard of 'Z' in my entire life. And I mean the building is USF recommended, so, not the hugest coincidence."

She doesn't turn to look at her best friend, but she can *feel* Isa's eyes rolling. "He's the one from the improv group I'm in on Thursday nights. Remember that story I told you about the Busch Gardens shenanigans? He lives in a triple a floor above you. Anyway, his roommate, mister tall, dark, and incredibly handsome jock man walks out, and you *definitely* have heard of him because he said you met a couple of times and *babysat Scar*. The nerve of you, not telling me." Shock is clear in her voice, tone peaking with the significance of Rose allowing someone else to watch her daughter.

Of course *Isa met Josh*. The man in question is entirely unlike Rose had anticipated him to be. As much as she likes to think she doesn't judge people by their appearance or a first impression, she never would've pegged the ripped bartender from upstairs to be so sentimental, have a paralyzing fear of alpacas, or be a pretty decent chef.

She's seen him a couple more times since he graciously babysat, and she is trying to convince her brain to be less skittish around him. Being half scared of the guy and half into him yields a pretty frustrating mess of emotions when he's around.

It's not exactly an accident Rose hasn't mentioned him to Isa yet. She's still trying to sift through her own feelings about the man before attempting to explain them to someone else.

'Z', then, must be the Zeke Bronte mentioned, who's like family to Josh. The elusive third resident of their apartment and the only one she's yet to run into in the elevator during an ungodly hour.

Kai she sees fairly regularly, thanks to his own crazy schedule, a mechanic's work hours combined with younger siblings he talks about the way Rose talks about Scar.

"I thought you only had eyes for Nick," Rose deflects, mentioning Isa's best friend back in New York.

Nick was a year behind Isa in school because of some kind of drama when he was younger involving a shit childhood and subsequent foster system screw up; Rose has never asked for the details because it's not really her business. But he's finishing up this semester, and she knows Isa's counting down the days.

And Rose knows her best friend; Isa tries to play it down, but it's clear she misses him like crazy.

(He's the only good thing from her former life.)

"Well, yes, of course, and once he graduates and moves down here, he will realize we're meant to be, and we'll end up married. But until that day comes, I am free to appreciate the scenery." The girls giggle, and Scar smiles up at them.

She's several months old now, but it still amazes Rose that her heart seizes every time her baby is happy, how every moment with her still feels so unbelievably precious no matter how much time she passes.

Having a child...it's something else entirely. Rose doesn't think she'll ever get over it, this feeling that envelops her at the mere thought of Scar, the radiant joy that wells when she holds her daughter, when she knows she's safe and healthy.

"You think Auntie Isa is funny, don't you, honey?" Rose gives Scar one last squeeze before reluctantly handing her back over to the woman in question, drawing her notebook out of her apron with a sigh at the thought of the rest of the shift before her.

You do this for Scar; everything for her. She's worth any number of shitty customers. The thought grounds her, and she steels herself, ignoring the protest from her feet.

"Alrighty, you two skedaddle before Marnie comes out and fires me for fraternizing on the job."

"We're going, we're going. Besides, I'm Marnie's favorite employee; she'd give you a bonus for spending time with me if she could. Anyway, we might order Chinese, so I'll leave the leftovers in the fridge for you when you get home, okay?"

"Thanks, Isa. You're the love of my life."

"Don't I know it." Isa winks. "Say bye to Mama, Scar!" She moves one of Scar's hands in a semblance of a wave, leaving Rose with a contented smile on her face as her heart exits the restaurant.

Marnie, Rose's manager and a woman in her fifties who's run the diner practically single-handedly for as long as anyone can remember, comes over and clucks her tongue. "You're in trouble when that one gets older. When they're that cute, you never want to tell them no."

Rose shakes her head. "Don't I know it. The doctor is telling me to start letting her cry it out when I put her in be. Trying not to cave is the hardest thing I do every day."

"It gets easier. When the attitude develops, you almost have to remind yourself *not* to say no when they're actually behaving," the older woman tells her with a resigned smirk.

Having raised five kids herself, Marnie is pretty much Rose's go-to where anything Scar-related is concerned, so she doesn't doubt it.

"But you're a great mom. You'll figure that all out." The words are genuine, and Rose can feel a bit of tension ease out of her at the affirmation; Marnie doesn't give compliments lightly, and anyone who's ever met the woman knows there's nothing she takes more seriously than the responsibility of being a parent. It resonates with Rose.

Because being a parent...it's the greatest privilege anyone could ever have. And not something to ever be taken lightly.

(She can never forget that.)

6

BEFORE | ROSE

She's in the back corner of the public library, logged in on a visitor's pass despite having had a library card of her own for years. She can't take any chances—there has to be no way to trace these searches back to her.

The more she reads, the tighter her clenched fists get; she doesn't stand a chance, even if she did try to tell. She already knew it would be pointless, entirely futile, but...

(The smallest part of her had hoped.)

She's old enough that it'd be considered legal in North Carolina—and she holds no delusions about anyone believing she hasn't been willing. She knows better than to hope to be believed in a world built on the shattered spines of women whose trauma is nothing but collateral damage, not worth a footnote in the history their abusers go on to be lauded for creating. A world where those in power have all committed such an exploitative crime that it's possible to choose between them based on who has less frequently contributed to something that eats her alive.

Not having full custody isn't an option, but that's exactly what'll happen if anyone finds out about Bean. Even if she did somehow get a conviction, all of her research agrees.

She needs out.

She has to get away from here. Somewhere else, anywhere else, but here.

Memories bubble up to the surface at the thought—shitty motel rooms and back alleys and Bronte's laugh and Evan's stories.

(Officers and crying, and Bronte pleading with them not to take her away.)

Rose tries to shrug it off; she's older now, almost eighteen. They couldn't drag her back even if they did manage to find her.

This time will be different.

(It has to be.)

———

A few months after moving to the new building, Rose rubs at her eyes tiredly as she slowly makes her way down the Walmart aisle.

Thankfully, Scar had stayed asleep when she took her out of the car and now snoozes obliviously in her car seat, snug beside the cans of peas stacked in Rose's cart.

Since living on her own, Rose has discovered that despite the joy she felt as a child when adding food to the pile, grocery shopping as an adult is more of a necessary evil. She only lets herself buy things the many coupon apps on her phone will apply to, and all the while internally winces at the thought of the hit to her bank account, however slim.

It's early November, though, and the candy sale prices post-Halloween are low enough that she caves, letting herself put an over-sized heart full of chocolates alongside her daughter.

"Now that's what I call a balanced diet."

The baritone makes her jump in surprise, and she turns to Josh with a bright if subdued smile as he gestures to the pile of vegetables and chocolate she's accumulated.

It's only been a week or two since she last saw him, but she'd started to get used to his constant presence, so even that feels like a while.

"Josh! Yeah, you got me; I don't know if a nutritionist would be proud or disappointed. How've you been?"

He gives a brilliant smile. "Doing alright. No work today, and we have a month between competitions, so practice is a little more laid back. How are you and the little one?"

"We're good. She's growing so fast; she's lifting her head all by herself now," Rose replies proudly, blush flooding her cheeks. "How are your classes going—you're a senior, right?" she checks.

"Junior, technically, but I'll graduate in December. I didn't take any time off, but I've been underloading a bit pretty much every semester; it's cheaper like that since I'm not paying room and board to the university anyway, and it lets me work pretty much full time."

Rose nods in understanding. "Oh wow, that's pretty ideal. I'm underloading too; I know they're all online, but I figured the more time I could direct towards this one," she motions to Scar, "especially while she's so young, the better."

"Absolutely," Josh agrees whole-heartedly.

It's nice talking to someone who gets it—who doesn't raise an eyebrow sardonically when she mentions that she's underloading, doesn't assume that to underload means she's inherently lazier or less capable.

He's an enigma, she decides. At first, she assumed the guy was pretty immature, nice enough, but the Marvel comments and the way he seemed to be constantly cracking jokes gave her the impression he was the type that didn't take anything seriously.

Since then, though, she's seen him be serious, seen the clarity in his eyes when the conversation grows heavy. Has felt at ease enough around him to open up a bit, has seen how free of judgment he is, how carefully he watches the people around him.

He's...complicated, she thinks, and she can't tell whether he's happy-go-lucky or severe at heart—or maybe some kind of hybrid of the two. There's a certain darkness in his eyes she recognizes from herself, a quality that comes from suffering.

(From trying your best but knowing at the end of the day your best might not be enough.)

That darkness is likely the only reason Rose doesn't assume the worst and lash out when the next words out of his mouth are, "So any friends or family of yours back home I should look forward to meeting eventually?"

She tenses up, eyes flicking to his defensively, but his face is devoid of judgment. The way he asks is casual, more of making sure what he thinks is true based on all their interactions thus far than prying for more information, so she gives him the benefit of the doubt.

"No, it's just us. Smallest, palest family you'll ever meet."

Josh shakes his head, giving her a bright grin. "Nope. You're part of our family now—Bronte says you don't have a choice; she's making you deal with the rest of us. Welcome to the island of misfit toys."

She smiles a little at the way he glosses over the topic of Scar's father, not pushing her for more information. Josh...he might be the rare actual *good* guy. The kind she's only ever known in Evan, the kind most nice guys only claim to be.

"Is this the part where you tell me the Thanksgivings are legendary?"

"Actually, no. Bronte came in raging one day back when Zeke, our friend Aaliyah, and I lived together and told us in no uncertain terms that we would never be celebrating Thanksgiving again for as long as she lived. So we do all of the food stuff the day before instead, and the day of, she hangs a 'Fuck Columbus' flag out the window, and we marathon Disney movies instead."

Rose raises her eyebrows. "I can get behind that."

"I thought it might be more up your alley than genocide glorification," he tells her with a laugh, reaching a hand back to scratch the back of his neck. "Anyway, I'm gonna head back now. Once the sun sets, it gets a little chillier than I like to walk home in."

She frowns. "You're walking back?"

It isn't *far* exactly between the store and their apartment building, but it isn't what qualifies as nearby, either. And while carrying bags of groceries, at night...

There are too many stories—too many innocent souls lost doing things just as innocuous.

"I can give you a ride," she says, the words coming out of her mouth before she's even really processed her intent to say them. "I have a few more things to grab, but if you're willing to wait maybe ten more minutes, we can just head back together."

Josh looks at her carefully, as though making sure she's serious, before nodding with a small smile. "That would be great, thanks. I can help you carry your bags up as payment."

"You really don't have to do that," she reassures him, and he grimaces.

"Believe me, my moms would roll over in their graves if I didn't, and I think Aunt Kathy would legitimately murder me on their behalf."

Rose figures him to have had manners ingrained in him from a young age, and sure enough, when they make their way out to the car, Josh has all of the bags loaded in by the time she's finished buckling Scar up. He refuses to let her be the one to take the cart to the cart return.

He jogs back to the car, sliding into the passenger seat with a shiver, and Rose winces at how run down the vehicle seems.

"It's not much," she admits, "but it runs, and the radio works, which is all I can really ask for."

"I mean, I've never had a car, and I grew up on my mom's salary as a housekeeper, so pretty much anything that gets from point A to point B is first class in my book." They sit in silence for a moment, awkward and unsure, and he clears his throat. "This must seem warm for you, coming from North Carolina."

"Yeah, as of right now, I'm a happy camper, but come summer...the heat and humidity and I don't get along very well."

"It can be a lot. Good excuse for eating a lot of ice cream, though; it'll be a big hit with the queen bee when she's a few years older." He winks, eyes soft as he glances at the baby in the back seat. "I'm more of a fall person—not that seasons really happen here, but it's not quite humid and not quite cold, so I count it as a win. When did you say you first moved down?"

"Last December; it'll be a year, soon. I moved about a month before my birthday." She pauses but continues despite herself. "I graduated a semester early and started doing the online classes for USF in the spring. Took the summer off, though, so I could work a lot before Scar got here and then have something resembling maternity leave."

"You're eighteen, right?" At her confirmation, Josh shakes his head in disbelief. "I can't imagine moving away and coming somewhere so new all by myself like that, especially before you were even considered an adult. And having a kid while you're at it. You're a badass," he declares, voice filled with awe.

Rose avoids making eye contact. "I don't know about that. I just did what I had to."

Josh hesitates, looking contemplative, and she just knows exactly what train of thought he's following.

He knows Scar was born in June, like him, putting Rose right at about a month along when she skipped town. He'll probably assume, the way most people do, that her parents found out and disowned her, kicked her out, and left her to fend for herself. Or that she knew before them even finding out that she wouldn't be welcome at home anymore and left without attempting to plead with them to let her stay.

Either way, they're not really close enough yet for him to bring it up directly, so she's saved from dealing with the excruciating nature of that conversation for the time being. "That must've been really hard. I can't imagine."

She laughs derisively. "Yeah. It was..."

It was sleeping in shelters or her car for the month until she turned eighteen, trying to get her hands on enough food to keep her developing baby nourished; it was applying to jobs anywhere that might take her, practically pleading with managers to take her on despite no work history, no references, and an unavoidable medical leave in seven months; it was being at last able to apply for apartments but not having enough credit or money to stay anywhere remotely secure; it was knowing no one would notice for weeks if something happened to her.

"It was not exactly the easiest time of my life," she settles on instead of telling him any of that.

"I'm sorry. Life is...so shitty, sometimes," Josh says, shaking his head. "I can't even imagine what you were going through. Right after my mom died, I was drowning in so much debt and grief, trying to figure things out...being alone in the world is just shit."

"You...you don't have to explain if you don't want to," Rose assures him, biting her lip as she makes a turn.

But she's watching him carefully, and she looks nervous. This is the most she's ever opened up to him, so he figures she's feeling vulnerable—and he can return the favor.

"My stepdad was...awful. Among a lot of other things, he gambled badly—and with my mom's assets, credit card, you name it, before she died. He's finally out of my life, but debt collectors came hounding her for two hundred grand, and since he put her name on every account too, it became legally her problem. I took out personal loans as soon as I turned eighteen to try to help us stay afloat, keep the creditors somewhat away.

"What was in her name was effectively expunged when she died, but the ones I took out that we planned to work through together... they're my problem now. Kathy has some, too. Bartenders make tips that I can put towards that after rent—not that much, though, being that I've been in college two years and barely made a dent. My credit score is trash. If I hadn't gotten the scholarship, I wouldn't have been able to get any kind of loan for college even if I tried."

Rose shakes her head, eyes closed with that righteous anger that always seems a step beneath her skin. "That's so fucked up. No one should be able to get away with...and I can't even imagine, if she was anything like Kathy...God, she's the sweetest human I've ever met. What the hell." She breathes deeply as she adjusts the AC more out of habit than actual discomfort. "Honestly, even if I weren't already planning on going to law school, shit like that would drive me to it for the sole purpose of putting monsters like that behind bars."

"You want to be an attorney?"

"Yeah. Family and human rights, ideally, although the two can be so different, I have no idea if I'll be able to bridge them." The urge to explain bubbles up inside her, unable to contain how desperately she cares about this, and she looks to him contemplatively, debating whether or not to say more. The thought of him baring his soul a minute ago wins out, and she adjusts in her seat, facing Josh just a bit more.

"My dad and I were never close," she tells him. "I don't think he really wanted kids, and after childbirth, I guess my mom decided she didn't either, so he was pretty much on his own and kind of clueless. He did the bare minimum, but I think he loved me, in his own weird way—whatever way he was capable of.

"He died when I was seven—like, a *month* after our relationship started getting a little bit better, and then it was just my mom and me. She'd never wanted much to do with me; I think it might have started off as postpartum, but by the time my dad was gone, she was just...*awful*. She liked to brag about my accomplishments, present herself as a PTA mom, but she didn't actually care, you know? She liked the idea of me, but...honestly, I don't believe she's ever really loved me.

"While my dad had been alive, I was a reminder of how easy life was before I came along, how much better their relationship had been, and once he was gone, I was just a mouth to feed and a responsibility she didn't want. She took everything I cared about—we moved from the only home I'd ever known, friends, she gave away all of my books, just..." Rose trails off, voice thick. "Everything. She tore it all down, did anything she knew would take away my happiness. Not even to hurt me, just because she didn't care, and as long as she was keeping me alive and I had good grades, she thought she was doing enough."

She clears her throat, leaving out the darker aspects that refuse to be forgotten. "By the time I was eleven, I'd had enough and figured anything was better than being there; that's when I ran away with Bronte. We met Evan a year later. They were the closest thing I'd ever had to a family, the way it's supposed to be, and the three of us made it almost a year in that last place before everything went to shit. Best time in my life, hands down.

"When CPS found us, I got sent back home. Bronte had been off the grid for too long, no diploma or GED, so they wouldn't let her have custody of me—not to mention how young she was. And she couldn't come back to North Carolina when they shipped me back there. Honestly, I have no idea what happened to Evan at that point. We made a pact that we would always stay in touch, gave each other emails and phone numbers, swore to talk every day.

"But Cheyenne – my mom, I mean – she was so pissed that I'd made her look bad, made her get investigated, that I'd run away, that I'd been so ungrateful. She trashed the papers with their information, had the phone company block their numbers, went to crazy lengths to make sure I would never be able to speak to them again. She said it was because they were bad influences, and she wanted better for me. After a couple years that, she said that even if I ever *did* find them, they would hate me for ignoring them forever, resent me for being so young and probably the reason we were caught—the reason everything went up in flames. It wasn't even malicious; it was...pitying. She said it was because she wanted me to stop keeping my hopes up for something that would end so terribly.

"And I believed her." Rose smiles bitterly, gaze far away. "Anyway, after her destroying everything I've ever had, I decided I wanted to be the one to stop things like that from happening—the one to believe kids, to remember that a child is the canary in the coal mine of a family, to know they act out for a reason. To fight for them."

Josh opens his mouth to offer his own condolences, even though she knows there are a lot of chunks of her story in between the lines of what she's told him, but she waves away whatever words he was about to attempt to string together. "Don't apologize; we're in the same boat. Poster children for the evil-parents-are-real movement."

Rose puts the car in park, walking around to the backseat to pull

Scar—now bright-eyed and bushy tailed, watching Josh with awe—into her arms before reaching for the groceries, only to see the other side of the back row empty.

"I told you: you drive, I carry. Seriously, it's no problem," Josh promises, his deep voice carrying amid the sounds of traffic nearby.

Reluctantly, she leads the way inside the building, glancing back at him with pursed lips intermittently, her disapproving looks only making his grin grow wider and wider.

They step into the elevator, and she reminds herself that she knows Josh now, that he's a friend, and has done nothing untoward, that he could've just as easily tried something in the car and didn't. That they just bared their souls to each other.

But her brain is just not on the same page.

All her muscles are wound tight as soon as the doors close, and she can *see* the confusion on his face. They've been talking, laughing, having a good time, growing closer...and suddenly, she's being stand-offish. They were in just as much of an enclosed space in the car, and she was *fine*, but now the close quarters have her unable to breathe.

(It makes her want to scream, how out of control her body's reactions are.)

Josh seems like the greatest guy she's yet to meet; in another world, he could be the love of her life. All the potential is there, all the chemistry and easy conversation.

If proximity to him didn't cause her to border the edge of a panic attack. If the enticing thought of his skin on hers weren't muddled with dread.

(In another world, alright.)

After a bit of the stifled silence, Josh spits out what she imagines are the first words that come to mind. "So, Zeke set off the fire alarm less than a week after we moved here." Rose doesn't comment, but her attention is on him, so he trucks onward. "It was just over three years ago, now. Bronte moved in with Evan, and this was before Kai would spend *any* time away from his family, so Zeke and I's third roommate was our friend Aaliyah—the one we've mentioned before. Aaliyah and I had gone to work and got home around the same time, and the whole building is outside; it's the middle of the night, so everyone is in pajamas and embarrassed, freezing their asses off, zit cream and glasses instead of contacts, the whole nine yards, and we overhear someone say something about *'the idiots on the fourth floor.'*"

Rose presses a hand to her mouth, eyes filled with laughter. She can feel herself trembling, feel how shallow her breathing is, but Josh is *trying,* and the smooth way he began talking and avoids making her contribute is enough to ease her hypervigilant reaction just the slightest bit. The elevator doors open at long last, and she rushes to step outside of the small space, and while still rattled, it's easier to engage in the discussion, easier to convince her brain they're going to be okay.

"And it was Zeke?" she clarifies, voice quiet.

Josh's eyes soften with what seems like relief when she speaks up, and he nods, his voice growing just a degree happier at the improvement. "And of course, there are plenty of us on the fourth floor, so there was no reason for us to *assume* anything, but we heard that, and Aaliyah and I looked at each other and groaned at the exact same time. We wander the crowd looking for him, but it's pretty packed, and eventually, we find him looking like a kid in detention with the landlord and a couple of firefighters. Come to find out, the imbecile put a fork in the microwave," he confesses, and Rose winces.

"He was nineteen at the time?"

"Yep. A whole entire adult and he didn't know better. Since then, he's terrified of using the microwave; he has a specific bowl he heats *everything* up in, nothing else. Hell, after the incident, he wouldn't use it at all unless someone else was home for at least six months."

"Poor guy. I hope he's not a big popcorn fan." Her voice is teasing as she unlocks the door with the hand not holding Scarlett, letting them inside the mostly bare studio apartment.

"He got lucky there, although he's big on easy mac, so that was a struggle."

"A man after my own heart."

Josh sets Rose's groceries on the rickety table while she sets Scar amongst musical toys in her playpen. "Alrighty, I'm gonna head up and get this stuff in the fridge." He pauses, the wheels in his brain visibly turning. "Te and Evan come over for family dinner with the whole gang on Sunday nights if you're not working," he offers. "I whip something up, and we normally watch a movie or play board games or do something equally tame afterward."

"Wholesome," she comments, lips twitching almost to a smile. "We'll try to stop by."

"Awesome. I'll see you then. Have a good night, Rose."

He crosses the room to smile at Scar, then hesitates before appearing to settle on waving before clicking the door shut behind him.

Rose takes a deep breath. "Get it together. This was good," she mutters to herself before moving to the kitchenette to put up the cold food.

A moment later, her breath catches at the sloppy handwriting across the notepad on the fridge: *Josh Brooks 813-788-3454. Call if you need anything.*

She has no idea how he had the time to jot it down without her seeing, but it sends a fluttery feeling through her body. Her mouth curves upwards.

He might be a good guy.

7

BEFORE | Evan

He didn't realize until years into his involvement—once it was far too late—that he'd become the definition of evil: that bad which thinks itself as good, which lauds itself as it ruins lives. He and Bronte reconnected, but he remained entrenched in that world.

When someone resembling Bronte cowers from him, he snaps. He grabs her, takes a partner's bike, and hauls ass to the nearest police station, begging them to help her and take him in, confessing as many crimes as he can remember alongside names and addresses indiscriminately, rarely pausing for breath.

He beseeches them for repercussions, offers up every detail he's ever known, but swears off any kind of plea deal. And on receiving his sentence (no plea deal, but far more generous than it might have been), he gets a knife between the ribs his first day in prison. He's several stab wounds in before guards catch a glimpse of him collapsed to the floor, conscious but not bothering to press a hand to staunch the flow of blood, believing himself to be receiving the penance he deserves for the hurt he's caused.

Upon waking again, the first thing he sees is the real Bronte—enraged, puffy-eyed, and beautiful. She tears into him without bothering to ask how he's feeling, livid after months and months of imploring him to stop what-

65

ever he was doing that he would never explain, to leave the dodgy people she'd seen him crossing paths with, to stop wasting the freedom they'd always wished for so long ago.

He hadn't listened, then. He'd only pushed her away, told her he knew what he was doing, fought with her for acting like he was an idiot. "Well, you're damn well acting like one, Hall."

She hadn't called him by his last name since she was eighteen and they'd first met and ended up back on the streets, when she wouldn't sleep because she didn't trust him, demanded to prepare all food they got ahold of for fear that he would leave her and Rose to starve.

And on she screams at him—calling him out on his bullshit as she always has, reminding him of the person he'd always wanted to be.

("You can always change. You can still be that guy.")

("You're right. Te—I fucked up. I'm sorry.")

No excuses. Confession, honesty, fessing up without cushioning the truth, as has always been their way.

They don't speak any more that night. The next day, they tell her why he'd been attacked, "snitches get stitches" written into his arm.

Slowly but surely, he grows into something new—not quite the hopeful child he'd been, not the man angry at the world, but something in the middle, somewhere in the grey. By the time he finishes his sentence, out early for good behavior with thousands of hours of community service, he wants nothing more than to go back in time. To talk to his younger self, to make him see that someone cared, make him understand all the things he was giving up.

To go back before it was too late and help himself or to have someone else do so is impossible, so instead, he starts trying to do it for someone else, to stop them from making the same mistakes he has.

On parole, he moves in with Bronte until he can get back on his feet; she's still pissed at him but knows he's moving forward, so she doesn't begrudge him a spot on her uncomfortable futon till he can get together the means and credit to get a place of his own. He snags two jobs: minimum wage, thirty-nine hours a week part-time so as to not have to provide benefits, the only kind that will take him with a criminal record, especially one so recent.

But he keeps finding himself drawn to the youth center in the shitty part of town where he talks to kids so full of anger and resentment and frustration with being unloved and unwanted, so familiar it hurts. Kids who initially hate his guts but slowly start to understand he's not going anywhere—that he's giving it to them straight, unlike anyone in their lives thus far had bothered to do.

The kids refuse to listen to anyone else, start to call him in the dead of night for a ride from somewhere that something bad is about to go down, for a place to stay when a parent is too fucked up for being home to go well in any meaning of the word, for someone to promise to watch their back while they sleep because the monsters haunting their dreams aren't just nightmares.

The center offers him a permanent position. The pay is shit, but the kids are the only thing a now-twenty-five-year-old Evan cares about, so all the money in the world elsewhere couldn't make him refuse.

By the time he gets together the money to start renting a place with friends, which has been nearly impossible with the way people treat ex-cons, he's not sleeping on the futon anymore, and it's decided he's already home.

———

"Don't you dare get any ideas." Bronte scowls at Evan playfully as he plays peekaboo with his niece on the couch.

"No worries, babe. Scar is the cutest creature on the planet, but I'm happy to be able to return her at the end of the day. We'll just be the best godparents there ever were." He winks, sliding an arm around her heavily inked shoulder, and Rose has to remind herself for approximately the hundredth time today that this is her new normal, that she's not just having the same dream of her adult life she's had since she was sent back to Cheyenne. Bronte and Evan are really here. Permanently in her life, from here on out.

It's funny to see them together. She'd never really considered it as a kid, and they physically seem so wholly like oppositional textbook stereotypes. Evan is a tall, lean, tan, brown-haired-blue-eyed All-

American boy, the only distinction from the archetype the savage burn along his arm from the time their seedy apartment building was set ablaze and he sent a younger Bronte and Rose ahead. He's devoid of muscle mass from a lack of food on top of growth spurts. Not visible is the brand haphazardly covered by a singular intricate tattoo that could never fully eradicate the image.

Bronte, on the other hand, is badass personified, the classic image of a twenty-something whose skin is entirely covered in tattoos save her face and neck, tall and lithe with a severe look and a strong case of resting bitch face.

Rose may never have considered it, but every time she sees them together, she has an overwhelming sense of *right*.

And of *course* they're Scar's godparents.

Settling back into the feeling of their presence in her life has been like slipping on an old coat: strange for a moment, but immediately comfortable, worn in all the right places, and shaped to your body despite the time that's passed since it was last worn.

"Food's ready!" Josh calls, and Rose practically drools in anticipation.

She's learned the man in question did not inherit his late mother's baking talents; he could find a way to massacre anything containing sugar and flour-even before putting it in the oven, a fact which came to her attention the day after their Walmart run-in when he stopped by with eviscerated brownies. Nonetheless, his cooking is some of the best that she's ever tasted, the few times she's been a recipient, and she's not above telling him so in order to convince him to cook more, especially as she grows more and more comfortable around him.

Isa takes her seat beside Zeke, who Rose has come to find out is not just *a* friend, but Isa's *best* friend, along with Rose herself. "You'd better not have been exaggerating, ma'am, or I will be thoroughly disappointed and will teach my niece to say the word 'no' extra early," Isa threatens.

Yesterday, Rose had been contemplating coming up with an excuse to miss family dinner, but when she'd hesitantly called Josh to cancel, he'd sounded so excited that she was coming that she couldn't bring herself to bail—and money was tight enough that a free dinner in and of itself was a huge incentive. She'd played off the call, asking if it were okay that she bring a friend, and Isa had been thrilled to tag along and meet Bronte and Evan.

"Hey now, I will not have doubters in my kitchen. My masterpiece does *not* need your negative energy," Josh sasses Isa, falling into the easy rapport the two of them developed the minute she'd walked in the door.

Bronte snorts. "The imbecile can't bake for shit, but I promise his cooking deserves the hype," she assures Isa. "I wouldn't let his ego get so big if it weren't worth it."

"Honestly not sure whether to be complimented or insulted."

"Take one of each, then. But hurry up already; my stomach is eating itself." Zeke grins at him.

Rose rolls her eyes. "Zeke, the stomach doesn't start eating itself till more than twelve hours after your most recent meal, and we all watched you scarf down three bowls of cheerios forty minutes ago."

"Come on, Ro, I'm starving," he whines half-heartedly. "Put the logic away so he'll get the food on the table faster."

"Don't call me Ro." The demand comes out harshly, and she feels the tension that filled her body at the nickname start to seep throughout the room. "Sorry, that came out too strong—but seriously, Zeke, just Rose. Please." She tries to blunt the remark, tries to make the *please* come out without as much desperation as she feels.

"Voila!" Josh's reappearance is perfectly timed to prevent further conversation—and if it wouldn't kill Rose's pride to admit how badly she needs it every time, she would confront him and find out how he always knows when she needs a *deus ex machina* intervention to get her out of conversations she'd rather not have.

(Every time any discussion veers towards something that sets her pulse racing, has her rapidly thinking up escape routes, there he is. It can't be an accident.)

Everyone else digs into the heaps of cuisine on the table, with way more chairs than intended pulled up to it, but Scar starts to whimper with hunger, and Rose picks her up to feed her before filling her own plate.

"Hey, I snacked while I cooked, and I have a hunch you haven't eaten all day." Josh gives Rose a look, and she can't help but grimace at the accurate accusation; he'd figured out early on that taking care of herself often falls to the wayside. "I can get her, go ahead and chow down," he says with a soft smile, reaching his arms out for the four-month-old. "We haven't gotten to bond since the last time I babysat."

The two settle into a comfortable position, which has become a regular thing in the weeks since the first time Rose allowed Josh to hold her. He's babysat once more and even gone to the park with them in the days since he left his number on her fridge, his eyes always lighting up at the sight of the infant.

Normally, Rose would be worried he's attempting to butter her up by showing interest in her kid, but Josh's whole demeanor changes when Scar is around in a way that's reassuring. He grows protective, face filled with genuine joy Rose doesn't have the heart to truly doubt.

"Thank you." She lifts her fork to her mouth and groans aloud at the taste, a burst of joy when she's otherwise exhausted after a long shift and a night of heavily perforated sleep due to Scar waking up a few more times than normal.

"So, Isa, how's the boyfriend? Need me to talk you up?" Zeke's teasing is clearly familiar to Isa, so she rolls her eyes and flicks him without pause before pushing her plate away.

The motion makes Rose frown, unable to draw her attention from the food that's only been picked at.

"He's just a friend, for the millionth time. Dating is...so far off my radar. And even if it were, I would keep you as far as possible from any prospects for at least a year." She scrunches her nose distrustfully, and Zeke practically cackles.

"We're going to be best friends forever, Castaneda, whether you like it or not."

Josh snorts. "You're the reason Aaliyah decided to move in with

Liza instead of us. I've known you since you were five, and *I* barely want to be your friend. "

"Okay, to be fair, because of that, she and Liza fell in love, and now they're getting married, so they should be thanking me for accidentally driving her away! And that's just because we live together, and you hold it against our friendship when I leave pizza crust in the couch cushions or break the pans."

"Because that pan was expensive, and you're an adult and should've known not to put cast iron in the dishwasher! And that was *after* you made the whole building hate us. And the pizza crusts attract bugs." Despite his words, Josh's tone is easy, and it's easy to see that Zeke was forgiven minutes after the incident occurred. "You're lucky I love you, Ezekiel."

"Damn straight. How else would I get such high-quality food for free? Also, you introduced me to Kai and Kathy."

"Kathy," everyone around the table except Isa echoes in confirmation, voices almost wistful.

The woman in question notified Josh that she'd be visiting the next week and had since been all any of them could talk about, such that they've roped Isa into coming over for a movie night for the sole purpose of being able to understand their references to the mother figure for practically the whole group.

Josh sighs. "Yeah, yeah, you only keep me around for my godmother, I'm aware. Next time we have a family dinner, you people can order a pizza."

"It's not our fault your aunt is the best thing about you, J," Bronte says, voice serious till she cracks a smirk after getting the whole sentence out. "Besides, if everyone didn't love you, we could get Kathy without engaging with you. You know she'd still talk to us, so clearly, we're voluntarily putting up with you."

The group chuckles, but Rose's attention is drawn to Evan, who's been uncharacteristically quiet for the last few minutes, staring down at his plate without actually eating. Rose watches him, waiting for his attention to flick onto her, and when it does, she draws her eyebrows together and mouths, *you okay?* Evan twists the edges of his mouth up and nods, and while it's clear enough that something is still bothering him, Rose knows the older man well enough to know when he's going to be okay. She'll talk to him about it when he's ready. When they were younger, Rose learned the hard way that pushing him would only make him hide things better thereafter.

Later, once everyone is uncomfortably full and has gotten in many more playful vocal jabs across the table, they settle throughout the living room, sprawled across the couch, the floor, and a couple of mismatched bean bags whose origin none of the apartment's residents seem to remember.

"He lives!" Bronte mock-cheers, and Rose turns to see Kai, who she's continued to run into only briefly and during inhumane hours when she's only up because of the baby because the guy is pretty much nocturnal when he's at the apartment. A prime example being tonight, wherein he's just woken up from a nap at eight o'clock at night on a Sunday.

He claims to just be a mechanic, but he runs his late father's auto shop and helps his mom with the four kids, so Rose figures the guy takes sleep where he can get it. She can't blame him.

Kai ruffles his hair, letting out a wide yawn. "Yeah, yeah, yeah, I'm a vampire, I know. If only I were as rich and pretty as the Cullens. Food, J?"

"Blue Tupperware in the fridge—don't heat it for too long."

"Roger that." Kai returns a moment later, glaring at Evan wordlessly until he reluctantly gets up from the netted, trampoline-like seat that anyone who has ever entered the apartment knows to be Kai's sacred place.

Zeke looks to Bronte with raised eyebrows, facing her expectantly. "Te, I have tickets for Rise Against next Friday—you in?"

"Hell yes!" She leans to high-five him energetically, but Evan shakes his head, apologetic.

"You have Aaliyah's bridal shower that day, bud. A little difficult for a bridesmaid to miss."

Bronte groans. "Shit, you're right. I forgot that was Friday. This whole wedding has just completely snuck up on me. Honestly, if you hadn't put all of the fitting dates into my phone, I would be wearing a paper bag at the altar."

Kai shakes his head. "Never thought I'd see the day someone won our ice queen's heart, but if anyone deserves it, it's Aaliyah."

"Ice queen?" Rose questions.

Bronte rolls her eyes for the umpteenth time; they get plenty of exercise when she's in the chaotic apartment. "Liza. Romeo here started calling her that when he first heard about her ages ago because she's never really been close to a lot of people and tends to be pretty straight-forward. Then he actually met her and became infatuated with her on sight, and even though they're friends now, he won't call her anything else. She hates it."

What she doesn't say but had disclosed to Rose during a movie night the week before is that it was pretty out of character for Kai, as her cousin doesn't really do relationships and hasn't in four years.

Rose can see the walls up behind his eyes.

Zeke sighs, mock-despondently. "Moving on. Josh?"

"I'm sorry, man, you know I can't afford to take off on a Friday night." Josh grimaces apologetically, holding his hands up in a helpless gesture. "I expect videos, though."

"I'll go," Isa offers. "I'm a fan, and I work the day shift that day since I don't have class."

"You're a godsend," Zeke praises, his face lighting up. "I have to work with my dad all morning that day, and I can already feel how stressed I'm going to be. This'll be awesome."

"Speaking of dads," Kai pipes up unexpectedly, and when his gaze turns to Rose, she tenses. "If there's anything you need help with regarding Scar's, let us know. Even if it's like a dad's coming to daycare day or something. I...it was something that really upset my youngest sister after we lost my dad; now I go with her for that type of thing, and it makes her feel better. Anything I or we can do."

There it is. Rose feels the blood rush out of her face at the question she's been waiting for, the one everyone has been oddly dancing around since Josh and his group of friends had walked into her life, since Bronte reappeared and suspected from the offset. The one she's been avoiding, even at the cost of making excuses every time Bronte tries to hang out one on one.

She should've prepared an excuse knowing this was coming, but somehow it still takes her off-guard.

Kai looks genuinely worried on her behalf, a scowl coming over his face as she fails to respond. "Or, I mean, if it's something where he's trying to get out of it...enough of us here have had deadbeats; if he is too, we can help you file for child support. Or kick his ass. Or both. Whatever you prefer. You shouldn't have to do this alone."

"Malakai," Bronte hisses, murder in her eyes.

Rose knows Kai means well, knows he would never have said anything if he had any clue how badly this topic would affect her, any clue how desperately she tries to avoid thinking about anything related to it. It's a sweet kind of naivety as though he can't imagine anything that bad. Good for him, really.

But she can feel all the eyes in the room on her after the question they've all been too understanding, too polite, too afraid to ask.

"He's not in the picture." *Good, that was good, Rose. Keep your voice that steady, and this will be fine. You won't have to say anything more.* The sentence is clipped, but the words don't break, and she's not shaking, so she counts it as a win despite the nausea and emotion preparing to overtake her.

Kai frowns, looking upset on her behalf. "He shouldn't get away with this. This loser is out there relaxing while you're working yourself to the bone to take care of his kid. You deserve better."

"She is not his kid." Rose takes a deep breath after biting out the words instinctively. "Being a father is more than just conceiving a child. Just...trust me on this one." *Don't think about it, Rose. He's out of your life. Forever.* "He is not a good person, and I don't want him anywhere near my daughter."

God, I don't want him on the same planet as my daughter. Or me. The thought is enough to make her blood chill.

"Sorry. I don't mean to overstep. I just know we all care about you, and doing it alone is hard. I get that. Let us know if there's anything we can do." Kai's tone is sorrowful and gentle, and small conversations awkwardly pick up around the room in an attempt to soothe the atmosphere that now has Rose feeling like she's suffocating.

Stop thinking about it; you're dwelling and making it worse. Think about something else-anything else. Convince them you're fine.

Of course, she can't distract herself. She should know better than to bother trying by now. That's not how this works.

(She's not that lucky.)

"I think Rose is tired," Bronte says quietly, that gentle voice she only ever used when Rose was injured while they were young and on the run. The kind of tone people use with spooked animals. "Let me walk you down to your apartment, kid."

Rose knows exactly what that means and is filled with absolute trepidation at the thought. Her heart is racing at the thoughts Zeke's words have unknowingly elicited, so much that she's almost glad the woman who was basically an older sister to her once upon a time is about to demand they talk about what they both know, what's been eating her alive for as long as she can remember, with no one to hear her screams.

As scary as it is, she's glad someone *cares* enough to make her talk about it.

"I'll walk you both to the door."

It's ridiculous, really, being that the door is approximately ten feet away and Rose lives a floor down, but she's noticed that Josh is always absurdly careful, something she suspects has to do with his mother. So she doesn't argue as he follows her out the door, Scar heavy and snoring in her arms and diaper bag strewn across her back.

"I'm really sorry about Kai," he mutters as they step outside, cheeks darkened. "He means well, but that was out of line. I don't know what your...situation is, but you shouldn't be uncomfortable like that when you're with friends, even if they're trying to help. His mouth moves faster than his brain sometimes. Not that that makes it okay," he hurries to assure her, looking worried she'll assume he's excusing his friend. "He just has such a cookie-cutter family doesn't always consider that not everyone does."

KAITIE HOWIE

"Honestly, it's fine, Josh. I really appreciate that he cares enough to bring it up. I'm not upset with him."

"But you *are* upset," he states, picking up on the words she doesn't say, looking to where Bronte stands nonchalantly by the elevator at the end of the hall rather than meeting his eyes.

"I—"

"Hey, Josh, did you—" Zeke swings the door open and lifts an arm as if to grab Josh's shoulder, but the motion is quick, and Rose reflexively finds herself flinching.

In the aftermath, out of the corner of her eye, she sees Josh flinch too. She sees the similar tensing of his posture as she straightens.

Rose pales, the knowing flooding through her, and their eyes lock in recognition.

(*Him too*, the little voice in her brain whispers.)

Shock and sorrow for Josh swirl through her brain as she re-watches all her memories of him with new eyes. The understanding with which he's kept his distance since the first time he sensed her discomfort, how carefully he moves around other people to avoid surprising them, the way his steps are always audible when he approaches, all of it crashing over her like a tsunami.

She turns away without another word, running away for fear of breaking down.

"Did it ever stop?"

They're the first words Bronte speaks after they've been sitting in silence in the apartment for ten minutes. Bronte had slammed two mugs of water into the microwave, practically stabbing the tea bags into them once the water was boiling, setting one before Rose and taking the seat opposite her at the shabby table while the music from Scar's mobile drifts up from the crib where she snoozes.

"No."

No pretenses or attempts to deflect, no avoiding the subject or

76

pretending either of them doesn't know exactly what she's talking about, exactly how Scar was conceived.

(Exactly who Scar's father is.)

Quiet words, whispered by a desperate and terrified twelve-year-old in the dead of night, long into their alliance, only once she knew Bronte was family and after making sure the others on the street were asleep. Words she'd only let herself say once before, to Cheyenne when she still thought there might be the slightest bit of decency left in her mother—*there wasn't*—before she completely gave up on that home and decided to run away. Words used to beg Bronte to do everything in her power to keep her, to never let anyone take her back. A plea.

Bronte's face had stayed blank—not devoid of emotion, but carefully controlled because, as Rose had learned early on, her would-be older sister goes lethal angry. So angry that to move a single muscle would have unleashed a tsunami of anger, and as she's since explained, to fly into a rage wouldn't have helped the traumatized and horrified twelve-year-old. She'd maintained a façade of calm, and from there on out, risked everything she hadn't already—which she insisted wasn't much but was worth the world to Rose—to keep anyone from finding the younger girl.

"Does he know about Scar?" Anyone else might ask the question more delicately, might slowly ease into it, but Bronte knows better—knows to get it out of the way.

"No. No, thank God, no. I found out a month in and was out the next day. The only symptom that had started was morning sickness, and only for two days; everyone assumed I had a virus. I...I had a feeling, and I didn't want to risk not finding out till later and him knowing, so I took the test even though I wasn't really sure." Rose's voice trembles, the memory and guilt palpable.

(If anything had gone differently, if either of them had come home early this *one* day, if anyone had seen her buying the pregnancy test at the store...any tiny factor going the tiniest bit differently, and Scar would never have had a chance.)

"God, Rose." Bronte doesn't look at her for a moment, and when she does, Rose is jolted by the sight of tears in her friend's eyes; it's only the second time she's ever seen them, despite the chaos and trauma she knows the older woman to have experienced, that she's experienced alongside her.

Even when Bronte's femur snapped wasn't the other occasion.

"I wish he were dead. I wish I had killed him a decade ago. Any prison sentence, any punishment would be worth knowing he was fucking gone."

The words are vicious, but Rose just doesn't have it in her to disagree. She lost the part of herself with enough compassion for that a long time ago.

"You know," Bronte starts, and Rose already knows what she's going to propose before the words leave her lips. "Scar is proof. Get a DNA test, and they'll know he's lying."

"It's not like I've never thought about it, but DNA will mean nothing if they think *I'm* lying. And women...women never win these cases. Even when they do, the sentences are so short, he could come after us in a year—or less. Especially if the prosecutor agreed to a plea deal; you know victims have no say in whether or not it's accepted?" She almost chokes on the words, shaking her head. "And anyway, odds are he wouldn't even be charged because the North Carolina age of consent is sixteen, and I was seventeen when she was conceived. And he would know about Scar. He could try to take her or hurt her—"

The oxygen seems to flee from her body even though she's thought through this a thousand times before because the prospect is still just as treacherous. What would happen to Scar if he found out about her, if he got his *hands* on her?

(She would do *anything* to prevent it. Had to. She would die before she let it happen.)

"If he got even partial custody..."

"Fuck!" Bronte practically roars in anger, and Rose gives her a warning glance at the volume.

But it's too late, Scar is awake, and Rose quietly walks over to press her baby—the entirety of her heart, her world—to her chest.

78

"Shh, honey, you're okay. Mama's here; we're okay. I love you." She whispers the phrases like a mantra, knowing Bronte sits in the other room, probably hating herself for knowingly letting Rose go back with Cheyenne as though she weren't only nineteen at the time and facing bullshit criminal charges, as though she hadn't done every possible thing she could think of to try to stop it from happening.

It was pressing in on her, making it hard to stay in the now, the memories and flashbacks closing in and threatening to overwhelm her. *"Ro,"* Zeke had called her jokingly, and the voice in her head murmurs *Ro*, slithering into the happiness she had tried to make for herself, far from him, from Cheyenne, from all of it, where she'd run to try to save her daughter—and herself.

"I'm really proud of you," Bronte says quietly, taking slow steps, knowing not to sneak up on her, even accidentally. "You escaped."

"I had to," Rose says, not being modest, just trying to make Bronte understand as that familiar sense of blame begins to flood her veins. "I couldn't...there was no option for Scar to be born there, for them to know about her. I—" The words almost choke her. "I didn't know if...I couldn't take the chance...and if they'd known once I found out she was a girl—"

And then she's crying, and Bronte's crying, and God *damn* it, the thought of it shouldn't still kill her like this, but even *considering* what might have happened in that house had she brought a baby girl into that world destroys her.

"But you made it," Bronte reminds her, voice strong despite the emotion laced throughout it. "You made it. You're so fucking strong, and Scar is here and okay because of it."

(And she is.)

Scar is here and safe, and that is all that Rose could ask for, even as the guilt crashes over her, strangling her heart every second.

A soft knock comes at the door, and Rose's stomach twists at the thought of talking to someone else even for a moment, of faking a smile while she's crumbling. Of trying to brush off the thing inside of her that's screaming at the top of its lungs and has been for a long time.

She straightens up, bracing herself to deal with whoever is on the other side of the slab of wood that somehow seems to keep her so much safer from the world around her as she returns Scar to her crib.

Before Rose can move to the door, though, Evan's head pops in with a sad smile, and in walks the only other person on this planet whose presence won't sent her into a downward spiral in this moment.

"Hey, squirt." Evan's voice is gentle, the way it always is with her—whether she's twelve and brandishing a baseball bat or thirteen and sobbing while clutching at the front of his shirt or eighteen and reminding him in a worried voice to keep an arm under Scar's neck *so help me God, Evan.*

The way Evan is with her, she'll never understand how the things that happened in his half-decade absence from her life did. She could never imagine someone this careful, this delicate, this caring, getting involved with a gang of the very monsters they'd once run from.

Defecting, going to prison, being attacked while he was there... after he was released, it had been purely by chance that he started volunteering at the youth center. He had only been hired on once the kids facing so many shitty circumstances trusted no one else.

Rose is pretty sure the careful honesty on Evan's face is a practiced look, one he probably uses often at work. When he gets a call at two a.m. and knows something terrible has happened and there aren't really words to make things right—that there never will be. There's not a way for him to get them through it. Only they can do that part, and it sucks, but he can be there to stand beside them when they break down along the way, trying to claw their way to happiness, to a better life they've probably never known.

His eyes are concentrated on her, and the coward inside of her is thrilled when Scar starts to cry, and she begins to stand again—*an out, thank God*—but he holds a palm up to her unapologetically, reaching to pick up the baby. For a moment, Rose is distracted by the way Evan grasps her daughter with what seems to her to be an oddly practiced grip, the unusual ease with which he settles the baby into the crook of his arm for someone who's never had a child or worked with such young kids. Odds are some of the kids at the center have young kids of their own—maybe even siblings they bring with them, unwilling to leave them alone.

Whatever the case, she doesn't have the wherewithal to focus on that at the moment, as he turns his attention back to her. *So, this conversation is happening,* her internal monologue mutters, resigning itself.

"It seems pretty clear to me that whoever Scar's biological father is, he was doing this to you for a long time," Evan says without preamble, his tone making it clear it's not a question, and Rose's head snaps up to him angrily.

"Did Bronte—" Even as she begins the question, she knows it's not a possibility, and Evan directs a lackluster scowl at her for bothering to voice the thought.

"Cut the shit, kid, you and I both know she would never betray your trust like that. I know because I see the same behaviors in you that I see in the kids I work with dealing with similar situations. If I were smarter—" He stops, swallows thickly, and her eyebrows scrunch together at the way he's unable to meet her eyes, closing his own with anguish. "If I were smarter, I would've figured it out half a decade ago and been filing for custody of you on my twenty-first birthday instead of drawing on the inside of my cell. But that's not the point. I'm sorry you've been dealing with this. That you've been alone."

Evan knowing—a man knowing, really—is enough to shoot Rose's anxiety through the roof, and she sits hunched, arms wrapped around her legs tightly enough that her knuckles are white.

"There was no reason for you to have known," she replies without emotion in her voice.

"It doesn't matter, anyway. We can't change it; we're here now. And I'm sorry you had to go through that.

Rose shakes her head, opens her mouth to interrupt and brush it all aside. "It's f—"

"Don't say it's fine because it's not. It will never be fine that you dealt with it—that it happened to you."

She nods, eyes watering because he *gets* it.

Bronte would rage for her, would fight the sun itself if it harmed her—and she needs that because even though she doesn't want anyone to fight *him*, it's nice to know someone cares enough to *want* to. That someone is so angry that they'd seek vengeance on her behalf were they able because they're *that mad* that she's been hurt.

But Evan...Evan would let her cry it out, would get her to talk about it when she doesn't want to face the truth, would save her from herself. And she needs that too.

"I—I've been dealing with it this long, I'll get through it," she insists despite herself, the words hollow as though she doesn't dwell on it constantly, as though flashbacks don't slam through her regularly interrupting any heartbeat of happiness, as though she's ever been able to do anything but drown inside of the crime scene that is her own body.

"No one just 'gets through' rape." His voice is gentle, but she flinches violently at the word.

Because *why would he say it, WHY, why would he say that word that makes her insides recoil and want to run in the opposite direction until her legs fail, that fucking word that haunts her.* She wants to scream because she hates that word, she hates it so much, and she hates him for saying it because if she can just not think the word, she can make an attempt at not thinking about everything. She glares at him as her whole body trembles.

Bronte's at her side in an instant, protective and giving her boyfriend a glare of warning. Her hands are raised as though to rub Rose's back, but she refrains. She knows better than to think it would help right now.

Evan maintains her gaze as soon as she meets his eyes. "It's an ugly word, I know, and I can imagine it's hard to hear. But not saying it is a disservice to you, it's downplaying the violence that's been done to you, and I won't do that. You deserve more than thinking the trauma you've been through is not a big deal. Whoever this monster is doesn't deserve to get away with you being afraid to acknowledge the reality of what you've been through."

But why should she? The first time she ever bothered to, back when she thought there was a chance telling someone would make it end, she'd feared her mother might not believe her.

But it had been worse than that.

Cheyenne had believed her without question—she just didn't *care*.

And therein lay the reality of why she'd never gone forward to the police and why she never would. She couldn't bare her soul again for them to wave him away, slap on a three-month sentence, if anything, and expect her to move forward, business as usual. For them to say that was what her years of suffering was worth.

"I don't...I don't want to talk about this anymore."

Evan starts to reach out, then pulls back as if seeing in her eyes that while his touch hasn't set her off before, hadn't done so in the time he'd been back in her life, in this moment, the feel of skin against hers would trigger something incredibly painful in her brain. She keeps telling herself it's Evan—just *Evan*, the guy she's practically worshipped for years, the one guy she knows she can forever trust— but even his proximity has her breathing shallow and her eyes dilated.

For a moment, the only sound in the apartment is him, humming in a gravelly voice as he rocks Scar.

"We don't have to. It's completely your choice. You're in charge here."

And he drops it, just like that, hard conversation over. The way he says the words, she knows it's something he's said before—but they're exactly the right ones.

Rose has been called a control freak a million different times by a million different people—and she is.

(Because when you have no power over what has happened to you, there's nothing you want more than to control everything else you possibly can.)

8

She's fourteen, in a blue dress Cheyenne got her for the occasion that makes her squirm.

It's not the grandest wedding in the world, but they've known the bride for years, and the groom goes to their church. It's the kind of thing that has a pretty big chunk of the community all coming together.

There's not a kid's table, so she's seated with her mother and a few of her vaguely familiar middle-aged friends, two of whom have spouses and all of whom are simpering like they know her.

"Oh, Rose. I know you've been working really hard in school lately, so I got you some gift cards to that store you like." Cheyenne smiles at her, eyes earnest.

Rose holds back a bitter laugh because this generosity, this kindness everyone else sees...it's fucking blood money. Her mother's money to make up for her silence as though it's a fair trade.

As though any amount of money and stuff could make this right, could make it okay that she's just standing by and taking his side when he's...

It's...almost worse, she thinks sometimes. He's the one hurting her, but Cheyenne is the one letting it happen when she's supposed to love her, protect her—even believing she's doing so all the while.

Rose wants to scream, but it's useless. Attempting to change anything is useless; she learned that a long time ago.

She just forces her lips to curve upward, says, "Thanks, Mom."

She keeps herself from crying out at the top of her lungs, from demanding to know how someone can claim to love her when they're letting this happen.

The table's conversation switches to the fall festival coming up, recent events, the usual gossip. It's not till twenty minutes later when Carolyn's eyes light up across the table. "Kyle! How are you?"

(Rose's entire body goes alert.)

"Hi, Carolyn. I'm doing well, thank you. How have you and Aiden been?"

She focuses on breathing in and out, the one thing in her control.

He's dazzling them the way he does the whole town, and her mother is laughing with him, and then he's smiling as he turns to them.

That smile that makes her sick, the precursor to the moments that make every cell in her body tremble and cringe and curl inward.

"Cheyenne, Ro-Ro, you both look lovely."

Don't look at me, please, please, God take his eyes off of me.

"Can I interest either of you ladies in a dance?"

Cheyenne squeezes his shoulder. "You're so sweet! I'm a bit too tired to attempt it, but I'm sure Rose would love to."

Rose nods obediently, getting to her feet because of fucking course, she can't say no.

(And when has her saying no ever made a difference?)

They're all saying how sweet he is, dancing with the daughter of a friend so she's less lonely and bored because he's just such a good guy, she just knows it.

His hand grips her waist with such familiarity, with a possessiveness she's grown accustomed to. It's all she can do to separate from herself, to wall away the feelings and thoughts and memories until she's numb to it all.

She sees a flash of white-blonde hair in the crowd, and it makes her think of Bronte—of happiness and the only family she's ever known. Of her two favorite people in the world, out there somewhere hopefully doing well because if anyone deserves to be happy, it's them.

She dreams up a world where they're both happy and safe and stable, and the three of them live together in a nice house in a good neighborhood far away from everything here. Bronte has an art studio, and Evan works in an office...

She so desperately dreams it that she's far away, so far she can almost forget where she is, can almost block out his breath against her skin.

———

In early December, Rose finds herself getting ready for Aaliyah and Liza's wedding nervously, Scar happily watching *The Wiggles* nearby.

"You're freakishly good at this."

Isa looks up at Rose with a smile in response as she does a practice run across the room in heels. "For whatever bullshit reason, my mother thought it was a crucial skill as a kid and made me practice every day for months. Turns out, strutting in heels is like riding a bike. The one good thing she ever taught me, I suppose, although I'm so tall already that half the time I don't bother."

"Useful skill to have," Rose responds with a joking scowl. "I'm short enough to actually make use of heels, but my ankles refuse to cooperate." Rose taps her foot nervously. "I feel kind of guilty that we're going without ever having met Liza and only knowing Aaliyah for a matter of days."

Two weeks ago, she'd woken to Bronte pounding on her front door unapologetically, a sheepish Josh in her wake. After making sure Rose had no plans the day of the wedding, Bronte had commanded her not to make any plans as she'd be Josh's plus one, and no, she couldn't convince her otherwise.

At the time, Rose had been terrified, but Zeke had already planned on bringing Isa since his boyfriend was out of town, and the four of them and Scar would be carpooling. Group efforts quickly quashed all her arguments for staying home.

Which brings her to where she stands now in a worn but nice

blue dress and two-inch gray wedges, getting ready with Isa in her apartment until the guys arrived. Scar's been in a good mood all morning, and Rose is just hoping it lasts through the ceremony.

"To be fair, most of the other plus ones have probably never met either of them," Isa points out.

Rose sighs, smoothing down her skirt for the tenth time since she's gotten dressed. "Maybe so, but most of the other plus ones don't have their *own* five-month-old plus one."

"Babe, relax; Aaliyah and Liza said kids are welcome, and anyway, she's been an angel all morning. You're going to be such a good girl for Mommy, aren't you, Scarlett? That's my Letty-love."

The child in question looks up at the familiar sound of her name, kicking her legs happily from her place in the self-moving swing that has become her favorite place.

Rose is pretty sure she's forgotten all the pain of childbirth immediately upon seeing how refined and adorable her little girl looks in her fancy yellow and white dress for the occasion; she's succeeded in preventing Scar getting any spit up on it thus far but is all too aware that luck will only last for so long and already rushed to take as many pictures as possible.

A fist raps on the door, just once, and then devolves into a beat that doesn't let up until Rose tugs it open with a singular raised eyebrow. "Were you a drummer in a former life, Zeke?"

"Not that I know of, but I'm hoping I will be in the next one," he responds cheekily. He steps inside without further ado, pressing a peck to her cheek. "You look gorgeous, Rose. You too, Isa. We need to put paper bags on both of your heads during the ceremony so everyone will be able to focus on the brides."

Rose flushes despite herself. "Thanks, Zeke. You're looking rather debonair yourself."

"Couldn't let down my date. Even though I know she pines for another, a woman as beautiful as Isa deserves damn nice arm candy."

"You're a true friend," Isa coos. "If you weren't so happily taken, I'd tell all of the single bridesmaids and groomsmen how very compassionate you are."

Josh snorts as he steps inside. "I think I'm going to speak on behalf of all of our ears and beg that you don't ever do that. Zeke already talks incessantly, but Zeke infatuated and *not* secure in the relationship is another beast entirely."

Josh's words make both women laugh, and Rose's eyes linger on the silver button-up's tight fit to his shoulders as he crosses the room. She'd never given much thought to the muscles cheer develops, but the way the suit highlights his biceps and chest holds her attention.

"Zeke's overdramatic, but he's right about you looking absolutely beautiful," he says to Rose quietly, Zeke and Isa already immersed in their own conversation.

"Thank you. You clean up pretty nicely as well." She catches his gaze flicker down to her mouth and has to stop herself from biting her lip.

A twinkle appears in Josh's eyes, and he grins at her. "I have to do my date justice. Although," he reaches to lift a squealing Scar from her buckle, "I don't hold a candle to this one's gorgeousness."

Something deep in Rose's chest throbs at how easily he smiles at her daughter, how natural their interaction is. It shouldn't be surprising, how attractive a hot guy with a baby is, but when it's *this* guy with *her* baby? Her reaction feels almost primal.

While she and Josh have become friends—really good friends, actually—she's not entirely comfortable with how badly she wants to see the two before her together more often, how loudly her mind is screaming at her that this is *right*.

"Also, change of plans," Josh says. "Bronte left by herself since she had to be there hours early to get ready with the others and help Aaliyah become bride-ly and do other bridesmaid things, so Kathy is picking all of us up. She should be here in a few."

Anxiety immediately flares in Rose. "But we won't all fit. A car will only seat five, and we have five and the baby—"

"Relax, Rosie, I know. I didn't forget Scar," Josh reassures gently, and her pulse spikes pleasantly with his use of the nickname. "She has Evan with her, and they're driving his minivan."

"I still don't understand why he has a minivan," Zeke says under his breath.

"Dude, he works with youth. How else is he supposed to get a bunch of them places?"

"Yeah, well, I'm taking so many pictures of this," Zeke mumbles. "Isa, darling, I hope you intend to dance the night away because there will be a full bar and a great DJ, and there's no way we're letting it go to waste."

Rose turns to Josh with a grimace. "I'm letting you know you ahead of time, I don't dance much," she warns him under her breath, but he merely smiles in return.

"Fine by me. Give me one number, and I'll call the night a success."

She bites her lip again as her entire face flushes, and Josh winks, hoisting Scar higher in his arms. "I have to have a turn dancing with this one as well, of course."

"I think we can arrange that," Rose concedes, and then they're all trekking into the elevator, Josh's arms full of child and car seat and Rose with only a diaper bag over her shoulder and a smile on her face.

Being around Josh...it's something she doesn't quite know how to put words to. Her heart speeds up a bit when he flashes her a grin, suited up and carrying Scar in a way so natural it hurts to watch.

(Maybe.)

———

Isa and Josh are taking turns kidnapping Scarlett, who's a big fan of the dance floor, the lights and music making her the happiest baby in the world. Currently, Isa is parading her around to look at all the colorful decorations. Kai's thirteen-year-old sister, who he's introduced as Peyton and the third oldest in his family, looks like she's having the time of her life. Rose can't remember having that kind of energy.

She finds herself being angsty with Bronte, seated at a center table from which she can always see the entire venue (and thus always have eyes on her daughter). She keeps worrying the light green tablecloth with her fingers, overwhelmed by the number of people. Bronte keeps grabbing her more wine, urging her to let loose just this once.

"You look so grown up." Bronte has a smile on her face, but her tone is almost mournful.

"Adulthood will do that to you," Rose jokes, hoping to lighten the mood. "You look stunning. And Liza and Aaliyah...you can just see how in love they are. It's nice to see a happy ending."

"It is. Especially after what they've gone through. Aaliyah...for a long time, I didn't know if she would ever be able to have this. And now she has that kind of love, the all-consuming, never-ending type." Bronte settles her gaze on Rose, lips turning downward. "I can't wait to see you have that one day. All of this...you're an adult, yes, but you grew up long before that. Too soon. And you're a kickass mom to Scar, but you have the weight of the world on your shoulders. I want more for you."

Rose swallows heavily. "I'll get there eventually. Besides, I'm already a million times better off than I was a year ago."

"That doesn't mean you're by any means okay. When was the last time you made it through the night with no nightmares?"

Rose squirms under her gaze. "It's been a while," she admits honestly, not meeting Bronte's eyes. "But don't you have them even still?"

"Yeah. Some things, I think will always...will always haunt me. But they're rare now. And when I wake up...I know that's not my life anymore. Working through your shit helps." Bronte eyes Evan across the room. "So does having someone to talk to when you're drowning."

Rose nods in understanding, heart warming at the sight. "I'm so glad you have each other. Although it's probably better that you and Evan aren't having kids. Any child of yours would be fit to burst with angst."

Bronte scowls at her playfully, but a laugh escapes her. "I hate that you're right. You know Josh never grew out of his emo phase either."

"I call bullshit."

"I swear it. That's why we get along so well. Why do you think none of them ever wants to give him the aux?"

"Josh Brooks, king of punk and culinary arts," Rose says, spreading her hands like she can see the title on a marquis with a laugh so free it feels out of character.

Bronte's expression grows serious again. "He's also a really good listener. If you ever wanted to talk to someone other than me or Evan...Josh would be a good choice. He's been through a lot. He's one of us."

One of us. The broken, the scarred, the ones whose reasons for not talking about their parents are much darker than fights about curfew and college major.

People like them find each other; they have to because no one else could ever understand.

(Trauma knows trauma.)

Bronte's words don't exactly come as a surprise. While Josh has spoken plenty about his early childhood, he's cagey about the more recent years, and though he's mentioned a step-father, the man's existence has come into conversation rarely enough for Rose to know he's not a person Josh wants in his life.

Still. Knowing what's there is enough that Bronte thinks he might understand, might be able to fathom the chaos inside her head instead of running from it. It means enough that when Josh approaches with a smirk, holding a hand out for her, Rose acquiesces to a dance.

"If I step on your toes, I'm sorry in advance."

"I asked you to dance, so if you do step on my toes, I brought it on myself," he replies. His hands slowly move to her waist; the song is slow and romantic in the way that's beautiful when you're someone in the audience watching a newly married couple, but while on the dance floor, it makes her heart pound with nervousness.

Rose reaches up to rest her arms on his shoulders, trying to remind herself to stay calm as his grip solidifies on her midsection, but her breathing quickens against her will, and she can feel herself tensing up ever so slightly.

"You okay? If you don't...if this is at all uncomfortable, we can go sit..." He trails off, looking at her with big brown eyes wide, filled with genuine concern. His wording, how quickly he's ready to stop what they're doing...it makes Rose wonder if Bronte told him that she was one of them, too.

She's not okay, not really, but she *wants* this, wants to dance with Josh and not let the people who ruined her life up to this point continue to have enough power over her to stop her from doing something that will make her happy. "No. Thank you, really, but I want to dance. I just...haven't really done this before."

"Well, luckily for you, I just go around in a circle. No fancy foot-work necessary," Josh teases, and Rose feels herself start to relax.

"I learned something about you just now," she informs him.

"I *knew* letting tipsy Bronte interact without supervision was a bad idea," he groans, shaking his head. "Okay. Hit me with it."

"Allegedly, you've yet to grow out of your emo phase."

"She's got me there." His tone is light, the confession not at all reluctant, and despite the love ballad Rose can hear in the background, the atmosphere doesn't feel at all forced or awkward. "Always playing throwbacks means everyone knows the words, though, which I personally like." Josh levels her with mock wide eyes. "Is it a deal-breaker? Am I a bad influence on Scar?"

"Never," she promises, eyes twinkling. "I'll just resign myself to her first words being *My Chemical Romance* lyrics now. Ideally, not the profane ones."

Josh looks jokingly offended. "Of course not. I made a playlist for while I'm babysitting, no cursing or overt sex stuff. You can blame any cussing by her on Bronte."

"You're not wrong," Rose concedes with a nod.

The song changes, but the tempo remains slow, and for a beat, they continue dancing until Josh abruptly straightens with a grin. "Wait right here."

He jogs away, and in the dim lighting of the reception room's high ceilings, she can't really tell what he's up to. Moments later, he stalks up to her purposefully, smile on his face.

"I thought the belle of the ball should get to dance with us too," he explains as he comes closer, the tiny bundle that is her daughter tucked into his chest. Across the room, Rose sees Isa looking put out, though she winks and wiggles her eyebrows meaningfully at Josh when she catches Rose's eye.

Josh turns Scar so that she can see Rose, and she feels a pang of guilt at the spot of drool now gracing Josh's tie, but he's not paying it any mind. Every bit of attention in his six-four, bulky frame is focused on the baby in his arm. His other arm wraps back around Rose's waist, and she returns one hand to his shoulder, slipping a finger into Scar's grasp. Josh begins to hum along to the song, and Rose closes her eyes, basking in the moment as the three of them slowly move in a circle, a contentment inside her like she had never thought was possible.

9

"Are you almost ready?"

Josh is lying on the hallway carpet, speaking into the crack between the bottom of the door and the floor.

"Not yet, honey."

He hums for a moment. "What about now?"

At twelve, he's inherently impatient, but more than ever when he's excited about their destination.

Mama laughs. "No, Joshua."

"Ugh." He gets to his feet, trudging to the kitchen. "Aunt Kathy, tell your friend to hurry up."

His godmother smirks fondly, pressing a kiss to the top of his head. "You and I both know that is a battle that is useless to fight, little man. Besides, you don't have room to talk; this is the first time I've seen you ready on time since you learned how to walk."

"I thought you were supposed to be on my side!" His expression is affronted.

"You know very well I am always on your side, baby boy. I will forever and always be on your team."

94

"*Except the actual teams I'm on because you really do suck at sports, Aunt Kathy.*"

A snort escapes her as her eyes roll. "*Yes, except for sports teams, thank you for that reminder. But even then, I'll be in the front row.*"

"*Stop spoiling my kid, Kath,*" *Mama chides when she comes into the room, ruffling Josh's hair on her way to grab a banana off the counter.*

"*She's not spoiling me!*"

"*Pft.*" *Mama gives him a look.*

"*She's not! She just loves me.*"

"*I know, JJ. That's why I know I'll never have to worry about you being alone.*"

Kathy raises an eyebrow. "*Morbid much?*"

"*It's the truth, isn't it? If something were to happen to me—*"

"*Mama! Can you not?*" *Josh beseeches her with a scowl of disapproval.*

His godmother nods in agreement. "*Honestly, shut up. You're not going anywhere for a few decades.*"

(None of them know, then.)

———

Scar gurgles, and Rose can't help but laugh, a full-body movement, at the delighted look on her kid's face.

Realistically, Scar is probably happy because she just finished eating, she's getting lots of cuddles and attention from her mama, and there are at least five bright lights in her vision. But that doesn't mean Rose won't try to tell herself her daughter is in such a good mood because they're in the library, where she's decided to camp them out for her afternoon off—on the first floor, right by the coffee shop, where noise and conversation are aplenty, and any temper tantrums won't invoke the wrath of hordes of other students.

Scar's too young to really care about books or libraries, of course, but there are few things Rose hopes for more than her daughter to inherit her love of books, because God, without it, she wouldn't have made it this far—couldn't have withstood the years in the hell she lived in for the last decade. It's the greatest strength she could possibly pass on.

"He's throwing up slugs, Scar, how icky!" While she doesn't use a baby voice with her daughter, she definitely tries to tone down her vocabulary for the infant. In the thirty-minute break from studying for finals she's allowing herself, using children's wording is a welcome change of pace.

"Starting her early, I see," Josh's familiar voice says from nearby, sounding amused, and Rose smiles as she looks up to see him leaning against the wall by the couch she and Scar are settled on.

She'd told him where they'd be earlier and invited him to meet up with them when his group project meeting was over. He'd said he would try, but she really hadn't thought he'd come.

"Are you talking about the library or the reading?"

"Neither—the Harry Potter," Josh teases. "Don't tell me you two already managed to get through all of Sorcerer's Stone."

"We did more than half of it while I was home with her for the first few weeks on maternity leave, to be fair."

Rose was already in a great mood, as being in the library curled up with her baby and a book is pretty much her favorite thing in this world, but the sight of her friend has her spirits rising even higher. Nothing romantic has happened between them since the wedding, but they've been growing steadily closer, and her heart skips a happy beat in his presence.

"What all do you have to get done?" she asks as Josh sits across from her.

The ever-present grin on his face flips to a half-hearted grimace. "Studying for ethics. I'm doing the required credit I should've done approximately three semesters ago, and it's killing me slowly—especially since all of my friends actually did knock it out way back when, so no one I know is in the class or remembers enough of it to help me. If I didn't need it to graduate, I would've dropped it a month ago—and I still have to take the second section next semester."

"Yikes. The athletics admin hasn't offered to spring for a tutor or something?" Rose asks, brows scrunched together. "I thought they would give anything to keep their athletes at a 2.0."

"They did—er, they tried, anyway. But I have a learning disability, and I missed some foundational stuff in high school because of a lot of absences; I ended up getting a lot of visits from truancy officers. Anyway, the moral of the story is that all of the tutors at USF we've tried haven't really known what to do with me. And I already get accommodations for classes and test-taking and shit, so I think I've used up all of the fucks they give." The admission makes him wince.

Rose feels her heart pause and then leap. She shouldn't. Should she?

"Actually," she starts, though she hadn't decided to offer before her mouth decided to act of its own accord. "I have a lot of experience tutoring; it was the only way I could make money in high school since I didn't have a way to get to and from...well, anyway, not that I'm any more qualified than the tutors you've worked with by any means, but I have worked with a lot of different learners with a lot of different learning abilities. I'm used to finding ways to make different things make sense to different learning styles. I took ethics last semester, partially for the requirement, but it's also pretty imperative to know the basic arguments and premises going into law school, especially if I decide to go into a more political field. But that's beside the point. I, um, I could work with you, if you want—if you're okay with Scarlett being there."

His eyes widen, face brightening—which is good because the dose of desolation that was showing reminded Rose too strongly of the way he'd looked weeks and weeks back after Zeke and the slamming door that'd made them both flinch. The moment that they still haven't talked about, that she gets the sense both of them are intentionally and actively avoiding.

She might be projecting, but she doesn't think either of them is excited for that reckoning or is in a place to have that kind of conversation together...or at all.

In real-time, Josh looks hesitantly relieved, enough that she's not berating herself for offering up time she doesn't have. "That would be amazing! Are you sure? I know you're super busy, and philosophy isn't exactly a good time—"

"Josh," Rose cuts him off gently. "I wouldn't offer if I couldn't make good on it. We'll probably just have to multitask while we work. Besides, I'm a lawyer to be; if I can't make arguments for things that aren't exactly fun, I'm screwed. Ethical arguments are going to be my entire life. And anyway, I can always use the review; you learn best by teaching."

She's trying a little hard to convince him, but she's resigned herself to how hopelessly enamored with the guy she's becoming despite herself, so she's not going to bother playing it cool. It's Josh. He's physically imposing, and being a college athlete makes him automatically suave, gives him the appearance of having his shit together, but the guy is as rambling and sweet as it gets.

(And he's one of them.)

"Okay," he relents. "I really appreciate it. The final is Saturday, and I don't understand anything even though I've gone to office hours every time I haven't had to work. I was just about to head out, actually; would you and Scar want to get lunch soon?" The question is directed to her, but before he's finished getting the words out of his mouth, he's scooping Scarlett away from her, spinning with the baby, who babbles a little louder at his familiar face.

Rose grins at the sight, stretches her arms as she stands. "We would love that. I've been putting off grocery shopping longer than any sane person and didn't have anything to throw together as breakfast this morning, so I'm starving."

He gives her a disapproving look as he buckles Scar into the stroller beside her while she begins packing up her notebooks and copious quantities of highlighters.

"You need to take better care of yourself. You good with pizza?"

Rose rolls her eyes. "Like I expect to eat anything else when I'm out and about with you."

She catches him staring at her mouth in the car and bites back a smile.

———

Rose hangs up the phone after her call with Natalya, who she's grown much closer to since the woman had both Rose and Scarlett over for Christmas dinner a few weeks prior.

Winter break means a much-needed break from classes, and Rose finds her apartment frequently occupied as Isa and Josh make use of the time off. By the time January and the beginning of the spring semester roll around, it's become a pattern, the refrain of music and playful arguments in her apartment familiar.

"You owe me five hundred, pay the hell up!" Isa demands, finger in Josh's face.

"I do not! You're a liar and a cheat!"

Rose crosses her arms and gives them a look from the kitchen table. "Didn't I tell you two no more Monopoly last week?"

Josh and Isa both forget their argument instantly and turn to her with guilty eyes from where they face off on the living room floor. Eyes that are begging her to let them continue even though it wouldn't be the first time that the game ended with something broken.

She raises her eyebrows at their position: Isa, raised up on her knees, leaning almost menacingly in Josh's direction whilst he tugs at his crew neck's collar, muscles tensed and nose scrunched in return.

Isa speaks first. "I'm so close to beating him, Rose, if you just give us five more minutes—"

"Okay, listen, she's totally bullshitting you, but I agree about the five more minutes, please."

"Five more minutes, my ass," Rose mutters with an eye roll. "Josh, you promised me dinner, so hop to it. We still have another chapter to review tonight, and I want to eat before I feed Scar."

"Ma'am, yes, ma'am." He salutes jokingly but stretches to his feet and heads to the kitchen to get cracking.

When they'd first started the tutoring arrangement, they very nearly had a shouting match when the topic of payment came up. Josh had wanted to pay her, even though he really didn't have the extra cash, and to not felt like he was taking advantage of her generosity; Rose had refused to take the money for helping a friend out when it wasn't even an inconvenience and was almost affronted that he wouldn't listen when she said so.

In fact, spending time with Josh, even pouring over a textbook, had slowly and without her noticing become her second favorite way to spend her free time, after cuddling with Scar.

Eventually, Isa calmed them both down and convinced them it was a fair trade to consider the tutoring a favor and for Josh to pay Rose back in favors.

(Hence the cooking.)

More often than not, Josh begs to babysit his debt away, making up excuses for Rose to nap or run errands so he can watch Scar, even once his 'owed' favor time is up. But with how much more time he's been spending at her apartment as the two slowly gravitate closer and closer, not talking about their growing attachment but not doing anything to stop it when they end up on the couch during a long conversation and Josh's arm drifts over her shoulder, her hand occasionally entwining itself with his, Rose has started taking advantage of his culinary capability.

The arrangement is better for everyone involved. On her own, she subsists on a ridiculous amount of pasta, mac and cheese, and ramen —in other words, noodles are her only hope in the kitchen.

The first time, she'd fallen asleep at the table while he cooked only to jerk awake from nightmares, Josh's hand on her shoulder and a look of worry on his face.

He'd been kind enough not to press the issue.

"What are you feeding us tonight, Chef Boyardee?" Isa asks as she starts packing the game pieces in the box, putting on background music with her phone.

Meanwhile, Rose watches her carefully, aware of the way Isa's been lately whenever they're eating. Isa's great at faking a smile, but Rose can see what she's doing, and... she's worried.

Josh smirks at Isa. "It's Jamie Oliver, thank you. Respect the chef or no food for you."

Isa sticks her tongue out in response, screeching a second later when Josh turns the kitchen sink hose her way with a flourish and sprays her directly in the face.

"Joshua Brooks, if you don't grab a towel right now and clean up that mess, I will help Kai cover your bedroom floor with mouse traps while you sleep," Rose warns.

Josh's eyes widen at the threat, shutting the faucet off immediately. "Damn, super genius, I didn't know you could be so violent."

"I'm a super genius, now, am I?" she asks, stepping around him to put the milk she'd pumped in the freezer.

There's silence for a beat, and without looking, she knows Josh and Isa are making faces about her behind her back, exchanging glances over the concerns they both often voice about her well-being. As though their own isn't equally worrisome.

Everyone's struggling, and they all think they're hiding it.

Josh heaves a disgruntled sigh and gives her a look she can't read. "Sure are—I saw your admission letters while I was getting Scar's pajamas the other day. You've been holding out on us, you brainiac. Harvard, Rose? And Stanford? And you're here?"

The confusion and frustration lacing his voice are palpable, and Rose can't meet his eyes, feeling her heart grow heavy.

She can understand why he's asking, can understand why he's so baffled and almost upset she let the opportunities slip away.

"It's complicated."

Her standard answer—one she knows Josh has heard plenty by now, whenever things scare her enough to have him waking her from nightmares when she falls asleep unexpectedly while he cooks or plays with Scar.

(Something that happens more often than she knows.)

"USF was the better option once Scar was in the picture," Rose finishes, clearing the table to avoid meeting his eyes.

Cheyenne didn't know she'd applied anywhere south of North Carolina, anywhere not an Ivy or other top ten—let alone to USF.

(Neither did he.)

He eyes her, and Rose is well aware her discomfort with the topic is clear, so Josh lets it go and offers her a smile. "Whatever the reason, I'm glad you ended up here, smarty pants. You and my six-and-a-half-month-old best friend. We're lucky to have you."

"I second that!" Isa chirps before Josh drops the dishtowel, now soaked from wiping up the puddle, on her head. She growls audibly. "I'll get you back for that, Brooks."

"No, you won't. I'm holding a baby; I have immunity." Josh's tone is cocky from where he again approaches the tiny stovetop, Scar tucked into one arm and a spatula on the end of the other.

It's a position Rose has found him in rather frequently as of late—and one she likes.

(A lot.)

———

"And you've been eating enough, right, honey?"

"Yes, Aunt Kathy, don't worry. And before you ask, yes, I've been making sure Zeke does, too. I think he's been doing a little bit better lately. We went to their graves last week with Aaliyah and Dmitri, and he seemed more...I don't know, peaceful?" Josh feels a little awkward, not sure how to put words to the friend that had barred himself off from the world several years before, who they'd all been slowly working to bring back to life.

But then, Zeke's life being lost had never been the root of the issue.

Zeke's recovery... it's no wonder he's struggling. No wonder he feels the need to play the jokester constantly lest anyone see the cracks.

"Good. You tell that boy I love him. Now, where are you and Rose going for your date tomorrow?"

"I already told you, it's not a date!" he says, exasperated, for approximately the tenth time. As much as he'd like it to be, Rose has enough going on without him getting any ideas. And worse, if he made a move and she grew uncomfortable or decided to end their friendship...it isn't a risk he wants to take.

"You're going on a picnic, just the two of you and the baby, and you made sure you had off work and have been asking me what foods you should pack for a week. Sweetheart, it's a date. That's not you getting your hopes up unnecessarily, that's plain fact," Kathy tells him, knowing just what to say to set his nerves just the slightest bit at ease.

If Kathy were able to see him, there would be no way to deny it; he feels his entire face flush, ears warm. "I just thought it would be a fun day for Scar and something to get Rose outside and relaxed on her day off. The last few weeks have been really stressful and busy, and she finally has a calm day. She needs someone to remind her to put herself first. She's... she's my best friend."

(And her eyes are pretty, and she never makes me feel stupid even though she's got the brain of a MENSA member, and I'm on the verge of falling in love with her but-)

"Josh, honey, I think we can both tell that sweet young woman has been through a lot."

Josh has never mentioned what he's mentally dubbed the incident wherein he'd realized he and Rose had a lot more in common than he'd thought—though it hadn't surprised him as much as he wishes that kind of thing would—but his godmother understands people, and knows something is up all on her own, just as his mother always had.

"And I know that because of that, you're probably trying not to scare her off or overwhelm her, but it seems to me she likes you too. And love...love doesn't always come when it might be convenient, but it's always worth chasing. Don't let yourself miss out—or her."

He wants to object, insist that she's seeing things because the chances of Rose liking him? Like that? Of her being ready for a relationship right now on top of being a single mother and working and taking classes and dealing with her past, whatever the hell she's been through?

But knowing Kathy, he figures she would have an excuse to fight almost any argument he came up with.

"I... I'll ask her. Soon," he promises. "And yes, I promise to give you all of the details and take at least one picture."

"That's my boy." He can hear the love in her voice, sense the smile on her face from through the phone—probably tucked into the worn and beloved throw blanket on the couch with the sudoku notebook she'll crack as soon as they hung up.

It hurts not being able to have this conversation with his mom—or even better, his mother and his godmother on that same couch together with him on speakerphone like they had any time he was away from home in high school.

Kathy's love means the world to him, always will, but it's not the same. And in some ways, it's a brutal reminder of what he'd lost when his mom had been taken from him, from this life that no one could possibly deserve more.

"I'm proud of you, sweetie. Your mama would be too—more than you know. You're exactly the kind of man Desiree always hoped she would raise you to be."

"Thanks, Aunt Kathy," he tells her, voice cracking even though he's never doubted it; his moms had never failed to make it clear that they were proud of him. Not when he was kicked off of teams or out of summer camps, put in school suspension for flunking classes or talking back to teachers; not when he picked a fight with Geoffrey knowing how it would end; not when he once gave money they'd really needed to put towards bills to an old man on the street without thinking. Never. They'd both loved him unconditionally, as Kathy has in Mama's stead since her loss. "I gotta go take a shower and get to bed, but I'll talk to you soon. I love you."

"I love you too, honey. Good night."

He hangs up the phone, rubbing his tired eyes before heading to the bathroom, his godmother and Rose both swirling through his mind.

(Soon.)

10

"How are you doing? The pregnancy, I mean... how's the baby? You don't know the sex, right?"

Rose stiffens at the inquiry, but Isabel's eyes are kind, face open and seemingly genuine.

She's only been working at the diner a month or so, but she and her coworker have an abundance of shifts together, and all of her interactions with the other girl have been positive thus far.

But that doesn't mean she can trust her, doesn't mean she can afford to stop being on guard.

"No, the little bean is being stubborn during every ultrasound. I have a hunch it's a boy, though, so I mostly refer to him as a he. Everything is good; he's good." Rose swallows but continues, encouraged by the other girl's soft expression. "Right on track for everything—growth, kicking my vital organs every hour on the hour, all the usual things."

Isabel laughs. "Delightful, I'm sure." Her head cocks to the side. "You must be so excited—hell, I'm so excited for you. A baby...and he'll be here so soon!"

"Yeah, I am." She bites her lip, debating whether opening up is the best idea, but...

(She's alone in the world.)

Her baby deserves more than just her—deserves a family, an entire village of love. Rose has to let people in to give that to them.

(It has to start somewhere.)

"I'm scared, too," she admits. "I've read everything I can and tried to do everything in my power to get ready, but... there's a lot I could mess up. And doing it all alone is daunting. It's...part of me doesn't want him to be born yet because at least while he's in utero, I can protect him from the world."

"That's fair. I mean, the world is a terrifying place. But kids are resilient, you know? They survive worse things than a mom who loves them trying her best and getting it a little bit wrong every once in a while." She reaches for Rose's hand, giving it a reassuring squeeze. "Worrying about your baby is normal—the most normal thing in the world, probably. I think most moms feel that way, you know? The good ones, anyway. Not like I know much about those."

"You too?" Rose blurts before thinking it through, surprising herself.

It's worth it for the wicked grin Isabel returns. "Yep. Funny how everyone with shitty parents finds each other."

Rose nods in agreement, her mind wandering to long-ago memories of Bronte and Evan, of all of them opening up about the darkness in their homes for the first time.

"Have you decided on a name yet?"

She blinks in confusion for a moment before realizing what the other girl means. "Oh, yes. Evan James."

Isabel's smile is warm. "That's precious. Do you have a backup, just in case he ends up being a girl?"

"Thanks. And yeah, I'm thinking Scarlett Bronte, although I have a really strong feeling he's an Evan."

"Better not tell the guys in the kitchen that," Isabel teases. "They've all placed bets on whether they think it'll be a boy or girl."

"Of course they have." Rose rolls her eyes with a snort. "I should collect the winnings for being the one growing the kid."

"Maybe the winner will split it with you."

They both giggle for a moment. Talking to Isabel is light and easy, in a way she hasn't had in a long time.

"Isabel, do you...would you want to come over after work one day this week and hang out? We could watch a movie or something. I'd say we could hit Applebee's for drinks, but..." She gestures to the bulge of the baby, earning another bright smile from the other girl.

"I'd love to! Honestly, I've been in Florida for months, and I think I've only done something other than work once." She gets to her feet as a table sits in her section but looks back over her shoulder before walking away. *"Also, call me Isa. All my friends do."*

———

Being a good mom at any time is hard as fuck.

Being a good mom when your brain is working against you...well, Rose spends hours those days thinking of how much more Scar deserves.

She's known this downswing was coming for a while. The things she normally enjoys have been losing their appeal; everything under the moon has been irritating. She knows the signs well enough by now to have an idea of what's headed her way a week before everything hits.

The last few days, triggers have been anywhere—a man seated in her section at work whose frame was so reminiscent of his, her entire body froze; a classmate offhandedly calling her Ro; a conversation overheard in passing with graphic comments too close to the words in her nightmares—close enough that she proceeded to throw up moments later.

The world is a rape victim's nightmare.

Some people like to refer to themselves as survivors because it's over, and they've made it, and Rose doesn't fault them for it; she's impressed by them, really, for letting the trauma make them stronger, for deciding for themselves exactly what they are in the wake of decisions being made for them.

But to survive something is to get through it, and she will never be 'through' this, will never be 'over' it. It'll keep affecting her for the rest of her life.

(Being a survivor means you're still alive; most days, she doesn't think that she is.

(Being a survivor means you're living, and Rose has only been existing for as long as she can remember.)

Every night, she wakes up, eyes flying open with an instant sense of alertness. To be awake should be a relief, should make her heart slow down with the reassurance that the nightmare she was trapped in seconds ago before over. Instead, she just feels empty and inexplicably sad.

Nighttime is always the hardest, always the most dangerous time, but waking is everything crashing down and not feeling okay. On days like this, the hours just before dawn are her darkest moments. Her pulse remains rapid, her reflexes hypervigilant, every sound eliciting her panicked full attention as Scar dozes peacefully.

Rose loves her daughter—loves her so fucking much it pains her, consumes her entire being; it feels impossible that Scar didn't exist for the majority of her life when she's now all Rose can see. It feels like an insult to her kid that she is so unhappy in this moment, like she's telling Scar she's somehow not enough, that being blessed enough to be her mother is not enough to make her life feel worth living—because Scar is everything.

Her daughter is every star in every galaxy, every smile she has ever worn, everything good and perfect in this universe.

(And yet Rose still feels so broken.)

Days like this, she doesn't understand how the human body can produce so many tears, how it's physically possible to spend so much of the day with a lump in your throat and lips pressed together, trembling. Every time she thinks she's done, it starts again—for absolutely no reason as she's staring at the wall or her threadbare sheets.

This wave of misery is inescapable. Refuses to leave her alone.

It's lucky, this time, that the swing is hitting on her day off. Other times, when she's had to go into work while fighting the ever-present need to scream, the cracks in her facade seem like ravines. The energy it takes to engage with anyone, let alone customers, is completely draining, taxing reserves that have already run dry.

(Lucky. If only.)

———

The day goes on. The apathy doesn't abate.

She gets it together enough to feed Scar, to change her and bathe her and play with her for a few minutes because, like work, those aren't things she gets to opt-out of. She's a fucking parent, and depression and PTSD and whatever the fuck else is rattling around inside her head don't make her exempt from those things. Even when doing them feels like crawling across rusty nails.

It shouldn't be this hard—especially now, when her life is in every way better than it's ever been, when she's not still facing the struggles she dealt with for a decade. There's literally no reason for her to feel this beaten down. No reason why the perfect little baby next to her on the futon, smiling like a genuine angel, should not be enough to make up for everything that has ever gone wrong in her life—which is how she feels, constantly, so incomprehensibly grateful for Scarlett that nothing else matters.

A knock sounds on the door, and Rose tenses, curling into a tighter ball, hoping if she ignores it long enough, whoever is on the other side will give up, but no such luck. They rap on the hardwood once more, and when she fails to respond again, there's an audible, if muffled, sigh from the outside.

The sound of metal on metal reaches her ears, and for a moment, her brain is moving a million miles an hour, thinking up scenarios in which someone is here to attack her, currently expertly picking the lock. But before she can get worked up further, the lock clicks with a resounding key turn, and Isa steps inside.

"Hi, love."

Rose looks up to her best friend, who gazes down on her with a sad smile before reaching to re-lock the door.

Isa steps to the kitchenette, dropping the canvas bag over her shoulder on the table heavily before coming over to the futon, climbing in on the other side of Scar and tugging the other half of the quilt over herself with a flourish.

And that's it.

She doesn't press Rose to talk, doesn't push for details, doesn't ask what's wrong or try to get her out of bed, out of the apartment—just joins her in the silence. Reminds her with her presence alone that she's loved, that she's not alone, and the simple action means more to Rose than she can ever express.

They lay there for an hour, each of them dozing off briefly, sometimes flipping through tabs on their phone until eventually, Scar gets antsy, and Isa rises to her feet with a stretch.

"Okay. So. I'm gonna do homework and play with my best girl for a little bit since that's the best way to procrastinate said homework. I brought food, which you're going to eat because I know you haven't yet today, and then you're going to shower because no matter how bad you feel, that will help at least a little bit. And then you can do whatever you want—paint or sit in the corner and listen to sad music, whatever floats your boat. Okay?"

She lays it all out gently without room for argument, and they've been here—and in the reversed positions—enough times that Rose knows she's right. She also knows that, while her heart might not be full of activity at the moment, when it is, Isa owns a prime piece of its real estate. Even if Isa were completely wrong, Rose would do anything for her.

Rose dips her head in a nod and leans forward to grasp her friend in a tight hug before standing to do exactly that.

She eats—only half of what Isa brought her, but it's progress. And she showers, taking advantage of the unlimited hot water for the first time since they moved to the new building, letting herself cry again under the spray, the hot rivulets soothing aching muscles. She steps out feeling just the smallest bit better, as Isa knew she would.

When she re-emerges, Isa is singing to a cranky Scarlett, who slowly calms down and proceeds to delightedly play with the toys before her, putting blocks in her mouth and smiling when Isa sings.

Part of Rose wants to run to her—wants to apologize in words

Scar can't yet understand for not being everything she deserves, not being the best possible mother, letting her down like this. Wants to pour all the energy she scraped together in the shower into playing with her and showing her how much she loves her.

But long term, that won't help. That will only drain her again, and she knows it. She'll be better off if she gives herself a little more time, a little more space to recharge.

So instead, she reaches into the cabinet for the paints she hasn't touched in months, grabs a piece of thick cardstock for a canvas, and settles herself in the corner. She hits play on a carefully honed playlist on her phone and takes a deep breath before throwing herself into the art.

It's not her best piece by any means; it's been months since she's worked on anything, and her technique is sloppier than she'd like, the details not coming out as she intends. It's visceral and not a work she would want anyone else to see.

But it's there. For the first time in so, so long.

It makes her feel in control. Independent. Art always has; for just a beat, she has unchallenged power, unquestioned authority over this blank canvas. What it turns out to be is entirely on her.

(It's a reassuring thought, that some things in this world can still be in her hands.)

———

It's evening when Josh makes his way down to Rose and Scar's apartment. He hadn't planned on seeing them today—hadn't planned on seeing anyone after the grueling workout he and his teammate and workout partner had put themselves through—but somewhere along the line, he'd realized he hadn't seen the familiar brunette in a few days.

She'd been a little off the week before, her responses to his texts more stunted and distracted. And maybe he's overreacting a little bit and really just looking for an excuse to see her, to see Scar, but nonetheless, he already knows he'll feel better once he's been near them.

The door opens softly after he knocks, and Rose bites her lip as she looks up at him.

Her eyes are swollen—the way his have only been once, sitting in a deserted courtroom and wanting to set the whole fucking world on fire. The way that eyes only get after hours of crying, heavy and tired and resigned to further tears. Her sweatpants are covered in splatters of paint, and the bags beneath her eyes are so dark it scares him. But she offers an exhausted smile, and everything else disappears.

He surges forward, bending down and pressing his lips to hers without a second thought.

Josh feels her sharp intake of breath against his mouth, but then she's kissing him back, and for a moment, this is the entire world; he's completely focused on sliding the fingers of his right hand into her hair. Rose leans into him hesitantly, lightly, and while he hadn't dared to hope for this anytime soon, it's everything he didn't know he needed.

The hand not knotted in her curls slips to her waist, her back, reaching for any part of her he can, and then she's jerking out of his arms, his eyelids flying open to see her a yard away, eyes wide.

"Sorry," she whispers, then clears her throat.

"No, I'm sorry. I totally sprang that on you," he cuts in before she speaks further. "That wasn't my plan for coming down here or anything, I just..." Josh trails off, shaking his head incredulously before meeting her gaze. "You opened the door, and...I don't mean this in a bad way, but you're kind of a mess today, and I realized that even a mess, you're still one of the most beautiful things I've ever seen."

Rose's lips part, surprise filling her face at his confession. "I—you —what? But...my hair is genuinely tied in a gigantic knot right now."

"It's endearing," Josh says, perplexed even as the words leave his mouth.

Scar lets out a cry, and within seconds, they're both standing next to the playpen, their attention alone enough to quiet her and put a mischievous smile on her small face.

"Don't worry, little angel. You're the other most beautiful thing

I've ever seen," Josh stage whispers, and Rose simultaneously blushes fiercely and beams at her daughter, pride visible. "Really, though, Rosie, are you doing okay?"

Her eyes cloud, and Josh mentally curses himself for ruining her moment of distraction, even as she turns her attention back to him. "It's been a rough couple of days. I think things are better now. Sorry I haven't answered your texts."

He frowns, breaching the distance between them to tuck a strand of paint-spotted hair behind her ear. "I'm not worried about that. I'm just glad you're doing better."

Her wording makes it clear she doesn't want to go into detail about what she's dealing with, and he doesn't want to push, so he chooses his next words carefully. "Anything I can do to help?"

The corners of her mouth tip upwards, and though her eyes are still sad, the set of her shoulder softens just the smallest bit. He hopes somehow it's enough to make her feel at least a modicum less alone. "You being here is enough. Thank you for coming."

"Netflix?" he questions, pointing to her laptop. She nods, setting them up on the futon with Scar and returning to their most recent episode.

They don't talk about the kiss further—not right now, at least. That's not what she needs at the moment.

But as soon as they're comfortable, his arm is wrapped around her; it's not the first time it's happened, but this time it means something else, and when she falls asleep with her head on his shoulder, Josh knows there's no going back.

———

Just a few days later, Rose glances down at her phone under the guise of checking the time from her seat intentionally across the room from Isa. She's been avoiding her friend a little the last few days, worried she would slip up or be too incapable of acting natural that Isa would know something was up. This, keeping herself and her phone away, is the last stretch but possibly the most important of all.

After all the work she and Nick have done to make this surprise happen, it wouldn't do for Isa to figure it out a minute early because she caught a glimpse of Nick's name on Rose's phone screen seconds before the reveal.

Nick had texted her three weeks ago, saying he'd managed to graduate and get things in order to move down and was hoping to surprise Isa. The timing is nearly perfect, and Rose is hopeful it will raise her best friend's spirits.

Everyone's upstairs for their fairly regular movie night in the boys' triple, Isa on the dilapidated couch squished between Josh (who knows Nick is coming, because Rose would've felt way too guilty bringing a random guy to his apartment without permission) and Kai (who doesn't because his mouth is the biggest thing on the east coast). Bronte is sprawled on the armchair with Scar in her lap, eyes excited as she relays stories of the baby's mother in her perhaps wilder younger days, not limited to the time twelve-year-old Rose swung on a two-hundred-pound man with the rusty kitchen frying pan because he took a step inside their apartment, toward Bronte, and it was the only conceivable weapon within reach.

It's a rare night when no one has to work or go to class in the morning, so Evan works his magic to make a few more drinks in the kitchen. While Josh might be more adept, they never let him play bartender on his night off.

It's already a good night, a reminder of this new home and that she's so lucky she can't comprehend it, but Rose's excitement for Isa's reaction is too hyped up to enjoy the familiar happy atmosphere this group that's become her family provides.

Headed up. The text hits Rose's phone with a ding, and she quickly hops to her feet, making eye contact with Josh before busying her hands with the tray of wings on the tiny living room coffee table. Normally, Isa would find this suspicious because Rose has never liked wings, and Isa is way too observant not to notice even the smallest actions that are out of character. But she's currently occupied with the movie, so she doesn't bat an eye.

Mere seconds later, a knock sounds on the door and Rose looks up apologetically; she spots Josh holding back a laugh at the devious-ness in her eyes as she holds up both arms helplessly. "I have sauce all over my hands. Could you get it, Isa?"

"I don't even live here; your go, Adkins," she tells Kai, gesturing to the door with a flourish.

"TV owner privileges; Kai and I are exempt," Josh zings without pause, deep voice carrying across the apartment but passing the intervention off completely naturally. "Sorry, Castaneda."

"Yeah, sorry, sweetheart."

The tongue Kai sticks out does nothing to convince Isa, but whoever is at the door has been waiting for a long moment, and Rose gives her the look—the same look she gives her when Isa 'happens' to disappear right when the table of bitchy middle-aged regulars comes in at work and Rose is left to deal with them.

Isa sighs, pulling herself to her feet and trudging to the door.

Before she has it open, she starts speaking, "Hey, if you're looking for Joshua or Kai, they're busy being lazy ass—"

Rose sees the exact second Isa actually zones in, the exact second she looks up to see her childhood best friend who isn't supposed to be in the same state as her for another month. She pauses dramatically before launching herself towards Nick, their closeness in height making the embrace easy.

"Oh, my God, you *didn't*! How did you do this? I can't believe you didn't tell me you were coming!"

"Suffocating here, Isabel," Nick (somewhat) jokes, and the girl in question pulls away to drag him forward. "I realized I had no desire to walk across a stage when I could be with my best friend sooner, and all of my courses are done, so I'm in the clear. You're the proud BFF of a high school graduate."

"Who says I'm proud?" Her face is so flushed with joy that the tease has no weight, and she spins to narrow her eyes at Rose with a suppressed grin. "You had something to do with this, didn't you? I knew you were acting weird all week! You were conspiring this whole time?"

"Guilty as charged. Nick called me a few weeks ago to start figuring out the details."

"I can't believe you two did this! Don't think you're in the clear for hiding this from me, Slider," she threatens, the warning holding no weight next to the delight in her eyes.

"I need the story behind that nickname," Zeke begs, and Nick smiles at him, amused.

"That's Zeke," Isa says by way of explanation, and Nick nods, understanding lighting in his eyes.

"Hi, Zeke. No story, really—just a skiing incident where we learned I should never be left alone in the snow again."

"He couldn't stand back up, so he took off his skis and used them as paddles to slide his way down a mountain. I have pictures," Isa informs everyone, overjoyed face full of mischief.

"What do I have to do to get you to delete them?"

Rose is pretty sure the answer running through Isa's brain is something along the lines of a long-awaited marriage, but Isa laughs it off and swears she'll keep the pictures until she's dead.

Rose leaves them to catch up and introduce Nick to the others and heads to the kitchen to sneak some of the ice cream Kai doesn't know about yet.

"What's all the commotion?" Evan asks from where he stands at the counter, two glasses in one hand and a handle of tequila in the other, working on the margaritas he'd promised Josh and Isa if they studied for all of their exams the week before.

"Isa's best friend from New York is here. She didn't know he was coming."

"Ah," Evan grins, giving a comprehensive nod. "That explains the squealing."

"Pretty much. You want a bowl?" Rose waves toward the carton of triple chocolate brownie in front of her and Evan nods vehemently.

"But not in a bowl, you heathen. Real adults eat their ice cream in cones."

"Says who?"

"Says me, and I've been adulting like ten years longer than you."

"I have a kid; I think that makes me extra-adult. For sure at least a decade on my actual age," she argues with a smile, turning to the cabinet for the cones.

"I took care of you when you were a kid, so I think I win."

"Fine, fine, whatever." Rose pretends to scowl at him, but they're too close for her to maintain it for long. She hands over his cone before hopping up onto the counter, and he joins her.

"Josh treating you alright?" Evan checks, eyes serious.

Rose bumps his shoulder but can't help the blush that rises to her cheeks. "We're not...just... we've barely..."

He raises an eyebrow. "Rose. Come on."

"Yeah, okay. He's—he's been great." A smile she can't help creeps onto her face. "I don't know where it's going, if it is going anywhere, but...I like him. He makes me smile, and he's good with Scar, and I... almost feel safe when I'm with him. It's..." Unfamiliar, terrifying, thrilling. "It's good. We'll see what happens. I don't know if he even wants anything serious."

"Please, that boy is so smitten he doesn't know what to do with himself. I think his angst might make the building explode if you two don't DTR soon."

Rose makes a face. "Don't say DTR, please. I'm begging you. Why is that even in your vocabulary?"

"I run a youth center, kid. I pick up some weird-ass lingo." He laughs when she mimes gagging. "Let me know when you two make it official, will you?"

"Sure thing." Her eyes narrow. "Why?"

"No reason. Just like to be kept in the loop."

"You're gonna give him the dad speech, aren't you?"

"Obviously." He grins before gently reaching to give her a one-armed hug. "You're one of the most important people in my life, Rose. Always. I'm going to do everything in my power to make sure no one ever hurts you again. Sometimes that means talking you down from a spiral; this time that means giving a guy I like a talking to and reminding him about the people in your corner."

She scrunches up her nose, not sure how to respond to the love, the familial intimacy she has so little experience with. "Thanks." Scooting closer to him, she leans her head on his shoulder, hoping the gesture conveys the gratitude, the love she struggles to put into words.

Evan nods like it's no big deal, giving her shoulder a squeeze.

Isa stumbles in a few minutes later, her entire face alight with joy at Nick's presence, her emotions visible enough that they cue Evan to leave the room.

She beams at Rose, grabbing her face to press a kiss to the other girl's forehead. "I can't believe you two did this. Thank you. I'm so glad you're in my life."

"Right back at you, love." Rose is quiet for a moment. Attempting to be nonchalant, she gets to her feet, eating a few chips before opening one of the pizza boxes. "You want a slice, Isa? I can make you a plate."

"No thanks, I'm okay!" Isa smiles, waving her away.

She says it so casually as though it's no big deal, like she just doesn't want any.

(Rose knows better.)

"Are you sure? You didn't have any wings, either. There's ice cream and stuff for sandwiches too."

"I'm really not hungry."

Rose bites her lip but doesn't relent. "Isa, you should really—"

"I said I'm fine, Rose," Isa snaps, visibly irritated. "Please just... leave it, okay?"

The fact that she's going for confrontation, instead of just placating everyone around her... It's getting worse.

Pushing her further right now won't do any good, Rose knows that, so she forces a smile, muttering an apology and squeezing Isa's hand before heading back into the living room.

And the rest of the day is wonderful, truly. Wholesome bonding and quality time with most of the best people Rose has ever known.

But a part of her is distracted, too worried to relax.

(If things don't change soon... something's gotta give.)

11

He rubs at his eyes as he pads into the living room, nearly tripping over a pair of Geoffrey's shoes.

He's been living with them for a few months now, but sometimes Josh is still surprised by the smallest things that have changed since his new step-father moved in.

The door creaks open, and Mama steps inside wearing the shitty flip-flops she mostly wears for taking out the trash and going to the beach, clearly having just done the former. "Morning, honey."

"Mornin'."

He lets her press a familiar kiss to his cheek without protest.

"Geoffrey's working a double today. I thought maybe you and I could go to the aquarium?" *A smile tugs at her lips as she suggests it, knowing full well it's Josh's favorite place in the world.*

"Hell yes!" *He gives a bashful grin when she levels him with a look.* "I mean, heck yes."

"Better. Go get ready, we'll leave in twenty minutes, okay?"

Josh beams, reaching to hug her, but she winces at the pressure. "What's wrong?"

"Nothing, sweetheart. I just bumped into a counter at work the other day, gave myself quite the bruise."

He doesn't have a reason to think she's lying, not really.

(But something about it just...feels off. Feels wrong.)

He hates the shadows that have become permanent beneath her eyes, the life that's begun to drain from her body. The stress she's begun to carry with her.

(And whatever it is that's dragging her down... it's only just begun.)

———

Things are beginning to feel like they're shifting closer to normal a week later, and in a rare carefree moment, Rose finds herself glaring at Josh, where they both sit on her futon.

"You're not going to convince me that Spider-Man is a better superhero than the Flash."

"You think that and can still call yourself a 'purveyor of truth'?!"

"Stop throwing my own phrases back at me, Joshua. The truth is that Barry Allen is unequivocally the superior hero. He could overcome literally any other power with his speed because by channeling and manipulating it, he can exert limitless force, become impervious to time—he's unstoppable."

Josh rolls his eyes as he stands, straightening the fabric of his work shirt with the hand not holding Scarlett. Too soon, sooner than he normally leaves, and Rose notices something is off.

"Since when do you leave early for work?" The words are joking, but she's actually kind of nervous because it's so out of character for him.

The intensity crackles between them.

"I'm not leaving yet; I wanted to talk to you about something, actually." Clearing his throat, he meets her eyes while Rose watches him with confusion and worry. "I—er...I was wondering if you would want to go out on Saturday. Like a date," he clarifies, scrunching his nose as though mentally face-palming.

"Oh."

The sound is brief and surprised, no other trace of emotion in her voice.

They haven't talked about the kiss since the week before—haven't talked about anything to do with their relationship, whatever the hell it is at this point, just rolling with it in the midst of the chaos.

They've known there was something between them for a while, of course, and since the wedding, Rose has been hyper-aware of his presence, but somehow his acknowledging it so directly is like a defibrillator straight to the chest. Words? Sounds? Breathing? Something, Rose, get it together.

Josh seems to scramble at her hesitation. "If you don't want to, that's okay. I just...I thought you might, but no pressure. I won't take it personally and abandon our friendship because I really care about you; I'll just leave now and—"

"Josh," she cuts him off, the corners of her lips turning upward. "Of course I want to. Sorry, I froze for a second there. I just..." *Wasn't expecting the closest thing to an angel I've ever known to have feelings for me too?* "I was surprised. I'd love that. I'll have to see if Isa or Bronte has off to babysit."

"No!" he says immediately, the pitch of his voice shooting upward until he clears his throat. "Sorry. I just mean that I'd like Scar to come, too. I really think she should be there."

"Really?"

Because of course she wants Scar with her, and it's no secret that Josh adores her daughter, but to actively want to bring her on their first date? Didn't see that one coming.

And how desperately he wants to make sure her kid is included... there's something he hasn't told her.

"Yeah. I mean, she's your kid. Dating you means in like a very, very long term way dating to be her parent, right? She's the number one permanent member of whatever family you go on to build. I mean, yes, I want us to have solo dates too, obviously, but I would never want to try to have a relationship with you around her."

Rose gives him a small smile. "Do I get to know what we're doing?"

"Well, I thought that since you're kind of a know it all genius, it might be good for you to be surprised for a change. I promise it won't be anything you'll be uncomfortable with."

"Fair enough." She accepts the jest and has to restrain herself from leaning forward to kiss him already.

She reaches out to take Scar so he can head to work, internally mourning at losing the sight of Josh holding her baby girl, a sight that has started to take over what few dreams interweave with her nightmares.

Ruminating over the way she's starting to fall in love with him, she catches herself wishing Scar could have a father as caring and devoted as Josh to love her as much as Rose does.

(Hoping, despite herself, that it's not too good to be true.)

———

"How long before we got here did you guess where we were going?" Josh asks with a smile, teeth shining in a bright smile that contrasts with his dark skin, having expected as much and holding back laughter at Rose's feigned surprise when they approached the aquarium.

The humidity is toned down a bit today, bright white clouds subduing the sun's intensity. For Florida residents, it's still a bit chilly, but tourists are exclusively wearing shorts and already hitting the beaches.

"Two hours after you left on Tuesday," Rose admits sheepishly as Josh slides his fingers through hers. Her other arm is tight around a practically giddy Scarlett who's been feeding off of everyone's excitement and good mood all morning.

"As long as I could hope it would take, really." Josh nods with resignation, leading Rose by the hand to the ticket window. "My thinking is, we take as much advantage of Scar getting into places free as we can while it lasts."

"You know I'm on board with anything free."

Josh chuckles at her smirk, glad she's not put off by the easy way he mentions the future, as though it's not a question for him that Scar will be in his life well past the age of free admission—which is what, three at the earliest? If he has any say in the matter, it's a given he'll be around the two of them that long.

"Okay, so we definitely have to start in the saltwater section; they're the coolest, and the sharks are there," he declares, pushing the empty stroller forward without pause.

It's cooler, inside, the lighting around them dim but inside the tanks bright, making the whole place feel as though it's underground.

It's not too crowded; most of the people who are there are parents by themselves or with other kids who look too young for school, all babbling excitedly at the bright colors and movement.

"I would've pictured you as more of a dolphin guy."

Josh practically shudders, stepping closer to the glowing tank before them in the darkened room. "Dolphins are assholes. They're genuinely cruel to other animals and humans, and jus—God, the articles I've seen... they're the worst. Sharks get a bad reputation because they have the potential to hurt humans, but they almost never do. They're like...underwater puppies. With extra teeth."

"Whatever you say, Mr. Expert. How do you know so much about marine life, anyhow?"

His expression turns almost bashful, as it's a question he doesn't get often, and he's trying to compose his response even as he watches Scar, the infant enraptured by the many colors and lights within the tanks. "I...my mom used to work here—not Mama, who was close with Aunt Kathy, the other one—so I got free admission. Came all the time, especially after she died. It was the place I felt closest to her. All her coworkers let me in free; they were great, honestly, always gave me lunch, took the time to see how I was doing."

He gives a bittersweet smile, lost in the nostalgia. "Although now almost everyone is new and doesn't really know me. Anyway, I could probably recite most of the exhibit descriptions from memory. I thought about going into marine biology, trying to work in Clearwater, where they do the prosthetics, but...I don't think that's for me."

Because as much as he likes fish and everything else under the sea, he cares about kids more. He has to help them.

(He just needs to find a way he can help them and still make enough money to dig himself out of his financial grave more than a pebble at a time.)

"Well, anywhere would be lucky to have you. If you settle around here regardless, you'll get to visit. Maybe you can chaperone if any of the teachers at your school bring students here on field trips. Pass on the passion," Rose suggests.

"Maybe. And we can—" He cuts himself off abruptly as his ears turn red at the realization that maybe it's a little direct to talk about them bringing Scar to Harry Potter world in a hypothetical future where the three of them live near Orlando and go to amusement parks on their days off. Together.

(In all fairness, the thought preemptively crosses Rose's mind too.)

It scares them both that they consider it so early on; normally, that kind of commitment would be terrifying, but...somehow, right now, it doesn't seem like such a daunting prospect.

The rest of their wandering throughout the aquarium follows in a similar fashion, easy conversation between them, Josh's happiness flaring every time Scar gets excited at the sight of the different sea creatures, the intertwining of his and Rose's fingers unconscious, and the most comfortable sensation either of them has had in ages.

(But this is Josh and Rose, and so neither of them is surprised when the content bubble is broken a few hours later.)

They make it back to the apartment building and post up in Josh's apartment as Scar snoozes peacefully on Kai's treasured beanbag. The guy in question is in his hometown today as he usually is on weekdays, and his brother has a school performance of some sort that's keeping him there till Sunday.

Josh stands at the stove whilst Rose sits on the counter beside him, legs dangling and occasionally poking him when he gets lost in the dishes he's working on putting together.

"There we go. You have twenty-five minutes of my undivided attention," he teases, sliding off his oven mitts after getting everything started.

"Finally, I don't have to compete with fish or food," she volleys back, snatching his hand and drawing him close to where she perches. Rose isn't especially short, but Josh towers over her, so him standing and her on the elevated counter is about as close to even in height as they'll ever get.

He smiles, leaning into her. "Really, though, did you have a good time? I know ocean stuff is more up my alley, but I figured Scar would like all the colored lights, and I know I always learn a lot when I'm there, which I figured you would like. I thought since you're still newish to Florida and I'm guessing you haven't really explored that much, it would—"

She can see that the more he speaks, the more nervous he gets, so without bothering to verbally reassure him, she reaches up to slide her hands across the planes of his face as she's been wanting to for months because good God is the man chiseled in a way that should be illegal.

Rose tugs his head toward her and finally—*fucking finally*—presses her lips to his.

For a moment, Josh doesn't react; she hopes it's just his brain short-circuiting at the feeling. She knows she's been imagining nothing but this since their first kiss, which was too short to satiate the need for him, can only dream that he's been likewise hoping for it so much that he's not quite sure it's real.

After a beat, though, he's himself again and carefully slips his fingers into the thick locks of her hair gently, so gently, as though too much force will shatter the moment, will send her running, and begins to move his lips with hers in earnest.

Rose's brain is a whirlwind of emotions as she processes the moment because going on a date with Josh is one thing, but making out with him? Entirely otherworldly.

Her heart is racing at the agency she feels after initiating the kiss, the tremor at being able to control who kisses her for once in her goddamn life. The series of pangs—excitement, anxiety, confusion—running through her have her in a tailspin.

Eventually, they both draw apart, breathless, but Josh doesn't stray far, pressing his forehead to hers as his fingers keep running soothingly through strands of her hair.

"Hi," he whispers, and a giggle slips through her lips.

"Hi."

"So...you did have a good time, then?" he asks quietly, their eye contact smoldering.

"I always have a good time with you, jock man," she tells him with a small smile. "But yes, the aquarium was perfect. It's my turn next time, though."

"Fair enough. I—" The ringing of his phone cuts him off, and he purses his lips without real malice, pressing it to his ear without checking caller ID, looking hopeful to get whatever conversation needs to be had over hastily. "Hello?"

Rose had guessed it would be Kathy calling, but the tension that fills Josh's body within seconds of the voice on the other end beginning to speak tells her immediately that something is off. Hesitantly, she runs her fingers down his forearm, hoping to help keep him calm, but the lightning flashing in his unfocused eyes is far too angry.

"Yeah, which has only happened because of the fucking protection order."

The outburst, the anger she's never seen from Josh, makes her eyes widen.

The caller says something else briefly, and Josh's muscles tense even further—and for the first time since she and Josh have gotten close, Rose truly reconsiders the strength he possesses. She feels herself inching backward, making herself smaller.

The familiar instincts take over as all the possibilities of how he might take this anger out on her run through her head, even as the logical part of herself reminds her that he flinched, Rose, he's been there too, and this is Josh—because don't an awful lot of victims go on to become abusers?

"Find a way to get us another hearing, something. Have you called Kathy yet?"

Another few remarks pass between his clenched teeth, but Rose is focused on curling in on herself, focused on making a plan of how she can grab Scar and get out without facing his wrath.

She's too focused to notice him end the call and tug on his shirt collar with anguish before looking down at her, taking in her hostile position for the first time.

"Fuck, Rose, I'm so sorry. I'm so out of line right now. I can't believe..."

(The horror flooding through him is visible, palpable to her, at the contained, resigned fear he sees on Rose's face that had been so familiar on his own mother's—on his own.)

She doesn't respond, and he takes a deep breath, careful not to come any closer or speak too loudly, she knows, for fear of spooking her. "My stepdad, the one I mentioned before...he used to hit my mom," he admits in a whisper.

"He would beat the shit out of both of us whenever the fancy struck him. For half a decade. Everyone who knew me till I got to college thought I was so clumsy..." Josh lets out a deep sigh. "Pretending to be made it a lot easier to get people to not ask questions. They got married when I was pretty young, and he seemed nice, and we were in bad shape, and then once he started to be this awful human being, it was too late because he was the only source of income. When it got bad, he threatened to kill each of us if the other ever ratted and...and then one day, he did."

He shakes his head in anguish, eyes closed. "And she was gone, and so I finally, finally got away, but the bastard only got a year's sentence. After he fucking murdered her." The bitter laugh that escapes him after the vulnerable words has Rose slowly inching out of the instinctive terror, listening closely as his words reinforce her mind's words that Josh is one of the good ones; we're safe with him.

(But what do we know about being safe?)

"And then he got out early for good behavior. We filed the protection orders the second we found out he would be out, one for each of us. Me and Aunt Kathy, I mean. He hates her; she knows too much about everything he did to Mom, was around all the time, and she was constantly trying to convince her to report, and...well, he's always had it out for her. And that was before she testified against him. The protection orders have to be renewed annually, and we submitted our forms as early as we could, but that was our lawyer. She said that 'as no aggression was made in the last year and the order wasn't violated,' the judge decided to deny the request to renew."

Tentatively, Rose reaches for his hand. "That's—that's horrible, Josh. What kind of justice system..." Well, she's done the research, she's well aware of how fucked the justice system is. But still, to think these people could allow that monster another legal chance to go after them. After he's already ended a life and ruined another. "Is there any kind of appeal we can file?"

The tension in his shoulders begins to lessen at the word 'we' slipping off of her tongue, her hand in his; she can only imagine what it had seemed like to him for a moment there, her pulling away as full-on survival mode took over.

"She said she's going to try. We still have a few weeks until the old one expires, and Kathy has moved apartments and jobs since the sentencing, but to keep him away from where she is, the protection order has to have her new residence and place of employment, of course. So he knows where she is. She's a sitting duck. If it doesn't go through, I don't know what we'll do. I will have to move her here, so she's not alone or hire a bodyguard. As if we can afford any of that," he whispers bitterly.

Rose squeezes his hand carefully. "I...I don't know what we'll do, Josh, but we'll figure something out. I'll start researching it as soon as I get off tomorrow; there has to be a way. And you know everyone else won't just sit by. We won't let him near you or Kathy," she vows.

Though moments ago, her body's instinctive reaction had her cowering, now she's the one holding him together as the fear, anger, and worry make him tremble. He presses his face into her shoulder without speaking further.

"We'll get through this," Rose whispers, hoping that if she says it enough, she'll believe it, to reiterate the cause for hope, to remind Josh that she'll fight with him every step of the way, somehow.

Because her monster might be states away for now, but his is roaming the streets, and she'll be damned if they both made it through the years of torment they did to lose now that they're finally together, finally free.

(Finally have a semblance of a chance at happiness.)

12

When Kathy finds him, his throat is raw from screaming into his arm.

"Oh, sweetheart." Her eyes are welling up with tears as she moves to embrace him.

He'd outgrown her during a wave of growth spurts two years ago, and yet in this moment, he seems so, so small.

(So young—*a ghost of the little boy he used to be, so hopeless and scared.)*

"I always said he'd kill her one day," Josh chokes out, eyes swollen. "I told them, and she begged *for their help, and they did* nothing. *And now she's gone."*

"I know, sweet pea. I know." Kathy rubs his back with shaky hands. "The world is...a terrible place, sometimes. She should've been protected," her voice breaks. "Your mama deserved so much more."

"Will it ever stop hurting, do you think?"

Josh's eyes are glassy and far away, face hollow.

His godmother bites her lip, searching for the right words. "I don't know that it'll ever stop; *that's the thing about love. You love someone forever, so you miss them forever, too." She squeezes his hand softly. "But grief takes different shapes. Right now, it's...all-consuming and overpowering. But time will morph it into something less sharp; eventually, we'll be able to talk about the good things, to think of her fondly without the missing her drowning us. Just like when we lost your mom."*

"I know, and I still miss her too, but—" His nose starts to run, and he rubs at it with the sleeve of his jacket, ignoring the scowl Kathy gives him. "That was unavoidable, you know? It was terrible, and—and it hurt, but it was out of anyone's control, and there was time to know it was coming. Mama...this could've been prevented, fucking easily, if anyone in power had bothered to give a damn."

Kathy nods, trying to hold back her own rage and frustration. "It's wrong. A corrupt system, in a corrupt city, in a country that doesn't care." She takes a deep breath. "But it's what we're working with, so we have to push through. Carry on. Do what we can to push for better and hope things change."

While we're still around to see it, *she doesn't say aloud, though they're both thinking it.)*

"I guess they're together, now," Josh mumbles, feeling almost drunk with exhaustion.

The pain both twists in his chest and almost becomes bearable at the thought of Mama and Mom reunited at last, wherever the hell they are in the life after this.

———

So much has been happening in Rose's personal life lately that it's almost jarring to find herself worrying about something as familiar as money problems.

"I have no idea how to make this work," she confesses to herself, fingers to her temples as she stares hopelessly at the mass of bills before her.

Normally, she wouldn't be too worried, as she tends to be the overcautious type when it comes to putting every cent she could into savings, but Scar has just had a crazy growth spurt and needed all new clothes. Even second hand, on top of diapers and formula and every other thing, it added up.

Worse, it had been slower at work, and the people who *had* been coming in had apparently decided that while they could spend absurd amounts of money on food, they didn't need to leave over ten percent even though she worked her ass off to keep them taken care of.

She's been pushing off dealing with the expenses, hoping things would pick up, but...waiting any longer isn't an option.

"Why do you have your overthinking look on your face?"

She jumps in surprise at Josh's voice, not having heard him come in, but relaxes at the familiar press of his lips to her forehead before he slides into the seat next to her, his jeans brushing up against her leg. He leans forward to read the pages crumpled before her, sticky notes with crossed-out math and random ideas of how to make the funds she *does* have stretch, and grimaces with recognition.

"Ah. One of those days?"

Rose nods, and he leans to pull her into him. Face pressed into his chest, she feels herself starting to relax, the familiar smell that's somehow so very *Josh* permeating her senses and somehow convincing her brain things are going to be okay.

"I'm sorry, Rosie. Dealing with this, with everything, it sucks. It's so, so frustrating."

Josh slowly releases her and pulls the dreaded pages closer to him. After a minute, he exhales heavily. "Okay, you get paid next Friday, right?" At her confirmation, he pushes all but one of the papers and sticky notes into one pile, the remaining two in another. "So, I think you should pay all of these now. Our building doesn't fine you until you're more than a month late, so you can wait to pay rent till the next paycheck comes in."

"I can't pay rent late!" She winces at how sharp her tone is, but the principle of the thing isn't even a question to her.

"Babe, I don't know that there's any other option. I'll go with you if you want to talk to the landlord about it and give him a heads up. I know the thought of having a late payment on your record stresses you out a lot, but at least this way, you can make all of the payments."

"Even if I do, that still leaves groceries. I get a free meal at work every day, but that's not enough with how much running around and pumping milk I have to do, even with WIC."

The last time she'd tried to cut down on costs by eating less, her milk production plummeted; Scar going hungry isn't an option.

"You can just join in our pool; everything is a lot cheaper when we buy in bulk for everyone and make meals that leave leftovers instead of eating individually. That's why I started cooking regularly," he confesses, and she can see the tell-tale scrunch of his face that happens every time his cheeks warm. "Anyway, we each pitch in like twenty or thirty bucks every two weeks. Saves us all a lot of money."

Rose bites her lip but knows she's going to take him up on the offer despite herself, desperately needing the alternative he's offering. She coupons and uses every trick in the book to try to make ends meet, but it's not working, and as much as she would be willing to skip as many meals as it took to take care of Scar, it's just not on the table when she's her daughter's main source of food.

The tiny part of her that spends pretty much all its time thinking about Josh flutters at the kindness in his willingness to take on her problems as his own without trying to offer her money they both know she won't take; the easy way he works to make her problems *theirs*.

Standing, grateful to leave the cluster of stress on her kitchen table, she and Josh enter the living room, where Scar babbles excitedly at the sight of them. Rose scowls at the sight of her daughter laying on her back, flipping Scar back onto her front for what has been long dubbed 'tummy time' and receiving a squeal in response from the baby in question.

Rose narrows her eyes at Josh. "Did you flip her over when you came in?"

"Nope."

"Don't lie to me, Josh, and don't flip her. You know her lying on his stomach is important for her learning to crawl!"

"Rose, I swear I didn't move her! I said hi to her when I came in, but she was already on her back."

"Well, you must've moved her. How else would she—"

"Rose," he interrupts her, his voice a whisper and his eyes wide.

She follows his gaze down to Scar, who is giggling and...on her back? But hadn't she flipped her?

"Did she just—"

"I think she did," Josh breathes. "Oh my God."

"Oh my God," Rose repeats, squatting down to pick Scar up, happy tears forming in her eyes. "Did you just roll over all by yourself, honey? Mama is so, so proud of you!"

She's so overwhelmed with joy, she almost doesn't notice the tiny pang in her heart at this sign of her daughter growing, becoming her own person. So, so wonderful, but the first sign of her eventually not being a baby.

Scar responds nonsensically, excited by all the attention, and Rose lies her back down. "Go on, sweet pea, do it again so we can see!"

She's so entranced with watching her it takes her a minute to realize Josh is almost as thrilled from where he stands behind her, his phone out and videotaping the kid as they urge her to demonstrate her new skill.

It crosses Rose's mind that while she's easily referred to the others who are close to her as aunts and uncles of Scar's, she's never addressed Josh toward her daughter.

(Probably because the title she wishes she could give him at heart is terrifying to consider.)

———

Josh finds himself on the couch with Isa, each of them typing away at homework while they wait for Rose to get off work.

They'd argued over who got to take care of Scarlett while Rose was at work and Natalya was busy ages ago and had compromised, making a habit of watching her together at Josh's place where Isa spends a lot of time anyway because of her friendship with Zeke and, more recently, with Josh.

Timers are being consistently set to switch turns because they both want to cuddle Scar while she sleeps without Rose there to remind them that she needs to get used to sleeping in the crib and not in someone's arms.

The news blares in the background, likely Kai's doing as he's the only one of them that would have bothered to put it on. It switches from sports to the financial segment, and Josh resists the urge to groan.

"And Julian Castaneda has done it again, striking a deal for yet another property and spiking Castaneda stock prices to an all-time high. Mr. Castaneda has also recently confirmed he and his wife, Karen, intend to again sponsor the local youth soccer team he backed last year, taking care of fees as well as providing cleats and other equipment for kids on the team."

As soon as Josh realizes who the report is referring to, he slowly turns to a tense Isa.

She's never *confirmed*, per se, that Julian Castaneda is her father, but Josh had guessed as much early on in their friendship between the uncanny resemblance and shared name. It's pretty clear that something not-so-great had happened between them, so he tries to change the channel whenever Julian is mentioned.

The damage has been done this time, though. Sorrow is leaking through Isa's eyes despite the sleeping baby she holds in her arms.

"You know," Josh says hesitantly, carefully making eye contact. "If you were to ever want to talk about it...that would be okay. I know it must be hard because he's...him, and people probably take his word because he's famous and wealthy, but whatever it is, I'd believe you. I know you, and I believe you must have had a good reason to run so far."

It wouldn't be the first time they got emo while hanging out. They've ended up trading a lot of background stories and deep secrets over the last few months.

Isa considers this for a moment, then sighs and turns to face him. "He was never...I mean, he never deprived me or mistreated me or anything, but he was never a very affectionate dad. He had his assistants get whatever they deemed I needed and figured buying me everything under the sun was a substitute for actual parenting or love or...any interaction whatsoever, really.

"But as I got older...his expectations got higher. It was pretty clear anything I did wasn't good enough, that I would never be perfect. My mother, too; she'd grown up in a socialite family, learned how to smile and gossip and navigate that almost-Hamptons culture. They expected me to be the same way. I wasn't. Nothing I did was ever enough. When I was younger, I tried...everything, became *everything* I could possibly imagine they would want from me. But it wasn't enough. Nothing was good enough."

"It was little things at first, and then they started restricting me the more I messed up. I mean, things like a Maserati or Michael Kors don't matter to me, and I don't need allowance larger than most people's paychecks, but then they both realized taking things away wasn't working, so they would lock me in my room until I mastered a skill. If that didn't work, the next time, it would be a closet. A restraint to bind me to my seat at the dinner table so that I wouldn't have poor posture. Any employee who tried to help me was immediately fired and blacklisted among all the other wealthy families of their status." She shakes her head. "I know it sounds fake—it's the kind of thing you only see on tv. But it was that level of insanity."

The more she speaks, the more Josh's eyes grow dark with horror, his fists clenching unconsciously.

"Not too long before graduation, they announced they would be adopting a son to take over the empire. I would be married in the fall, and I should be fucking *grateful* to have parents who loved me so much."

(*"How can you call this love and still live with yourself?"* she'd demanded of her father when the edict was leveled, and he'd looked at her like she was disgraceful.)

(*"I have given you everything a child could ever wish for, Isa."*)

Divulging her story to Josh was so cathartic, she couldn't stop herself from continuing.

"My older brother..." She trails off, and Josh closes his eyes with a wince, having forgotten she'd had a brother.

Having forgotten the TMZ reports so many months ago.

"We were so close. Have to be when your parents are awful and you don't have anyone else, you know? With their reputation...no one else would've believed us. He was in the Army. Enlisted as soon as he turned eighteen, got the hell out before our parents could ever catch wind. He was so much happier, and I knew he felt guilty for leaving me behind, but I was just so happy he was out, you know? I just had to last a little bit longer. I'd been stashing away allowance, setting things up to leave once I graduated...

"And then we got the call," she croaks, and Josh immediately knows what she's referring to; he wraps an arm around her shoulder firmly. "A week before graduation. He was gone. It had always been a possibility, with him being in a combat zone, but he was my whole world, and he was gone, and my parents...they had the nerve to pretend to mourn, to give a eulogy at his funeral. I was pissed. I left early and beat the shit out of my father's Lambo with Diego's old baseball bat at home. Found some precious heirlooms and smashed those, too, for good measure."

"Never knew you were such a badass." Josh's comments break the tension, and Isa bursts out laughing through the tears.

"Yeah, my one and only felony. Not that they'd ever press charges —wouldn't want the world to know their own daughter was a delinquent." A bitter smirk crosses her face. "Anyway, I left for the airport straight from the ceremony. Took all the jewelry and expensive shit I'd accumulated over the years and pawned it on the way. I don't care that it was blood money; it got me out. Got me here. Even if I have a ton of debt now because out-of-state tuition is a monster."

"Damn, Isa. That's... that's so shitty. Really, just...heavy. You've been through a lot."

He'd been through something terrible, too, but to think about his mom not believing him? Being the one to make him feel inferior? A different kind of terrible. Painful, right down to your soul.

(When someone who was supposed to love you more than this world cares so little.)

"Tell me the truth, honey; has he been a gentleman? You know I'll come up there and give him a talking to if he hasn't." Natalya's voice is serious as it comes through the phone, so ready to fight on Rose's behalf, it makes her heart sing.

"He's been perfect, Nati," Rose promises, shaking her head with a smile. The man in question is currently babysitting—what Rose has begun to affectionately refer to as 'kidnapping'—and had taken Scarlett to the park so she could run errands and take a nap after pulling three doubles in a row at work.

It's only been a month or so since that first date, but it's been as easy as breathing to turn their friendship into a relationship, the main difference being that they now make out a lot more. And Josh absentmindedly whispers about how beautiful she is like an awestruck preteen whenever he thinks she isn't paying attention.

(It's Josh, though; she's always paying attention.)

Regardless, it hasn't been long, but...it feels like so much longer. She and Josh just click.

"Good. That changes, and you just let me know. Now, really, how are you doing, sweetheart? You sound awfully tired."

Even through the phone, Nati sees right through her, refusing to discuss her own illness and plans to visit the grandkids soon, no matter how much Rose pushes it. The second they'd gotten on the call, as they do pretty often outside of when Nati watches Scarlett, the older woman could tell something was not right with Rose.

Something being the nightmares perforating her sleep even more frequently, because as much as she loves her newfound physical affection with Josh—had never realized how much she desperately craved it, how much she loved human contact and holding hands and falling asleep curled up together on the futon—her brain only has one thing to compare it to, and so her life before Florida has been a lot fresher on her mind, in waking and in dreams.

Rose purses her lips before replying. "I'm okay. I... there's kind of a lot going on in my brain, stuff that I really just have to work through with time, I think. Josh helps, though. He makes me really happy. I'm so lucky to have him."

"You deserve all of the happiness in the world, Rose, sweetheart. Don't you ever forget that, okay? I don't know what you've been through, but what I do know is that you are so strong and such an amazing mother. I can't imagine anyone being better for Josh, but more importantly, I can't in a million years imagine any way you could possibly be a better mother to Scarlett."

Rose swallows thickly, accepting the compliments and telling Nati she loves her and she'll talk to her soon.

(But the buried part of her hiding in her chest that's been mourning for the better part of two years, the part that sometimes aches when she looks down at Scar, sobs for hours.)

———

"I think I want to get a tattoo," Rose tells Josh nervously, watching him out of the corner of her eye for his reaction.

She'd planned the date this time: a battle of the band's event in the bandshell at a public park nearby, the best kind of date because it's free, which they had intended to bring Scar to until Isa had snatched her up while wagging a finger at them. Isa claimed they needed 'alone time' every once in a while, and besides, Auntie Isa hadn't gotten nearly enough Letty-love lately, what with the second round of midterms crucifying them all.

"Really? Do you have something specific in mind, or do you just want one in general?" he asks, head in her lap as she runs her fingers along his cropped hair.

"Something specific." Rose swallows. "A large sunflower covering my shoulder, with two smaller buds leading away. One of them..." She trails off, not making eye contact. "I-I don't really want to go into what it means right now, if that's okay, because it kind of hurts to think about. But I'd like to tell you someday."

"Whenever you're ready, I'll be ready to hear it," he promises, squeezing her knee lightly.

She opens her mouth to respond, but before a sound escapes her, she catches sight of golden blond hair, some three rows ahead of them.

She gasps in air without meaning to, feeling her heart rate rise and terror fill her.

He's here. He's here, and Scar isn't with her, and now she's put Josh in danger.

She sputters out, "He found me, he found me, he found me," too quiet for Josh's ears, but he must realize something is wrong because of the way she's violently shaking against him.

"Rosie? Rose? Hey, what's wrong?" Sitting up, worry floods his face, and she knows she must look horrified, her skin paler than he's ever seen it. "Rose, you have to breathe, okay? Just breathe, baby, you're okay, come on."

By now, *he's* turned around. Though his face isn't the one from her nightmares, Rose can't feel the relief she wants to, and she's too lost inside her own mind to acknowledge Josh.

Because it *could* be him; maybe it's not this time, but it could've been.

(One day, it will be. He'll find her.)

Overwhelmed, Josh keeps whispering without a clue as to what will help, saying what seems like every possible thing he can come up with to comfort her but to no avail.

(She can't truly hear any of it.)

"Let me," Zeke says, appearing in front of them.

While they'd bumped into Zeke shortly after arriving, he'd gone off to experience the concert on his own, so his voice is the last one Rose expects.

She hears their interaction through a fog, as though she's underwater.

"I don't know what happened, man, but I'm really worried. I don't—"

"Panic attack," Zeke says by way of explanation, no preamble, scooting next to Rose on the grass. "Hey, Rose, I don't know where you're at in your head right now, but you're here, okay? We're in the park, you, me, and Josh, and we're completely safe. We're gonna get you home now, so you feel more secure, but I promise we're here with you, and you're okay, alright?"

She forces herself to breathe in and out, and Josh haphazardly shoves their sprawled belongings into the canvas bag they'd lugged along, helping Zeke pull her up from the grass and to her feet.

Slowly, they make their way back to the apartment building, Josh holding onto Rose's hand to remind her he's there silently as Zeke keeps reminding her that she is okay, that they're with her. By the time they approach the complex, she nods in response to his words, feeling less liable to fall apart despite the exhaustion and shakiness throughout her body.

They step inside the apartment to a smiling Isa, whose expression quickly turns to concern as Josh moves forward to fill her in.

Without a word, Rose holds her hands out, and Isa places Scar into them, and it's this, this visceral reminder of where she is and of Scarlett's safety that really makes Rose feel like herself again.

"I'm okay," she assures them all quietly. "Honestly, you can go ahead home, Isa. I need to be with her right now, and I think after the guys leave, we're both going to take a long nap."

(*A nap likely to be ridden with nightmares, but a modicum of rest, at least.*)

It sucks the energy out of her, these moments, her entire body readying for an attack.

Isa presses a kiss to Rose's cheek softly, grasping Scar's tiny fingers before heading out, her features mirroring Josh's pained expression.

Zeke steps towards the door. "I'm, uh, gonna leave you two to it, but...if you ever want to talk about panic attacks or anything, I get it. I got them really bad for a while...still do, every once in a while, if I get stressed enough."

"Thank you, Zeke. Really."

He shrugs before leaving as well, and Josh carefully sits next to Rose on the futon, pausing as though unsure as to whether or not she wants to be the first one to speak.

When she doesn't, shoulders still curved in her body a bit like she's scared, he starts to talk like he always does when she gets nervous; she's pretty sure he figured out day one that it's easier for her to open up without feeling weak once someone else has.

"I... I've never had one," he admits. "I have no idea what you're feeling right now. But I *have* been that kind of scared before, and I know it takes a lot out of you, so I really want to make sure you eat and drink something before you lay down, and then I can head out, okay?"

Rose nods without making eye contact, then asks in an undertone, "Is Zeke okay?"

"He's had a rough time of it," Josh replies, eyebrows scrunching up. "It's, uh, touchy for him to talk about. He was in a really bad fire a few years back; his older brother and best friend were there too. Zeke was the only one who made it, and that was complete luck. He was in the ICU for weeks."

"God, that's awful," Rose whispers. "He must be in so much pain..."

"We've each had our very own hell, haven't we?" Josh says with a bitter tone.

So many times over. "Yeah. Yeah, we have."

Josh hesitates, fidgets beside her. "We, um, we don't have to talk about today if you don't want to. I mean, if you do, I would love to be here however you need, but I kind of get the feeling that you aren't ready yet, and I just mean that that's okay because I know you're still kind of mentally dealing with a lot. But I sort of don't want to leave you here alone after that. If you're not feeling super safe. All I know is, if it were me, I would feel better having someone else here, and now I'm just rambling," he ends abruptly, nervously scratching the back of his neck.

"You...you want to stay?"

"Of course." He reaches out cautiously to tuck a stray lock of hair behind her ear; she can see him gradually calm as she grows more and more functional. "I can lay down on the floor, and I don't...we don't have to, er, do anything, that's not...I just, really think it would be good for you to not be alone. I also don't want to leave you while I'm worried about you."

He fumbles over the subject, them not having had a real conversation about sex yet, but Rose doesn't take it the wrong way. She just moves to lay Scar down in her crib before responding.

"Okay."

Josh's eyes widen in shock, but Rose nods deliberately, knowing he's doubting his ears.

"I...you can lie on the futon with me, but I...I need you to be in front of me." The words slip out of her mouth unintentionally, desperately, and she stares at her feet to avoid seeing his reaction to the odd request.

Because she wants to lie down with Josh. Thus far in their relationship, his presence has always soothed her, made her feel the slightest bit safe, and truly, after today, she wants nothing more than to curl into him.

But to wake up with a man in bed behind her, unable to see his face and remind her razor-edged instincts that it was Josh...few things would be more terrifying.

She knows without question she can't handle that.

"Whatever you need," he reminds her softly before helping her to pull the futon out into bed form.

Slowly, he climbs on and over to the far side, hoping that to not be boxed in against the wall by his body might make Rose more comfortable, and she slides beneath the worn, thick quilt already half on him.

Breathing shallow, she lets him delicately hold her close, lips touching to her forehead before she tucks her head into his chest.

"I've got you," he promises in a quiet whisper.

It takes Josh ages to fall asleep.

He has no idea what it is that haunts her, and as much as he wants her to open up to him whenever she's able, wants to help her through whatever this is, the thought of finally knowing scares him stiff.

(Because whatever fire it is that she's had to drag herself through, whatever someone has done to traumatize the mind-blowingly strong creature he's lucky enough to hold in his arms, it's something bad. Really, really bad.)

It makes him quiver with rage in a way that frightens him just to think about, makes him want to hunt down whoever dared take a sliver of the light from her eyes.

(And he doesn't know how well he'll handle knowing the extent of it.)

13

BEFORE | **ROSE**

She's curled on the bathroom floor, trying to breathe and focus on the cool tile against her cheek.

It hurts so badly, she'd think she was dying if she didn't know better.

But it's worse than that...because her baby is dying.

Rose had only been eight weeks along as far as she'd figured out, so she knows she most likely will be fine even without going to the hospital. And it's...technically they're not even alive yet. And if it were someone else and they were getting an abortion at this stage, she would support them wholeheartedly.

(But it's not someone else. It's her, her baby, the life that would've been —should've been.)

Rationally, it's almost better. She's sixteen and in no way in a position to take care of a baby. God knows she'd rather die than bring another person into this house that's more hell than home. But Kyle could've objected to her putting them up for adoption. And if it had been a girl...

But rational doesn't matter.

Logic doesn't make it okay—it doesn't make her heart break any less at losing the baby she already loves more than anything in the entire world.

They were hers, a part of her, and she can't look at her body and not think of how they're supposed to be there.

They were tangible; Rose was supposed to have them in her arms, and she never will, and it hurts.

She's gutted, and it's... she's had plenty of dark moments before, but in this instant, everything is meaningless. She can't be bothered to care about anything. Nothing matters. How could anything possibly matter when her baby is dead?

(A part of her wonders if it's possible to die from a broken heart. If such bone-deep sorrow might kill her.)

She hasn't prayed in years, but she finds herself crying out for anyone and anything, begging any deity for any way to bring them back, even if it hurts ten times as much. She'd do anything.

(Does anybody hear her?)

Regardless, there's nothing to be done.

The baby was only here for a little while, but for the rest of Rose's life, every decision she makes... she'll always imagine how it would've been different if they were here.

Later, she whispers into her pillow, as though her baby can hear, "I was supposed to love you for all of your life. But I'll miss you all of mine."

———

Life goes on.

Rose and Josh grow closer and closer, and getting to hang out with her and Scar becomes one of the best parts of his day.

They don't really talk about it much, the fact that both of them are dealing with monsters from their lives before. The fact that neither of them can sleep through the night most days.

The fact that some days, one or both of them can't stand another human's touch.

They're both exhausted; their friends see this, but they're climbing their own mountains, and there's only so much they can all do for each other when it takes each of them everything within them to stay afloat. Their mental health is a disaster, money is tight, and some days, it feels like there's no end in sight.

But they power through.

They do family dinners at least twice a week, but most days, whoever is off meets up for a meal anyway; they might bring along homework, and whoever needs to do chores at home hosts so they can be productive, but they're together.

Everything feels lighter that way.

Scarlett grows slowly, and since most of them see her pretty often, the differences can seem negligible, but every once in a while, someone blinks at the difference between the fresh out of the womb alien they first met and the giggling blue-eyed baby with them today.

Rose works and works and worries about Isa—worries about her more and more every day as it becomes harder and harder to believe she'll start taking care of herself on her own.

Sometimes Rose's eyes flutter of their own volition, her body attempting to fall asleep where she stands without her permission, but she fights back. She tries to see Bronte and Evan as much as she can. Her grades aren't the perfection they were in high school, but that doesn't matter anymore, only that she passes and keeps a roof over her daughter's head. That, and making sure Scar knows she loves her, however young she may be. She's busy enough to distract herself from the chaos inside of her head, and most days, by the time things slow down enough to think, she's collapsing in bed.

It's as much as she could hope for.

And having both Scar and Josh in her life... it's *everything*.

(*They're* everything.)

Josh works, too, but the mountain of debt doesn't flinch—especially not now when he's again swamped with legal fees as he tries to petition for a new protection order; he's given up on his own, but Kathy going without one isn't an option.

The end of the semester's gradual approach means work is busier, which equals more tips for him but also means being there an extra hour of cleaning after close and then coming home to attempt to run through homework like a zombie. Things are solid, though. He's making it. He's *going to* make it.

They're surviving. But things aren't perfect.

(And they'll fall apart before they can put themselves back together.)

———

"Did you really think I wouldn't find you, Ro?" His hands slide along Rose's body where she lies, and she flinches violently, mentally screaming, trapped in his arms as she has been for so many years. His touch feels like slime and rusty nails and everything dark in this world.

"Let me go! Please, please, just let me go," she begs, her voice breaking.

Scarlett begins to sob. Real, chest-heaving sobs of fear, the kind any parent can only dread, Rose despairing as she slams against his grip to get to her baby.

"What is that?" His voice is ice, and he drags her to the crib where Scar lies screeching.

"Please, you can't hurt her. Please. She's-she's a friend's daughter. I'm just watching her, I swear."

"If that's the case, why are you so defensive?"

She screams as he reaches for her helpless baby girl, who's without any idea as to the danger she's in, screams as her dream morphs into his weight crushing her, kneeling over her and muttering obscenely in the home she grew up in.

"Rose!"

She jerks alert, wetness on her face and her heart racing a million miles an hour as she takes in the dark room, the dim light of the tv stuck on the *"Still Watching?"* screen. Josh lays beside her propped up on an arm, having spent the night—a habit that's grown to almost daily, as they both seem to sleep better when they're not alone.

He eyes her worriedly.

"I...sorry if I woke you," Rose pants breathlessly, fanning at the sweat on her neck. She feels especially bad given that Scar's already been up twice, and while she'd tried to soothe her quickly, Josh is a pretty light sleeper and was awakened both times.

"Baby, I don't care if I have to wake up ten times a night if I can help snap you out faster." He frowns, gently stroking the side of her face. "That sounded like a bad one."

"Yeah, not my most peaceful rest ever," she acknowledges.

You're here, Rose. You're with Josh, Scar is safe, and he is nowhere near you. Get it together. You got out. You got her out.

She repeats the reminder, but the part of her that learned a long time ago escape was impossible denies it.

"Do you want to talk about it?"

"No," she snaps instinctively, curling in on herself.

But she thinks about it for a moment—actually lets herself consider the idea, for once. What would it be like to have this person that's grown so close to her heart know this hardest truth about her, to be able to talk to him about what she's feeling with complete honesty?

It's a terrifying prospect, but at the same time... wouldn't it be such a relief?

Into the silence, she makes herself whisper, "I...I think I might, actually."

The confession is hesitant, and she physically feels her pulse beginning to hammer faster as she voices the thought, but...he needs to know. *She* needs him to know.

Josh's eyes widen in surprise, but he quickly straightens, moving into a sitting position with his legs crossed, all his attention focused on her.

The only noise in the room is the whirring of the fan and Scarlett's quiet breathing.

"It...fuck, I have no idea how to do this," she admits, and she and Josh both let out an abbreviated laugh, the tension minimally lessening before she sighs and tries to get it together.

How does one put it into words, calmly explain the horrors of their life? Josh has done it, opening up about the monster that was his stepdad, and she'd never stopped to appreciate how well the words flowed. How difficult it must've been to try to explain.

"My home situation..." She breaks off, shakes her head, tries again. "Scarlett's conception wasn't intentional," she begins. "She...it was..." Rose bites her lip, beginning to tremble, but she remembers Evan's words from months ago: *Acknowledge the reality of what you've been through*. She can do this.

Just say it.

"I was raped."

The words are out, and it hurts, really hurts, to say. She'd never had to with Isa; some women just know. She hasn't said the words since she was a child, pleading with Bronte to never let anyone take her away.

Josh's intake of breath is sharp, but she can't face him, can't see what must be running through his eyes, so she continues. "It wasn't, um, the first time. My mother's best friend... he's the superintendent of the school district back home, and he...he started coming over all the time right after my dad died—even got his own guest room. To help out with the estate and whatever bullshit excuse they gave. I was eight at the time, and he started pretty soon after.

"I told Cheyenne—my mom—a year or so later. She didn't care." Rose says the words without emotion, but then tears start slipping down her face before she can stop it. "Didn't want people to know, thought that it was...my fault, somehow? I don't know."

Josh reaches to wipe at the tears softly.

"That's why I ran away. I told Bronte while we were on the run, and she tried to tell the police when they sent me back, but...Cheyenne has a great reputation in the community. Him too, of course; no one wants to believe the worst about a man they trust with the fate of their children, you know? And Bronte was a runaway who they thought would claim anything and didn't trust authority. No one believed it.

"I was set to go Ivy League, as far as they knew, but as soon as I found out about Scarlett, I had to get out. That's why I ended up at

USF. If he'd found out about her...if he'd ever known that she's a girl... I got lucky with the timing. Any sooner..."

Trailing off, she nervously looks up at Josh, only to find tears welling in his eyes.

"Rosie," he whispers, voice cracking.

He's always known the statistics—one in five women is assaulted in her lifetime, a number and a concept his mom had drilled into his head since he knew what girls were. Has always known there was a chance someone he knew had been through it.

But knowing about this abstract atrocity done to women around the world doesn't mean you would ever guess the one you've fallen in love with has survived it. Doesn't mean you could ever begin to fathom what happens to a person who's been through it. Doesn't make it any easier to reconcile.

"I can't...I can't even imagine. You are so, so strong. That bastard... hell isn't good enough for him."

He reaches for Rose in that slow, careful way of his, the way he's tried to since he picked up on her aversion to unexpected physical touch months and months ago, and she lets him hold her, basking in the righteous anger splayed across his face on her behalf.

"I'm sorry," she whispers back, and he recoils, locking eyes with her.

"What the fuck could you possibly be sorry for?"

"I don't know, I just... it's a lot to take on, and it's heavy, and a lot in a girlfriend who already has a kid when you're dealing with your own shit."

"Yeah, it's *heavy*, Rose. And you've carried it all alone on top of everything else you've been through, and you've loved Scarlett like nothing in this world, been the most amazing mother—"

A horrible sob tears out of Rose's throat, and she shakes her head vehemently. "I'm not, I'm not, I'm really not."

"But you are, baby. Scar is the luckiest—"

"No!" she shouts, her tone rising two octaves. "You don't understand."

"Then tell me, Rosie. I promise there is not one thing you could possibly tell me that will affect the way I feel about you. I love you."

Her heart stutters in disbelief that he could possibly, in joy and in gratefulness, and she wants to say it back, wants to admit that she's loved him for a lot longer than she probably should've. But that's not the topic that wants to consume her mind at the moment, so those aren't the words spilling out of her mouth. She can't stop herself from speaking as though he hadn't even said the last three words—those most important words.

"I...about two years ago..." Raspy, nervous, pained, suffering more than he's ever heard in her, she speaks. "I found out I was pregnant. It shouldn't have been surprising; I'm lucky it didn't happen sooner, realistically, given that he almost never used condoms. I was stupid, thought I could hide the baby, thought I would be able to..." She trails off, throat thick and unable to meet Josh's eyes. "But he figured it out when I started to show. I don't think he even told my mother, just took care of it himself. He plied me with alcohol and pushed me down the stairs, so I miscarried after I fought him trying to take me to get an abortion. I-I support anyone who wants to, but it wasn't for me, you know? I wanted that baby."

The last words are ground together, between the heavy sobs escaping her. "I loved them already. That's what the tattoo is—the one that I want. One little bright sunflower for Scar, and one pale and not wholly present for the baby that died. All my fault. That's what I mean, timing is...timing is everything." A heavy swallow. "Why I was so quick to get out as soon as I found out about Scar."

Because my baby had already died because of me...because how could I fail another? she wants to beg of him. Wants him to hate her too, on behalf of the child she let down in the worst way.

"My God, baby...no wonder you're so sad. That kind of loss, that kind of guilt, even though you don't deserve to carry it...to lose a kid is the worst pain in this world. Especially after everything else. I'm so sorry you went through that."

"But he...you didn't sign up for...I just feel like a chaotic mass of wreckage. I'm an unnecessary complication, you have enough going on, and you don't need to deal with my problems."

"Did he tell you that?" Josh's tone is venomous, angrier than she's ever heard him. So livid she's almost scared. "Rose...to know you, to love you, is the greatest thing I've ever done. You're a mess because someone *hurt* you, my God. And yeah, I want to kill him, but that has no impact on my feelings for you, okay? I love you, I love your daughter, I love the unborn child we'll never get to know, and nothing anyone has ever done to you changes that."

And Josh's presence might not wish away the nightmares, might not wish away the monsters that still haunt her every second of the day, always waiting behind her eyes, but it sure helps her fall asleep.

(Even when the nightmares come again, a whisper in her brain reminds her that she might not go through it alone anymore.)

14

She's anxious as she leaves her shift at the diner, desperate to get to her daughter though she knows she has no reason to worry.

Nonetheless, she can't breathe until she's in the familiar apartment building, and Isa opens the door with a smile. "Hey, love. She's asleep—has been for thirty minutes or so."

"Perfect. Thank you again; I don't know what I would've done if you hadn't offered to take care of her."

Her heart unclenches at the sight of Scar passed out with a bottle, trapped by a wall of pillows to keep her from rolling away from the center of Isa's bed.

"It was no trouble at all," Isa promises. "She was a little grumpy right before falling asleep, but other than that, we had a great time. Honestly, I never do anything but work; it was nice to have a little excitement. Feel free to hit me up whenever you need someone to watch her."

"I—I just might." Rose gives her a half-smile, nervous at the prospect of trusting someone enough, but over the last few months, Isa has been there for her like no one has in years.

(Having a friend who feels like family, someone else who knows what the darkness looks like...)

"I'm really glad to have you," she admits to Isa in a whisper. "Doing this alone has been terrifying, so it...means the world."

"Of course." Isa reaches to squeeze her hand. "You're my best friend. I'm here whenever you need me."

She must be curious, and yet she's never pressed the issue—never asked the question Rose knows they all wonder. It's what made her warm to Isa in the first place.

And it makes Rose want to tell her. Almost.

It's been so long since she confided in anyone.

(Memories of whispers in a motel room, Bronte's hands tightly gripping hers, cross her mind.)

Isa opens and closes her mouth before speaking hesitantly. "Honey, it's clear you've been through a lot. I know there are some things weighing you down. If you ever want to talk about it..."

Rose nods. "I...yeah. It's..." She takes a deep breath, finds a spot on the wall to focus on. "It started after my dad died."

———

Rose had worried telling Josh would change the dynamic between them, but it's just made their relationship more cohesive. Made it easier for her to be honest about what she needs in small moments, and...overall, she just feels freer, having him know.

He's supportive and understands that he doesn't understand, and it just—

(She never knew this kind of love was out there.)

She's at a cafe with Bronte, who's mostly pretty quiet, and Liza, who she's been meaning to get lunch with for ages. It's busy, plenty of patrons coming in and out as an indie pop station plays in the background.

"I never got the story; how did you and Aaliyah meet?"

Liza's eyes drop to her ring, and she practically glows at the thought of her wife before looking back up at Rose.

They've been attempting to meet up for months, now, ever since the wedding, given that they have about a million things in common *besides* wanting to become attorneys, but law school and work and childcare have made it almost impossible for them to find a time that worked for both of them. Even so, Rose feels a connection to the other girl as both of them work to figure out where they fit into the convoluted family they've been adopted into. Everyone has always done their best to include them, but...well, it's just different, in a way only Liza can really understand. And something in her eyes—

"On the bus, actually," Liza responds, her entire face full of joy. "It was crazy hectic, but she was just sitting there stoic as ever, buried in a criminal law textbook. I couldn't take my eyes off her. The bus jerked suddenly, and the book went flying, and I lunged for it; it's embarrassing, honestly, how far out of my way I went to be the one to hand it back to her. I'd been thinking about law school for ages, though, and it had seemed like a dream, but I finally had the credit to apply for a loan. So I started to ask her about it, and she was getting off at the next stop, so we agreed to meet for coffee so she could give me more detail, and –"

"And according to Josh, Aaliyah wouldn't shut up about the hot girl she'd met on the train," Bronte interjects.

"And rest is history," Rose finishes with a warm smile. "It's amazing how the love of your life can come when you least expect it. Life is...something else."

"Honestly," Liza agrees, and while her gaze is technically on Rose, Rose can tell the other girl is far away. "I would have laughed if you'd told me a year before that it would happen. I mean, I was actually on my way home from an AA meeting that day. My relationship with my last boyfriend..." Her jaw tightens, and she swallows perfunctorily.

Rose's stomach clenches at the familiar darkness flashing across her face, as though Liza's memories are eating her from the inside.

"It didn't end well. I couldn't handle...everything and went on a bender. Pushed everyone away, lost a job, and another... Bronte dragged me to my first meeting after months of me being practically a ghost."

Bronte's face darkens at the mention of the dark time, and Rose catches Liza shooting her a reassuring look.

"And then I saw Aaliyah, and I just... couldn't stop looking. The odds that she was a friend of a friend of Bronte's...I don't know how that kind of coincidence happens. I hadn't come to terms with the fact that I was bi before then, but from the moment I met her, I just wanted to know everything about her."

"And now you're spending the rest of your lives together."

"I can't imagine a better life," Liza admits, and Rose feels her heart stutter at imagining that kind of love, that kind of commitment. *Forever.*

More specifically, imagining it with Josh.

As though she's summoned him, her phone begins vibrating incessantly, the man in question's name lighting up her screen. While she knows she would've answered anyway, always eager to hear his voice, a bigger part of her answers before she can even process the ring in the ever-present need to make sure everything was okay with Scarlett. "Hello? Josh...why are you face timing me?"

"Hey, baby, I'm sorry—sorry Liza!" he says apologetically, but his voice is calm and his eyes lively, so Rose knows nothing is really wrong, feels her heart rate start returning to normal. *"Not sorry to Bronte, of course. She can suck it up. Anyway, I know you're at lunch, Rosie, but I had to call; you won't believe this,"* he promises.

Rose watches with raised eyebrows as he lifts Scar into the camera's range until her chubby face takes up the entire screen.

"Come on, Simba, show Mama." He prods the infant, who looks at him quizzically before beginning to babble, at which point Rose understands the reason for the call.

"Oh my God, oh my God, really?! Josh, is that real?"

"Sure is. Our girl has her first tooth all the way in—and she's already tried to put it into every single one of the shoes, a pillow, a toy, and my phone."

"Of course she has. Little overachiever. She's growing up so fast."

Rose can see Scar's confusion at seeing her on a phone screen, at hearing her mother's voice without her being there, and while it initially excites Scar, she can see her starting to grow agitated at the *almost* of her presence.

Josh sees it too and pulls the phone back to include his grimace in the frame. "We'll let you get back to your lunch, I don't want her too cranky, but I'll see you later. Bye, Liza!"

"Thank you for calling. Really, it means the world." Rose can't control the bashful smile on her face. "I'll see y'all in a little bit."

For a moment, she stares at the wallpaper of her phone, a picture of a smiling Josh holding Scar weeks ago. *Our girl. He called her our girl.* The words give her chills, send heat down her spine, and make her lightheaded all at once.

Her giddiness doesn't go unnoticed.

"And what about you and Josh?" Liza asks with a smirk.

I did this to myself, Rose internally groans. "We're... we're really good." She feels the corners of her mouth turn upward and stills her fidgeting hands, attempting to quell the need to check for a text from him. "I never imagined myself in any kind of romantic relationship, *ever*, so to feel so strongly for someone, so comfortable around him... it's strange. I don't really know how to handle it."

Meanwhile, Bronte scowls. "You're too grown-up; I feel old."

Rose knows she claims this because it's easier than discussing all the years missed between them, how much the mention of her age is a reminder.

Liza nods slowly in understanding. "When I first met Kai—and eventually Josh and Zeke—I was skeptical and wanted nothing to do with them. Half the time, I would bail whenever any of them were involved. Because of Bronte, though, and eventually Aaliyah, we ended up around each other quite a lot, and they were all much more than I expected. Kai especially; he's become as close to me as Bronte. And Josh...I mean, he's probably the best man I've ever known. They're the first I've trusted in...in a very, very long time. They give me hope. Make me believe there are good men in the world."

Rose knows that tone so well, knows the fear with which the other woman speaks of trying to trust the men in her life, and when she makes eye contact with Liza, she's sure their emotions stem from a very similar place. Sure the two of them might eventually be much closer than they are now, bonded in suffering, in survival. Sure they've both been forged in fire.

"Yeah," she says softly, relishing in the undercurrent of emotion flowing between them. Knowing Liza can feel it too. "Me too."

15

It hurts when he comes to.

There's a beeping sound, and even through his eyelids, the lights are bright. A hospital rather than the prison infirmary, then.

Days like this, he wants to laugh bitterly. Of course, this is where he is. How his life has ended up.

(He never stood a chance, did he?)

His mother had been a prostitute—not that that in and of itself made her a bad person. She was a single mom trying to pay bills. Had her own shitty hand before he ever came into the picture and was trying to make it work. Trying so, so desperately.

She was doing her best.

His sperm donor had bailed after he was born, said he couldn't handle the pressure like the piece of shit he was, naturally.

That was when the guy she worked for told her he could get her something to help.

She'd gotten hooked on heroin—the black tar kind, fucking cheap and accessible and specifically designed to prey on those vulnerable to anything that makes the world just a little bit more bearable. And the more addicted she got, the more she was willing to work, so it suited the bastard responsible, of course.

(Ended up murdered by a client, but it was like it never happened. There never has *been any justice for sex workers, has there?)*

There was no one but a child who didn't know how to report her missing; no one to identify the corpse, nothing, till the landlord found Evan cuddled next to the body hopelessly when he came to yell at her for not paying rent.

(CPS got involved, then, and...well, nothing new there. It's the story of thousands of children.)

His eyelids flutter, and he imagines someone who almost looks like Bronte sitting beside him. Reminds him of way back when he thought he could be more; him, Bronte, and Rose, hungry and struggling but safe and loved.

Once upon a time when he mattered, when he had a semblance of a family—just the three of them but with enough love and trust and pain to hold their broken pieces together.

He'd thought he could be more, then.

Now he wakes up handcuffed to the bed, knowing the nothingness everyone else sees.

Shitty foster dad, addict hooker mom—the most he'd ever been was a hungry, distraught, "troubled" kid from an at-risk neighborhood with a juvie record.

(He'd never stood a chance.)

———

A week or so later, they're in Josh's apartment during the downtime between shifts, and Josh has been off all day. His smile isn't reaching his eyes, he didn't sing along when Green Day came on in the car, and he hasn't laughed in hours.

Rose knows something is wrong.

"I met a girl." Kai's words are quiet, the closest to nervous she's ever heard him, and she's immediately distracted, head snapping to stare at him.

"I'm sorry, did I hear that right?"

"Someone alert the press!" Zeke yells, pressing a hand to his heart dramatically. "Florida's most eligible and active bachelor has been wrangled."

"Shut up," Kai rolls his eyes, throwing a crumpled-up piece of paper at his friend.

It's a big deal because Kai hasn't actually even mentioned dating everyone since things imploded with his last girlfriend—childhood best friends turned high school sweethearts, and he'd thought she was the one.

(That was before it all went up in flames.)

Kai clears his throat and continues, "Her name is Lacey, and she...I mean, we've been friends for a little while, but I feel like I just woke up one day and *bam*. I didn't realize how much I like hanging out with her, and it hit me like a truck. I haven't really considered dating anyone in so long that it just...took a minute for it to register."

Rose waits a beat to see if Josh will respond, if he's even on the same plane as them, but when he doesn't, she immediately speaks up to distract his best friend while Zeke elbows him in the gut. "What does she look like?"

"Gorgeous." He stares off into space, eyes out of focus, face slackened.

Rose snorts when he fails to elaborate. "That doesn't help me much, lover boy."

"Right. She has green eyes, and her hair is black, and her skin is so soft and..." He sighs. "I don't know why she's not a model, honestly."

"You've got it bad," Rose observes, leaning down to scoop Scar up in her arms. "Uncle Kai is in *love*, Scarlett! You'll be the cutest flower girl there has ever been."

"Don't jinx me on this, man," he tells her, flushing. "I have no idea how to go about this. Any time I think of dating, I just...think of *her*. I don't really know how to be with anyone else or even *start* a relationship. And what if it's not mutual, and then I lose Lacey as a friend, too?"

The angst in his voice makes it clear it's a pain he's felt before.

"If she's been your friend this long, unrequited feelings won't send her running. It would only be awkward for a little bit. But if she's smart, she'll feel the same way; you're a catch, Kaister. *I'd* date you if my man weren't so hot."

The jab earns a slight uplift in Josh's lips, which Rose assumes is the closest thing to a reaction she'll get today.

"Thanks, Rose." Kai squeezes her in a one-armed hug, pressing a kiss to the top of Scar's head. "I have to go. I'm meeting Evan to play Call of Duty while Bronte's having girl's night with Aaliyah and Liza, but I'll see you guys later."

"Oh, I'm so coming with," Zeke says, hopping from his chair. "You driving?"

"Dude, no one said you were invited."

As Kai closes the door behind them, Josh rises to his feet, meeting Rose's eyes for the first time in hours. "I'm gonna head out, too."

Her heart drops out from beneath her. He's avoiding communicating, avoiding *her*. Not even attempting to come up with an excuse.

"So, we're doing this?"

"This?" he asks, voice saturated with guilt as he tenses up.

"Pretending like everything is fine. What the hell, Josh? Your best friend just poured his heart out to us, and you sat there like a brick. You haven't picked up Scar all morning, and now you're just heading out?" Her voice cracks and she blinks back tears. "Josh, I don't want that to be our relationship. I want us to talk to each other. You're always there when I need you, and you're not even trying to let me do the same."

"Rosie, I don't want to burden you, it's better if I—"

"It's not a burden! I know putting up walls has always been how you protect yourself, but it just comes across as you not trusting me—and I know that's not it, babe, I know it's just your way of coping. You can build walls if you need to, but...I need to be inside them. It's so far from a burden, Josh. I love you, idiot. There's nothing I want more than to be the one you go to when you're struggling. You shutting me out like this? *That's* what hurts."

A pained noise comes from the back of Josh's throat before she registers what she's said, and then she can feel her entire face, neck, chest turning bright red. *I love you, idiot. Shit.*

Before she can figure out what to say, he speaks. "The protection orders expired yesterday."

"Oh. Fuck."

"Yeah." He offers a bitter grimace. "I just... I'm really worried about Aunt Kathy. And that bastard hates me too—really, really has it out for me. So until we know what's going on, I just think it might be best if—"

"Please tell me you're not about to tell me it's best if we break up for my safety." The sentence comes out in a whisper. "I swear to God, Joshua, if you're breaking up with me for my own good, I will never forgive you."

"What? No, of course not, baby. That's the dumbest thing I've ever heard." He steps closer, pulling her into his chest without a second thought; it's only then she notices that he's shaking from the stress, the frustration, the fear of the threat Geoffrey poses. "Everything in me wants to never fuck this up."

"You promise?" The words feel juvenile, but she needs him to say them.

"I promise, Rosie. I love you too. And Scar. I don't want anything to happen to you, and if it were because of me...I couldn't bear it. So I was just going to say, I'm going to be around less the next couple weeks, at my own place more just in case he does come after me, so you two won't be in danger. And so he doesn't catch Kai and Zeke there unsuspecting and take it out on them. If anyone got hurt instead of me, *because* of me..." He winces at the thought. "Once it seems safe, you won't be able to get rid of me."

"I'll hold you to it," she warns him, pressing a kiss to his collarbone. "You'll still call?"

"Yes ma'am. I've got to make sure you don't forget about me," he teases. "This one too." He steals Scar from her arms, spinning her above their heads until she's giggling uncontrollably.

"Please," Rose snorts. "You know you don't have to worry about her forgetting you. If I weren't her food source, she'd like you more than she likes me."

"As soon as she's on solid foods, I'll have favorite in the bag." His lips touch Rose's softly, and they both grow serious again. "I should go. I'm making Kathy let me stay with her for a few days, keep an eye out. But...I do love you. Sorry we couldn't tell each other romantically the first time on either end, but I really do. Although," his eyes light with amusement, "I will enjoy telling everyone that you said it first for the first time paired with calling me an idiot. Bronte's gonna get such a kick out of that."

"Oh, God," Rose moans. "Can't we just come up with a different version to tell everyone else?"

Josh shakes his head with a wide grin. "No way. I like our version." They kiss again, mouths moving in sync until Scar releases an annoyed squeal, and Josh pulls back with a sigh. "*Damn. I don't want to go.*"

"We'll make up for lost time when things settle down. Tell Kathy I'm thinking of her. Call if you need anything. Even if you don't, call anyway," she admonishes him, opening the door for him.

"I will," he promises. "Talk to you soon as I can. I love you, Rosie."

"I love you, too. Stay safe."

———

The time without Josh drags on, but Rose tries to stay busy. She hadn't realized how used to his presence she'd grown, how integral the brightness he brings to her day had become until she's without it.

Scar misses him too, Rose knows; in the little moments, when her wide eyes search the room, befuddled by the absence of the man she's come to love.

They Facetime at least once a day, most days talking into the receiver until one of them passes out mid-sentence.

(But it's not the same as having him *there*.)

"Honestly," Bronte complains, "I just want the bastard to show his face so the two of you can cut this shit out and stop moping all over the place." She collapses onto the couch in the apartment she shares with Evan, where Rose has been hanging out to try and distract herself. "I haven't seen you this angsty since your emo phase."

"Please, her entire life is an emo phase," Evan comments from the table where he sits, working his way through paperwork for the center.

Rose rolls her eyes, twirling a toy for Scar with one hand. "The irony of either of you commenting on anyone else's emo phase is absurd. You're the definition of scene kids that never grew up."

Bronte scowls. "I'll remember that whenever you decide to do your first tattoo, and I get to stab you with a needle several hundred times."

"That might be sooner rather than later, actually. I've been thinking I want—"

Rose's sentence cuts off as her ringtone begins to buzz. She hurries to tug the phone out of her pocket, expecting it to be Josh. Instead, she feels all the blood rush out of her face.

The number isn't in her contacts, but the area code is familiar. North Carolina.

(They found me. He found me.)

"Rose?" Evan asks, concern in his tone. "What's wrong? You look like you've seen a ghost."

"It's nothing. I just..." *He found me, he found me, he found me.* "I forgot, I have to go."

"No."

She looks to Evan incredulously, hackles rising. "Excuse me?"

"No. You don't want to tell us what's going on? That's fine. But you don't need to sneak off to have a mental breakdown alone when you're already stressed and worried about Josh and Kathy. And don't think I haven't noticed how on edge you've been lately, even before this started going down. You don't have to talk about it, but fuck if I'm gonna sit here while you go off and panic yourself into a stupor."

Rose glares at him wordlessly. "A psychopath has it out for my boyfriend and his godmother, and I have my own truckload of trauma to deal with. I think I deserve the occasional breakdown."

"Of course you do. And you can have it out all you want. Just not alone. Come on, kid." Without waiting for confirmation, he reaches down to steal a cranky Scarlett from the play blanket in front of her. "Put your shoes on. We'll be in the car when you're ready to go."

"Asshole," Rose mutters under her breath, packing Scar's things back into the diaper bag. "Needs my keys to get the car seat out of my car anyway, so I don't know where he gets off being so bossy."

Bronte snorts before waving bye, caught up in doing a markup for a client later in the week.

When Rose gets outside, though, they're not standing outside of her aged sedan; she approaches Evan's grey Chevy minivan to find him smugly sitting in the driver's seat, Scar strapped into a brand new car seat in the back and already passed out.

"Since when do you have a car seat?" Rose demands.

"Since last week. Would have had it way sooner, but Bronte and I took a while to come to an agreement about which one had the best safety features."

Rose swallows heavily. "You bought a car seat." *For me. For my* kid, *because you love her that much.*

Evan leans across the center console to press a kiss to her forehead. "Of course we did."

As if it's not even a question that he and Bronte would spend the money, that they would be in Scar's life enough to have a need of it.

(*This is what family feels like.*)

She can't voice her thoughts, can't put into words how much she appreciates him being there, how much she appreciates him loving her daughter enough that she knows Scar would be okay if something happened to her.

She merely reaches to squeeze Evan's arm before clearing her throat and changing the subject. "Where are we going, by the way?"

"The center. I think it's about time you met my kids."

———

It's not the nicest building in the world, covered in faded paint and dilapidated signage, but as soon as they're inside, it's clear that's because Evan directs all funding to make the interior a place where kids feel safe—a place they can feel at *home*. There are air hockey, ping pong, and pool tables, a giant screen and a projector with a VCR and DVD player, and a well-stocked kitchenette, all amidst a bunch of couches, beanbags, and hammocks. None of the stuff matches, but it seems clear that's kind of the point. There's something for everyone.

"Go ahead, grab a snack if you're hungry," Evan encourages.

Rose cocks her head at the stocked pantry, memories of her own time in youth groups rolling around. "You don't ration the snacks?"

"Not at all," he shakes his head, eyes sad. "I budget more than they'd like me to and end up spending some of my check on food sometimes. It's...after the kind of things we went through, what these kids *are* going through...some things shouldn't have rules, you know? Necessities shouldn't be a reward or a punishment or something kids aren't sure is coming."

Rose nods in agreement. "Even if all but one take advantage of it, it's worth it for the one. This is...amazing, Evan."

Things are much less chaotic than Rose had expected when they arrive; a few teenagers are sprawled across couches and bean bags watching a movie, two play an aggressive game of ping pong, and one girl is sitting in the corner with earbuds in.

"Evan!" One of the guys on a bean bag springs to his feet and skips up to them. "What the fuck, is that a *baby*?"

"Yeah, Will, it is, don't act like she's a goddamn alien." Evan rolls his eyes. "Rose, this is Will, one of the blessed lucky enough to see me almost every day. Will, this is my goddaughter Scarlett and her mom, Rose."

"She looks like a potato," Will observes before giving Rose a sheepish grin, looking a little terrified of her reaction. "A really fuckin' cute potato, I mean, and all babies look like potatoes, so that's not a comment on her personally, just in general."

"William, stop insulting babies and saying fuck so much, or I'll fuck you up."

Will rolls his eyes at Evan's admonishment. "Great role model, isn't he? Nice to meet you, Rosalind."

"I swear to God," Evan says under his breath, but his body is so relaxed, his face so full of love and joy, Rose knows he's only reprimanding the kid for the sake of propriety.

"It's fine. As long as you think she's the cutest potato you ever saw, we won't have to fight," she teases, earning a wicked grin.

"*The* cutest," Will confirms with a nod. "And you're the reason they call it hot potato if baby daddy doesn't mind me saying so."

Rose's smile freezes on her face, and Evan frowns as her eyes darken. "He's not in the picture. Although I'm sure my boyfriend won't feel the need to fight you for my honor if that's what you're worried about."

"He work out?"

"College athlete."

Will's eyes widen to the size of saucers. "Then yes, I would say that's exactly what I'm worried about. I'm gonna get back to my movie now. I'm suddenly much more invested."

"Yeah, you do that, punk," Evan snorts, ruffling his hair before leading Rose to his office. "I don't honestly spend much time in here; unless I have to take a private phone call or talk to one of the kids one-on-one, I'd rather be out there in the midst of them."

"They're so lucky to have you."

"I don't know about that. Sometimes I worry I'm only screwing them over worse than life already has."

"No." Rose shakes her head desperately. "You could do the wrong things nine times out of ten, which I know you don't, and they'd still be lucky to have you. Knowing someone cares, knowing someone is always there and ready to drop everything to be what you need, knowing you're so unconditionally loved... that's the most important thing a kid could ever have. *Especially* one of us."

"If I can be a sliver of that for just one of them, I'll die happy," he admits. "I just think about myself, at that age...about you, and

Bronte...can you imagine how different things would've been? If we'd had someone?" Rose shakes her head sadly, and he continues, almost mumbling to himself. "We deserved it. *They* deserve it. How could I not?"

(The words he leaves unspoken ring through her: *I couldn't save us. How could I not try to save them?*)

"I am in awe of you. Every day," she promises him. "And I know you're making a difference for them. Just like you did for me, Ev. I would've never had any kind of experience that let me know a better life was even *possible,* that let me have any kind of hope without you. I couldn't...I don't think I would've been strong enough to make it through the last few years if I hadn't met you and Bronte. I don't know if it would've felt worth it. But knowing y'all, knowing the happiness and love and good that could exist in the world? It gave me the will to go on. Light at the end of the tunnel and all that."

"I think you just want to make a grown-ass man cry," he replies gruffly, pulling her into a bear hug.

"Icing on the cake."

They pull apart, and Evan releases a sigh with a glance at the haphazard stacks of pages on post-it notes strewn across his desk, unopened envelopes and to-do reminders throughout. "I really do need to get this done, but...mingle. I think it would be really good for you to talk to some of them."

"Yeah. Sure thing."

Rose re-enters the main room with a deep breath. Most of these kids are years younger than her, and she knows she's probably intimidating, having entered with their idol, but somehow, she's still terrified that they'll hate her. The thought of approaching them, of attempting to initiate any kind of conversation, is terrifying; Will's exuberance already surpassed her ability to interact for the day.

I can raise a child, and I work in customer service for a living, but God forbid I try to talk to teenagers.

It's a pathetic Achilles' heel.

The girl in the corner catches her eye, despite not moving a muscle—visibly, at least. The way she sits, isolated but still a part of the group... it's familiar. Achingly so. The way of someone who doesn't have it in them to socialize but can't bear to be alone; one who can't fight past their demons long enough to pretend but finds a home in the presence of other misfits, others drowning in their own lives.

(She's her.)

Slowly, she approaches the girl, who, upon further inspection, doesn't seem older than fourteen. She doesn't attempt to start a conversation, merely waves when their eyes meet before setting Scar down on her play blanket and curling into an armchair across from the girl, pulling out her own phone to scroll aimlessly.

None of the books Rose tries to start catch her attention, none of the social media can keep her preoccupied for long, but still, sitting near this girl, each of them so alone and yet not, something clicks softly. She's doing nothing at all, and yet it feels like everything.

(Some days, the very air itself seems to flow differently between two people so similar.)

Odds are, she's getting ahead of herself, and maybe she and this girl are nothing alike; maybe the girl will go home and tell whoever's there about the freaky young woman who settled down in a worn armchair with her and acted like they were friends when she'd rather be anywhere else.

But just maybe...maybe they'll recognize something familiar in each other.

The girl meets her eyes again, not looking away immediately to escape to her own world, and Rose is pretty sure it will be the latter.

16

BEFORE | ROSE

She's numb as she makes her way through the store, shivering despite having been inside for at least twenty minutes. The fear, the anxiety, the lack of food she's taken in from being so fucking nervous she can't eat... it's all coming together to make the perfect storm.

It's an unfamiliar building; she'd gone far, the opposite side of the county in a part of town no one in her life has ever stepped foot in an attempt to take every possible precaution.

Still, she finds herself looking over her shoulder every other moment, just in case, so desperate to make sure she's not seen.

Nothing in this life would be worse than what happens if she's seen.

(If she's right.)

If she could, she'd buy several other things to distract from her purpose. But if what she thinks is true, she can't afford to waste a single dollar.

Her hands shake as she plucks the box from the shelf. It's not the cheapest one, but it's worth it for the reliability. She can't afford for it to be wrong.

She scans the area twice before approaching the register; she doesn't meet the cashier's eyes as she places the test on the conveyer.

She can feel the girl's judgment, the burn of her scalding gaze. Rose knows what she assumes.

(You have no idea, she wants to scream, wants to sob, wants to beg someone to believe.)

The total pops up, and before the cashier can read it out, Rose is counting out the ones and change she'd carefully snuck with her for this.

She tries not to look at the girl's face as she does so but catches her distaste all the same.

But Rose doesn't have time to nurse the wound. All that matters is getting out of here and getting to a bathroom.

She's trying to imagine every contingency, every way she can escape and make this work, even as she hurries to the gas station down the block, hoping she's wrong. Just thinking and praying and hoping with everything in her.

She tries to force a smile at the gas station attendant as she steps inside. He's clearly seen more wretched-looking people and doesn't seem to care.

And then it's positive, and everything changes.

(Nothing in this world matters beyond keeping her baby safe.)

———

A knock sounds on Rose's door just as she's about to walk out, and she scowls before setting down the diaper bag and keeping a grumpy Scar tucked into the other arm with keys in hand. When she looks through the peephole, though, her demeanor changes completely.

She flings open the door and throws her free arm around Josh without a word. "I thought we wouldn't see you for another week," she tells him, the sentence muffled by his chest.

"I couldn't stay away." When Rose pulls back to level him with a look, he laughs and continues, tucking a misplaced lock of hair behind her ear. "I'm kidding. We haven't seen any sign of him in three weeks, and we hired a decently priced P.I. to go check on him, and it seems like he is where he's supposed to be and hasn't done anything more dodgy than usual since the expiration. It seems no less safe to go on with life."

"Translation: you kept being overly cautious beyond the realm of every rational person, and Kathy kicked you out?"

"I really need to date someone dumber," he mutters without meeting her eyes.

Rose laughs and kisses his shoulder. "It's not that I'm smart, baby, it's that I know you. There's no way you'd voluntarily be anywhere but by Kathy's side when her monster is on the streets. You're way too overprotective—like a mama bear."

"Her monster?" Josh inquires, and Rose hesitates.

"It's just...how I conceptualize them. In my head."

"Both of our...monsters?"

She nods. "And Bronte's. And Evan's. And Isa's."

He hums, resting his chin on the top of her head. "Our monsters. I like it."

"Thanks." After a beat, she slides out from his arms, waving away the frown that flashes across his face. "Come on, I need to run a few errands. You can come grocery shopping with us."

"Oh, damn, this relationship is serious," he teases, reaching to grab Scar and press her tiny face to his own as they walk down the hall. "Hey, little angel. I'm so glad to see you. I don't know which one of you I missed more."

"I do, and it sure wasn't me," Rose volleys with a smirk. "Don't worry, she missed you too. We're both glad Kathy kicked your ass to the curb."

"Me too...even though it's making me crazy," he admits.

They sing in the car on the way to the store, not much to update each other on that they haven't already relayed on the phone. Rose can feel herself relaxing, can feel how much lighter she is when Josh is around, how much brighter the sun seems to shine, how much easier it is to feel happy.

(It scares her.)

She doesn't want anyone to have this kind of effect on her other than Scar, this kind of sway over her mood and well-being. It's terrifying that Josh has really only been around a smattering of months and has this kind of hold on her heart.

If something happens, if anything changes, if Josh wakes up one day and decides he doesn't want this anymore...she knows she wouldn't handle it well. Knows her daughter would be devastated, too.

She'd still have her family; Bronte and Evan would never leave her, and honestly, she's close enough to Zeke and Kai by now that they would probably try to see her even if she and Josh fell apart.

But she doesn't think she'd feel whole, and that's a petrifying prospect.

The only thing more intimidating is the fact that she really doesn't think she'll ever have to worry about that; she's pretty sure this is forever.

It's a lot to take in before her twentieth birthday.

"Anybody home?" Josh asks, tapping her forehead gently as they enter the grocery store. He slides Scar's cushion into the kid-seat of a shopping cart.

"Sorry. Just...I missed you. I'm really glad to have you back."

He smiles, and it lights up his whole face. Rose had never known a person could be so attracted to teeth, of all things, but when Josh gives her that open-mouthed grin, eyes so full of love...it doesn't get any better.

"Back at you, baby. Life isn't the same without you in it. You want me to take her and swing by the bakery and meet you by the deli?"

Rose narrows her eyes at him. "Joshua, are you plotting to use my daughter to get a free cookie?"

"Do you think it'll work? I mean, I feel like most people can't tell she's not quite eating crunchy solids yet. Unless they've had a kid."

"You feel free to do your darndest to convince them, hot stuff, but I feel like most people would know based on the fact that she only has two teeth."

Josh purses his lips at her. "We'll see. May the best man win."

"Good luck." She watches him walk away, Scar lively and clapping instinctively in his arms, and her insides melt. *My favorites.*

She catches two middle-aged women whispering, glancing at her and quickly away, but it's nothing she hasn't heard before. She just makes her way down the aisles, shopping mostly from memory but occasionally consulting the list on her phone.

A few minutes later, she overhears a mother on the same aisle as her, muttering to the teenager at her side.

"So, Jamie's got a new boyfriend—and no, it's not the baby daddy," the daughter says, making a face.

"I don't know how she lives with herself," the woman says. "She's already far too young to be a mother, she's not marrying the father, and now she has some other man taking care of her child?"

They're not talking about her, but Rose goes tense all the same. It's gossip she'd grown up hearing from her mother a million times over; it's a sense of superiority and moral righteousness that's all too familiar.

"What kind of example is she setting for that baby?"

Rose's frustration simmers; because even though this time it's not her, if they'd seen her with Scar and Josh a moment ago, it would be.

She's so *tired* of everyone assuming the worst, making judgments when they have no *idea*.

The daughter nods in agreement. "Poor kid. Shitty mom and God knows what kind of revolving door of father figures in his life." There's such visceral disdain in her voice.

Rose half wants to laugh and is half tempted to cry. Plenty of people have whispered it behind her back before. She's well aware it's what they all think.

(And yet it still kills her, the reminder of where it all started.)

She doesn't know anything, Rose tries to remind herself, although she can feel the color leaching from her face even as she moves to grab what she needs from the shelves. *She knows nothing about me, or Scar, or her conception. I've done nothing wrong.*

Without another word, Rose turns and stalks away with the cart as fast as she can, the words blurring together as she leaves the women in her wake.

By the time she reaches Josh and Scar, she's managed to calm the shaking some, but she knows Josh will be able to tell that something is off. Sure enough, as soon as she's in range, he turns to give her a crumb-covered grin, but it slips into an expression of concern once he's looked her over.

"What happened?"

"Nothing, I'm fine. I grabbed you Oreos."

He ignores the sweets and reaches an arm around her, rubbing slow circles on the small of her back. "Baby, you're white as a sheet. Did someone do something?"

"No. Yes. This woman...it wasn't bad, really. I don't know her, and she has no idea what she's talking about. She wasn't even talking to or about me. It just took me by surprise." She meets Josh's eyes, forcing a small smile. "I'll be fine, I promise. Just give me a minute."

She's still a little out of it as they meander through the store, tossing bulk packages of necessities in and arguing with Josh about whether cookie dough ice cream counts as a necessity half-heartedly.

It's only once she's put the car in park outside the apartment building that she turns to face Josh, where he sits staring at her in the passenger seat that she lets down her walls, comforted by the subdued noises of the world outside.

"Do you think I'm a bad mom?"

"What?" Josh's tone is flabbergasted. "Of course not, Rosie. You love Scar more than anything. More than your own life. She's so lucky to have you."

"You're not just saying that because you love me?"

"No! What the hell, baby? You're the best mom I can imagine, and honestly, you could probably have even given my own a run for her money. God, I hope she didn't hear me say that. I bet she's gonna haunt me now." He cracks a sliver of a grin before growing solemn again. "Is this about what happened in the store?"

"It's just...people are always going to look at me differently. Look at Scar differently. And they don't...I just hate—" She chokes back a sob. "There's nothing wrong with having a kid young, you know, as long as you're going to love and take care of and do what's best for the baby. But I...I never *wanted* this, I never got to choose to have sex and then have a baby due to those decisions, and...and a baby should never be a negative consequence; they're so fucking precious.

But it just...it wasn't my *idea* to do the things that led to Scar's existence.

"I wouldn't trade her for the world, you know that, but I...I hate that people will always look at me that way, will never consider that I might not have had any say in the matter until she was already on the way. It will never cross their minds. And Scar will face that her whole life; I can only imagine the stuff people will say about me when she's in high school, you know? And if she ever finds out about...about how she was conceived, will that make it better or worse?

"Will she stop thinking less of me, or will she hate that that's who contributed half of her genes?" Rose sucks in a breath heavily, pressing her hands to her face and feeling the wetness drenching her eyelashes. "I just hate this," she whispers, so quiet she's not sure if Josh can hear.

It's hitting her harder than it normally would, she knows, most likely because of the missed call she'd found on her phone after work the day before – an unknown North Carolina number, a voicemail she'd deleted without listening to. Her hands were shaky as she forced herself through a panic attack the whole drive home.

"Scarlett will *never* think less of you," Josh begins, the timbre of his voice reverberating through the car. "She will know that you've always loved her, that you've always worked as hard as you possibly could to take care of her, that you put her before everything else. And nothing, no revelation or lack thereof, can take that away.

"And yeah, Rosie, the circumstances are shit. I wish...I so wish for you that she had been conceived differently, that this didn't have to hang over you forever. I hate that things that bastard did can change the way people look at you. You should have so much more from the world. If anyone deserves more, deserves better...God, it's you.

"But the people who matter, the people who love you? Our opinions of you would be the same even if you'd voluntarily slept with a hundred men before Scar was born. And it's shit that other people can't see that, but honestly, baby, they don't mean anything at the end of the day. Me, Isa, Bronte, Evan? We think you're a kickass mom. Nati thinks you're a kickass mom. Your boss, even—everyone who knows anything about you."

Rose ponders this for a moment. "You're probably right," she concedes, voice scratchy. "I know you're right...but it doesn't feel like it."

"That's okay." Josh leans across the center console to peck her on the lips once, quickly. "Sometimes nothing makes it better. It just...sucks until it doesn't. *C'est la vie.*"

"*C'est la vie,*" she repeats. Such is life.

(And it is.)

———

Hours later, they're curled up on the futon, Scar passed out in her crib with a stuffed elephant locked in her arm while Rose rubs Josh's neck where he lies across her lap, muscles tense from the hyper-vigilance Geoffrey's freedom has heightened in him.

"Mmm, I don't understand why anyone wouldn't want a girlfriend. This...this is heaven," he mumbles, and Rose lets out a giggle.

"It's ironic because you're not getting the main benefits people expect from a relationship."

"Doesn't bother me. Who needs sex when you can get massages? I could live like this." After a beat, he sits upright, locking eyes with her. "While I am one hundred percent on board with waiting as long as you want, I said that in jest. Please don't actually believe that I never want to have sex. Because I really, really do. Just not till you're ready."

Rose bites her lip, blushing but amused. "Don't worry, I didn't believe you. But thanks for the clarification." She takes a deep breath, then goes ahead. "Actually...I wanted to talk to you about that."

"Sex?" His eyes are wide with surprise.

"Yeah. As in, us having it. Soon."

"You've got my attention," he confirms teasingly, though she can still see the apprehension in his face. "Are you sure?"

"Very. I...you probably already know this, but I don't think it'll go well the first time. It's going to be really hard for me."

"Then maybe we should just—"

"No!" Her eyes widen at her own near shout. "Sorry. I just...I want this, I have for a while, and I don't care about the fact that it's going to suck. I choose this. For once in my goddamn life, I want to *choose* to have sex. Period. That's all that matters."

Josh still seems hesitant, unsure, and she doesn't know how to convey to him this need she has to replace the memories, to reclaim her body as her own, to do what she wants with it solely because she *wants* to.

"Joshua," she says quietly, bringing her face close to his, eyes inches from his own. "I want this. I want it with you because I love you and trust you, and I couldn't bear it to be anyone else. But...I also think I need this personally to heal. To know that I *can* make the choice to do it or to not. To stop feeling like my body belongs to someone else."

He swallows heavily, eyes wet even as he nods. Rose leans forward to press a kiss to his jaw, pressing into his side tightly.

"If we...when we do this," Josh corrects himself, "you have to tell me immediately if anything is wrong. If we need to stop and try again another time. I don't care if it takes fifty tries; we can't...I won't do anything to risk becoming part of the trauma. I couldn't handle it if you associated me with..." He trails off, squeezing his eyes shut.

"I will. I promise."

They sit in contemplative silence for a while until Rose can't handle the quiet. "So what are you going to do with all this free time, Mr. Almost College Graduate?"

He graduates in December, as soon as he finishes two summer sessions and one more semester.

Josh rolls his eyes at her, one hand playing with strands of her hair. "I haven't decided yet. Well, I mean, I *know* what I want to do, but I haven't decided if I can." Rose waves a hand impatiently for him to go on, and he sighs. "I really...the more I think about it, I *do* want to go to grad school, become some kind of advisor or guidance counselor."

He'd wavered back and forth for a while, not excited for several more years of both working and going to school and likely more debt, but...it feels right.

"I think...helping people like that? Would make me feel like my life means something. Like Evan. What he does is so freaking great for those kids, and I want to help them the same way, but I'm not good at that kind of thing. But advice, working the personal in with necessities, I could do. I could try to help kids find scholarships, try to do things that are more accessible for people in the neighborhoods I've grown up in, for the kids who fall asleep in class because it's not safe to sleep at home. I want to be there for them."

"Of course you do. You...Josh, you are everything good in this world."

He shifts uncomfortably at the praise, and Rose continues to smile at him wholeheartedly. "I can't imagine anything you're more suited for. Then why wouldn't you...oh."

The debt.

The debt that hangs over him every day, that would virtually ensure he get no financial aid even if he did try to go to grad school; debt that would only be compounded with the one-hundred thousand or so grad school would tack on, barring any grants he could magically get.

"Damn." Her face scrunches up, pained, but Josh's is resigned.

"Yeah. So...I just have to figure out if it's worth it long-term. I mean, I *know* it would be worth it, but...the kinds of loans I would be able to get would have insane interest rates. I have to decide if I want that much more hanging over me for the next couple of decades."

Rose can see how desperately he wants it—God, he wants that future *so* badly—but they both know better than most that you don't always get what you want. That life isn't fair.

"I think," Rose says carefully, "that you should at least take the GRE. That way, if you decide to apply in the next couple months, you can. Give yourself the choice. Maybe find a counselor to shadow the rest of the summer?"

Josh nods contemplatively. "Yeah. I don't know. I guess I just feel like it'll hurt that much more to not be able to if I've really let myself consider it."

"Maybe that's a sign that considering it is worth whatever it takes to get there," she whispers, and Josh presses his hands to his face.

"I just..." He winces. "All I've ever wanted to do is make the world better, in any way possible—the way I could with power and resources, you know? The example I would be able to set for all the little kids like me who've never seen a teacher or anyone in a position of authority that looks like them, the kids who assume that future isn't an option for them. They've never had anyone tell them what they're capable of, that everything out there is within their grasp. So I just...if there's *any* way I can be that for them..."

(The pain in his eyes—Rose knows he wants it like fucking oxygen.)

But neither of them has the luxury of making choices based solely on what they want.

———

Some days are good.

Since Rose opened up to Josh about her life pre-Scar, the good days have seemed to be more frequent. Knowing someone knows everything about her and still loves her absolutely makes her feel lighter.

But the good days are still limited.

(Today is not one of them.)

Josh slept over, and she'd come to panting and crying when the sun had yet to rise. He'd stirred beside her, reaching to soothe her and remind her that her nightmares were only just that, but the feel of skin on hers made her flinch and hurry to sit across the apartment from him. She sat near the trash can, overcome with nausea and frustration, wanting to have a normal morning with her boyfriend, for God's sake.

Scar wakes up less than twenty minutes later, cranky and impossible to calm, and while Josh offers to try to soothe her so Rose can go back to sleep, she refuses, unable to withstand the thought of further nightmares, all the while hating herself for feeling too overcome with darkness to care for her daughter properly.

She presses her lips to Scar's hair as she gently bounces her in her arms, holding her warmth to her chest.

"Can I...is there anything I can do?" Josh's voice is sad but full of understanding.

Rose shakes her head without speaking in reply.

"Do you want me to leave?"

Another silent head shake.

"Stay but keep a little distance?"

A slow nod.

"Okay. I love you, baby. Tell me if there's anything you need."

She watches as Josh makes his way to the kitchen, taking just long enough to put sliced banana on toast and place it near her with water before stepping away. He seats himself back on the futon, pulling his laptop towards him and pretending to do homework—though, every time she glances his way, his attention is trained on either her or Scarlett.

Eventually, he has to leave for work. He kisses Scar's forehead where she now sits amongst pillows and toys, whispers a farewell to Rose, and locks the door behind him.

Using the key she'd given him two weeks before, her hands shaky and a nervous smile he presses a kiss to.

The day passes, and Rose sits in a daze. Occasionally, she starts crying for no particular reason, jolted out of staring into nothingness by her own sobs.

The heaviness consumes her, and she doesn't know how the hours slip away with her doing nothing but lying down, getting up only to feed and change her daughter, trying to rally the energy to play with her but knowing she's not doing enough, knowing she needs to break through this for Scar's sake and hating herself further in the moments she can't.

Everything feels hopeless today. Yesterday was fine, and the day before, and so on, but here she is, feeling more broken and emptier than ever.

She's never been one to kid herself—she knows she's not completely okay—but lately, things have seemed somewhat better. *She'd* seemed better. She wouldn't say she'd been thinking she wasn't depressed anymore, but—well, she hadn't felt like she was, at least.

After all these years, she'd thought she might be on the road to recovery. Free at last.

(She should've known better.)

This is how her mental illness works, the parasite inside her; weeks ago, she had it together enough to stage an intervention for Isa, and now she can't lift herself from the floor. Can't see the light at the end of the tunnel.

And if it's this bad now...what happens whenever things come to a head with the North Carolina number that keeps calling?

And she tries the strategies she's learned over the years of fighting herself—reminding herself of the people who love her, of the clear evidence of them caring; that she has a daughter, and a doting boyfriend, a family of friends she loves more than words, a stable job she's good at, and a strong GPA.

But the words she tells herself don't matter. Her brain won't believe any of them, despite the rational evidence standing tall in their defense. Life itself seems pointless.

She knows it's her brain chemistry, knows given the environmental stressors she's been exposed to, it's no fucking wonder she's a mess of imbalances and wonky brain activity. But she only feels weaker knowing Josh, and Isa, and Bronte, and Evan, and hell, probably Zeke and Kai—they all have shitty pasts, too, scars and nightmares and experiences anyone would wish away, and yet they're strong enough to not fall apart. Strong enough to not let their demons win, even as hers consume her.

Her friends deserve better. Scarlett...Scar deserves so much better, so much more than Rose is giving, so much more than she will ever be able to give. Josh, too; he deserves more than not knowing whether he'll be able to kiss his girlfriend good morning or if the action will make her scream. And really, what 22-year-old guy wants to be with someone who can't handle sex someday? Who hadn't even broached the topic for months of dating seriously, preceded by even longer of being best friends, together every moment they could? Bronte and Evan finally have their shit together, are happy and stable, and she came stumbling back into their lives, the incapable little kid who got Bronte into trouble for taking care of her so long ago still making their lives more complicated. Isa, gorgeous and worldly and capable, working beside Rose in the diner when she could've probably secured a modeling gig by this point if she didn't feel obligated to stay with her. Zeke, Kai, Nick...people she isn't even that close to but knows she's managed to inconvenience.

Do any of them really like her? Would they be better off without her in their lives—if she just kept to herself and stopped intruding on their lives?

She spirals and spirals, her chest growing heavier and heavier, thoughts more and more hopeless as the hours pass, and none of the facts and figures about her life can convince her mind anything is okay.

Josh returns seven hours later to a snoozing baby and girlfriend curled up together. Gently, he slips Scar from Rose's arms. Rose's eyes fly open immediately, but calm when they see him moving the kid to her playpen.

"Hi," she greets him quietly, rising to a sitting position. He gently sits a few feet from her, observing her carefully, knees tucked into her chest and not meeting his eyes.

"Feeling better?"

"Not really," she admits quietly. "I'm sorry. I want...I hate...feeling like this. You don't have to stay if you don't want to. I know you have a lot to do."

"Nothing I have to do is more important than making sure you're okay," he says firmly, then hesitates. "Unless you need space. If you want me to leave, I can."

"I just...my head is dark right now. I don't want to make you be around that."

"I want to be wherever you are. No conditions or exceptions. Can I...are you okay for physical contact right now?"

Rose bites her lip but nods, scooting closer to him, then pressing her face into his chest. His arms wrap around her solidly, and he feels the coil in his chest that's been cranking tighter and tighter all day relax at long last.

"Hey," he says into her hair.

"Hey."

"I love you."

"Yeah?"

She sounds unsure, and he wants to scream at the thought of her still not feeling worthy of love, of not being able to believe someone could love her. It makes him want to kill her shit excuse for a mother and the bastard who hurt her for so many years whose name she can't bring herself to say.

"Yeah, baby. More than I knew was possible. You and Scar both."

She hums without speaking further but eventually moves one of the palms curled into her to his chest, gently tracing invisible shapes. Tension slowly drifts out of her body, and he sighs in relief at the start of this wave's end.

It won't be the last, he knows; his own bad days are just around the corner, too. They'll never be fully healed, most likely. It's the reality of the lives they've lived. But that's okay. As long as after the bad day ends, they can come back to each other, he can handle it— this life that seems like too much sometimes.

"How was work?" she asks eventually, and he presses a kiss to her curls.

"It was okay. A couple guys on the team came in, which was good, but there was this group of douche frat boys...anyway, I'm glad to be home."

He worries that he's overstepped, for a moment—but then a smile curls at the edge of her lips, and his heart warms at the thought that she agrees, that this complicated, imperfect, beautiful thing they have as home, however pained each of them may be.

"Have you eaten anything since I left?" He knows the answer already, knows the thought probably hadn't even crossed her mind despite her giving Scar his feedings right on time.

"No. Damn. I need...I need to work on that."

He nods but doesn't push. Knows it won't help. "I brought you home some stuff from work; we were pretty busy, so the kitchen cooked us all up something to take home. It's in the fridge whenever you want it."

"I love you," she mumbles into his shirt, and he just squeezes her lightly in return.

"You and me against the world. And sometimes ourselves."

"Brains are the worst," Rose nods, humming against his skin.

And maybe, hopefully, tomorrow will be a good day, and today will feel like a distant memory.

But maybe it won't. They'll work through it all the same and hope for the same the next night.

(Such is life.)

17

"This is ridiculous; the other guy was clearly better." Evan scowls like the rom com's love triangle ending has personally offended him. The light yellow of his sweatshirt makes his tan skin stand out, and he already looks at home in the soft fabric of the armchair.

Kai nods in agreement, one hand absentmindedly rubbing his youngest sister's back where she's fallen asleep beside him.

He and Evan keep ranting about it, the conversation evolving into a discussion of superhero movies; Kai's teenage sister Grace meets Bronte's gaze and rolls her eyes.

Bronte had worried before introducing them all for the first time; she'd spent so many years searching for her family and had gotten even luckier than she'd ever expected. An aunt that emanates kindness and love, five cousins—three of them so young she still gets to see them grow up. Kai, who's naive about the darkness in the world, but still one of the sweetest and most thoughtful people she's ever met.

Her family.

But Evan is family just as much. Even all these years later, he and Rose.

(God, does she hope Rose is okay. Thinking about her, not knowing what happened to her after everything went to hell...it's excruciating.)

She'd worried there would be animosity between Evan and Kai, the family she made for herself up against the one she was born into.

But that's not her boys. Instead, they mostly seem grateful to each other for being there for her when the other couldn't. They're so different in so many ways, but they're making it work because they both love her.

(It's the kind of life she never thought she'd be able to have.)

Her second youngest cousin, a little boy named Micah, pulls himself up onto the couch beside her. He wedges his way between her and Evan and curls into her side, giving her a smile that flashes his missing teeth when she puts his arm around him.

"I've been replaced, I see," Evan teases, and Bronte scoffs, knowing he'd drop her for a cute kid in a heartbeat.

She's still broken, in a million ways; still healing, missing a piece of her heart.

But moments like this make the rest of it bearable.

———

Summer arrives, and Rose is not even half as stressed as she had been.

Her scholarship doesn't require that she take summer classes, and while in the future she might try to knock out some requirements, in the meantime, there's nothing better than spending all of her time outside of work completely devoted to Scar.

She's started taking her to a *Mommy and Me* group that Natalya had recommended on Thursday mornings, and while she loves her friends more than anything, it's so *nice* to spend time with other parents. Others who understand the main chunk of your brain always being devoted to this tiny human's existence, who understand what it is to wake in the middle of the night and hold your hand before your child's face to make sure they're breathing.

Five times a night.

Some days, she looks at Scar and bursts into tears at how big she seems, how quickly she's growing up. She now babbles much more than she used to, the beginnings of her language forming; she loves seeing dogs at the park, she absolutely hates the mall and still adores the aquarium.

As Josh reminds anyone who will listen.

And while money is tight, the apartment is barer than Rose would like, and the threat of Cheyenne someday finding her—the voice-mails she continues to receive and delete without listening—still hangs over her head, she's...happier than she can ever remember being.

Something will go wrong soon, she's sure. Regression to the mean, and all that. Story of her life. But until then, she might as well enjoy life surrounded by family.

"Oh my word, Rose!! I can't believe you didn't tell us!"

She grins at the shock on Ampara's face as the older mother stares at Scar, who had just sat up—completely unaided.

"I thought it might be more exciting for you to witness her new trick firsthand. She just did it for the first time on Monday. I swear, I cried for at least an hour."

"That's one of the things I always thought would be less emotional after the first kid, but Moises is number four, and I already know when he does, I'll bawl just as hard as I did when Valentina did," Ampara confides, referencing her firstborn wistfully. "Being a mother...it's unlike any other experience."

"That it is," Rose agrees with a small smile. "We're so lucky we got it on camera." She pulls out her phone to show Ampara her new background: Scar, looking extremely pleased with herself, sitting next to a shocked Rose, the beginnings of tears running down the tops of her cheeks.

"Your young man took the picture?" Ampara's voice is knowing, and Rose can't look her in the eyes, instead focusing her attention on her daughter, where she sits hitting light-up buttons on a musical toy gleefully.

"He did. He...I think he loves Scar almost as much as I do. It's incredible. I'm so lucky to have found him, that he wants to be a part of...of this. With us."

"Till little Scar is grown up and becomes a daddy's girl, and then it's two against one, and they out-vote you for what to watch on tv," Ampara teases. "At least until you and Josh have another one or two. Maybe then you'll get one to back you up."

Rose's jaw drops at the insinuation, stuttering and feeling everything from her ears to her collarbone flush. "I don't...we haven't discussed...I don't even know if—" She cuts off abruptly, face still flaming, at the amusement coloring the faces of all the mothers—and one father, a single dad who lives near her—around the room.

"I get not wanting to jinx it," Naziyah confides across the circle from her. "But honey, barring a nuclear apocalypse or something equally crazy, that boy is not going anywhere."

But something equally crazy could mean a lot of things. And while Rose likes to think she and Josh have been through enough in their own lives to not let circumstances change their feelings, that they've been through enough shit that anything that could happen wouldn't rattle their relationship...that's not how life works.

(Especially not for people like them.)

The odds of something happening, of something from their pasts coming into play, are high. And with Geoffrey on the streets and no renewed protective order, with Cheyenne and *him* always potentially on her tail, who knows what could happen in their lives?

Still...they'll try. And while Rose occasionally freaks out, doubts that anyone could love her or want to be with her forever, rationally she knows that nothing short of her, Kathy, Zeke, or Scar's safety being jeopardized could take Josh away from her—or her away from him.

And after what they've been through, what they will always be dealing with internally, they deserve this. They deserve a happily ever after where their relationship is concerned if nothing else.

She'd fight God himself for it.

———

A few days after the revelation, Bronte and Evan badger her to let them kidnap Scarlett for the night. Rose had been reluctant, as she always is, to have her daughter out of her sight, and especially for such an extended period of time.

But it's been *so* long since she had eight hours of sleep, and the prospect of date night and being able to actually sleep uninterrupted is too enticing for her to refuse them.

Josh offered to take her out to dinner, but they're both such home-bodies anyway that he doesn't suspect anything when she suggests a movie night in. It's not until she takes a bottle of sweet wine out of the fridge that his eyebrows scrunch with confusion. "What are you doing?"

"I thought it would be romantic; candles, wine, the usual things, the one night we don't have to worry about the hazards around Scar."

"But you don't like to drink."

Rose crosses her arms in mock-irritation. "I've never said that."

"No, but you hate feeling out of control." He's staring at her like she's lost her mind. "You panic anytime you start to lose agency; I'm not saying that's a bad thing; obviously, that's so fair, and I support you. But I'm a little concerned as to why you want to drink right now."

She finds herself scowling even as her cheeks heat with pleasant surprise; her man notices every little thing, even when she doesn't say anything. Knows her well enough to figure out exactly why she does everything she does, exactly how she ticks.

(God, does she love him.)

A sigh escapes her, and she moves back to the futon with the chilled bottle in hand. He pulls her towards him until she's on his lap, and he's staring into her eyes—his usual tactic for making sure she's being honest, not waving away her own feelings in fear of being a burden like she's used to.

"I..." Putting down the bottle, she wraps her arms around his neck, letting him pull her closer. "I love you. And I *really* want to fuck you."

His pupils dilate, but his gaze stays on hers. "I love you too. And you know I would really, really love that. But baby, if you have to drink to want to actually do it, it just seems like—"

"No," she interrupts sharply, squeezing her eyes shut like doing so will stop him from thinking it. "It's not that I need the alcohol to want to. I think about it all the time, Josh; God, I'm obsessed with the idea of being with you. Of knowing you every way there is to know a person. It's just..." Opening her eyes, she scrunches her face with frustration. "I'm going to be anxious, no matter how long we wait. All the bad is all my brain has to compare it to. But I don't want to keep waiting; I don't want him to keep controlling me and impacting my life when this is something I want with the man I love. So I think if we have wine...I'm not trying to blackout; I just want my inhibitions to be a little lowered and my anxiety about it all not to consume me so that I can actually enjoy it."

Josh runs his hands up and down her sides slowly, expression worried. "I don't know, baby. I don't want to disrespect you or keep you from making your own decisions about what you do with your body. I'm just worried you're doing this because you feel like you should and not because you actually want to and are mentally in the right space to. A lot of people who've been through what you have use sex as a form of self-harm, having it when they don't want to for the sense of control even as it is actually incredibly damaging."

"Did you just—" Rose's jaw drops. "Did you *research* this?"

"Of course." The way he says it is easy, as though it was never a question in his mind. "I also, you know, almost have an entire degree in psychology. But I wanted to make sure if there was anything specific about your experience that I could do to prepare or make it better..."

"I love you so fucking much." She presses her face into his chest, arms tight around his back. His fingers trail up and down her back in soothing motions while she tears up into his shirt, overwhelmed with gratitude for this man who has somehow become the second-brightest spot in her days.

And it's not just that she loves him, but also that she feels so constantly loved *by* him. She can't imagine how long this has been weighing on him, how many other times he's taken the time to research things like this with her none the wiser.

She pulls back eventually, looking up at him. "I won't lie—I like the idea of being the one deciding what my body is doing for once. I would really like to cover up every memory of the feeling of him with you. I want your touch to be the only thing in the world. Joshua, I love you. I want all of those things with you because your arms are the only place in the world I feel safe. This is...the first time it will count. The first time it will matter. And I want that to be with you."

He nods slowly, tucking a flyaway hair behind her ear. "If you're absolutely sure."

"Please."

(She's rarely been so sure of anything.)

So they make their way through the bottle of wine while they talk through the movie like usual, cuddling close in the darkroom, the tv the only source of light.

After, they turn on another. The wine is gone, and Josh's skin is warm, and her gaze keeps catching on his mouth.

She leans a bit closer, and then he's pressing his lips to hers, arms gentle even as they pull her tighter against him.

This much they've done before, and a bit more, so it's comfortingly familiar. After a few moments, she tugs at his shorts, basking in the safety of being with him. "Please."

A shaky breath of relief escapes him, and then he's kissing her like nothing else. Like he's been restraining himself, for her benefit.

It's the most complicated kind of wonderful; so different than anything she's known before, so *good* when it's something she so desperately wants.

She has to fight back the harder memories all the while, of course. At one point she has to ask him to stop, has to breathe and walk through reminding herself where she is and who she's with. It's incredible—and yet terrible that it's tainted in this way, the fear and godawful memories she works so hard to suppress every day taking over in some moments.

After, she's quiet, so glad to have done it, already looking forward to doing it again, but also unequivocally reminded of all the times it wasn't this good. Unable to hold back the tide of feelings the experience has stirred within her mind.

Josh helps clean her up and then tucks them both back under the soft fabric of the blanket. He's worried, she can tell; she knows he's panicking about her out of character quiet, the timid way she curls into him.

"You okay, baby?"

She hums in response and hides her face in his chest to avoid his eyes.

"Okay. Tell me if you need anything, okay?"

She nods, clinging to him tightly. "Just you. I love you."

One hand strokes at her hair, gently soothing the anxiety in her chest. "I know," he promises. Because even though she hasn't said, she knows he can read her that well—he understands she's not saying it to hear it back, only to try to convey how much he means, all of the things she doesn't have the words to express.

And then he lets her be. He holds her tight, loves her, pressing the occasional kiss to her hair, legs tangled up with hers.

Josh falls asleep first, while Rose panics and overthinks and tries to come to terms with the fucked-up mess of emotions roiling through her, the gratitude and sorrow and frustration and elation battling in her chest.

Eventually, the exhaustion wins out, and she too is lost to dreams, curled up against his chest with an arm holding onto her.

(It's the best sleep she's had in years.)

———

Rose drags herself and Scar out of the apartment on her day off; it's a Wednesday, which means Josh, Isa, and the rest of her family all have work.

Something tugs at her, though. An antsy need to get out of the apartment, a feeling that there's somewhere else she should be.

They drive around aimlessly for a while. Run a few errands, stop by the bank, hang out at the park for a bit, but something itches at the back of Rose's brain until she finds herself parked outside of the youth center.

She feels so at home here. She spent so much of her childhood in the one where she'd met Bronte, and those were some of her best memories even though the surrounding circumstances were garbage. She thinks centers like these will always feel like a safe haven.

School hasn't let out yet, so the place is mostly deserted, but a few kids lounge around the place, the sound effects of some video game the main activity. She wanders for a moment, trails her fingers along the shelves of secondhand books and DVDs stacked to the ceiling. Let's Scar down so she can crawl, as obsessed with being independent as the kid's grown the last few weeks.

One guy who looks maybe sixteen smiles at the sight of her, a suave expression overtaking momentary joy as soon as he spots Rose

He can't fool her, though. Lip ring, scowl, and all, she can still tell he's got a soft heart.

Will isn't here, this time, but her mini-me is, tucked into a corner again, book in hand, tuning everything about real life out.

Rose lays out Scar's blanket, some toys for her to play with, and a sippy cup full of water, then folds herself into a threadbare armchair across from the girl. "Hey. I'm Rose."

The girl eyes her for a moment, and Rose knows the girl is debating trusting her. Whether it's worth it to let someone in. If she can afford to.

(Rose knows the feeling.)

"Imani." She doesn't offer anything else, just her name, then returns to the tome in hand.

But the distance between them feels smaller.

When Rose gets up to grab a snack eventually, she grabs one for Imani too. When Imani gets up to leave, she bites her lip but sends a wave Rose's way. She even pats Scar's head softly on her way out.

(It's a start.)

———

"Now, your mom probably wouldn't approve of this, so we'll call this you and me day one of many, okay, little one?"

Scar smiles back up at him and says something nonsensical, which Josh takes as a yes before carrying her into the animal shelter.

"Hi, how are you today, sir?" the woman at the counter asks, and Josh responds in kind.

"Is it possible for us to play with one of the dogs? Her mom would kill me if I tried to adopt one, but I figure she'd have some fun playing with them, and they can use the love, right?"

"They certainly can. You and your daughter are more than welcome to play with one of them. I'll try to find one with a little less energy so she doesn't get too overwhelmed, but if you two decide to come back again, we can pair you with someone more outgoing, okay?"

Josh nods, trying not to blush at the assumption that Scar is his daughter. It's not the first time it's happened, not by a long shot, and he doesn't mind at all. Scar is the most perfect kid. Anyone would be lucky to call her theirs.

But he doesn't want Rose to assume that's what he thinks when they haven't had a conversation about it. They haven't really had to have any of that kind of conversation before because the two of them are almost always on the same page, and now he has no idea how to bring the topic up without coming off as expectant or overstepping.

"Alrighty, kiddo. If we're lucky, I'll be able to talk your mom into letting us get one of these of our own by next Christmas," he informs the baby, seating her on his lap just as the worker allows an older mutt out of his kennel. "Here, boy," he whistles softly, watching Scar's face carefully as the animal approaches. She doesn't seem scared, only curious, and she lets out a giggle when the dog licks her tiny hand.

"You're such a sweet boy, aren't you? How have you not been

adopted yet?" he almost croons at the dog, cuddled up to them and occasionally nuzzling a joyous Scar. "I wish I could convince Zeke and Kai to help me take you for walks when I'm at work. The pet fee for the building really isn't *too* bad..." He trails off, lost in thoughts of himself curled up with Rose while Scar plays with the dog—Domino, according to the kennel—on the rug before them. *I want that life.*

Almost as if she hears him thinking about her, his phone lights up with his girlfriend's name, and he quickly presses it to his ear. "Hey, baby, how's work?"

"Really good, actually," she says, sounding surprised. "What are you two up to?"

"Oh, you know, not much, just going for a walk, and—"

Domino chooses this moment to let out a bark, too close to the phone for Josh to play it off as a dog across the street, and Rose's voice grows suspicious. "Joshua...was that a dog?"

"Busted," he whispers to Scar, whose eyes are now fluttering closed. "Er, we may or may not be at the pet shelter."

"Josh," she groans, and he can almost see her rubbing her temples in his mind. "What if she'd been allergic? Or the dog had leaped on her? The plates of bone on her head still haven't fully formed, and she's so vulnerable to illness, and—"

"The dog's name is Domino, and I promise he's super sweet and hasn't shown any inclination of leaping on her," he swears earnestly. "I really think it's good for her to interact with animals early on, to teach her not to be afraid of them. Besides, in some cases, exposing kids to things early on helps them not develop an aversion. It's like a non-painful vaccine! For dogs!"

"I don't personally know enough about the science to refute that statement, but I'm almost positive that's not how it works."

"Rose," he pleads, "this is a good thing. Domino is just so gentle and adorable, and we could both use something so anxiety-reducing, and I was thinking...I mean, my birthday is only a month or so away... what would you think about fostering a dog?"

"Yeah, if by a month or so you mean four, and after Bronte and

Zeke's birthdays, in case you'd forgotten," she teases. "I don't know, Josh. I mean, we don't really have time to care for a pet right now."

"I know, but for now, it would be just fostering when we can. Domino is low maintenance; I can already tell!"

Rose sighs. "I don't know, babe. I know you want this, but the fee could be a little hefty, and the cost of a dog on top of it...do you think it's a good idea?"

The question isn't rhetorical or condescending like it would be coming from someone else; she genuinely wants to hear if he thinks this is worth the effort. She will genuinely consider it if he does—and that alone warms him.

"I really do. I know it's a little while off, but eventually. He's short-haired, so less of a mess, and honestly, Rosie, I think you would sleep better with an in-home security system. And Scar is loving being here; I swear, I'm not just saying that."

It's funny because though they haven't moved in together and this dog is his idea and would predominantly be his, they both know Domino would stay in Rose's apartment whenever they have him.

As Josh practically does, with the exception of cooking for them plus his roommates in his own apartment for at least one meal a day.

"Listen, I understand why you're apprehensive, and I know this is a lot to ask, but I promise I wouldn't even be suggesting it if I didn't think it would be good for all three of us. That's why I'm saying let's start thinking about it. I'm gonna go ahead and send you a picture of him with Scar, and then we revisit the subject in a while, and you have the final say, okay? Whatever you decide goes, and I won't argue or bring up the idea of a pet again."

Rose snorts. "Never again?"

"Okay, not for at least six months."

"Yeah, that sounds more like it."

After they hang up, he snaps a photo of the two, Domino resting his head on Scar's stomach as she sleeps peacefully like she has been almost since Josh got the call. He can almost *feel* how happy his heart is. And yes, Rose and Kai both would roll their eyes at him for attributing feelings to the organ that only deals with blood conduction, but that's really not important right now. He can't control the smile lighting up his face as he sends the picture with a question mark.

It's not the most responsible decision they've ever made, but it's a rare one solely to bring them a little more joy and security. The way Scar claps her hands upon seeing Domino every morning leaves little room for regret.

18

BEFORE | **BRONTE**

Evan finds her sitting on the floor outside while Rose is fast asleep inside their shoddy motel room.

She'd left the room not too long after the younger girl fell asleep and after peeking at Rose to check on her. The sight of her curled up and unconscious sent her back to months prior, their first night on the run when it took Rose fifty hours to fall asleep with Bronte watching her back.

When it had been clear she was about to jet, Rose confronted her and said she was leaving too. The urgency in her movements, the fight in her eyes...

(The choice to take her in was almost unconscious.)

"You look like something's weighing you down," Evan prods gently as he sits down beside her.

Another unexpected light in her life—one she'd initially been suspicious of, but who's wormed his way into her heart.

"Rose," she admits, voice cracking. "I worry about her...all the time. And sometimes I worry her being with me is a bad idea.

He gives her a look. "You're already way too attached. You couldn't leave her even if you wanted to."

A grimace forms on Bronte's face. "I know. God, do I know; I love that girl more than I've ever loved anyone. And it's not that I want to leave her. But..." She takes a deep breath, wishing the world would feel a little less heavy. "What if she's better off without me? What if she'd be safer if I left, and I'm...being selfish, keeping her with me because I love her?"

Evan makes a face, rubbing at his jaw. "I don't know. But what if she'd be worse off without you? Besides..." He reaches to squeeze Bronte's hand reassuringly.

It's an unfamiliar motion, but it doesn't shock her.

(It's the kind of comfortable she could get used to.)

"Everyone is better off with love in their lives," he insists. "Especially people like us that have never had it before."

Bronte concedes with a nod. He's right; she knows he is. But she can't help but second guess herself.

Rose means more than anything; Rose is her family.

(Bronte can't afford to give her anything but her best chance in the hell that is this world.)

———

By the time he gets to leave work, Josh is exhausted and in an objectively shitty mood. He wants nothing more than to be home with Rose and Scar, whom he's seen maybe once in the last week after working doubles almost every day.

His back hurts from hours spent on his feet, and the tips he pulled tonight won't cover half of what he needs them to, what with the additional legal fees and costs for security measures he's had to shell out recently.

He lets himself into the apartment, ready to take the fastest shower the world has ever seen and collapse on the futon, but pauses at the sight that meets him. Domino rushes to greet him as soon as he's over the threshold, and on the futon, Rose is semi-reclined as though she'd just meant to sit down for a moment before falling into the slack-jawed sleep she's currently in. Scar is snuggled into her chest, their cheeks pressed together as they breathe deeply in tandem.

The sight warms his heart. These two people who have become nearly his whole heart, laying together so untouched and wholly in their own world. It's strange to suddenly have these feelings and relationships that had never been a thought in his mind so recently.

The idea that a sleeping baby's smile would be the highlight of his week? Would eradicate every moment of frustration from a shitty day? Would become his life's goal to cause?

(No one could've seen it coming.)

He gets a shower quickly, out in a jiff and with eyes struggling to stay open. If the next day weren't his day off, he thinks he might've had a mental breakdown.

Domino is curled up in his bed, eyes following Josh's movements but otherwise seemingly content to be done for the day.

Josh walks to the futon, intending to relocate Scar to her crib and pull the futon itself out into bed form to get Rose into a more comfortable position, but by the time he approaches, Scar has started to squirm. One drawn-out whine makes it to his ears, the tell-tale sign of waterworks to come, and he carefully maneuvers Scar out from her mother's arms, pulling her to his chest to see the little girl looking back at him with lively eyes.

"Hey, little one. You think you'll go back to sleep soon?"

Scarlett merely blinks in response, then begins to babble a few of her favorite sounds with a smile, and Josh lets out a raspy laugh that's probably louder than it should be.

"Yeah, I figured as much. You're the definition of bright-eyed and bushy tailed." He sighs with a yawn, setting Scar on the floor. "You hang out here for just a minute, angel, so I can get Mama more comfortable. Then you and I will find something to do so she can get some rest."

Scar had recently had a sleep regression; the doctor said it wasn't at all uncommon, but she's been up all hours for a few weeks now, and Rose refuses to let Josh be the one to stay up with her most nights, despite him not being the one who has to work morning shifts.

He understands why—understands that she doesn't want to

depend on him, can't bear not to be the one spending time with Scar, and doesn't want to leave the raising of her daughter to another, anyway. But...Scar doesn't feel like just his girlfriend's kid anymore.

And he wants this. Wants to be someone Scar knows she can rely on, someone who she knows will be there to take care of her and love her always.

Carefully, he lifts Rose and rearranges her so that she's fully lying down. He cautiously pulls the futon out, cursing under his breath when it clangs loudly into place. Relief floods through him when she stays asleep, the bags beneath her eyes still attention-grabbing. He winces at the sight, wishes getting her to take a few fewer shifts or some time off were an option.

He returns to snatch up Scar, bringing her to the kitchen quietly. Grabbing both a bottle and a book, he settles into a chair for the long haul.

———

A few hours later, Rose comes to and jerks upright, silently stretching and confused at not having gotten up with Scar at all throughout the night.

Not that the night is over, really; she's opening today, which means it's currently 4:15 a.m. Enough time for her to get ready, set out Scar's things, and get to work by 5. No hint of sunlight comes through the window, though of course, the streets are never completely silent, despite the hour.

Even more confusing, Scar isn't beside her, where Rose *knows* she was when she fell asleep, and she starts to panic until she hears the cadence of Josh's voice floating out from the kitchenette.

Domino head butts her legs gently, tail wagging when she leans down to pet him as she gets to her feet.

"*I do not like them, Sam I am,*" Josh articulates carefully, and Rose slowly walks up behind them in time to see him press kisses to a giggling Scarlett's face, dropping the book to join several others on the table.

"Josh?"

He swivels in his seat, looking up at her with a tired smile. "Morning, baby. I didn't hear you get up."

"I beat my alarm by a few minutes," she confesses, grabbing a banana and joining him at the table. She sets the fruit down, leaning to kiss Scar good morning until her daughter reaches out her arms for her excitedly, and Rose helplessly picks her up, holding her tightly with closed eyes.

Seeing Scar first thing in the morning...it's the best. *She's* the best kid ever; Rose knows it.

"Were you...Josh, were you reading to her?"

Josh nods somewhat sheepishly, blushing and not meeting her eyes. "I mean, technically, I don't know that it counts as reading. Most of these I have memorized from when I was a kid. Took them ages to figure out I still hadn't learned how yet, till one day I was reciting the next line before I remembered to turn the page."

"Of course you did." She shakes her head, a knowing smirk on her face. "That's so sweet of you, though. You really didn't have to—especially when you're watching her all morning."

"You know I love hanging out with her. Besides, I don't have class today, so she and I can both ruin our sleep schedules and snooze till the afternoon together. I just really thought you could use the rest, Rosie; you've been so stressed lately."

Rose internally winces at this, doing her best to maintain a straight face. She's kept the main cause of her inner turmoil from him, not wanting to burden him while he's so worried about Kathy and on edge about Geoffrey, but she knows soon enough she'll have to face the music.

She will have to tell him—and Bronte, which will be arguably worse.

"Well, thank you. I appreciate it." She leans her head on his shoulder with a yawn, wishing she could freeze time and stay in this moment forever; tired, but happy, untouchable by her problems.

(It won't last long.)

. . .

It's a few hours later when the morning rush is gone and she's sitting on a metal chair in the back on her break, skimming the pages of a book from the library about parenting during the infant-to-toddler transition through half-closed eyes, when her phone starts buzzing away in her pocket. Assuming it's Josh, and always half-expecting something to be wrong with Scar and ready to sprint to her car, she accepts the call without a second thought, pressing the phone to her ear immediately. "Hey, everything okay?"

For a moment, there's silence on the other end before a throat clears, and she's tensing as an unfamiliar male voice speaks. "Hello, I'm calling to speak to Rose Simmons?"

No. This must be it—the mysterious number with a North Carolina area code that's been calling her for weeks, changing lines each time she blocks a new one without listening to the copious quantities of voicemails left behind.

It's because of them; she knows it is. There's nothing else in North Carolina to do with her.

(No one else who could *find* her. No one else who would try to.)

A part of her wants to hang up immediately and just block this number too. But she knows that will only make it worse now that they've heard her voice—now that they know for certain she's at the other end. She doesn't let herself consider what they would escalate to next if she ended the call now.

"This is she," she responds robotically. "May I ask who's calling?"

"You're quite the difficult person to get ahold of, Ms. Simmons. My name is Robert Sullivan; I've been hired by your mother."

Rose's entire body is live with electricity. "I have no contact with my mother, Mr. Sullivan, and that is not unintentional. I am legally an adult. Whatever this is about does not involve me."

"I'm sorry, but I'm afraid your family needs you, Ms. Simmons. They're going through a trying time right now."

"I can assure you, sir, there is no one in your entire state who I consider family."

The brazen man carries on, undeterred—or used to defending clients with negative reception, she supposes. "Whatever the case may be, your mother and those close to her could use your help. The elder Ms. Simmons has hired me to represent Mr. Kyle Sherwood, a close friend of the family, in his upcoming trial. That is to say, I'm his criminal defense attorney."

All of the blood rushes out of Rose's face, and for a moment, the world is only her and the phone her fist is clenched around, as her breathing hitches. "His...his attorney?"

"His lawyer, ma'am," he clarifies, the condescension in his voice palpable. "Everyone knows it's defamation, of course, but Mr. Sherwood has been falsely accused of the most egregious of charge. Two blasphemous young women have come forward alleging that he raped them during the last year and are proceeding with a trial."

His tone is static throughout the sentence, but the word— that *word*—it echoes in Rose's mind as though he's screamed it.

"Excuse me just a moment," Rose whispers into the phone, dropping it to the counter before lunging to empty the entire contents of her stomach into a nearby trash can.

Two young women.

Two others, hurt because of her, because she *left*, because he had to find new targets.

(*I did this.*)

(*They went through this because of me.*)

Pale and shaking, stomach still churning, she picks the phone back up with a trembling hand. "Mr. Sullivan, I fail to understand what this has to do with me." She's proud of how evenly the words come out, how little she sounds like someone in the beginnings of a nervous breakdown.

"Well, you have to testify, of course. You need to speak as a character witness to attest to the fact that Mr. Sherwood could never commit that kind of atrocity. You'll come in and talk about the quality of his character, that he's an upstanding citizen, the best uncle— pardon me, your mother said you had always considered him that— you could never imagine, wouldn't hurt a fly, etc."

Wouldn't hurt a fly. Rose chokes at the words and has to hold back a sob at the idea of going before a courtroom and defending the bastard who tortured her for years. The backdrop for every night-mare, the reason her own body will never fail to feel like a fucking crime scene.

Of having his eyes on her, knowing the kind of thoughts that would be running through his head.

(Of him potentially catching wind of *Scar*.)

"The trial has been ongoing for several weeks now. We've been trying to reach you for a while, Ms. Simmons; it's truly made things difficult on our end. The fees our private eye racked up...well, none-theless, since the trial is so soon, we'll need you to head here immedi-ately, from—where *is* it you are, Florida? You'll need to be here within a week at most."

"I..." She can't get the words out, knows if she speaks any further, all that will come out is a cry. She has to physically press a hand to her mouth to hold back the screams.

"I have to go to a meeting now, Ms. Simmons, but we'll talk soon. Cheyenne and Kyle will be thrilled we finally got ahold of you."

Without another word, the call clicks to an end, and Rose collapses to her knees on the floor as her life disintegrates around her.

———

Josh's head jerks upward when the door creaks open hours too early, instinctively sensing that something is off. When Rose closes it behind her and rushes to lock herself in the bathroom without a word to him or Scar, he *knows* things are very much not okay.

"You wait here, buddy. I'm gonna go see if I can make her feel better," he tells Scar, setting her in her bouncer and carefully walking to the bathroom door. He taps it lightly with his knuckles. "Baby? What happened?"

Rose doesn't reply, but he can hear a heart-wrenching sound escape her, mournful and pained.

"Rose? Did someone hurt you? Please tell me what happened. What can I do?" he begs.

"I—" She hiccups, clearing her throat before stumbling through the words. "I got a call today. From an attorney. He—my—" She breaks off, devolving into sobs.

"Can you...baby, can you just let me in so I can hold you?"

"You touching me right now would make it worse," she whispers honestly, and he can picture her curled up on the floor on the other side of the thin plank of wood.

"Okay." He swallows heavily, clueless as to how to handle the situation. His fists clench at his frustration, his inability to do anything useful. His inability to *help* her when she's drowning like this.

He sits down, pressing his hands to the door as though she can see them, can tell he's there for as best as he can be.

Josh hears her suck in a deep breath before attempting to continue. "Scar's...my mother's friend. The one who..."

His blood boils, his fists clench. The mention of the man he would happily take the prison time for murdering already has him livid, and he now knows the conversation is only going to get worse.

"He did it to other girls. They came forward; they're taking him to court. It was his attorney that called me." Rose releases a bitter laugh, so hopeless and betrayed and unsurprised all at once that it fucking *kills* him. "They expect me to testify as a character witness. To talk about how I couldn't *imagine* a better man—a better family friend, uncle in everything but blood. How he's such an upstanding fucking citizen."

"Are you kidding me right now? This actually happened?" Josh demands. Scar begins whimpering in the other room, not happy to be alone and probably growing scared of the angry voices, and Josh calls out to her. "We'll be right back, sweetheart! You're okay."

Attempting to use a pleasant tone in this moment is one of the most difficult things he's ever done.

On the other side of the door, he can hear Rose crying desperately.

"Josh, I...I have no idea what to do. Those girls deserve their justice, and I want them to have it—me testifying on their side could be a game-changer. But I don't know if I can do it. Being in the same *room* as him...or having to use Scar as evidence? I can't risk him knowing about her. *God.*

"And I—" A shuddering breath escapes her. "I came home today, and I came straight in here because I don't think I can look at Scar right now—her eyes, I mean. They're the same. They're *his* eyes. And I *love* them on her; I love her more than I could ever love anything else in this world, and I will never let the way she was conceived affect anything about the way I love her. But right now, I just...I think seeing her eyes will kill me," Rose confesses. "What kind of mother am I? How can I—how can I live with myself if my daughter grows up thinking I might not love her when I can't look her in the eye sometimes? Do I even deserve to be a mother?"

"Rosie," Josh begins, attempting to calm his temper long enough to soothe her when really, he wants to go ram his fist into a brick wall. "Baby, you are a *wonderful* mother. I know that's hard for you to accept—I know it's something you worry about a lot—but I promise you that Scarlett is a happy, healthy, safe baby, who could not be in better hands, and she knows it. That's why her whole face lights up when you walk into the room. She knows that if you're there, everything is going to be as good as it possibly could be.

"And I'm so sorry that she has to share genes with that monster. But baby, she's only been here for a matter of months, you know? You've had years of nothing but suffering and violation associated with those eyes, and even though Scar is the best thing on this planet, it makes sense that it would take a while for her to reverse that instinct, the way you associate her eyes. You're not a bad mom for that; you're human, Rosie. You've been through a lot, and you're still healing.

"The trial...I don't think there's a right answer there. You have to figure out what's best for you and what's best for Scar—what you can live with going forward. Hell, I can't imagine trying to decide what to do, baby; you just need to take some time for yourself, to really let yourself think about it."

"You're right," she says in a small voice. "I just don't...it brings back so many bad memories. And this, everything, was part of my life for so long; it changed who I am before I even figured out who I was. I don't know if I'll ever find the person I would've been—or the person I am. I never really got the chance to grieve her, to process what I was going through, and it's just crashing down on me right now. On top of everything else. And the fact that my *mother* is the one orchestrating this. I—I shouldn't be surprised by it anymore, you know? She's always picked him over me. But I still hope. I still catch myself wishing she would decide she actually cares about me."

Josh nods, mentally groaning when he remembers that she can't see him, but he presses a palm to the door anyway. "I'm sorry, baby. I don't think there are any words, anything I can say that could ever help. You deserve so much more. In every way."

This—the fact that a mother could stand by and let this happen to her *child*...it's the kind of thing that makes him lose faith in humanity.

"You've made it this far because you are so *strong*, and you shouldn't have to put that to the test anymore. You shouldn't have to go through more trauma for the sake of growing even stronger, but I know you will. The world is trying to drag you down, but you are so much more than any of the shit you've been through." He lets her take that in for a moment. "I love you. And Scar loves you. Whatever happens...you will always have us."

She doesn't respond, but then he hears the tell-tale click of the lock being undone, and he quickly opens the door, hesitating before she gives him a shallow nod of permission. He steps forward to wrap her in a hug, lips against her dark curls. "You're a badass, Rosie. We're gonna make it through this. All three of us."

She's still not okay. She won't be for a while.

But having someone to hold her while she cries, while she attempts to scramble together some semblance of sanity as she goes to lift her daughter apologetically, while she tries to make the hardest decision she's ever made...it helps.

(Not enough, but it's more than she's ever had on her team when facing her monster before.)

19

She's fifteen, at dinner at the only fancy restaurant nearby with her mother and several of her mother's friends—a local business owner, a lawyer, a hairstylist.

They're familiar faces Rose has seen a million times before, self-centered conversations she's heard so often she could recite them in her sleep.

She distracts herself by aimlessly folding and unfolding the napkin in her lap, counting the number of sips in a glass of water, focusing on the French music trickling out of the restaurant's speakers.

Loretta's wrapping up a story about her husband, and then Sadie jumps in.

"Did you see about that tennis coach in the news? How horrible." She shakes her head, taking another sip of wine. "And to think we almost let our Robbie join the team—he could've been one of them!"

Rose's blood runs cold, chest tightening in the worst way.

"My friend Sharice's son is actually the first one who spoke up," Paula confides; she's grinning as she says it, not sorry for the boy's suffering but gleeful for the social capital.

It doesn't surprise Rose, the callous way her mother's friend mentions something so awful, the way these women make anything about themselves.

(She knows all too well how easily they'll silently enable the monsters that hide amongst them.)

"It's just horrible." *Cheyenne nods in agreement, pressing a hand to her chest.* "All these years, the whole community has trusted him with their kids at their youngest, and all the while, he was doing something so sinful."

Rose forces herself to tune out and drinks heavily from her second glass, this one full of sweet tea, to try to distract herself.

To keep from screaming.

It's so in character, so typical of her mother to bemoan the very atrocity that takes place in her own home.

It's not the first time she's seen Cheyenne pretend as though it's a wrong she cares about.

And of course, this is the only context in which these women pretend to care. If it weren't children involved, they wouldn't be victims. They'd be asking for it or lying because 'women can accuse you of anything these days.'

(It's enough to make her stomach churn. Fists clench.)

"And that restaurant they busted last year!" *Loretta chimes in, earning nods from the rest.* "Human trafficking, in our own county!"

The women keep talking about it—mention how terrible it is, how messed up the kids must all be, how unbelievable it all is.

And Rose dissociates because there's something so incredibly dehumanizing about it. Something that fucks with your head, hearing that what you've been through is worse than anything others can imagine, hearing them speak about it like it's the kind of thing that doesn't happen to 'people like them.'

Something about your worst moments being dinnertime gossip.

Your own memories spoken of as so far away, they're almost unreal.

When your violation is another's storytime, your nightmares things they'll cluelessly throw in your face without any idea of your own suffering...

(It's enough to make anyone go mad.)

It's been three days since the call, and Rose has been on edge and in a dark place ever since.

He could be lurking around any corner. Cheyenne could be here. Both.

It's only a matter of time.

Rose forces herself out of the apartment, not letting Scar out of sight for a moment, body thrumming with anxiety. By the time she gets to the youth center, her heart rate is rapid enough that she can feel it in her chest, and she's feeling lightheaded.

The place is mostly even more deserted than usual; even Imani isn't here. Will nods to her as she enters, but she doesn't have the energy to strike up a conversation.

She makes her way to Evan, and his eyebrows jump up at the sight of her.

"Rose! I didn't know you were coming. What's up?" He reaches to take Scar from her carrier, holding her close, and then looks at her—*really* looks at her. "Is everything okay?"

"Honestly?" she says, voice a raspy whisper. "No."

Evan immediately heads towards his office, closes the door, and pulls her to the cushy couch next to his desk, a soothing hand on her shoulder that she unconsciously shoves off. "What's going on?"

"I—I'm sorry to just show up here like this. I just...I don't know what to do, and I know Josh loves me, and it's not his fault, but I just feel really alone right now. I don't know what the right thing to do is, and I feel like I'm going to disappoint everyone." She sucks in a rattling breath, eyes beginning to tear up and body beginning to tremble.

Evan's frowning, heart so visibly on his sleeve. "Rose, we're *family*. Being here for you is never a burden. You'd kill me if I tried that shit when I was struggling. So, tell me what the hell is going on and whose ass I have to kick."

"He's going to trial," she breathes, not bothering to specify who, knowing Evan, of all people, will know. Will *get* it. "Two others are pressing charges. I got a call from the attorney Cheyenne hired. She wants me to testify as a character witness."

Evan's eyes burn with anger and hatred, the knuckles of his free hand white. "You're fucking kidding me."

"Yeah. I mean, *that's* obviously not happening, but...I don't..." She closes her eyes and shakes her head, swallowing heavily. "I don't know what to do. Because I could testify against him, you know? I *want* him locked up; I want him off the streets, not able to hurt any more of us."

(*Not able to make another person feel like their body isn't their own.*)

"And I feel like I owe it to these girls. I know, I didn't hurt them, and I didn't do anything wrong, but...if I can help them lock him up, I should. But I also...I so, so don't want to see him. Don't want to be near him. Don't want him to know *anything* about my existence.

"And if he finds out about Scarlett...if he's not convicted, or he gets a short sentence and then gets out and comes after us or goes for any form of custody..." She practically convulses at the prospect.

Evan nods. "You're between a rock and a hard place."

"I know my testimony would strengthen the case; I have *years* of diary entries I jammed under my mattress all along. And while I don't want to use Scar as evidence...a paternity test would be solid proof that *something* happened. While I was a minor." She leans her head against the back of the couch. "But I don't know if I can bear it. Being in the courtroom with him, telling strangers everything he did to me...and if they find him not guilty?" Her voice rises three octaves. "My own mother not caring was one of the most painful things I've ever gone through. If the justice system does the same..."

She begins to break down into sobs.

"Listen. If you want to testify, then you should. We will support you. Bronte and I will testify too—about how you were when she met you, everything about when the two of you ran away, when we met, about when you told Bronte then, about going to CPS to try to stop you from having to go back to it. All of it—anything and everything we need to disclose. If this is what you want, we will do *anything* it takes. No questions asked." He locks eyes with her, so she knows he's serious before continuing. "But honestly, Rose? It sounds more like you're scared to not testify. And more than anything, I need you to understand: it's *okay* to not."

Her eyebrows press together, and she bites her lip with uncertainty, so he powers through.

"You don't owe *anything* to *anyone*. And yes, your testimony would strengthen the case, but fuck that. It's *yours*. It's your life, your trauma, and you don't have to tell it to anyone—*especially* if you think it will jeopardize your daughter's well-being.

"But even if Scar weren't in the picture, what that bastard did to you is no one's business unless you want it to be. And there is *nothing* wrong with you not wanting to bring it to court. He terrorized you for years, Rose, and you survived that, fought your way through it. There is *no* fucking shame in not wanting to put yourself back there.

"You have every right to not testify, and that's not any less right. There is nothing wrong with putting yourself and your mental health and your goddamn comfort first, kid, and fuck anyone who says anything different. The *only* reason you should testify is if you want to."

"Are you sure?" she whispers, not meeting his eyes.

"I am. And I'm not saying that because I think you shouldn't testify but because...if you do, it shouldn't be because you don't feel like you have a choice. Enough choices have been taken away from you. If you decide to testify...that should be all you. Because it's what's best for *you*."

Rose slides her head down onto his shoulder. "Love you."

"Love you too, kid. Family. Always."

———

"You're lucky to be *alive*, Aunt Kathy. Staying there isn't an option anymore!"

Rose pales as she approaches Josh's apartment a few hours later and hears his words through the wood of the door, the fear in his voice palpable. She enters quietly, dropping Scar's empty carrier immediately and carrying her daughter across the apartment to the tense kitchen, footsteps soft with hopes of not intruding.

"Rose!" Kathy exclaims, her face lighting up.

Her eyes remain filled with worry.

"Hi, Kathy. It's so good to see you."

The older woman pulls her into a hug, pressing a kiss to the top of Scar's head without hesitation.

Kathy opens her arms in question, and Rose hands Scar over. "It's good to see you too, sweetheart. And if Josh gets his way, you'll be seeing a lot more of me."

Josh scowls, hackles still raised, but he slides an arm around Rose, and a bit of the tension seeps out of his body. "Hi, Rosie. How was your day?"

"It was…good," Rose says hesitantly. "I went over to the center and talked to Evan about…everything. I feel a lot better about it."

"It's so good that you have him," Kathy simpers, rocking a babbling Scar in her arms. "I always wished Desiree or I had an older brother. Figured as long as one of us had one, we would share. I always wished for one to help me through life—protect me from the world, and all that."

"Why would it matter when you don't want to let anyone actually *do* anything to protect you!" Josh snaps. He shoots Rose an apologetic glance when she jumps at his raised voice, pressing a soft kiss to her shoulder. "Aunt Kathy, please, just move in here. Kai and Zeke both want you to, and you know we need to acknowledge the gravity of the situation.."

Kathy smiles at him sadly. "Honey, I appreciate the offer, and I love that you care so much, but I don't think it's a good idea. With you is the first place he would look for me. And besides, I don't want to stop living my life out of fear. If I do, is it really a life worth living at all?"

"*YES!*" Josh shouts, looking more upset than Rose has ever seen him. "Jesus fucking Christ, Aunt Kathy, I know the movies make it out like it's so noble and brave to not let your aggressor change your habits or the way you live your life, but it's not! It's not courageous or right or any of that bullshit; it's just *stupid*! He broke into your apartment; he left death threats at your workplace. Staying isn't just reckless, it's practically suicide! You know he wouldn't hesitate to if given a chance, and he's already proven that you're not safe where you are."

Rose's eyes widen, and she turns to Kathy. "Josh is right, Kathy; it's not worth putting yourself back in that situation. I can get you a job here at Metro or the little cafe I was at part-time too before I turned eighteen. The pay might not be what you're used to, but it's something."

"Even so, Josh, he'll come here first."

They talk it through, and eventually, Josh convinces her that here is the best place for her to be. Geoffrey's going to come after him anyway, and at least this way, there's strength in numbers.

"Did you file a report?" Rose eventually asks, frowning with worry. She knows reporting is almost never helpful but that the documentation will be what everyone points to later on.

Kathy snorts. "Yes. As if it'll make a difference. The legal system wasn't made for people like us."

She's not wrong.

20

It's the middle of the afternoon, and eleven-year-old Rose crumbles in the passenger seat of the car.

"I'm sorry, sweetheart, but you know he doesn't mean anything by it." Mom gives her a half-hearted smile. "Sometimes people have bad habits, but you love them anyway. Like Jesus. Everything else in your life is good, isn't it? We can move past this."

Cheyenne says it easily, as though her reaction—the lack thereof—is no big deal. She puts the car into drive without hesitation.

(As though she hasn't just shattered every bit of good Rose was still capable of believing in.)

She's been bracing herself for this for weeks—planned the exact words she would use, timed it knowing he's out of town till Friday.

But now, her entire chest is moving with the force of how rapidly her heart pumps. She can't hear anything outside of herself, wouldn't notice if a tree fell down right beside her at the moment.

"But—Mom, I—" Rose chokes, has to take a deep breath before continuing. "I don't think this is okay. I don't—I don't want to be around him anymore. Or see him. Anything."

Her mom's mouth contorts into a disappointed frown. "Rose Elizabeth, *he is as much a part of this family as you are. How could you say something so awful? I won't choose between the two of you."*

Rose swallows, blinking tears back rapidly.

When she doesn't respond, Mom sighs. "Well, that's enough of the heavy. How was practice, honey? There are some of those crackers you like in the glove compartment."

She hands her daughter a water bottle with a smile like it's any other day—like she cares, like she's a loving mother, like she does all the right things.

And the kicker is that she does, in plenty of ways—checks all the boxes of what a mother 'should' do, goes out of her way to meet the socially understood definition of a good parent. Which has always been frustrating and so far from what Rose actually needs, but believable, at least.

But this is the one time Rose has ever needed her—the one time she's needed her comfort, her defense, her love.

Rose knows her mom genuinely considers herself a good mom, genuinely believes she's doing what's best for her daughter. It's both heartbreaking and comical, all at once.

Her mom keeps prattling on about her day, updates Rose on work and their plans for the weekend. It makes her want to scream. This woman is supposed to be her mother, and she doesn't care that someone's hurting Rose? Thinks she's capable of caring about something as fucking unimportant as an annoying coworker when she's not even safe inside herself?

"I can't do this," she whispers to herself.

She says it so softly, Mom doesn't notice. But it means something—it's an admission, to herself, that she can't be in this life knowing her mom isn't on her side.

(Can't keep going through this, can't live in this place that's not a home, where what should be her refuge is the source of the worst kind of pain.)

She has to leave, has to find somewhere else.

Anywhere but here.

———

Rose lets herself into her apartment briskly, walking into the kitchenette without a second glance.

So her entire body jolts when someone clears their throat from their seat on the futon.

"You know, Rose, I really *do* wish I could rid myself of you."

Her heart stops. *No.*

No, no, no.

Rose turns around slowly, unable to breathe at the sight of Cheyenne cocking an eyebrow at her.

Here.

Inside her apartment—the one place she's ever been safe.

Rose clenches her fists, trying not to let the horror show through. "How did you get in here?"

"Oh, the landlord was only too happy to let in a mother surprising her daughter with a visit from out of state." Her mother smirks, crossing her legs. "That's how we figured out where you were in the first place. Clever of you, leaving so many brochures throughout your room and letting us think you'd go to an uppity school. A piece of mail came for you, though, and the ruse was up."

"That's impossible. I redirected all of my mail, changed my address, opted for email—nothing from the school should've come." She's surprised she manages to get the words out.

(*Cheyenne. Mom. **Here.***)

"Well, apparently, someone messed up. And when a stressed mother called to make sure her daughter's address was updated, the registrar was only too happy that the address they had on file—which they were kind enough to read aloud—was the correct one, so the frantic woman would get off the phone. How else did you think our attorney managed to get ahold of you?"

Of course—because her mother is charismatic and knows all the right things to say, believes the lies she tells so thoroughly she can convince anyone.

"Ingenious," Rose replies sarcastically. There's no room to be angry at the school or mad at the invasion of privacy, just pure terror at her mother's presence. At wondering if he's here, too. Her heart races, her entire body shakes. She feels faint and on fire all at once, and the fear is visceral. "What do you want, Cheyenne? Why the hell are you here?"

You're free, she reminds herself. *She doesn't control you anymore.*

(It doesn't feel like it.)

"Seeing as you spoke with the attorney three days ago, you know exactly what I want, sweetheart. You need to come testify for Kyle."

Revulsion slides through her body at the sound of his name. Most of the time, she tries to avoid even thinking it, so this...God, this is her nightmare.

"Why the fuck would I ever testify for him?"

"Because you owe it to me," Cheyenne says without hesitation, raising an eyebrow like this is obvious. "You've always been so ungrateful, Rose; I birthed you, I clothed and fed you for a decade and a half, kept a roof over your head, and the one time I need something you have the *audacity*—"

"You think I should be grateful?" Rose demands. "You tormented me, stood by and watched me suffer and want to die, let your friend–" She presses a hand to her mouth, unable to say the words. "How dare you? How dare you ever say that I owe you anything when you enabled my suffering—when you let me be *used* from the time I was a *child*."

"There's no need to be so melodramatic." Cheyenne rolls her eyes. "Of course, you're making me out to be the bad guy. Say what you like, but you always had everything you needed. Besides, honey, I looked around this apartment. I mean, I know you've always been a little promiscuous for obvious reasons, but really, a child so soon? I'm surprised at you. How can you claim things were so bad when as soon as you left, you picked up right where you left off, whoring around?"

All of the blood rushes out of her body because *Cheyenne can't know about Scar.*

Somehow, her mother hasn't put the pieces together, has assumed Scar was conceived after she moved to Florida.

It *needs* to stay that way.

The reminder is all it takes to eliminate anything else from her body—the anger, the outrage, the hurt, none of it matters; there is nothing but keeping Scar safe. All that matters is getting her mother to leave before she figures it out.

"Cheyenne, whatever the case, there is nothing you can do to make me—"

"Hey, babe, everything okay?" Josh's voice is careful as he enters the apartment. He looks around and freezes at the sight of the unfamiliar face, at his girlfriend pale with a clenched jaw.

He moves to her side, arm around her back as though he can lend her his strength. "Sorry, I don't mean to interrupt. You were just gone for a while, and I wanted to make sure you were alright."

"Who is *this*?" Cheyenne exclaims, putting on a dazzling smile for his benefit. "He's not baby daddy, is he? You're awful handsome to be palling around with Ro, here."

Rose flinches at the nickname, and it's this, this visceral reaction and the ease with which the woman speaks that make it click for him.

"You're Cheyenne," he says—not a question.

"Oh, so you've heard of me! Wonderful. And you are?"

"Not interested in speaking to you," he says, tone cold. "You should leave. Now. Before I call the police to escort you out."

"Young man, that's no way to speak to a lady," Cheyenne reprimands him. "Whatever Rose has told you, I can assure you, is an exaggeration. She's always been one to play the victim, as much as I tried to teach her otherwise."

The door opens again, and though Rose had thought the situation couldn't get any worse, it does: Kathy walks in with a screeching Scarlett.

(Scar and Cheyenne. In the same room.)

"Sorry, sweetheart, I can't get her to calm down; I think she just wants Mama," Kathy tells Rose apologetically, handing Scar over.

Rose shushes her quietly without looking at Cheyenne, focused on Scar. She's all that matters.

(All that has ever mattered.)

"Ah, is this your bastard?" Cheyenne asks, and Rose watches Kathy recoil out of the corner of her eye.

The kicker is she doesn't even mean it as an insult—just literally, because of *course*, out of everything that's happened between them, the part she has a problem with is Rose having a child out of wedlock.

"Get the fuck out and never speak a word about her again, you piece of shit excuse for a mother." Josh's voice is low and almost terrifying, but Cheyenne doesn't react.

Just leave, please just leave, Rose begs in her mind.

"I'm not going anywhere until Rose agrees to be a character witness—and I doubt you could find an officer to arrest me. My reputation is pristine."

Rose sees it almost in slow motion, this moment that changes everything. This moment that alters her future irrevocably.

"Then *I* will remove you, you bitch," Josh says, beginning to shout.

Josh is Scar's favorite person; she's never heard him upset. So when she hears the man's voice raised, she turns her little head to look at him in confusion.

Turns to where Josh stands inches from Cheyenne.

The movement draws both of their attention to her, wide-eyed in Rose's arms. Cheyenne sees her for the first time. Sees her eyes.

(Kyle's eyes.)

"Oh, my," Cheyenne says, brows rising upward, lips curving all too happily. "Isn't that interesting?"

———

"Testify for Kyle, or he'll file for custody of the baby."

Cheyenne's next words, spoken through an unapologetic smile—vindicated, that things went her way.

(Rose can't get them out of her head and has *no idea* what to do.)

It's an impossible catch-22 that's only gotten worse.

"You know exactly how it will go, darling. He's an upstanding member of the community, impeccable record, reliable income. You're barely an adult yourself, with a history of instability. Running away from home when you were eleven, really? And now, raising a child in this hovel on a diner salary?" Cheyenne clucks her tongue, and Rose can feel all the fight inside her dying out.

Is it a choice, really? He'll get at *least* partial custody, even in her best-case scenario, and even that is too much. Any time with him is time Scar isn't safe. Rose will die before she allows her daughter to go through what she did.

He can't be allowed near Scar. Ever.

And the thing is, Rose knows she has no leg to stand on. The North Carolina age of consent is sixteen, and they'll never believe her up against someone like Kyle. They wouldn't care or convict him even if they did. It'll all be viewed as legal; he'll get her daughter on the weekends.

(She'd looked into it all before. She knows how this story ends.)

Letting Scar into his and Cheyenne's grasp, allowing her to endure what Rose did, Scar *not being with her*...it's unfathomable.

But to testify that Kyle isn't capable of assault, after so many years of violation at his hands, to help to put him back on the streets and hurt others the way he hurt her...

There's no right answer. Neither option is okay.

Josh looks to Rose to see how she wants to handle this; when she doesn't respond, he steps between her and Cheyenne, his entire body quaking with anger. "Leave. Now. Or I call the police on you for trespassing, and that impeccable record goes out the window."

Josh's tone is darker than Rose has ever heard it. She feels herself shrink instinctively, even as he does it for her defense.

Cheyenne smiles, unfazed. "Oh, don't worry, I'm on my way out. Flight to catch after all. Rose, honey, I'll see you at eight a.m. sharp Tuesday morning a week from now. Our attorney will need to coach you before you take the stand."

She slinks through the door without further ado.

Rose slides down the wall till she hits the ground, holding onto Scar tightly—probably too tightly. Scar wiggles in her arms, waiting for her to kiss her, speak to her; Rose knows her daughter is confused at her silence.

"I'm so sorry, honey. This is all my fault," Kathy apologizes gently, sounding devastated. "I should've sensed something was off and walked right back out with Scar."

"It's not your fault that Cheyenne and her piece of shit friend belong in hell, Aunt Kathy," Josh says with a scowl, ignoring her half-hearted reproachful look. "Fuck. I should've started recording audio the second I knew it was her. If we could have evidence of her black-mailing you..."

Rose tunes out as the two of them go back and forth, bemoaning the situation and brainstorming ways for Rose to get out of the predicament, but she can't bring herself to chime in, to tell them both it's not their fault.

Of course it isn't. They've never done anything but love her. They're the first since Bronte and Evan to do so.

Rose is out of the apartment before she can really register that she's moving; it's lucky it's not too cold, she realizes, as she hadn't even considered putting a jacket on Scar.

Her keys are in her pocket, but she doesn't want to be in the car right now—doesn't want to have that kind of power, that kind of potential to destroy other people's lives if she gets distracted.

(She already *has* too much potential to destroy other people's lives, come the trial.)

She wanders aimlessly down side streets, her feet rapidly hitting the sidewalk. Passerby move at the sight of her, the shattered look in her eyes.

Her nightmare since the day she found out about Scarlett's existence has been Kyle knowing. Having to go to court to argue that the monster who ended her first baby's life before it even began shouldn't be allowed near her second—near the one she'd managed to keep from him for so long.

She was so *careful*.

And yet, the horror has come to life.

It begins to rain, of course, because what would her life be if not dramatic?

At first, she continues to walk, but the sheets of icy water come down harder and harder, so she ducks inside the first café she sees, Scar tucked inside her now-drenched cardigan in hopes that the proximity to her body heat will keep her warm.

She looks into her daughter's wide eyes—her precious, inquisitive eyes. The little face she loves more than anything in the world.

Rose hates herself for considering it, hates what her testimony for Kyle might mean for other women. The concept of character witnesses for rapists makes her so fucking angry in general, and now she might serve as one? Might serve as the piece of evidence that stops other women from getting their justice, if there is any in this world?

Scar begins to babble again, and tears drip down Rose's face.

Because she hates the idea of it. Might vomit at the thought of taking the stand and saying the things Cheyenne wants her to.

Of seeing Kyle's other victims and hearing her own voice say there's no way he could've done that to them—that they're *lying.* Jesus, it hurts viscerally to consider.

But she loves Scar.

So she makes two calls.

The first is to Liza.

By the time they hang up, she feels completely empty. Hollow. She dials Bronte's number, and her would-be older sister answers on the first ring.

"Josh called already. Tell me where you are, and I'll come pick you up."

Rose lets out a sob. "Café on Fowler. Don't tell the others yet."

"You're the only one I care about, kiddo. I'm grabbing the car seat from the van, and then I'll be there to get you two, okay?"

The way Bronte does this—knows exactly what she needs, gives it to her without question...it's *everything.*

"And Bronte?" There's a pause on both ends of the line. "I need a favor."

21

JOSH IS PACING MADLY when Rose comes home late that night, crazy worried despite the text from Bronte five hours earlier that read, *'I've got them—will bring them home when she's feeling better.'*

And that was it. All he had to go on regarding Rose and Scar's well-being for the whole day.

He's starting to think he might go insane when she finally walks in at almost midnight.

"Rose, thank *God*."

He notes her puffy eyes, messy hair, the imprint of the seam of Scar's car seat left on the baby's cheek before pulling them both to him in a desperate hug.

"Sorry if you were worried," she says timidly. "I just needed... some time away."

"That's...whatever you need," he reassures her. "Just, after what happened, I—I don't know. It doesn't matter. Are you feeling better?"

"A little bit. I—I think I know what I'm going to do." She closes her eyes in anguish but lets out a deep breath. "Thank you for still being here."

"I'm not going anywhere," Josh promises. He starts to say more but is interrupted by a knock on the door that makes them both jump. "What the hell?"

"It's probably Liza," Rose tells him, looking through the peephole briefly before letting the other woman in. "Thank you for getting this so quickly."

"Of course—I know the sooner, the better. If you have any questions or need any help with it before you go to file, let me know, okay?" Liza checks, handing her a manila folder.

Rose squeezes Liza's hand while accepting the paperwork. "I will. Really, thank you—you have no idea how much this means to me."

"I hope it works out."

They lock eyes; it's clearly meaningful in a way Josh doesn't really understand.

"What—" Josh begins to inquire as to what the hell is going on, but his phone starts to buzz, and he presses it to his ear with confusion. The caller not in his contacts, but it's a local area code. "Hello?"

"Joshua Brooks?" asks an unfamiliar but gentle male voice.

"This is he. Can I ask who's calling?"

"My name is Ahmed, sir; I work in registration at Tampa General Hospital. You're listed as the emergency contact for Katherine Wilson."

The world wobbles beneath his feet, and he feels his stomach twist.

She'd only left to stop by her place a couple hours ago, and yet some sixth sense inside him writhes with the *knowing* that something terrible has happened—something that changes things.

His nightmare come true.

"What happened to my godmother? Is she okay? What room is she in?" he fires off in rapid succession.

"Your godmother was attacked, Mr. Brooks; she's currently in surgery. If you can come to the Emergency Room, we can give you further information as well as get some more of her paperwork completed."

"I'll be there as soon as I can," Josh whispers.

He hangs up and spins around to look at Rose and Liza, everything inside him numb. "Aunt Kathy...she's in the hospital. I have to—have to go." His knuckles are white with how tightly he grips his keys.

"Joshua, breathe," Rose says, spine immediately straightening. "You shouldn't be behind the wheel right now. Put on your shoes, grab a change of clothes in case you're there for a while, and I'll drive you, okay?"

"Shoes...right...okay...five minutes," he confirms, a hand tugging at the shorn-tight curls of his hair. "Okay. I'm gonna go grab stuff from upstairs—be right back."

The second he and Liza are both out the door, Rose sucks in a deep breath before pulling out a duffel bag and shoving in outfits, toys for Scar, the whole nine yards. She has no idea how long it'll take, so she overdoes it, finding it easier to focus on packing than thinking about why she has to go.

By the time Josh rushes back in, the bag is slung over her shoulder, and she squeezes his arm reassuringly as they walk down to the car, footsteps loud against the wet pavement.

He has a panic attack on the way to the hospital.

As they sit in the waiting room for hours, Josh prays for the first time in years, willing to do anything, beg anyone, if only he doesn't hear the worst.

———

Eventually, a doctor comes out and tells them Kathy's going to make it. That she's stable.

But things are not good.

Josh relaxes, though, after hearing from the doctor. He's finally able to fall asleep, drooling in the chair beside Rose, as she bounces Scar in her lap, too riddled with anxiety and adrenaline to even remember what being tired feels like.

She hates herself for it as she gets up, pressing a kiss to Josh's forehead. Leaves a note next to him, full of regret.

(*I love you. I'm sorry. Let me know how she is when you wake up. I'll keep you updated. Tell Kathy I love her.*)

She texts Bronte to tell her she's on the way, calling into work as she drives to give Marnie a heads up that she won't be in the next few days, that she's so sorry.

Family emergency, she tells her.

By the time Rose picks up Bronte with puffy eyes, she's drained of tears, mentally bracing herself before starting the long drive.

Her mind is hell. She doesn't know if she's doing the right thing, doesn't know if there *is* a right thing.

(Doesn't feel like it.)

But she keeps driving down the interstate, eyes flashing to the rearview mirror to look at Scarlett.

A mother is a protector.

She has to do whatever it takes to keep her safe.

(How could she live with herself any other way?)

22

ROSE DROPS Bronte and Scar off at a hotel, a Best Western right off the highway, where she has to pay an extra fee to get them to let them check in so early.

The tears probably help, too, but those are unintentional. They come from being so emotionally haywire, so overwhelmed and anxiety-ridden that she feels both drunk and as though she's had an entire pot of coffee.

She doesn't bother to sleep herself despite having driven all night. She knows it wouldn't do any good. Instead, she goes straight to the courthouse; Cheyenne had told her to be there Tuesday, but the public record Rose looked up confirmed the trial started late the week before, and she thinks a day of being just a bystander might do her some good.

Might keep the day from making her implode.

Hair in a messy bun and sunglasses obscuring her face, she takes a deep breath before pushing open one of the doors, nauseous and already full of regret and self-hatred.

(*Am I doing the right thing?*)

The second she's inside the room, she can't breathe, and she's hit with the realization that she has to choose which side of the room to sit on. She's not even on the stand, and yet the pressure is on.

It's largely full, faces familiar and not milling about and chatting. Odds are Cheyenne might not spot her amidst the crowd.

But if she does...if she's caught sitting on the prosecution's side of the room...

No.

She might have to sell her soul and testify on the bastard's behalf, but she can have this one, small rebellion.

She sits near the back, jacket on, arms crossed, and by all accounts radiating '*stay away.*' It's all she can do to hold herself together—knowing Cheyenne is here, knowing *he* is here. She thinks if she opens her mouth, she won't be able to stop a scream from coming out.

Then it happens. She knew it was coming, she braced herself for it the whole drive, and yet it still surges through her body like poison.

He's here. Her monster, in the same room as her. The awareness is a punch to the gut, the golden blonde of his hair triggering a primal fear within her.

It's been so long, the memories fly through her mind all at once. The fear, shame, and pain fresh as ever. She tunes out most of the proceedings; it's a lot of nonsense and official business, statements from either side. Technical questions. Recitations from the police report, recaps of the testimonies so far.

None of it matters with her fight or flight instincts fired up. She can't think about anything but the fact that he's *here*. It doesn't make any sense; she knew he would be here. Has been forced to be in his presence a thousand times before.

Why is it affecting her so badly?

He's not taking the stand yet—if he is at all. Though he's a skilled enough pedagogue that she can't imagine the defense not using his charm to their advantage.

Rose sees *them*, too—the others like her. Two of them, sitting together with the prosecution attorney, jaws tight and bodies stiff.

(She knows the feeling.)

Seeing them, knowing their suffering firsthand, and knowing what she's about to do tomorrow...it's a different kind of pain.

She's so lost in thought that she doesn't notice him taking the steps, placing his hand on the Bible. Instead, she feels her eyes go wide when his voice reverberates through the courtroom.

He's on the stand, giving the crowd he's drawn a winning smile. Delicate, slightly harried, and tired.

Human.

He's trying to convince them he's human.

Because surely, no one so human, so relatable, could do something so awful.

She's frozen the entire time he's speaking. Part of her wants to run, to be anywhere but here, but mainly the idea of trying to move is laughable. She can't even *breathe*, let alone convince her legs to function.

(That *voice*.)

The words he's saying don't matter, although she can guess; she knows him better than she's ever known anyone. Figuring him out, learning his tics, what would provoke him and what wouldn't...it had been a vital skill to pick up years ago.

He's talking about how he could never hurt a fly, the pro-bono work he's done in the community, the glowing references from everyone who's ever met him. How he's so worried for these *misguided* young women. How he hopes they get help and is sorry that defamation of his character is what they think will help them.

She knows. She's heard it all before.

It's the same bullshit he and Cheyenne spewed when CPS came around after she ran away so long ago.

And she just *knows*—knows he's not even worried. That he assumes a not guilty verdict is a given, that he's getting a full night's rest every night, that somewhere in the community, there's probably a fund being raised to *help an innocent man shoulder court fees*.

A fund, a movement, made by people who assume a man can't

wear two faces. That because their interactions with him have only ever been positive, anyone else *must* be lying.

They have no fucking idea what he's really like.

Eventually, recess is called, and Rose is immediately up and out of the room. She finds herself in the bathroom, splashing water on her face and attempting to take deep breaths.

They're coming rapidly and far too shallow. She's pale as a sheet.

"You okay? You look about how I feel."

Her head jerks up as the other person speaks, and she makes eye contact with a seemingly friendly but exhausted woman, probably around her age if not a bit older.

"I—I'm fine, thank you. I drove up from Florida this morning, so...it's just been a long day," Rose says, trying to give a small smile.

"You're telling me." The other woman nods in sympathy. "We knew going in that this would be hard, but..." She sighs, rubbing at her eyes. "I'm just glad our lawyer got the heads up that he would be testifying today. Without warning, it would've been so much worse, and he hasn't even talked about...well, anyway." She blushes like she's said too much.

With a jolt, Rose realizes this is one of the women pressing charges.

(One of the women she's about to betray.)

"I'm so sorry," she says softly, wishing she could pour every bit of energy into the three small words.

The other woman shrugs as if to say, *what can you do?* and gives a sad smile.

Before Rose can say something else—*anything* else—the door swings open, and her stomach drops.

"Rose, darling, so glad you could make it—and early, too." Cheyenne's words are light and airy, the smile on her face unsurprised as she turns to the blonde. "Casey, I see you've met our newest witness; it's too bad, really. I think in other circumstances, the two of you might've been friends."

Revulsion floods Casey's face, and though their interaction was momentary, Rose would swear she can see the hurt on the other woman's face.

"I didn't realize."

"I—" Rose opens her mouth to explain, somehow, but the glare Cheyenne sends her is a vivid threat.

For Scar.

"Yes," Cheyenne says, "It was so sweet of her to come back home to testify on Kyle's behalf. But then, kindness begets kindness, don't you think? And he's always been like family to her."

At the sound of Kyle's name, Rose and Casey both flinch. Just barely, but it's there.

Cheyenne continues talking, but neither of them is paying attention anymore; Casey eyes Rose suspiciously.

"Shouldn't we g-go back in?" Rose stammers, and without looking at the other two, she practically trips over herself, leaving the bathroom that suddenly feels far, far too small.

———

The trial goes on. Rose hasn't had the time to look up the specifics of the case—a lie she tells herself; she could've made the time, but she couldn't bring herself to face the facts of the traumas she still blames herself for—so she learns them now. Kyle's defense claims his liaisons with both women were consensual; only one had a rape kit performed, which his attorney claims was rooted in regret and shame after their interaction, wherein the alleged victim couldn't acknowledge her own actions and instead chose to blame someone else.

It's a mentally and emotionally draining session, and by the time the court lets out for the day, Rose is severely over-caffeinated but still dead on her feet.

She waits outside during the mass exodus, pretending to be occupied with her phone as chattering members of the public leave the room.

Though big for their small town, the case isn't high-profile enough to draw much media presence, and by the time the audience is gone, the place is nearly silent.

"It's been too long, Ro."

She nearly convulses at the sound of the nickname he's always used and can physically feel her heart slamming in her chest as she looks up at him.

"I knew you couldn't stay away."

She clenches her jaw but steels herself. "Just stop. I'm sure you know exactly why I'm here." She opens the manila folder in hand and thrusts it towards him. "Just sign the damn papers, I'll testify tomorrow, and then we never have to see each other again."

"She has a backbone now, does she? What, because you live in a big city now, you think you call the shots? Not so fast." He pushes the papers back at her, then takes a step forward.

Rose steps back in an attempt to maintain the distance between them but finds herself pressed against the wall.

"You know that's not how this works. I'll sign them *after* you've done your part; I don't trust that you won't have a change of heart otherwise. And if you *were* to decide to work with the prosecution... well, who's to say I wouldn't decide to pursue custody of our child? I've always wanted to be a father."

Her eyes close as she holds back a scream.

Hearing him say it, the thought of him convincing a judge he cares about his child after the baby he'd caused her to lose...it *hurts*.

"I've got it, okay? You know I wouldn't risk...I obviously didn't move states away because I was unwilling to do whatever it takes to keep the two of you apart."

(*Please, please, just get away from me. I'll do anything if you'll get away from me.*)

"Good." Kyle's lips curve upward, and he reaches a hand out to tuck a lock of hair behind her ear. At the contact, the paperwork drops from her hand, sprawling across the tile.

She can't be bothered to look at it whilst his skin is on hers.

"Get your hand off of me," she says through clenched teeth.

"Ro's all grown up," he says wistfully, stroking her hair once more.

"Well, alright. I'll see you tomorrow. I've missed you. You're still such a good girl."

She doesn't even notice him leave, his parting remark striking her so hard, she runs to the trash can three yards away to throw up.

Then she's on the floor. Just sitting there, head on her knees, hyperventilating, ignoring the continued light of her phone as she receives calls and texts from Josh, Bronte, Evan. She knows they mean well, knows they want to help, but she can't handle it right now.

She screens Bronte's texts just in case they're about Scarlett; they're not, so she silences the phone and puts it back down.

She doesn't know how long she's been there when she notices footsteps approaching.

"Are you okay?" Casey asks her for the second time that day.

Rose braces herself as she raises her head, but she still feels a pang at the way Casey's face drops when she sees her face. "Oh. It's you."

For a moment, they just stare at each other. Rose can feel Casey taking in her haggard appearance. Hair oily at not having showered, face red and streaked with tears, crumpled papers fanned around her.

"I don't understand."

"Sorry?" Rose asks, brows pulling together in confusion.

Casey crosses her arms, staring her down from where she stands. "Well, in the first place, I don't understand how women can serve as character witnesses when it's so clear assaulters don't seem like bad guys to the people they're not assaulting. It's ridiculous on principle.

"But you...our attorney looked into you. Ages ago. Found out you'd moved away, figured good on you for getting away from them, but we always thought you might've been...well, if you *had* been here, we probably would've tried to find out if you might testify with us."

Rose swallows heavily, feeling herself pale as Casey circles closer to the truth.

"And now you're here. Drove all the way from *Florida* for this? I knew something was off to begin with, even before we met; people don't just move states away with no contact back home if home is a good place. And I've been watching you since the bathroom. The way you acted when he was speaking, sitting on our side, and now this... having a breakdown? I *know* you're one of us."

It's not a question—and honestly, Rose can't bring herself to deny it. She dealt with this for almost a decade. She *deserves* to be able to not deny it.

(Just this once.)

"I can understand not wanting to press charges of your own; the process is awful and hard, and I could never hold it against someone for not wanting to go through with it. But to testify *on his behalf*?" Her voice rises two octaves, nearing hysterics, and Rose is holding back tears. "How could you? What kind of person *does* that to other people he's hurt? Are they paying you or something? Or threatening to withhold your tuition? Do you just not care about what he's doing to other people now that you're not the one within his reach?"

At that, Rose's eyes blaze with agony. "You don't know anything about me," she whispers. "I am so, so sorry for what you're going through. And I wish the situation wasn't this, but...but I *have* to do this."

"Bullshit! What could possibly make this necessary? Don't you want him locked up too?" Casey's crying now, so hopeless and frustrated and drained from the toll the trial is taking on her.

"Of course I do!" Rose snaps, getting to her feet shakily. "But sometimes...something more important...I have to..." She wipes her face and begins gathering the pages of paperwork back into the folder.

She's already said too much. If Casey relays any of this to her attorney, it could mean the invalidation of her testimony, and she has no doubt Kyle and Cheyenne would renege on their deal.

The final sheet is beneath Casey's foot, and the other woman gives her a disappointed look before reluctantly reaching down to pick it up. Casey glances at it as she hands it to her, and Rose's stomach churns as the other woman's eyes widen with understanding.

The day continues its cascade of nightmares.

"Oh," Casey breathes, her voice so, so much more tender. "Oh, no."

"Please don't tell anyone," Rose begs, mouth trembling. "*Please*. I know testifying is wrong, but it's the only way I can get him to sign... I'm so sorry. If it were just about me—"

"This is why you left?" Casey asks, looking shaken.

"Yes," she admits. "They didn't know, but when Cheyenne came to try to get me to testify the other day, she saw her. Now that they know...if I don't do this..."

"He can go for custody," Casey finishes for her. "And she's a girl." The significance of it is heavy on the other woman's face, the understanding of *exactly* how bad him having custody would be. "How... how old is she?"

"Ten months." The smallest of smiles forms on Rose's face at the thought of Scar before dissipating. "Please...Casey, please, you can't use this. I know you want him to be convicted, and I hope he is, but... but this can't be part of it. This is my daughter's *life*," she pleads desperately.

(Her voice breaks.)

"I don't...I don't know," Casey says, face contorted in indecision. "I have to go."

Without another word, she pushes the offending page into Rose's hands and hurries away.

Rose's phone continues to ring, the frequent calls bypassing *Do Not Disturb*, but she makes no move to look at it. She sits back down on the pavement outside and doesn't leave for another hour, letting the tears and snot pour out of her.

She sits, distraught, the bolded *Petition to Terminate Parental Rights* at the top of the page laughing in her face, just the latest in the cosmic joke of her life.

23

Josh has never felt so helpless.

The love of his life disappeared in the middle of the night, and has refused to answer his calls all day. Which he can't fault her for; he just wishes there were something he could do—some way he could possibly make this easier.

When she finally picks up the phone, it takes all of thirty seconds for her to begin bawling.

He's viscerally aware that this is the hardest thing she's ever done —the most brutal, in ways he can already feel chipping away at her. It's for Scarlett, he knows; Rose would do anything for her daughter.

But he can't imagine how hard it is to remember that when you're in the room with your monster.

(When you have to pretend to be on their team.)

There's no way Rose is going to come out of this okay. She's only been back in North Carolina for a day, and her voice is already devoid of hope. Her testimony hasn't even begun.

It's only going to get worse from here, a downward spiral into hell.

From the moment she'd told him about Kyle, Josh had picked up on the fact that she couldn't say his name, that even hearing it affected her. That was what scared him the most. As heinous as Geoffrey was to him, Josh says his name with rage. With malice. For the manner in which you were hurt to be so disruptive that the perpetrator's name alone is like a fist to the gut...

Well, it's different. Makes him understand that while their traumas largely brought them together... they're still so, *so* different. Wounds of an entirely different sort.

And now, she's there. With her monster.

And he knows about Scar.

Everyone always wishes they could time travel, but the moment Cheyenne saw Scar is one Josh knows he would sell his soul to eradicate.

He can't imagine a more hellish situation for Rose...and he's not *there*. He can't support her, love her, glare at the fucker who did unspeakable things to her and make sure he stays the fuck away. He wants to be there with her more than anything in this world, but—

The beeping of his aunt's heart monitor. Her slow and rattling breaths.

The doctor's report, not the least of which included a broken spine.

He should probably try to get some more sleep. The chances of Kathy waking up in the next few hours are apparently less than zero.

But her life feels so fragile now.

He should've *done* more. He got too relaxed, too comfortable, too sure that if Geoffrey were to strike, he would've done it already. He'd started to believe they were safe. That it was actually over. After the bastard already killed his mother.

(The idea is laughable, in retrospect.)

Naturally, the officers who arrived on the scene of her attack found no traces of the perpetrator, and *"Given the year of no contact since his release, we have no evidence to indicate that Mr. Paulson was involved."*

Bullshit. No one else had reason to attack her. No one would have done it so cruelly.

A detective postulated it might've just been a robbery gone wrong, but anyone on the streets would've been able to spot the faded and worn nature of Kathy's clothes. Would have known better than to bother attempting to make any sort of profit from her. The detective had then suggested intent of rape; after restraining a roar, Josh carefully enunciated that the attacker had spent an awfully fucking long time inflicting injuries with her incapacitated for there to be no evidence of sexual assault, were that the goal.

They can't rule anything out, but he knows.

Geoffrey's a white man with the law on his side, with smooth talk and the implicit favor of the entire system. He won't be held accountable.

(They never are.)

If the circumstances were any different, Josh would be almost glad Rose and Scarlett weren't around. Two fewer people's safety at risk whilst Geoffrey is near.

He has to figure out a plan before they get back. Immediately. To get Geoffrey locked up or out of the picture, to get them all in Witness Protection.

Something.

———

Josh squints when he comes to the next morning, unsure why he'd woken given how bone-tired he still feels until a faint cough brings his attention to the hospital bed.

"Aunt Kathy!" he breathes, jamming his thumb on the nurse call button.

"Th—" She coughs again around the tube down her throat, clearly distressed at the intrusion, at the lack of mobility she currently has.

"Don't try to talk; the nurse will be here soon, okay? You're okay."

Not strictly true, but in moments like these...well, sometimes honesty and cruelty share a face.

The nurse runs in, and though her voice is light and soothing, her eyes meticulously comb over Kathy's body, her charts. She's quickly followed in by another woman who, though ten years younger, Josh knows to be the doctor. The doc gives the okay for the breathing tube to come out, eventually, and once more pain meds have been administered, Kathy falls back asleep almost instantaneously.

The doctor turns to Josh with sad eyes, dark hair plaited down her back; they've grown familiar over the brief but intense time Kathy has been in so far. From what one of the men who work in registration told Josh, the doc came into the shift early specifically when someone mentioned his godmother's case to her.

The way she meets his eyes, the careful way she handles the situation...

(*She's one of us*, Rose's voice whispers in his mind.)

"Do you want to tell her, and I can come in and give specifics after, or do you want me to do it?" she asks gently.

Josh closes his eyes, bracing himself, knowing that the kindness she's offering him is probably very much against protocol, against the law even. "Let me do it, please. She...yeah."

Coming from him won't make Kathy's reaction any better, won't make it easier for her to accept, but the truth of it is that he doesn't want anyone else to see her that vulnerable.

Doesn't think she would, either, but then, if she had it her way, he would think her invincible, too.

———

"Josh?" Kathy mumbles when she comes to a few hours later. For a moment, he thinks she's sleep-talking, but then her eyes drag open.

Despite everything going on, some tiny part of him glows at the reminder that even without knowing where she is, without being fully conscious, he's the first person she calls for.

"Hey, Aunt Kathy. I'm here."

Her lips are chapped, spots of bruising all across her skin, both visible to the eye and not.

"What..." She trails off and begins coughing again, esophagus still irritated from the throat tube despite its absence. After a moment, she seems to realize where she is, remember what happened, and her eyes widen in terror. "Josh, you have to go. He found me, and he'll come for you too!"

He sees her shoulders move, and he knows—he *knows*—she's realizing something's wrong.

(Realizing she can't move her legs. Can't feel them.)

"Josh, I can't..." She doesn't finish the sentence.

They both know. They both know what it means.

"He broke it, Aunt Kathy," Josh croaks, tears already forming in his eyes even though he's not the one who's supposed to be upset here. He's supposed to stay strong for her. "And he...he stabbed you between two of the vertebrae he didn't break, near the bottom. The doc called them lumber vertebrae or something; I don't remember. I —I'm so sorry, Aunt Kathy. I don't know if it's because of the break or the tear, but she said...she said barring a medical miracle the likes of which haven't been seen, you won't walk again."

And shit, Josh knows he said it wrong. There are more eloquent, better ways he should've done it. But how can there ever be a good way to tell someone they'll be paralyzed for the rest of their life?

Someone with a known enemy hunting them, who they have to run away from?

Except she can't walk. She won't be *able* to run away from him.

"Oh," is all she says, eyes downcast. It's clear she doesn't have the energy to pretend that's okay in front of her godson.

There's more he should tell her. She has a shattered hand, a broken femur, a punctured lung.

And no health insurance.

Realistically, it's a miracle she's alive. But now that her survival is ensured physically, Josh can focus on the fact that he has no fucking idea how they're going to make it through this financially—as if they weren't *already* drowning in debt.

"You're gonna be okay, Aunt Kathy. We'll make it through this. We always do." He's reassuring her, but he doesn't believe the words he's saying.

She nods and attempts a small smile, but it doesn't reach her eyes. "I'm tired, honey. I think I just want to rest for a little while."

Josh plays along, presses a kiss to her forehead, and closes the door behind him.

Pretends not to hear her sobs start through the door the second he's outside the room.

He slides to the floor, leaning against the hard surface of her door. Guarding her the way he should've been when she was attacked.

It hurts to hear her mournful crying—it doesn't stop.

But he deserves it. He needs the reminder of what's important.

His phone rings, and while he wishes it were Rose, he knows exactly who it is even before he double-checks.

"I can't afford to pay you," he says monotonously as he answers, no preamble. "Everything I have has to go to medical bills now, and while I wish I could ask you to reapply for the protection order and start a lawsuit against the state for previously not giving her one and allowing this to happen...I can't pay for your services. And I'm told there's no evidence that it was him, the usual bullshit, so it doesn't seem like it would help much, anyway."

Their lawyer is quiet for a moment before she speaks. "I know I'm a shark, Mr. Brooks, and that I benefit from our professional relationship, but I didn't want to see your godmother suffer. I don't want to see her go undefended now." A beat of silence. "I can't promise anything, but... I'll try to see if we can find a way. If I can afford to do it pro-bono, I'd like to, but Josh...I have kids of my own to think about. I need to be able to feed them, too."

It's all-consuming, the rage and grief inside him. It's been on his mind already, as he and Rose's relationship has progressed; every moment is a reminder of when his own mother started dating.

A man who always tried to push him further and further away, who separated her from all her friends, who took all the money and power and control into his hands, who had them both trapped.

Josh thought being trapped was the worst thing that could happen to his mother.

(Until it wasn't.)

And now it's happening all over again, right before his eyes.

While they've never been especially close, relief floods through Josh at the sight of Evan—and even more, at the sight of Zeke, Kai, and Isa behind him.

Kai's carrying flowers—not allowed in ICU, but once Kathy gets a long-term room, they'll brighten her day. The gesture isn't lost on Josh, as hopeless as everything feels.

"Heard you could use some company," Evan says, clapping him on the back.

He says it like it's no big deal, just friends hanging out, but the reaffirming way he grips Josh's shoulder...well, he can understand why Rose looks up to him more than almost anyone. Why a bunch of would-be punk kids from every horror story of a home do, too.

After a while, Kai and Isa go off in search of a vending machine. Josh can feel Evan and Zeke watching him carefully. The waiting room is nearly empty except for them, just for a few minutes, the one other person there asleep in their chair.

"Do you want to talk about it?" Zeke asks, no judgment in his voice.

"No. Yes. I don't know." Josh forces himself to take a deep breath, knuckles white where he clenches the edge of his seat. "I'm such an idiot. I can't believe I left her vulnerable. This is all my fault."

He can feel his temper rising, the frustration and sadness and age-old sorrow mixing into anger because getting mad hurts less than feeling how terrified and hopeless things seem.

Evan looks him dead in the eye. "Josh, the only person at fault is Geoffrey. *He* hurt your mom; *he* hurt Kathy. You're not responsible for their safety, and it's not on you to protect them. It's on him to not be a fucking psychopath."

"Yeah, but I *knew*! I sat there and watched him hurt my mom, watched him kill her, knew he was going to come after Kathy and I next and did...fucking nothing. I should've known better. He killed my mom." He blows out a deep breath. "And fucking Kyle is fucking blackmailing Rose, and I'm not there to protect her either when she has to go up and say that she *likes* him when he's a fucking piece of shit pedophile, and I just..."

It's years of wrath and anger, a lifetime of frustration with the systems not protecting the people who are vulnerable. It's his mother's death that he's still not okay about, it's Kathy being hurt and having to worry about how to pay for it rather than getting better, it's Rose being exploited and him unable to help her when God knows what Kyle's going to do when he's near her.

He's so full of rage, angrier than he's ever been, and he just wants to *break* something or punch the wall and feel it give just to know it's all real. He's unconsciously grabbed a stack of magazines off the side table, and then he's just ripping it in half with fury and—

And he freezes, blood running cold.

He'd wanted to *break* something—gotten violent because he'd gotten mad.

"I'm going to become him," he whispers with horror, the same words he'd said months ago, this time so much truer.

The anger's gone, now; all he can feel is terror, disgusted by himself.

"Woah, hey, calm down," Evan demands. "Look at me. What's up? Why is that what just came to mind?"

Josh holds up the ripped magazines as his breathing quickens. "I just...so mad. I was feeling so mad, and I wanted...to break something, to feel. I—"

"Breathe, man," Zeke says as Josh borders on hyperventilation, rubbing his back gently.

Evan meets his eyes. "Josh, wanting catharsis when you get upset on one of the worst days of your life does *not* make you anything like him."

"But—"

"No buts. Look at me. Is this the angriest you've ever been?"

"Yes." He swallows heavily, clutching at his armrests.

"So you're *as angry as you've ever been*...and you had no impulse to hurt anyone." Evan gestures to himself and Zeke meaningfully. "We're right here; you could've easily come at one of us or tried to start a fight. We're sitting closer to you than those magazines were—you had to lean out of your way to grab them. But you did because your impulse is never, ever to harm. Even unconsciously, you know you'd never hurt anyone, no matter how pissed off you are."

Josh's jaw tics, considering this. "I still ripped the magazines, though. I caused physical damage because I was mad. That's how it starts."

Evan snorts. "Dude, if it were that simple, I'd have a lot of teenagers at my center beating the shit out of each other. Why do you think I keep punching bags and a bunch of glass plates there? It's instinctive to seek out catharsis. It helps release some of the pent-up emotion. Logically you know this, man, you're a psych major. Being human, wanting an outlet for the hurt and frustration you're feeling right now...that is exactly what separates you from Geoffrey."

Zeke nods in agreement. "And I would argue that the fact that you're at your worst and still never considered hurting anyone—even him—proves that you're nothing like him. You never will be. I know you're terrified of ever causing that kind of hurt, but this is...evidence that you're not capable of being that person."

"He's right. And the fact that you're aware of it means you're better able to control it," Evan says. "If you ever did have the impulse, you would immediately make a change, do whatever is necessary to keep from doing anything like that. Thoughts and intentions are nice, but actions are what matters most—actions determine actual impact. And you're willing to take whatever actions you have to to keep from becoming like him. At the end of the day, that's what matters. And that's how I know you'll never even remotely start down the path Geoffrey has."

"You're going to be just fine," Zeke promises in a whisper, hand on his other shoulder.

And as disinclined as he is to believe them, he thinks they might be right.

———

A bit later, the anger has faded into fear and sadness, overpowering worry, and angst so painful, it physically hurts in his chest.

"I don't think I can do this," Josh confesses quietly, soft enough that only Evan can hear. "We can't afford any of her treatment. We're already in debt. There's no way to stop him coming after her again, and...and *Rose*." His voice breaks on her name. "It's all too much. The best people in my life...why do they have to get fucked over? Go through so much?"

"I wish I knew." Evan shakes his head, running a hand over his buzz cut. "And I wish there were any answer that could make it okay. But there just isn't. People suffer who don't deserve it, people are successful and lucky who don't deserve it, and...and we just have to hope that sometimes it works out."

He adjusts his seating, so he's facing Josh head-on. "I struggle with this every day—trying to reconcile myself to it for the kids I work with. I love them so much. And they deserve so much more than they have ever gotten. Their hearts are beating, and that's supposed to be enough, but it isn't."

Josh nods in agreement.

Living, surviving, they're not the same, and all of them... they've only ever known one. Odds are they only ever *will*.

(Such is life.)

24

THERE'S a moment when she wakes up—just the briefest of moments —that Rose feels okay.

She's disoriented, hasn't really processed where she is, what she needs to do when she gets out of bed, whether or not Scar is awake yet.

She takes a deep breath, keeps her eyes shut in the *if-they-stay-closed-I-might-still-fall-back-asleep* fashion.

Then she remembers.

Thirty seconds later, she's in the bathroom of their hotel room, puking. Shaking. Hyperventilating.

She can't do this.

Scarlett begins to whine from the playpen they'd brought with them.

She has to do this.

Bronte rubs Rose's back soothingly. "You know, you can still change your mind."

Bronte hasn't questioned her once since she explained why they had to go to North Carolina—hasn't tried to talk her out of it or convince her there's another way.

Which is why Rose knows Bronte's only reminding her of this, in this moment, so that she feels like she has a choice.

"I really can't," Rose whispers, wiping at her mouth. She gets to her feet, making her way to Scar, and holds her to her chest; her baby squirms but hums happily.

This. This is why she needs to do it—for the tiny human in her arms who means more than anything in this world.

Letting anyone hurt her will never be an option.

"I love you," Rose tells her.

Scar grows antsy as they stand there and starts screeching until Rose puts her on the bed, where she can crawl around on her own.

She can't help but pause, just watching her daughter *live.*

The way Scar's face lights up when she sees something new, her gurgles as she throws herself face down onto the pillows as though playing possum...this is why she needs to do it.

"As long as you're sure," Bronte says carefully, coming up beside her to squeeze her in a rare hug. "Call if you need anything."

"I will."

Rose gets dressed robotically, not thinking of what she's about to do. This day will suck, and then it will end, and that will be that.

Just another bad day. Nothing special.

She doesn't eat anything; she knows it wouldn't stay in her stomach long, anyway, what with the anxiety and dread coursing through her. Gets to the courthouse an hour early, hoping the silence will soothe her.

(It doesn't.)

The judge is the next one to arrive, nodding to her as he passes. Then Kyle's attorney; his big smile makes her shudder. When he calls her inside, *to prepare her to testify,* she has to hold back a sob.

Rose wonders if this is the last moment she'll ever be able to live with herself.

He walks her through the motions of how the procedure will go, what things she shouldn't answer, how she should phrase her comments about the defendant.

She knows the moniker defendant refers to the accused

defending themselves, but for a moment, she perceives it as the one *doing* the defense work; she can't help the hysteric giggle that escapes her at the idea of Kyle defending anyone.

Rose doesn't really have many memories of a time before he began tormenting her—before going to bed meant hiding under the blanket in fear, squeezing her eyes shut, and praying that this time it would be enough to keep the doorknob from turning.

(It never was.)

The attorney is still talking, but she's drowning in flashbacks and memories. Falling asleep in school because she couldn't fall asleep at night, awkward games of *never have I ever* where everyone would smirk and ask how far you'd gone, but the question made her cringe and unsure of her answer, the weird looks when she flinched from physical contact.

The first time—waking up to heaviness on top of her, crying out, bruising and searing pain, screaming again and his hand covering her mouth until she passed out. Waking up confused, still a child, hoping it was a dream but sore in all the wrong places. A part of her gone forever—not the literal virginity itself that mattered, but the innocence, the piece of her that was her own.

Everything from then on, every experience, every friendship, was tainted. Seen through different eyes.

Sixteen, realizing something had changed, hoping he wouldn't notice when he came for her those nights. For the first time in her life, being more terrified than relieved when he suddenly stopped that night, flashes of him beating her and forcing her to down more alcohol. More pain than she'd ever felt and then bleeding and then not being sure which hurt more, what was actually happening inside her, or the knowledge that the terrible ache was her baby's life fading from this world.

Years and years of wondering whether life was worth it. If it would ever end. If her skin could ever feel like her own, if she would ever get to be the one who decided who touched her—and even *if* they did so.

Wondering why anyone bothered to invent the word "no" in the first place when it was completely useless. Made things worse most days.

Long nights. Days of being sore and classmates asking why if she winced; questions about the hickey she didn't have a way to hide when everyone had been so sure she was single. Sitting still when he stroked her proprietarily.

(*Mine* and *good girl* and *shhh, you like it* over and over and over and over.)

When he was angry, the days he turned the light on as he entered her room. Knowing it would be worse. Knowing he would revel in her pain a little extra.

(*I love when you whimper for me* and smirks and *ask me to hurt you* and calling her beautiful as he made it sting and burn and bruise and *hurt*. The time she pissed him off so badly that she winced every time she moved for a week.)

Something being off, again, biting her lip in line at the store, not making eye contact with the judgey cashier eyeing her left hand as she scanned the pregnancy test.

Said cashier's lip curling when she paid with carefully counted ones and change.

Panic. A day of planning, the shitty car she'd made a deal to get the day she turned eighteen and bought early with money she'd squirreled away so, *so* carefully. Torn between driving as fast as the engine would take her and driving reasonably so as to not draw the attention of law enforcement.

Trying to find places to park at night where she could sleep, though never soundly. Keeping a toothbrush in her purse, attempting to clean up in the bathroom at work before her shifts. Constantly on high alert.

The nightmares constant all the while. The feeling of hands on her skin, an invader inside her...they didn't go away, even as the days away from him grew into months.

The glares of everyone around her. The comments about *foolish teenagers* and *if you're going to be a whore, don't be too stupid to use a condom* and *you should be ashamed* and all the while wanting to scream that she never chose this life, has never had a say in any of it.

This—testifying—shouldn't really come as a surprise. Her being on the stand at Kyle's behest.

(What her body does has never been her choice, anyway.)

"Do you understand all of this, Ms. Simmons? Any questions?"

"No, thank you. I understand perfectly. I'd like a minute, now."

Finds herself in the bathroom again, clutching a torn journal, pages wrinkled and blotted and in every shade of ink. To bring it today, when she will illegally give false testimony, was idiotic.

But Rose needs it here. Needs to remind herself that the years of pain were real. The little girl that started writing down what was happening to her, desperate to just get the words out, even if no one but her would ever read them...she needs to be here today.

She's over the toilet again, dry heaving since there's no food left in her to lose. She cries, considers slapping herself to snap out of it.

When she finally calms down enough to leave the stall, she's face to face with Casey *again*.

"Please, you don't have to do this," Casey begins, expression desperate, but Rose is desperate too, and she *does* have to. Her will to do so is already too weak, and she won't jeopardize her conviction to do what's right for Scarlett, what she has to do to keep Scar out of Kyle's hands, so she pushes past Casey without hesitation, the blood rushing through her head deafening, drowning out the sounds of her flats on the tile.

She feels like she can't breathe the whole time she's sitting with Cheyenne and Kyle, and he gives her a hug and what the crowd probably reads as a reassuring smile before she takes the stand.

(Everything hurts.)

Before she can blink, her hand is on a bible.

"Ms. Simmons, how long have you known the defendant?"

The defense attorney's questions are no surprise; he'd run through all of them with her multiple times this morning, as well as those the prosecution would likely ask.

"Twelve years."

"And in those twelve years, has the defendant ever made any sexual advances towards you, Ms. Simmons?"

The third time today she's heard the question, but it still makes her heart stop. "No, he has not."

The lie burns her lips.

"Your mother has mentioned previously that the defendant has been a surrogate father to you all these years." *Bastard.* Of course that old claim comes back. "Do you believe the defendant capable of any manner of violence or forced sexual contact, Ms. Simmons?"

"Of course not." Her soul is cracking with each question. She can't believe she's actually doing this. "The closest K-Kyle could come to hurting anyone is when he used to kill spiders for me."

A few laughs from the less bothered members of the crowd.

It's been ten minutes, maybe, and yet Rose feels like she's been on the stand for hours. Her mouth is dry. The world is heavy.

She braces herself for the next question, but before the defense attorney can get the words out of his mouth, the prosecution calls for a recess.

The entire time, it's taken everything in her not to look to where Casey stares her down with sad eyes.

She can't avoid her now, though; the other woman holds out a pleading hand as she takes the few steps down.

"*Please*, Rose—I know you have no reason to trust me, but please. Just...just give me five minutes. I promise it's important."

"Casey, you have to stop trying to talk me out of... it's already too late to—"

"Please. Just listen." The terror, the pain, the exhaustion in her voice... it's familiar. So familiar it hurts.

Rose gives in, already knowing it will only make it harder to get back on the stand. "Fine. Start talking."

"Not here. Trust me, you don't want..." Casey trails off, shaking her head, then gestures for Rose to follow her into the hallway.

"Rose, darling, don't be long," Cheyenne calls.

(A reminder.)

As soon as they're outside the courtroom, Rose shudders, the adrenaline fading, the reality of what she's doing sinking in.

"Whatever it is you're going to say, you have to understand—"

"You have to protect your daughter. I get it. I do," Casey swears, pushing hair out of her face hurriedly. "But I couldn't sleep last night thinking about it, because, well, your testimony would mean everything for our case, but also because... it's not fair that you have to defend him. That your child's fate is in his hands. So I—I did some research. And I talked with our lawyer to clarify—without telling her it was about you, of course. I wouldn't take that choice away from you."

Casey understands, after everything, how important it is that the decision is *hers*.

"And I mean, if you don't believe me, you can look it up yourself, it's all on government and legal sites, but..." Casey shuffles through the canvas bag on her arm, pulling out different papers hastily. "Here. Just...look."

Documents regarding laws and protocol in both North Carolina and Florida. A spreadsheet. Data on custody law, age of consent, in which state custody is determined.

It's several minutes before Rose puts together what Casey's laid out before her—what all of these documents are referring to.

"Am I reading this right?" she hesitates. "If I pressed charges...but I already researched it all ages ago. I didn't think it was possible."

"Our attorney did some digging," Casey explains. "With a conviction, both North Carolina and Florida have statutes that dictate he couldn't get custody. But it can't be a conviction for us. It has to be for the one that conceived her specifically. I mean, I'm sure you could press for all of the times—that is, I'm assuming it wasn't just once," she whispers the end apologetically.

Rose gives her a sharp nod.

"I thought it might be. I'm...really sorry." Casey takes a deep breath, then continues. "And I figured that would be a gamble for you because if he weren't convicted, he'd be even more vindictive and likely to go for custody, and obviously, that's the worst thing that could happen."

She pulls the spreadsheet to the front of the sheaf. "But, see, the age of consent in Florida is eighteen, so even if they decide that he's not guilty and we're lying sluts, which I'm trying to mentally prepare myself for if we're being honest because we all know women never win these cases...but anyway, even if they decide it was all consensual, even you, it doesn't matter, because yours was still statutory—at least, in the state you currently reside in, which is normally where parental rights and custody things are determined.

"And that's the one that conceived your daughter, anyway, and if they have a paternity test as proof, it's undeniable that he was... *with* you before you were eighteen, his rights should get terminated even without his agreement. And in Florida, if the parents aren't married, the mother automatically gets primary custody unless ruled otherwise in court."

Rose narrows her eyes, letting herself actually consider what Casey is saying. "And this would be...worst-case scenario? I can..."

But she's already given false testimony. To retract her statements now might discredit anything she does say. On her record...it would look horrible. What could that mean for her future, even with regards to Scarlett? Could they argue she's an unfit parent?

She begins pacing away from Casey, lost in her own thoughts.

"There you are." Cheyenne's voice is poison when she corners her in an empty hallway a moment later.

"What do you want?"

"Just wanted to make sure you're not getting any ideas. You *should* know better than to go back on our deal, but then, you've never been very smart, have you? Sometimes I really do think you do these things just to spite me."

It's so *familiar*—her mother berating her, this bone-deep feeling of betrayal.

She's an adult now, and yet she still feels like the quivering twelve-year-old who wishes Mama loved her enough to save her. Cheyenne giving her updates on how Kyle's doing constantly, expecting her to give a fuck, not caring that the sound of his name makes her insides twist, jaw clenching to keep from screaming.

"I have a daughter," Rose says quietly. Cheyenne raises an eyebrow and looks at her like she's babbling, but she carries on. "And from the moment I knew she existed, I've loved her more than anything. I would do anything to protect her. As you know, since that's why I'm *here*. And I can't... can't *imagine* what I would do if someone hurt her. I'd die before I let it happen. I would set the world on fire to stop it from happening again. If anything like this happened to her...my God, I would lose my fucking mind."

"Is there a point to these dramatics?"

"How could you?" She means for it to be a scream, but the words come out as a pained whisper that almost chokes her. "How could you let him keep hurting me? How could you take his side? How could you let this happen and make me keep pretending everything was okay? You're my *mother*—if anyone is on my team, it's supposed to be you! *You were supposed to protect me.*"

Her mother crosses her arms. "I kept you fed and sheltered, paid for all of your things, for school and activities. *That* is my job as a mother. Need I remind you that you were admitted to a host of top ten schools because of me because *I* enabled you to get the grades and be involved? I'm the reason you made it so far."

"The only role you played in my education is that I worked *so* hard to get *away* from you," Rose spits, feeling herself tremble. "You wouldn't be claiming the credit if I'd killed myself the way I thought about a million times, waiting for him to slink into my room. Your child shouldn't have to *beg* you to love them enough to stop a monster from hurting them. You should want to stop them from being hurt more than you want to breathe."

"You were appealing to him, Rose; how was he supposed to stop himself? And anyway, you seem to be doing well enough for yourself now, so clearly, things weren't that bad. I really don't understand why you feel the need to make yourself out to be such a victim, sweetheart."

Rose almost retches. At the implication that a child could be responsible for a grown man coming on to her, that because she's alive and functioning means she's okay, that if she's making ends meet now, years of violent assault are water under the bridge.

"You disgust me. There...there is not one semblance of humanity in you." Spinning on her heel, she runs—anywhere else in this godforsaken courthouse, anywhere she doesn't have to look at the face that should've been her lifeline or the one that taught her exactly why she should be afraid of the dark.

(The things, the people that lurk and thrive in darkness.)

She squirrels herself away in a dark alcove, secluded enough that no one finds her for the rest of the hour-long recess.

She knows they must be trying to. Knows Cheyenne won't rest until she's reminded Rose exactly what's at stake after her outburst—will worry that the anger might make her do something reckless.

It very well might.

Eventually, her time is up. She has to go back.

(Back to that horrible room, with Cheyenne and *him* and his voice and her memories and the desire to scream and the slimy attorney and the judge who has no idea how wrong all of this is.)

Her phone buzzes from inside her purse. She thought she'd turned it to do not disturb already but nonetheless pulls it out to turn off the ringer.

A text from Josh; he's sent so little correspondence since she left.

(It's not like him. Something is very, very wrong.)

She wishes she had the energy to find out what, but everything in her is trying not to fall apart. She doesn't have anything left over.

```
I love you, baby. Whatever you do, I'm so
proud of you. You're so strong. Give Scar a
hug for me.
```

She's crying again. Jesus Christ. She's not exactly the *I've-cried-once-in-my-life* type, but she hasn't been this emotional since...well, maybe ever. It's like it needs to escape her, the pain and disgust.

It has to find a way out of her, or she'll explode.

She makes her way back to the courtroom, where for the first time in her life, she's two minutes late. The court is in disarray, and Cheyenne and Kyle both look beyond livid.

Rose shakily climbs back up to the stand, and while still awful, and horrifying, and the last place on the planet she wants to be, it seems...different.

"Are you ready to begin again, Ms. Simmons?" the defense attorney asks between clenched teeth.

Rose looks up into the eyes that haunt her.

Those eyes. Her *daughter's* eyes...but on her little girl, so full of love and light.

Eyes she could never get out of her head. Eyes she used to dream about stabbing out—truly, gouging them in the most awful of ways.

But then, she looks to Casey, and to Casey's side, the woman a few years older than them whose name she's learned is Alexa.

Casey, who knows her secret. Who isn't telling it despite knowing how it would help her case.

Because women have to stick together—especially those who've survived the same monster.

Whose monster still roams the earth.

She thinks of Scarlett—the reason she's here. Because keeping her safe is all that matters.

(But if she could do something else and still keep her safe...)

"Your honor?" She turns to the judge with watery eyes, her voice raspy. "I'm so sorry, but I...I have to retract my earlier comments."

The tension in the room skyrockets—the gasps from a few members of the audience, for whom this is just entertainment; a sob of relief in a voice that sounds much like Casey's; outraged hisses from the defense table.

"Objection!" Kyle's attorney demands, but the judge waves him away.

(Something about the shattered, desperate look in her eyes.)

"Please elaborate, Ms. Simmons."

His voice is not gentle, but he is not cruel. The picture of neutrality.

"I thought..." She presses a hand to her mouth, a rattling breath into her lungs. "I was under duress, Your Honor. Extortion. I'm so sorry that I gave false evidence, but...it was to protect my daughter."

It's out there, now, and there's a wrenching pain in her gut. *No going back.*

"Cheyenne—Mrs. Simmons, I mean. She and the defendant, they threatened to file for custody if I didn't support their case. They agreed he would sign the paperwork to terminate parental rights after I completed my end of the deal."

The judge leans forward in his chair, eyebrows raised. There's knowing in his eyes, but he maintains procedure. "Ms. Simmons, please clarify why the defendant and his associate would be in such a position as to pursue custody of the child."

"My daughter..." The tears are pouring down her face now, and she can't believe she's letting herself say the words, prays to whatever God there might be that what she's doing won't hurt Scar. That somehow what seems like the right thing to do for the world can be the best for her baby.

"My daughter is biologically—and only biologically—the child of the defendant." She flinches at the shocked sounds from those who hadn't put the pieces together. "She was conceived just over a year and a half ago when I was raped by the defendant, for what was not... not the first time. While I was still a minor."

Chaos ensues.

25

KATHY'S BEEN in the hospital three days when she convinces Josh to go home for the first time. He doesn't think the whole commute; he blocks out the world, every thought in his head.

The second he closes his front door behind him, he falls to the floor.

He almost lost her. Even now, things might look okay, but he's heard stories. He knows nothing in life is guaranteed.

(Nothing except pain.)

Domino's not there, despite Rose having dropped him off before driving to North Carolina. Zeke had offered to take care of him while Josh was at the hospital with Kathy before Josh had even thought to arrange for someone to watch the dog, which had been a godsend, but. His absence only exacerbates the wrongness of the circumstances. The apartment feels more empty than it ever has while uninhabited before; something about it rings with finality.

Later, he'll wonder why that didn't strike him—wonder how he could know something was so wrong instinctively from so far away. As though the very walls already knew something would change irrevocably.

He doesn't question it now.

He drags himself into the shower, turns the water to as near-boiling as he can get it. Falls asleep standing up after a few minutes. Manages to make his way to his bed, collapses in it, putting his phone near his pillow in case Rose calls.

He forgets it's on five percent; by the time anyone calls, it'll be dead.

Josh closes his eyes and slips into REM almost instantly. No darkness touches his dreams, and he's like a stone for hours.

He's woken prematurely by a heavy pounding. Bleary-eyed, he opens the door without checking the peephole, too tired to be on guard until the door is fully open, and he's met with a knife to the gut.

Geoffrey slams the door shut, the navy-blue threads of his clothes all Josh can see.

———

Recess is called for the rest of the day.

Rose is swarmed immediately, a tightening in her chest as the room converges.

She can't think about the masses, though. Can't think about the prosecution's wide eyes and rapid speech, the defense's anger. The gratitude and pride and pain in Casey's face.

What she *can* think about is the acute anger in Kyle's eyes. The promise of retribution. The way Cheyenne has to grip his tensed muscles to stop him from getting to her.

She fucked up. This was the wrong thing to do; she's put Scarlett in danger. Kyle won't allow this to stand.

Casey and Alexa begin telling her all the details of the case she'd yet to hear—how they'd initially pressed the charges a year ago, not too long after she'd left. The delays in court, the check they'd been offered to drop the charges.

They look to Rose with subdued hope, sorry for her suffering but thinking their case might finally stand a chance. Their monster could actually be put away—for *good*. Some semblance of justice is *so close*.

She doesn't hear a word they say.

They end up at a restaurant in town she can't afford, wincing as she knows the waiter does internally when she asks for just a glass of water.

(She doesn't want to be here.)

"Well, Ms. Simmons, while the circumstances are heinous... welcome to the team." The prosecution attorney says, a middle-aged woman with graying hair in braids that are pulled into a ponytail, accompanied by an unblinking stare. "Luckily, charges can be added at any point throughout the trial prior to deliberation, so we don't have to worry about waiting for an entirely separate trial to also come to fruition and repeat all of the same preliminary information we already have.

"To be honest, I'm not sure how your prior testimony will affect any subsequent ones, but the rights termination paperwork seems like a valid demonstration of proof that you were under duress. You're virtually guaranteed to be re-examined by the defense and, of course, by us, but we'll discuss ahead of time so there will be no surprises. What the defense is going to throw at you...it won't be pretty."

Casey cringes, and Alexa's jaw tightens whilst her skin pales.

"I can't afford to pay you," Rose says bluntly. The first words she's spoken since leaving the stand.

"That's not an issue; I'm working this case pro-bono. As soon as we're done here, we'll go file for an Emergency Protective Order. That goes into effect immediately, so he'll be mandated to have no contact with you long enough to get an actual Temporary Protection Order. Hopefully, that will last long enough for the rest of the trial, but if not, we'll file for another."

Rose feels fear creep higher in her chest because she's seen exactly how well protective orders have worked for Josh and Kathy. It's no guarantee.

The attorney, whose name is Amira but everyone just calls by her last name, Davis, has already proven herself to be someone who's unafraid to be honest with them—brutally so because it's what's in their best interest.

If anyone is going to be real with them about the likely outcome of the trial, it's her. Rose should just ask her, just ask their odds. How much worse it's going to get.

But she doesn't. Can't bear it—can hardly bear the thought of what she's done.

Without explanation, Rose drops her dilapidated journal onto the table; it smacks onto the wood too loudly, and heads around them turn, but she couldn't care less.

Davis raises her eyebrows expectantly but picks up the crinkled and stained notebook when Rose merely stares her down silently. She opens to the first page and begins reading, and Rose can see the exact moment the older woman realizes what she's holding, the moment her shoulders jerk and her jaw drops, lip curling up with disgust though the possibilities race through her mind. "This is..."

"Nearly every incident for roughly a decade. Documented, dated —I'm sure they can have some expert date the ink if they don't believe it." The only possession she'd held onto since it started. The rest of it...brutal reminders.

"This could be a game-changer." Davis thumbs through the pages carefully. "I don't want to guarantee anything, but...I don't know the last time I saw something so promising."

"A decade?" Casey whispers, pressing a hand to her mouth.

And Rose would never begrudge someone their pain, would never try to say her experience was *worse* or *more* horrifying because no one's trauma deserves that kind of disrespect. None would be "better" to have gone through; no one should have to go through *any* of them. That's not a thing.

But there's something so fucking validating about a complete stranger seeing her pain so viscerally—something so gratifying for the eleven-year-old whose mother said the thing eating her alive was "no big deal" and let her be another human's plaything for years afterward.

The recognition that this part of her, this innocence and happiness and belief in the good of the world that's been gone for so long, that everyone *should* have throughout their childhood...it was *taken*.

That she deserved more.

"Let me speak with a colleague, and we'll figure out where to go from here." There's something quiet in Davis's face. Something that worries Rose as the professional steps away, immediately pressing her phone to her ear. Something not quite right.

(She doesn't trust it.)

Before she has time to think about it, her phone rings, and she winces at the sight of Bronte's contact. "Hi, Te, I'm sorry I'm running so late, is she okay? I—"

"Rose." Bronte's voice is more pained than Rose has ever heard it, and it scares her. Something is very, very wrong.

No. Not when things are finally coming together.

"He said he...he tried to call you." She can almost see the way the words are sticking in her friend's throat and closes her eyes. *Which he?* "Rose, I...we have to go home. Something's happened."

And Bronte hasn't even said it yet, but she crumples out of her chair because for Bronte—solid, unflinching Bronte—to be this upset, someone must be gone.

———

It's all a blur when Josh comes to.

He remembers being stabbed. Unfortunately, *that* part couldn't be part of the trauma-induced amnesia. As soon as he thinks about it, the generalized pain he's noticed in his abdomen grows stronger.

He remembers the door swinging open slowly, his friend ambling in before taking stock of the situation.

Evan rushing Geoffrey, even as he starts to dial 911.

Geoffrey pulling a gun. Collective tension.

The sound of a gunshot. Evan's gasp of pain, the sight of him collapsing.

Passing back out.

Coming to again, seeing Evan on the floor across the room.

The only sound is Geoffrey mumbling to himself, tossing the gun to the ground as he goes to the bathroom, presumably to find cleaning supplies to erase his trail.

Josh can't move.

The stab had become a slice before they arrived, across his stomach and inches deep. So much blood lost, already.

Evan whimpering, biting down on his lip as he crawls to the gun. Josh's eyes sliding closed again.

The bathroom door opening. Two more shots fired. Geoffrey's thump to the floor.

Unbeknownst to a now unconscious Josh, a struggling breath from Evan. His thumb finally hitting send.

"911, what is your emergency?" to a silent room.

Only one heart still beating when the paramedics arrive.

———

Rose probably shouldn't be behind the wheel, but she has to get to Bronte. To Scarlett.

(Evan. *Gone.*)

She can't even cry, the whiplash of emotion of the last few days too much for her to do anything but shut down.

Bronte, puffy-eyed and shaking, cannot say the same.

They sit together through the night, unable to start the long drive home but too drained and heartbroken to do anything else.

The story is that Geoffrey came after Josh; Evan had intended to pop by and visit him and Kai, not knowing Kai was at work.

That was the last anyone heard from any of them until Kai came home to an apartment full of personnel and two body bags and was told that Josh was airlifted to Tampa General.

Rose can't imagine what Bronte's feeling. Her *soul mate*, gone, protecting her family.

Let alone Josh's injuries which Rose has next to no information on.

How are any of them supposed to move past this?

Bronte finally passes out after crying for hours, wordlessly, but Rose can't bear to.

She knows what will join the cast of her nightmares the next time she does.

Scarlett doesn't understand—obviously, the kid's not even one—but she can sense something is off. She can tell her mom is sad as much as she tries to hide it, so she's been crying more than usual, too, because if Mommy's sad, of *course,* she should be sad too. That's love.

The best, the purest love Rose could ever be lucky enough to receive. A love she could never deserve or even begin to live up to.

Her phone rings—Davis, again—and she would put it on silent if she weren't constantly worried she'd receive an update about Josh from Zeke, the only one at the hospital still able to properly function.

She knows Isa and Kai are together. From what Zeke overheard, they're breaking every fragile thing they can get their hands on in an attempt to handle their grief.

She'd never realized how close Kai had gotten to his cousin's boyfriend, but all the time they'd spent together...it had built up.

Now Isa's left to try and soothe him, despite her growing fear that she's the reason people in her life keep dying.

In Isa's apartment, as Kai's is a crime scene currently under investigation.

(The scene of a murder.)

Even thinking about it hurts.

Her phone vibrates again, and she considers chucking it at the linoleum in the hopes that it will break. Every phone call in the last week seems to have been the source of bad news and pain, and she can't handle anymore. Another piece of bad news will break her.

It's actually Zeke this time, though, and she hurriedly accepts the call.

"How is he?"

"He's okay. He just woke up a few minutes ago; he's on hella pain meds, but he seems somewhat present. Asked about you. He remembers...what happened. The police kicked me out to take his statement as soon as the doctor okay'd it."

"But he's okay. He's..." The word *alive* is the one on the tip of her tongue, and a tsunami of pain and the reminder that one of her best friends was just lost consumes her.

"I know. And it doesn't help to hear now, but... it'll get better. The missing them won't, but...eventually, you can live with it."

For a moment, the sting of guilt overcomes her. She hadn't even thought about how this must be for him, how reminiscent of his brother and friend's deaths. Isa, too.

But she can't hold onto the shame for long. There just isn't any more room for hurt inside her.

"Thanks, Zeke. I have to go."

She hangs up without remembering to say goodbye. She realizes it a second later, but it doesn't seem to matter much, anyway.

"How's Josh?" Bronte whispers. She's in the fetal position in the corner of the room, and Rose knows it's because it reminds Bronte so much of her childhood—her mom high out of her mind, grabbing her worn stuffed bear and hiding in a closet until all her mom's "friends" left or they fell asleep. Making herself as small as possible.

All Bronte's mother had ever wanted her to do—take up less space.

"He woke up. Talked to the cops. Zeke said it looks like he'll make a full recovery." The words are hollow, though. Can a recovery really be full when there's a hole inside of you, the shape of the two lives lost?

"Thank God. Something...something good. Fuck."

The pain is visible in Bronte's body—the set of her shoulders, her tightened jaw. The way she refuses to look Rose in the eye.

And finally, *finally*, for the first time since finding out her would-be older brother died, Rose cries.

"He deserved so much more," she whispers angrily. "We all deserve so much more. We've been through so much."

And sure, maybe religion explains it away with the *"blessed are they who mourn"* because they will rejoice in the afterlife, and maybe she believes that or maybe she doesn't, but right now, it doesn't seem to *matter* either way.

He's dead. One of the best people who has ever fucking lived, someone who dedicated his life to nothing but helping the people around him...gone. Josh hospitalized. Kathy paralyzed. Bronte grieving. Rose having to argue that the man who assaulted her for years did anything *wrong* and fight for him to *not* be allowed near a child.

(What the hell is this world? How is any of this okay?)

A knock sounds on the door, and at the sight of Davis in the peephole Rose is only further enraged, not even bothering to wonder how she found out the room number.

She heaves the door open with a sob, Scarlett balanced on her hip, and glares at the attorney.

"Ms. Simmons, I've been trying to contact you—"

"And my ignoring your calls was no accident. Why are you here?" she demands.

"We need you to come meet us; it's vital for the case." Davis's face is earnest.

"There is nothing you could say right now that could get me to come," Rose says, voice empty. "One of the most important people in my life is *dead*. I could care less about my next time on the stand right now. Plan your battle strategy alone."

"Ms. Simmons, I'm so sorry for your loss, but... there's a plea deal."

26

FOR WHAT FEELS like the thousandth time in the last twenty-four hours, Josh regains consciousness and has to stop himself from immediately crying out in pain.

A memory floats through his head of a nurse reminding him to press the call button for more drugs, but he knows he won't; too much has happened for him to continue being unable to hold coherent thoughts. He needs a few minutes to process, to get his shit together.

"Hey." Isa's voice is raspy—which for her equals worried—and quieter than Josh has heard it.

"Sup," Josh rasps, wincing at the movement of his diaphragm. Isa eyes him and reaches for the nurse call button without another word, but Josh attempts to paw her hand away. "No. Don't want...meds. Fucking with my head."

Isa lets out an exasperated sigh. "Fine. You get a five-minute head start before I tell them you're up."

"Fair." Josh takes a deep breath, then looks into the eyes of his girlfriend's best friend.

Before he even gets the words out, Isa visibly tenses, like she knows what he's about to ask—knows exactly what Josh wants to know, the first time they've really talked since everything went down.

"He's gone?" Josh's voice wobbles in a way he didn't know it was capable of.

(*He died protecting me. For me. My fault.*)

A nod of confirmation from Isa. "Geoffrey too. The only good thing to come from this…" In the silence, *massacre* is the only word to come to Josh's mind. "Kai's sorry he couldn't be here. Zeke too; he and I are taking turns keeping him company."

Sorrow fills Josh. "God, I could never expect him to be. Not when he's processing. Shit, Bronte? And Rose's case, Jesus." *Everything…gone to shit.*

They deserved so much more.

"Bronte is…coping."

Isa frowns. "Rose…a lot has gone down where that's concerned— in a good-ish way, *stay in the bed* God damn it, Joshua. You were *stabbed*, you dumb fuck."

She restrains Josh from jumping to his feet, though the motion involved in sitting up alone is excruciating, so Josh relents and lays back.

"What do you mean good-*ish*? And if Bronte's out of commission, who's watching Scarlett?!"

"Rose made some…revelations yesterday, before what happened to you. I guess the court decided to call a recess for a day or two while both sides reconfigure. Anyway, she's not in court, so she can watch Scar."

A relieved breath pushes out of his lips. "Thank God. I…" *Can't bear to lose anyone else.*

(*Especially* not them.)

"Oh, honey, thank God you're awake!" Kathy's voice breaks the spiral of darkness Josh's thoughts are spinning into, and he jerks his head up without remembering he's injured until his body screeches at him to stop.

"Aunt Kathy, what the hell are you doing out of bed?"

It's then that he realizes she's in a wheelchair, pushing herself unsteadily towards him, the movements still unpracticed. Because she's paralyzed now.

(For a few moments, he'd been able to forget.)

"My baby," she says wistfully, laying a hand on his cheek—and briefly, everything feels right in the world. His godmother is here. Safe.

It doesn't last.

"I'm so sorry, Josh." Her voice is heart-wrenching, and he has no idea what she's apologizing for until she continues. "This is all my fault. I didn't stop Desiree from bringing him into your home; I didn't do enough to keep him away once she was gone, and now he's hurt you again. He's—" A sob escapes her. "Your friend—your poor, noble friend, so brave and trying to help you. All my fault."

"Aunt Kathy, no, you know that's not true," he pleads with her.

"I can never thank Evan; you would be gone too if he hadn't called the police when he did. He saved you." Kathy lets herself have thirty more seconds of grief, then sits up straighter, attempting to even out her breathing. "I talked to Saba," she says, referencing their lawyer, and Josh feels himself tense.

"I tried to tell her we wouldn't be able to—"

"Joshua Brooks, I know your mother didn't raise you to interrupt someone speaking." He closes his mouth guiltily. "Obviously, we no longer need her help with getting the protective order, although I did let her know Rose might have a need of her services when she gets back, depending on how things go. Saba said she can help us with a case for reparations and compensation against the state for not giving us the order before, and on behalf of Evan, honey. She... she's willing to do it at a lower rate, although that means we'll have to work around her schedule a little bit."

"Even at a lower rate, between the medical bills for the two of us, on top of everything we already had..."

He'd always used to think the term "crippling debt" was just a metaphor.

"Well, actually...before I even told her about you being here too, honey, she found something."

Josh tries to remind himself not to get his hopes up, but the look in his godmother's eyes...if she can look even mildly relieved, with everything that's happened, what Saba found is a big deal.

"This hospital has a really strong financial assistance program," she explains hesitantly. "They offer lower rates and some aid, honey. We have to get approved, and it's based on biological family, so we would be applying separately, but Saba thinks we have a pretty good chance; it's a full charity care discount for people who qualify as below the federal poverty level."

A halfhearted snort, followed by a wince, from Josh. "Well, that is *definitely* us."

"That it is." Kathy smooths a cool paper towel she'd made Isa grab over Josh's face, and he can see the exhaustion in her eyes beneath the strength she's trying to project for him.

The way she's hiding each time she tries to cross her legs, each time she forgets she can't stand up to press her lips to her godson's forehead.

He knows he won't let him see how much she's hurting for a while yet, not with everything he's already dealing with. She's here to be his rock, regardless of her own struggles.

(That's what it means to love someone.)

The door to the room reopens, and a nurse steps in. Isa trails behind her—Josh hadn't even seen her leave, the snake—and he tries to scowl at his friend, but Isa raises her eyebrows blamelessly and mouths, *'Five minutes. Told you.'*

Josh squeezes his godmother's hand tightly as the nurse begins to administer another round of meds, and he can tell he's starting to fall back asleep despite himself.

(Despite how badly he needs to hear Rose's voice, assure himself she's okay; how badly he needs to beg Bronte for forgiveness, that the man she loved gave his love to save his own.)

As the world begins to darken, he's torn. It's bittersweet in the worst way. The problems that have haunted him for the longest time have been made irrelevant. Geoffrey is gone. *Finally*. His godmother is safe, and he won't have to worry about her not getting the treatment she needs because the spare change he can scrape together isn't even enough for a consultation.

(It's hard to feel like it matters, though. Hard to feel like anything matters.)

———

"What's going on?"

By the time Rose bustles into the coffee shop behind Davis, it's clear the other two women have been waiting a while.

Scarlett sits on her hip, wide-eyed, Rose too distraught for her daughter to be anywhere but attached to her. She can see it the moment the others realize Scar's with her—the way they carefully take stock of her tiny body, looking for signs of the man who'd terrorized them.

Scar stares around the room, too distracted by the bright lights and colorful wall art to notice the tension. But then, the kid has been holed up in a hotel room for days, now, so the change of scenery is practically another world for her.

"Davis refused to tell us anything until we were all together," Casey says nervously, setting down an empty coffee mug.

"A plea deal's been struck." Davis uses her no-nonsense voice. "I wanted to tell you all before I formally accept it, but the defense has agreed to plead guilty."

Alexa's face lights up, and tears of joy begin to fill Casey's eyes. Months and months and *months* of thinking this will all be for nothing, but he's pleading guilty.

It's a miracle.

(Rose has never believed in miracles.)

She can see the look in Davis's eyes—frustration, guilt, something she's not telling them. There's more to the story.

Rose's grip on Scarlett tightens.

It's unsurprising, really. And no matter, because she hasn't bothered to get her hopes up. She learned better long ago.

She's not the girl who gets a happy ending.

"What are the terms of the deal?"

Davis grimaces. "No additional charges; he pleads only to those initiated at the start of the proceedings, and he agrees to sign the papers to terminate parental rights." A nod to the infant in question, who hums nonsensically.

So the rest of it, what Rose has gone through...off the table. The years of abuse and degradation. Extortion, which would've kept him locked up for so, so long.

"Mmma," Scarlett babbles, as she's been doing for a few days now. Rose had thought it coincidence, but the way Scar pats her face as she says it—"Ma*ma*" she repeats—Rose knows she's saying it intentionally.

Not her very first word (*hi*), but... it's everything. And it's happening now, in the midst of chaos and pain and frustration.

The moment is magic, wrapped up in pain and fear, but *there*.

"There's more," the attorney tells them, her face morphing back into stone. "We agree to recommend a two-year max sentence to the judge."

"Are you fucking kidding me?" Fire runs through Rose's veins, and she can see outrage and shock on Casey and Alexa's faces at the pronouncement as Alexa rants, the raised voice making Scarlett jump. "How can you even consider agreeing to that? A slap on the wrist and without half of the ammunition against him now that Rose's joined the case?"

"I'm not 'considering' it, I'm accepting it. My notifying you prior to doing so is merely a courtesy." Davis's voice is icy now. "I know this seems like garbage to you, and I know it's not nearly justice if such a thing is ever even possible when the crime has altered you permanently. But believe me, in the American justice system? This is as good as it gets."

"We don't have any say in you accepting this?" Casey demands.

"Nope. Just the prosecution," Rose comments, devoid of emotion. "Convenient for her, another win on her record without all the tedious work that would've come next, and none of the risk of a loss."

Davis fumes. "Don't you dare imply that I'm making this choice at all lightly." A tone of warning laces the sentence. "You have no idea how rare of a win this is. Him being convicted and agreeing to revoke his rights... it's a *huge* deal. From here on out, he'll have to register as an offender, it'll be on his record, and any future charges—"

"But there shouldn't *be* any future charges!" Alexa argues. "He should be locked up until he's a shriveled corpse. How is it fair that he gets to go on hurting people?"

(*Nothing about this has ever been fair*, Rose thinks to herself.)

"I thought you were on our side—that we were in this together. But you don't give a damn, do you?" Casey's laugh is bitter, and Davis slams a hand to the table in response.

Scarlett begins to whimper, and Rose rubs her back gently, making clicking noises with her tongue until Scar calms.

"I don't take cases pro bono because I 'don't *give a damn*,'" Davis hisses, the words acid. "Did you never consider why I agreed to do this case for free—why *I* approached you about me taking it on? Attorneys don't do that when they don't give a fuck; the time I've spent on this case could've gone to others that would've brought profit and bolstered my reputation, but I am *here,* where I have been for *months* because there is nothing I want more than that monster behind bars.

"I'm agreeing to this deal because it is a *win* for us—yes, us— whether you get that or not. I'm agreeing because I had all the evidence in the world, but *my* attacker was found not guilty; because in the twenty years I've been practicing law since then, I've seen too many of the disgusting men I've prosecuted walk away scot-free when they should be in solitary. You're being offered an actual conviction. The rest of us aren't so lucky."

And she's right. This is as lucky as it gets.

This 'lucky' equals two years in a cushy cell for Kyle, after which the three women with clenched fists will look over their shoulders every day in fear of him. In fear that if it's not them he's attacking, it's someone else.

(*Lucky.*)

"I know this doesn't feel like a good thing to you," Davis says, tone apologetic. "I know it's not enough. I know it's not nearly what he deserves. But this is as good as it gets. This is a win."

Part of Rose is relieved, of course. The custody battle she's feared as long as Scarlett's existed is no longer an issue, the daughter in her arms safe from the beast who'd destroyed everything she'd ever held dear before her. And however short the sentence, people will *know*. That he did this, that he's *capable* of this, however sweet and charming and generous he may seem.

But it's a bit hard to care about that side of things.

This is what her government, her country, thinks her violation is worth. Two years, if that.

Three women's bodies no longer seem their own. She doesn't know that there's ever been a day since it all began that she hasn't thought about it.

Every. Day. For so many years and countless to come.

The justice system thinks that's worth two years.

She's so *lucky*.

"I have to go," she tells them, throat constricting as she pushes away from the table, Scarlett's tiny fingers curling into a haphazard curl of her hair. It's all too much—this, seeing Kyle, the grief, Josh's injuries...she can't *do* it. "I need to get home for a funeral."

27

THE SOUND of Scarlett's crying seeps through the bathroom door, and Rose takes a deep breath, locking eyes with herself in the mirror one last time.

She'd known better than to put on makeup—she's already cried three times since she woke up and knows there will probably be less than a sum total of an hour throughout the rest of the day wherein she's *not*. She's done her hair nicely, though, an intricate braid, multi-purposed to both make her look a bit nicer and keep the curls from tangling in front of her face when she inevitably breaks down.

The black of her dress is bright, a thrift shop purchase specifically for today. She hadn't had an occasion to wear all black since over a decade ago.

(It was her father's funeral, then.)

Of course, this isn't technically a funeral. That entails actual burial, and what with cremation being less than a third the price, it wasn't much of a choice.

Scar's crying abates, and for a moment, Rose is filled with illogical terror until a familiar hand taps on the door. "You almost ready, baby?"

No. The not ready-ness permeates every cell of her body; she's not ready to say goodbye.

(How could she ever be ready to say goodbye to the first man she ever trusted?)

A shiver, and she opens the door, not meeting Josh's eyes.

"Yeah. Let's go."

His hand trembles as it reaches for hers; she knows this is hard for him too. He's been trying to be there for those of them closest to Evan, let alone dealing with his own grief.

(How is Bronte ever going to move on?)

And he blames himself, Rose knows; however much she and the others have tried to reassure him that Evan knew what he was doing in protecting him, he feels entirely responsible for the other man's death.

It's not something anyone can talk him out of.

By the time they arrive at the church putting on the service, the one Zeke's a member of, most of their friends are already there.

Isa kneels near the altar, hands clasped and face pressed into the steps but shoulders heaving enough for the rest of them to figure how well she's doing. She's the only one of them besides Zeke and Kai who's religious, so Rose's best guess is that she's praying.

Demanding an explanation. Not understanding why, what purpose could be worth this. Thinking that God knows best but not comprehending what could possibly make this the right thing.

Nick's not there—hasn't been anywhere lately.

Isa had mentioned in passing three days prior that he'd decided to move, and they weren't talking as much, but his abrupt departure, the fact that he's not there on this of all days...it speaks volumes about how much she's going through outside of them all.

(How much she's bottling up, still refusing to talk about because she just doesn't have it in her to process yet.)

On the other end of the spectrum, Kai lies sprawled on the front pew. He lifts his head as they approach, smiling at Scarlett and handing her a shiny coin from his pocket, but where they're close enough, Rose catches the scent of tequila rolling off of him in waves.

No one had realized how close he'd grown to Evan until he was gone.

How much Evan had been the first to truly understand him, the first he could be completely real with.

"Kai...man, how much have you had to drink? When was the last time you showered?" Josh asks gently.

(They're all just doing their best to keep from crying before the service even starts.)

"I have done nothing but drink since he's been gone." Even as he says it, he pulls the flask out of his jacket and takes a swig. "None of it matters. And don't you dare tell me he wouldn't have wanted this. We'll never get to know what he wanted. Because he's *gone.*"

And after the way Kai's dad's death had thrown everything off course, it's no wonder this is sending him spiraling again.

Rose nods, eyeing him speculatively. She hands Scarlett to Josh carefully, pressing a kiss to the little girl's forehead, before dropping down next to Kai and snatching the flask from his hand. His and Josh's eyes both widen as she chugs from it.

"Yeah?" Kai asks, eyebrows raised as he drags himself to a sitting position. Relaxing with her, knowing he's with family, as she'd hoped he might.

"It's been a hell of a week." She can see the worry lining Josh's face and motions for him to relax. "I won't get hammered, I promise. You know I won't let myself out of control while Scar's here."

She presses her shoulder to Kai's, and he scowls like he knows what she's doing but gives her a nod of respect and leans against her in return.

Bronte makes her way back from the fellowship hall where she's been hiding out, alone, earbuds in and blasting Breaking Benjamin loud enough for them all to hear.

If it were any other day, Rose would reprimand her about the damage to her eardrums, but...not now.

"Where the hell *is* Zeke, anyway?" Bronte snaps, pain creeping into her voice.

"He's on his way, Te," Josh promises. "You know he wouldn't miss it.

Rose finds herself staring at the extra-large pictures of their lost friend, a giant collage across the altar. Shots of he and Bronte together recently, looking so happy to have each other, they wouldn't know if the room was on fire.

Some of Evan laughing, sprawled out beside Bronte. A pang goes through Rose at how weary and hopeless he'd looked right after getting out of prison. The more recent pictures show a bit more energy and light in him. Hope in his eyes, despite whatever he'd been through after they were all ripped apart, bouncing around the system the rest of his life. Rose had finally found them, the kind of love that didn't forget her even though it had been half a decade. He had finally built a stable life with Bronte.

He was *just* on his way to the happy ending he deserved.

Rose looks back at the collage, at the shots of him grinning at Scarlett and attempting to teach her to walk, clapping when she crawled. She lets out an excruciating gasp—there, in the middle of it all. A faded image of her, Bronte, and Evan.

Bronte comes to stand next to her, a giving Rose pained look of knowing. "I didn't know he had it till I turned his stuff upside down last night. Had a bit of a breakdown," she confesses, rubbing at her face. "Found it sticking out of the book he kept with him while he was in jail."

"I can't believe he kept it safe, all these years," Rose replies, unable to take her eyes off the picture. "I'll have to get a copy to frame for my wall."

A one-armed hug comes from Bronte—as much as she could hope for, really.

The door swings open with a slam, the kind in a league all its own, powered by the all-consuming rage of a teenager with a reason to be upset.

Twenty or so kids, ranging from twelve to twenty-two, trail inside. Many of them wear ill-fitting clothes, bags beneath their eyes, expressions sullen.

At the end of the procession is the only person Rose knows who could rival them for angst.

(Seeing Zeke in black is nothing out of the ordinary.)

"What..." She starts to ask until she begins to recognize them.

Evan's kids—so many for whom he was the only positive role model they'd ever had.

Imani's with them; she moves to Rose's side like she knows she's safe there, though her expression is cold and guarded.

(Shut down, because that's the only way for girls like them to make it through when the roof caves in just when you thought it couldn't get any worse.)

Zeke gives Rose a half-hearted attempt at a smile. "My boyfriend, Dmitri...he used to come to the center when he was younger, stuck around when he was out of his own hell. That's how we met," he says, nodding towards the familiar man at the front of the bunch. "It was his idea. Knew they'd all want to be here. Sorry we're late."

Of course—*of course,* they wanted to be here. Rose wants to beat herself up for it not crossing her mind, but... she's so exhausted and empty already, it's hard to be any more down on herself.

And it's the kind of thing that reminds everyone how important Zeke is—how important the quiet ones who listen more than they speak, who truly *see* the world around them, are.

Even on this darkest of days, somehow, there are specks of light that make her think maybe things can be almost okay again. Someday, anyway.

———

The rest feels like a blur.

For a while, Rose feels cried out, too drained to feel any sadder. Not many more people show up; they hadn't broadcasted the service because they wanted it to be real, personal, and not everyone who'd ever met the dead bemoaning what a tragedy it was when their lives won't change in the slightest.

Bronte more than anyone, as she's the one bearing the brunt of the mourning, the brunt of the impact this will have.

Almost everyone takes a turn speaking. There's no need for a microphone, and they sit in a circle on the floor, sharing favorite memories and the characteristics and habits they'd all miss most. There's almost as much laughter as there are tears in the end.

They share pictures of Evan looking out of his element with Bronte and Zeke at a *Three Days Grace* concert, the time Kai challenged him to arm wrestle without the latter considering the former's hand would be slippery with grease from work.

Bronte tells a story Evan had relayed to her of his childhood while drunk, muttering about a little boy chattering away and somehow picking up both rudimentary Spanish and French from cartoons when his dad got a crappy TV; Zeke mentions Evan renting a bounce house for a youth group event and the kids informing everyone he had only done so because *he* wanted the contraption.

Bronte recalls the time Evan joked that she'd have to marry him someday, and she realized she wanted nothing more.

Liza learning to trust Evan when every instinct within her told her to run. His unfaltering loyalty and kindness. The kids he taught to ride bikes—one he picked up from a dealer's place when a shootout erupted.

The day Evan found Rose and Bronte. He approached Bronte in their doorway, and Rose's twelve-year-old self considered throwing a chair before biting him hard enough to leave a scar until he mentioned that he'd brought cookies.

The love with which he looked at her and Scarlett, despite having been gone from her life much longer than he'd ever been in it.

Kai's voice cracking when he talked about the pranks he and Evan pulled on each other. Opening up about how each of them felt so, so inferior, so responsible for holding it together and staying in control enough for the people around them, their problems seeming pale in comparison.

Josh talking about Evan's words to him in the darkest hour, his aunt unconscious. The first man older than him he'd ever had to truly consider family.

(They don't talk about what led to him being gone.)

They finish by blasting music, an amalgamation playlist of their lost one's favorite songs, so different and yet somehow fusing into something familiar.

Rose isn't the type to believe in ghosts, but if she did, this is the moment she would swear there's a warmth with her that's not her own.

And she loves Josh, loves Bronte, and wants to grieve with them both...but not right now. This grief is all her own, not one she can bear to share or reconcile, collective pain being somehow different.

This...this is all-consuming.

She slips away from the crowd under the guise of going to the bathroom but makes her way to a quiet hallway, staring at the bible verses plastered along the wall in confusion.

It's just so *hard*. She lost her dad when she was young, of course, but...she was young. They'd never been particularly close, and she'd started feeling alone in the world long before then.

And when she'd been separated from Bronte and Evan, she'd at least known they were *okay*, but this...

He'd only just begun changing the world the way he was born to.

She hears the footsteps ten seconds before he says, *hey*, but she's pretty sure that was intentional; Zeke has always been good about noticing who gets jumpy if you sneak up on them.

"You should be in there," she rasps, but he shakes his head.

"I think you need me more than they do."

Rose snorts but doesn't argue further. Instead, she stares at the cross hanging across the hall from her.

"I wondered if it'd be you or Bronte," he comments offhandedly, and she turns to him, confused.

"Come again?"

"Having an existential crisis about the universe. Death always brings them out—makes people either come to God, whichever one they're suited to, or turn from religion altogether."

"You...losing them was what made you 'come to Jesus'?"

He smirks. "Well, actually, it initially made me refuse to believe in God. I decided even if there *was* one, I didn't want anything to do with them. Not after they'd let Gus and Angie die. But then..." He sighs, looks at Rose pensively. "Then I realized I couldn't handle life if this was it—if not believing meant they were just...gone. I have to believe in a god because I can't handle the world if they're not happy somewhere out there, somehow." He makes a meaningful motion to the semi-colon tattoo on his wrist—the one he'd gotten just after his attempt.

Rose swallows, lips wobbling. "I...yeah. Both of those concepts are fighting in my head right now." And they both *hurt* because either she *does* believe in a God who was willing to watch the most wonderful person go for whatever reason that she doesn't think could justify it, or she *doesn't*, and every ember of his existence has been snuffed out. Both conclusions are painful. "I don't think I know where on the spectrum I'll end up falling," she admits.

"That's because both rationales make sense. And I mean, you can always change your mind, you know?" Zeke shrugs. "I'm religious. But I wasn't always. Isa, she grew up as Catholic as can be, Liza was Jewish, but now she's a diehard atheist. Aaliyah's Muslim, Kai's family is Baptist, but he doesn't practice much... there's room for wherever you wind up. Just know you're not alone in the indecision, yeah?"

He hugs her, at which point Rose realizes this is possibly the most physical affection she's ever gotten from him.

She makes her way back to the sanctuary, where Josh patiently sits with puffy eyes, Scarlett crawling about on the floor in front of him.

By this time, almost everyone has headed out. Bronte lingers long enough to give Rose a hug before leaving without a word.

They're silent on the way back to the apartment, both lost inside their own grief, when a song comes on—one of Evan's favorites. The kind of pop hit every teenage girl wants to deny liking at some point before they realize being like other girls isn't a bad thing.

Rose starts humming it under her breath, and Josh squawks out the lyrics, and by the time they park at home, they're both smiling and crying and belting out every word, hands clasped over the gear shift—trembling, but together.

They sing another as they make their way upstairs—obnoxiously, giggling and knowing this is *exactly* what Evan would want them to be doing. Unequivocally.

And Rose says, "Evan would be disappointed we're not using his death as an excuse to eschew social etiquette."

"Hold that thought." Josh runs off to his apartment before he slides back into the room minutes later in a onesie, handing her a can of half-full whipped cream and his fluffiest blanket despite the fact that it's not even three in the afternoon.

They watch *The Walking Dead* for Evan, *The Flash* for themselves, and *The Princess Diaries* for the hell of it. They only move from the futon to go to the bathroom or get more snacks, Scarlett crawling across them to get into a new position every so often, and... it's so *good*.

Rose is in so much pain, so much turmoil, and the need to write her victim impact statement sneaks around the fringes of her mind, but *life is short*.

And she hates that this is what it took for her to realize it, but it doesn't matter in the end. She's here, with the little girl she made and the guy she loves and a fuck ton of popcorn and rom-coms. She's allowed to be happy, to relish in these little moments of pure love. Evan would've kicked her ass if she didn't.

When Scarlett falls asleep, she practically jumps Josh, consuming his mouth and virtually molding her body to his own, and he looks apprehensive until she rolls her eyes and reassures him that she doesn't want to have sex for the first time since the trial, since reopened wounds and triggers, on the day of their family's funeral.

But soon. She likes sex with Josh—likes *it*, likes that it's with him, likes that she knows she's safe, likes that for once, it actually feels like she gets to decide what her body does and does not do.

She's not "over" Evan's death; when she wakes up the next morning, when it hits her again that he's gone—as it will every day for the next year or two, and then slightly less often, maybe—she loses it.

(Again.)

Breaks down, crying and pressing her nails into her palms until they draw blood.

(Again.)

But she picks herself up. Pulls it together. Makes her way to work, touching the photo of the one she's lost hanging on her front door.

(For them.)

28

"Rose, honey, you've got three at 107," Marnie's voice jolts her, and she jerks from where she's been standing by the coffee pot, lost in thought.

"On it, sorry," Rose apologizes with a half-hearted smile, and Marnie nods at her with soft eyes.

She knows what it's like to miss someone, too.

It's been a month since they've been gone, now, a month since Isa moved away for a "change of pace" because that's how she outruns her grief. But it's still Rose's instinct to look for Isa. To want to catch her eye and make a face at the creepy old men that come in every Thursday. Throw dirty dishrags at her. Scowl when the other girl avoids brewing new tea because she hates to.

It's the little things she misses the most—the ones that are voluntarily missing, that are easier to think about missing than rants about legal reform with Evan, afternoons sprawled across the couch in his office.

Classes have started back up this week, and after much convincing, she's been conned into taking one on campus. Josh, Kathy, and Bronte all spent hours coercing her, but Zeke was the one who really talked her into it, who reminded her not to let the darkness in the world win.

(*"It's a once-a-week seminar, Rose. You care about this too much to not be able to be there and discuss it with your professor. We can all take turns watching Scar that day. Your life didn't end, too—act like it. Make the fact that you're still here mean something."*)

She'd fought them on it, but within the first five minutes of the first day, she felt so *alive*, getting to argue with other people as passionate as her. She's already completely enamored with the professor.

It doesn't hurt that Josh signed up for the class, too, somehow putting it towards his major, though she's entirely sure he's there primarily for her benefit.

Kathy's recovery is going well, though it's making them all much more aware of just how many of the places they go every day aren't accessible.

Rose is at the grocery store with Bronte one night, and somehow, they end up in front of the avocados.

Neither of them likes avocados.

(Evan does. *Did.*)

It's bittersweet; they're so used to what he did and didn't care about, which speaks volumes about the quality of their relationships with him, but this is just the first of many times cruel reminders that he's gone will smack them with the realization that they don't *need* to buy something, do something, anymore.

But they're making it—picking up the pieces, finding ways to fit them together despite the gaps that can never be filled again. They can remember the one they've lost, love and cherish his legacy, without losing themselves along the way.

It's a slow process.

And it's not without painful nudges that drive home the loss...the most visceral of which is the victim impact statement Rose has to write weeks later.

How does one sum up what years of brutality can do to a person, the way nearly a decade of violation and hurt and invasion and trauma have impacted them?

(The way they'll never be the same, no matter how much healing they do.)

She sits down to write it several different times, but each devolves into a mental breakdown. It's just too *much*.

She tries consuming all the different media dealing with sexual assault and the aftermath, and moving on—reads all the books, watches all the movies, listens to all the songs.

After, the protagonist is always *stronger* for what they've gone through, always forgiving the perpetrator even if they don't deserve it, wishing that they'll go on to become a better person and change their ways.

She doesn't feel *stronger*. She feels fucking hollow, exhausted, and she wishes Kyle and everyone like him everything they have coming to them for what they've done to other people. She will never forgive, forget, or any of that lovely bullshit; she'll probably feel relief when he finally dies rather than any sort of grief.

(Does that make her a bad person?)

Josh finds her at the table during the fourth of these incidents— legs crossed, teeth clenched, looking devoid of any kind of hope.

He looks at her—really looks at her—and reaches to squeeze her hand; slowly, so she sees the contact before it comes.

"I love you," he says softly. "And you know I want to be here for you and that I'm happy to talk to you about anything you want. But I don't think I'm the person you *need* to talk to right now."

She tilts her head questioningly, but before he can continue speaking, the door swings open, Bronte and Liza stalk inside.

Bronte nods to Josh. "We've got this. Get out."

Josh gives Rose a lopsided smile. "Scar and I are gonna go to the park and get ice cream. Call if you need me, yeah?"

"Bye, Mama!" Scar calls as they head out, using 2 of the 15 words now in her repertoire and making Rose's heart burst. She feels like Scar was just born, but she's becoming a whole *person* by this point. She has likes and dislikes, and every day Rose can see her personality begin to take shape just a little bit more. Can see her daughter becoming whoever it is she'll be.

Rose did that—that happy, happy little girl. She made her, raised her, and she's going to be an awesome person. Her eyes are as close, as similar, as she will *ever* get to Kyle.

Liza clears her throat, and Rose turns her attention back to the table. "What exactly did Josh tell y'all?"

"You were getting angsty and conflicted writing your victim impact statement, and he knew you wouldn't believe anything he had to say because it was coming from him." Bronte squeezes her hand. "I love you, and I'm here for you, and I'm one hundred percent on your team. But I'm not the one who can understand what you're feeling right now. I figured I'd bring someone more equipped to understand."

When Rose raises an eyebrow, Liza continues, "I figured you were getting into a guilt spiral. The kind of thing where you start to wonder if your anger is even justified. If you've become so vindictive that you're the one at fault."

"You too?"

"Rose, I'm gonna tell you something Aaliyah has spent all of our time together beating into my brain, okay? Listen to me. You don't owe anyone forgiveness. *Ever.* That's the whole point of forgiveness. It's a gift that you *can* give someone, but you are in no way obligated to do so.

"And not giving it doesn't make you better or worse. That's why people have to *ask* for forgiveness because it's not something they just *get.* People who've been wronged can give it if it makes *them* feel better, not the perpetrator. You're... you're allowed to feel relieved, you know? You don't have to feel guilty because you're glad what you went through was recognized. You *deserve* the validation."

"Cognitively, I know that. But it just...it still feels wrong, you know? Like I should be the better person, move past it. A million other people have." Rose clenches and unclenches her fists, feeling aimless.

"Every person's story is different. And every person processes differently. And more power to the ones who find it in their hearts to forgive those who assaulted them, but honestly...fuck that." Liza locks eyes with Rose unapologetically, and Bronte snaps in appreciation in the background. "Someone who's done this kind of thing doesn't deserve forgiveness; if they did, we wouldn't have to give it to them. They would have it automatically—but they don't. We have the power to forgive them *or not*. And beyond that, you were wronged, and you have a right to your anger."

"I have a right to my anger," Rose repeats softly, testing it out.

It's the kind of thing that might just fit.

———

"You're going to do *what*?" Rose says for the third time, looking back and forth between Bronte and Zeke. Beside her, Kai looks equally surprised, which is a bit of a consolation. They'd gone to Applebee's for half-priced apps, to catch up and be around people equally devastated and healing, and now she's staring at them across the table with raised eyebrows.

"Honestly, you'd think we planned this." Bronte looks to her friend with a soft smile. "But yeah. Liza and I are starting a women's club that meets weekly, and I'm leading a Girl Scout troop. I just...I think about us at that age. How much we could've used someone older who *got* it, that our biggest problems weren't our parents refusing to buy a toy we wanted. Someone to just care and be real with us and a good female role model. I want to do that for someone else."

Rose's heart swells, but her and Bronte's relationship isn't a mushy one, so she just nods. She knows Bronte sees everything in her eyes. With a deep breath, she turns to Zeke. "And you?"

"I already talked to the city council and had my interview with the sponsor and everything," he tells them sheepishly. "Dmitri and I start next week."

"There's no one Evan would trust to take over more," Bronte says with authority, looking overtaken with emotion for half a second before forcing it down. "No one else I would trust with his kids."

The moment is tender, bittersweet, and Rose would worry she's intruding if not for Bronte's hand clenching hers under the table.

"There's no one else I would believe could do it justice," Kai agrees, giving a firm nod with a sad but proud expression.

He, at least, has no major life changes; he'd ended up deciding he didn't want to date the girl he'd caught feelings for, so it's just him at the shop and with his mom and siblings as usual.

This is moving on—this is the new normal, figuring out who they are when pieces of themselves are gone. And it's scary, but... it's okay. *They're* going to be okay.

And Evan is gone, but his legacy isn't. His kids will know how much he loved them, and Zeke will carry on the legacy at the center to make sure they're still loved in a way none of the rest of them had ever gotten to have. A way every kid *should* have.

———

"Standing there longer won't make it any easier." Imani's voice is no more gentle than usual despite the circumstances, as Rose stares up at the entrance sign with her heart in her throat.

It's her first time back at the center since Evan's been gone. Five minutes she's been standing here filled with trepidation. Entering feels wrong.

She'd been heartbroken when Isa said she was leaving, even felt a little betrayed. But in this moment, she can understand the need to run away.

It'll be different once Zeke takes over. This is one last thing she needs to do before then.

Rose tilts her head at Imani and seats herself on the step with a sigh. "Want to sit out here today?"

"You don't want to go inside?" Even as she asks, Imani seats herself beside Rose.

Rose bumps Imani's shoulder with her own, chest heavy. "You know I'm only here for you, anyway."

"Yeah?" The younger girl quiets, looking pensive.

Rose gets it—gets being surprised that anyone would ever care enough to do something like that, something they don't want to.

"Yep. I care about you, kid. Evan or no, you're stuck with me."

Imani eyes her, the hope and fear in her wide eyes strong enough to sear Rose's skin.

Rose worries at her lip. "I want you to call me whenever you need anything. Ever. And..." She hesitates, nervous the big step will send Imani running, but pulls the card with her number and address out of her pocket nonetheless. "This is for you. If you just want to come over, or—or if something's not okay and you need to get away. No questions asked unless you want to talk about it. You're always welcome. Okay?"

Imani nods, eyes far away. "I...okay. Thank you."

"Of course. Girls like us have to stick together."

Rose slings an arm around her, and they stay like that for a while.

———

Rose groans when her phone rings; it's not actually very early, but the bed is comfy, and she's nestled into Josh's chest in a way that makes her feel safe. No part of her wants to move.

"I got it," he mumbles, throwing an arm to snatch the offending technology from the bedside table. "'Lo?" he greets and whispers, "It's just Zeke, don't worry. Go back to sleep, and I'll deal with him."

He's been over every day since everything went up in flames, which she loves, but also made hiding his present a challenge before his birthday two months ago. She got away with it, but she's pretty sure that's only because he was so focused on Scarlett turning one that he forgot about his own celebration a week later.

Rose starts to drift off again when Josh snorts, the motion jolting her body.

"Seriously?" he asks, then sighs dramatically as he hangs up the phone. "Well, apparently, I'm being evicted."

"Huh?" Rose sits upright, pulling the quilt with her to cover her bare skin.

"Their apartment reminds Bronte too much of Evan, and she doesn't want to live alone, so Zeke and Kai decided that she's going to move into my room since I already live here anyway. We're still expected to show up to family dinners, but I think that's more because they can't cook than because they want to make sure we still come."

"I guess we might as well save the money on rent," she says casually, watching his reaction carefully from under her eyelashes. "You know, it'll cut down our expenses enough to maybe adopt Domino..."

"You just don't want to have to walk of shame when you forget your work clothes," he rolls his eyes, pulling her into his side.

"It's a perk," she concedes. "Mainly, I think Scar would like to have you around more."

"Oh, Scar would, would she?" He presses his lips to Rose's neck, and her back instinctively arches, quilt falling to the bed forgotten.

"Are you indifferent to the idea, then?" she asks breathlessly, fingers stroking the hair at the nape of his neck as his mouth trails down her chest.

"I'm very much in favor," he mumbles against her skin. "I want this—you—twenty-four seven. Forever."

She turns to face him, bringing her lips to his jaw. "Okay, good. We can move your stuff in tomorrow and—"

It's at this moment that Scar squeals the happy "*Hi!*" with which she likes to announce that she's woken up every morning from across the apartment, and both Josh and Rose burst out laughing.

"Hi to you too, hon," Josh calls to her. "We'll be right there."

"Hope you want that twenty-four-seven, too," Rose teases, pecking him before donning his over-sized t-shirt.

"More than anything," he replies seriously.

And he means it. She can see the light in his eyes as he

approaches the crib, picking up Scar and carrying her back to where Rose sits on the bed.

"Hey, you," she says fondly, grinning at the way her daughter holds her arms out to her without hesitation. "What do you think? Is there room in our little family for this troublemaker?"

Scar by no means understands most of the words her mother's saying but claps her hands together nonetheless and gives Josh a toothy grin, which Rose interprets to be her approval.

"Probably the worst decision you'll ever make," Josh says cheerfully, one arm around Rose and Scar's fingers wrapped around the other.

"Oh, for sure," Rose agrees. She pulls out Scar's storybook—the worn one, the only one she'd had when Scar was born. "Alrighty Miss Scarlett, are you feeling Goldilocks or Red Riding Hood?"

"Eenah!" Scar babbles with all the confidence in the world, and Rose nods sagely.

"Goldilocks it is."

She and Josh take turns reading the story, inserting commentary about imperialism and entitlement along the way, and being all-around goofy and ridiculous like always.

"See, honey? There's the mama bear, the daddy bear, and the baby bear—he's just like you!"

"Dada?" Scar repeats because she's too damn smart for her own good and knows this isn't a word she's heard before except in stories.

Rose freezes, a thousand different scenarios of how to handle this running through her head. They haven't talked about this.

But Scar saves her the trouble. She looks back at the picture, says, "Mama," and points to Rose, as she's done a million times. Then she points to Josh and says, "Dada"—not a question, saying it with the confidence only a one-year-old can muster.

Josh looks to Rose as if to check that this is okay, and she nods rapidly; he wipes at his eyes. "Yeah, sweetheart. I'm your Daddy." He says it without hesitation, looking at the baby he's been helping to raise for nearly a year like she's the most precious thing in the world.

He presses a kiss to the top of Scar's head, and the toddler claps her hands together with a giggle.

Rose takes a deep, shuddering breath, tears sliding down to the smile on her face.

Life isn't perfect by any means. And she has no delusion that everything from here on out will be easy.

But they're on their way to healing, to happiness, and whatever else happens, her daughter is so, *so* loved. It's all she could ever ask for.

EPILOGUE

As a kid, Josh had always hated the idea of going to school on his birthday.

As an adult, going to work on his birthday isn't much better, dream job or no. The whole day, all he can think of is getting home to Scar—their daily ritual of watching *Masterchef Junior* with snacks from their secret stash while they wait for Rose to get home, the way his wife's face will light up when she sings happy birthday to him over a misshapen cake, the promise of the emerald negligee she's let hang visibly in their closet all week.

He loves his job, loves the kids he works with, but he'll always want to be with his family more.

When three o'clock hits, he's waving the teenagers away as they clamber into cars without hesitation, blasting Green Day the whole way home. By the time he careens through the front door of the cozy townhouse they'd moved into about a year ago, he's keyed up and ready to be far earlier than necessary to Scar's bus stop.

It takes him a minute to notice that Scar is already there, curled into Rose's side on the couch, her legs sprawled across Bronte and Kai's laps.

It's the kind of thing he comes home to every once in a while, on *Game of Thrones* new episode days, the two currently hogging his furniture interchanged with Liza and Aaliyah or Zeke for wine nights or *Brooklyn Nine-Nine* marathons, respectively, although Kai usually has his wife with him.

There's no sign of Imani today, but it's pretty much a given that if she's not there one day, she'll be over the next, so Josh isn't too worried by her absence.

"Did you guys have a party and forget to invite me? On my birthday?" he asks curiously, plopping onto the arm of the couch and sliding a familiar arm to ruffle Scar's hair as he presses a kiss to Rose's temple.

Domino leans his head against Josh's leg until he pets him, making Scar giggle.

"Scar and I decided to play hooky today," Rose explains, smiling up at him. "We had some last-minute things to get for you, so you couldn't come, but don't worry. We have lots planned for the rest of the night."

"You're gonna love it, Daddy!" Scar promises earnestly. Rose gives her cautionary look, and Scar rolls her eyes in a way that is adorable as it only can be while she's seven. "I know, Mama; I promise I won't spoil the surprise!"

Josh has to hold in a laugh at the strain evident in Scar's face at holding in the secret. "And how exactly did Auntie Bronte and Uncle Kai get roped into this?"

"They came over to see me and Uncle Evan on TV. We're movie stars," Scar says sagely.

Rose strokes a thumb along her cheek. "I was going through old stuff earlier and found the home movies from when she was a baby; Evan is in almost all of them, and after I saw him again, it just made sense for them to come over to watch with us."

She's staring off into space, and Josh watches as she taps her forearm almost unconsciously, where the chain link tattoo she'd gotten in Evan's memory sits, the twin to that adorning Bronte's skin.

"And you started without me—the disrespect."

Scar clambers over Rose to throw her arms around Josh, and Rose lets out a grunt when a bony elbow grinds into her thigh. "Scarlett Bronte Brooks!"

"Sorry, Mama," Scar says and pats Rose's leg gently.

Both Rose's favorite humans look over at her with innocent expressions, and she purses her lips with a sigh but turns the video back on.

"Hey, little one!" Evan's voice fills the room, and a crooked shot of Scar in a swing lights up the TV screen. *"You're six months old today, so we're commemorating with all of your favorite things while we wait for Mommy's shift to end. Yay!"*

Hearing her cue, baby Scar puts her hands towards each other in her best attempt at a clap, which makes seven-year-old Scar scrunch her nose.

"He loved you so much," Rose says wistfully.

It's instinct for Josh to worry she might spiral at the bittersweet words, but he knows it doesn't hurt her the same way anymore. She'll always miss Evan, but life goes on—has *been* going on—and they're so much better having had him in their lives for even the briefest of moments.

"He's the bestest guardian angel." Scar punctuates the words with wide hand gestures, and Josh ruffles her hair.

Bronte nods in agreement, pressing on her own tattoo. "That he is."

Rose smiles too. "By the way, Isa's flight gets in at five a.m. Saturday. How much do you love me?"

Josh groans. "Why do *I* always have to pick her up when it's a red-eye?"

"Because you always lose rock paper scissors," Rose says unabashedly.

"Can Aunt Isa sleep in my room, Mama? Please, please, please?"

"We'll see," Rose promises Scar. "As much as she loves your *Frozen* tent, she might be in the mood for a grown-up bed if she's tired. We'll ask her when she gets here, okay?"

They finish the videos (Rose cries twice), and Josh heads to the kitchen to get a snack, wincing at the boxes all over the floor. "Babe, did you bring more than just the videos out of storage?"

"Yeah, I needed some other stuff, so I figured I'd put these two heathens to work." She says it casually, but Josh can *tell* something's up.

Scar whispers in the too-loud ineffective way most kids do, such that Josh can hear, *"Can I do it now?"*

He doesn't hear Rose's response, just the pitter-patter of his daughter's feet hurrying to her own room.

By the time he makes it back to the living room, Hot Pocket in hand, Scar has returned to Rose's side looking giddy. She's trying so hard to suppress her excitement at whatever the surprise is; she's doing her patented *figured-out-my-Christmas-present-two-weeks-early* mouth clamp, the only way she can physically keep herself from spilling secrets, and the time when both of her parents' influence is most obvious.

Josh sits back down, biting into the Hot Pocket; it sears his mouth, but he's hungry enough not to care. It takes him a minute to notice Scar has changed from her school polo into a t-shirt, her arms obscuring the writing. "Is that a new shirt, honey?"

"Yep! Nana and Ms. Nati helped me pick it out this morning."

"You played hooky *with my Aunt Kathy and Natalya* without me?" he demands, turning to Rose with a playful scowl. "What the—"

"Swear jar, Daddy!"

Rose gestures for them both to quiet down. "I needed them to help me psych myself up for your surprise."

She's smiling, but Josh can see the nerves in his wife's eyes. He knows nothing is really wrong—she would've already told him—but he hates that she's feeling anxious if he's not doing anything to help.

"Everything okay?"

A depressive episode, maybe? It wouldn't be the first time she's had to take a mental health day, but she's been reading, cleaning, not irritable, which all normally show up *days* before the downswing hits.

She reaches over a hand to squeeze his reassuringly, opening her mouth to explain.

"Daddy, don't you like my shirt?" Scar interrupts.

Josh turns his attention back to the bright blue of the cotton, making himself actually read the thing—and then he does a double-take at the white lettering. *I'm so cool, I'm being promoted to big sister.*

For a minute, he just blinks, mouth open. "Oh my God. Oh my— oh my god."

"Words would be good, J," Bronte advises with a laugh, watching Josh's heart explode, and Rose's anxiety mount all at once.

"I...I *love* your shirt, kiddo." He barely gets the words out, voice thick. "Best shirt I've ever seen."

Rose meets his eye, biting her lip. "Yeah?"

"I—yes. God, Rosie, I can't believe this is real."

"The baby is in her belly," Scar informs him, leaning her head onto her father's lap. "She says that's just how they grow, but I think she really ate it."

"I wouldn't put it past her," Josh whispers conspiratorially.

Replaying the moment constantly for the rest of the day, Rose just feels her heart *swell.* She loves her family so much she can't believe it sometimes.

Josh is the best dad ever (she's completely unbiased), and Scar is going to love this baby with her whole heart, is going to protect her younger sibling fiercely, Rose already knows.

And they're *ready.* Scar is the best kid in the world, but there were so many moments of terror, so many times Rose worried about the circumstances of her conception or about being able to keep a roof over her head. This time, she and Josh are graduates, have careers and stable income, have a crib she already conned Bronte and Kai into setting up in their room for them, the whole shebang.

Later, when they're curled up in bed together, sweaty from making good use of the green negligee after Scar fell asleep, Josh trails his finger back and forth across Rose's stomach.

(Unbeknownst to them, she'll start showing a mere week later.)

"You're growing our kid right now," he whispers.

"I'm growing our kid right now," she confirms, draping her arm across his chest. "Is it bad that I only thought to take a pregnancy test because I've had to pee constantly?"

"I would say yes, but considering you're up almost a cup size and neither of us thought anything of it, I have no room to talk."

She nods her head in agreement. "Yeah, that should have given it away a month ago." She weaves one hand through the short waves of his hair. "I... I'm really glad it's you, this time."

The words are quiet. She says them like she's nervous to bring down the mood, to bring up something so dark in this happiest of moments.

But it's her only other experience to contrast this with, and it's a world of difference, being *excited* to tell someone you love that you're having a child. To not be terrified of them finding out, to know they already love the baby as much as you do.

"Me too." He rubs her back gently. "I'm sorry you were alone before. You know I'll wait on you hand and foot this time around."

She smiles softly. "I know."

And she does. She knows these blue lines mean nothing but joy for them (even if it's made her think more than she'd like about some of her harder memories).

She presses her lips to his neck, gently and then more insistently, and Josh raises his eyebrows at her. "Someone's full of energy today," he comments, even as he immediately begins returning her affections.

"It's not my fault; this is one hundred percent the baby's fault. Hormones," she states, and he snorts even as he joins their bodies together, knowing that's going to be her excuse for everything under the sun until the baby is born.

"Love you," Rose reminds him softly afterward, voice breathy in his ear, every inch of flesh still pressed up against him.

"I love you, Rosie" he promises in return. He sits up just enough to press a kiss to her abdomen. "And you," he says, voice wobbling.

———

Six months later, they name him Evan Andrew, and Scar refuses to let him out of her arms for nearly an hour.

Zeke brings a teddy bear (which little E will keep with him till adulthood). Isa shows up with her fiancé and sobs over little E for three days straight with joy. Kai spoils them rotten, claiming it's a godfather's duty, and always happy to help when they're bound to get themselves into trouble otherwise. Bronte will teach him karate, and Josh gets both Scar and E's names tattooed on his chest (which Rose makes fun of him for but secretly makes her cry).

Josh tells the kids stories, and Scar sings Evan to sleep (wobbly and off-key), and the dog guards them both like they're his own puppies.

Evan will hate math (which breaks his mother's heart), and Scar will think history is a bore (which makes her father proud). Their family will always go way too crazy for Halloween and Christmas, and their weekly movie night is sacred. No fighting is allowed on birthdays, mental health days are encouraged, and everyone gets home immediately when Nana says she's heading over with cookies.

The bad days are still there, all the time. She still feels broken, sometimes.

Things aren't perfect, but there isn't a single moment Scar or Evan ever doubts that they're loved. Not a single occasion that Rose ever doubts Josh loves her.

Being broken is okay when they're together.

(Rose can breathe, now.)

ACKNOWLEDGMENTS

This book started as nothing but thoughts and feelings, *what-if's* and *what-might've-been's* that I had to write down because I couldn't get them out of my head otherwise; not a work in progress, but a need, something I had to pour out of myself to keep from being consumed.

I had no idea how far it would come, but it was the book I wished I could've found, the one I so desperately wanted to read—and so it was the book I *needed* to write. The book I needed to put into the world.

Even now, I can't believe this story made it this far.

And it wouldn't have without so many people: thank you to my found family, first and foremost—you've kept me sane long enough to write this piece of my soul into existence.

To all of my initial readers, who loved and supported this story when it was only a skeleton of a book, who were the first to believe in what it could become and made it feel worth pursuing.

To everyone who poured time and love into beta reading—I am so eternally grateful for your love and feedback; you shaped this story in ways you'll never know.

To Isabelle, for your thorough and incredibly helpful thoughts and suggestions, and to Charlie, for your constant kindness and for making the editing process I was dreading as painless as possible.

To Brooke, the first to read the first draft of this book in its entirety—thank you for your support, your love, your willingness to answer random plot-related questions and texts about whether a different scene might be better in the middle of the night for the last two years.

To my Commons family, who spent I don't even want to know how many hours listening to me ramble throughout our shifts as I worked my way through this story; love y'all like crazy.

To Alexandria, Cherie, Omy, and all the members of Arts Theme House who have spent so many mornings and afternoons and evenings encouraging and supporting me through the process of bringing this book into existence.

To Mr. Lester, the first to ever believe in me at all—I could never thank you enough for the years you've impacted my life.

To those older than I, parents and mentors alike, who've been the best role models I could ever ask for and embody unfaltering love—I am eternally grateful for your presence in my life.

To Jake and Kaylee, for the years of friendship and light in hard times, and being forever on the other end of the phone in a heartbeat. To Cass and Jess (and Bailey), for the jokes and check-ins and call outs and always being able to tell when I need them even if I won't admit it. To Dylon, for being my person and forever knowing exactly what I need to hear (and for dropping everything to spend the day reading my horcrux the moment I sent it).

To Chloe and Faith, for staying with me and somehow loving me in every iteration of myself I've been—I don't know where I'd be without you. To Rachel, for being the kind of friend who crawls into bed beside you to keep you company when you can't bring yourself to face the world.

To Ariana, for over a decade of discussing books and writing, for your never-ending support, for pouring your time and love into the beautiful cover art for this book; I am forever in awe of your talent and ability to understand the thoughts I can't put into words.

To Emily, Brandon, and Mikey: you are forever my world.

And to anyone else who has their own monster—I hope despite it all, you find every bit of light and love there is in this world.

ABOUT THE AUTHOR

Kaitie Howie grew up in a small town in Florida, and is an avid reader of anything but nonfiction. Holding a Bachelor's Degree in psychology, she frequently goes on tangents about the intersection of psychology and fiction writing, and is a big believer in fiction reading as the number one way to learn about humanity.

While residing in North Carolina, she served on the summer reading selection committee for Duke University's incoming first-year students for several years. She has a history of arguing the morals (and lack thereof) of fictional characters at parties, and lives for pop culture trivia.

Kaitie currently teaches middle school social studies, and when not scrolling TikTok or consuming fanfic she spends most of her free time reading or writing, curled up with coffee and her cat.